From the Abyss

Other Handheld Classics

From the Abyss

Weird Fiction, 1907–1945

by D K Broster

Edited by Melissa Edmundson

Handheld Classic 27

This edition published in 2022 by Handheld Press
72 Warminster Road, Bath BA2 6RU, United Kingdom.
www.handheldpress.co.uk

ISBN 978-1-912766-56-7

1 2 3 4 5 6 7 8 9 0

Series design by Nadja Guggi and typeset in Adobe Caslon Pro and Open Sans.

Printed and bound in Great Britain by Short Run Press, Exeter.

FSC
www.fsc.org
MIX
Paper from
responsible sources
FSC® C014540

Contents

Acknowledgements

My thanks to Kate Macdonald of Handheld Press, for commissioning me to curate the stories in this book.

I would also like to express my gratitude to Oliver Mahony, the Archivist at St Hilda's College, University of Oxford, for providing copies of D K Broster's typescript of 'The Taste of Pomegranates', as well as for graciously allowing permission to reprint the story in this present volume.

I also wish to thank Jeff Makala for his feedback on the introduction and for his editorial assistance.

And my gratitude, as always, goes to Murray, Maggie, Kitsey, and Simone for their furry support.

Melissa Edmundson is Senior Lecturer in British Literature and Women's Writing at Clemson University, South Carolina, and specializes in nineteenth and early twentieth-century British women writers, with a particular interest in women's supernatural fiction. She is the editor of a critical edition of Alice Perrin's *East of Suez* (1901), published in 2011, and author of *Women's Ghost Literature in Nineteenth-Century Britain* (2013) and *Women's Colonial Gothic Writing, 1850–1930: Haunted Empire* (2018). She also edited *Avenging Angels: Ghost Stories by Victorian Women Writers* (2018).

She has edited these Handheld Press titles: *Women's Weird: Strange Stories by Women, 1890–1940* (2019), *Women's Weird 2: More Strange Stories by Women, 1891–1937* (2020), Elinor Mordaunt's *The Villa and The Vortex: Supernatural Stories, 1916–1924* (2021), and Helen de Guerry Simpson's *The Outcast and The Rite: Stories of Landscape and Fear, 1925–1938* (2022).

Introduction

BY MELISSA EDMUNDSON

If the name 'D K Broster' is familiar to contemporary readers, it is most likely due to a popular trilogy of historical novels she published in the 1920s. These books, known as the 'Jacobite Trilogy', are the bestselling *The Flight of the Heron* (1925), *The Gleam in the North* (1927), and *The Dark Mile* (1929). Throughout her decades-long career as a professional writer, from the early 1920s until a few years before her death in 1950, Broster enjoyed critical and commercial success as a novelist, with most of her novels published by William Heinemann. The normally reclusive Broster, who tended to avoid the public spotlight (see Spear 2012), made headlines when she attended London parties hosted by Heinemann and visited areas of Scotland made famous in her fiction.

Broster's contributions to short fiction, and especially weird short fiction, received less attention during her career and those who have read her novels might be surprised to discover this facet of her writing career. Broster's short fiction represents an even broader span of her writing career, with stories appearing during the first decade of the twentieth century until the 1940s. Many of these stories are similar in theme and setting to her novels and are centred on historical characters and events from the eighteenth and nineteenth centuries. Yet Broster also published weird and supernatural tales in several major magazines of the day, including *Macmillan's*, *Chambers's*, the *Cornhill*, and *Good Housekeeping*. Several of these stories later appeared in her two collections of stories, *A Fire of Driftwood* (1932) and *Couching at the Door* (1942). These weird stories represent only a small portion of her output as a writer, but they reveal a very different side to the author. *From the Abyss: Weird Fiction, 1907–1945* highlights this other side to Broster's career – and perhaps the more shadowy undercurrents of her own psyche as well. The stories in this volume are wonderfully varied and include incidents of pure horror, subtle psychological studies of obsession, haunted houses, and tales of ghostly doubles. These stories reveal a true mistress of the form, one who could craft a deceptively quiet narrative where fear is just around the corner, lying in wait to catch us off guard.

Dorothy Kathleen Broster was born on 2 September 1877 at Grassendale Park, Garston, in Liverpool. She was the eldest of four children born to Thomas Mawdsley Broster, a shipowner, and Emily, née Gething. Broster received a private education until she was ten years old, and then attended a boarding school in Lancashire. After the family's move to Cheltenham when she was sixteen, Broster became a day student at Cheltenham Ladies' College. At nineteen, she was awarded a scholarship to St Hilda's College, Oxford. While an undergraduate, she was secretary of the St Hilda's College Debating Society and contributed to *The Fritillary*, a magazine of the Oxford women's colleges, which she edited from 1898 to 1899. Broster excelled at her university studies, and in 1900 she achieved a second-class honours degree in modern history. Yet because women students were not at that time permitted to be awarded their degrees, she had to wait until 1920 to receive her BA and MA. On 15 October 1920, the *Times* reported on the historic ceremony, listing Broster (as well as Dorothy L Sayers, who graduated from Somerville College) among the first 29 women to receive an Oxford degree (Anon 1920, 7).

After completing her studies Broster spent thirteen years working as the secretary to Sir Charles Harding Firth, Regius Professor of Modern History at Oxford. During this time, Broster also began publishing poetry and fiction. Her first historical novel, *Chantemerle* (1911), was co-authored with Gertrude Winifred Taylor. This was followed by *The Vision Splendid* (1913), once again co-written with Taylor.

During the First World War, Broster, who spoke fluent French, volunteered as a nurse. In late 1914, she was working in Belgium and by 1915 was working with the British Red Cross and stationed at an Anglo-American hospital in Yvetot, France. However she was forced to return to England at the beginning of 1916 after suffering from a leg infection.

Broster's post-war novels showcase her continuing interest in history, with most being set in the eighteenth and early nineteenth centuries. These include *Sir Isumbras at the Ford* (1918), *The Yellow Poppy* (1920), and *The Wounded Name* (1922). A 1923 visit to Lochaber in the Scottish Highlands inspired Broster to write her Jacobite Trilogy. Their publication marked the beginning of a long professional partnership with William Heinemann as well as a lifelong interest in Scotland and its history. During her fifth visit to Scotland in 1928, a newspaper article about her visit opened with, 'The Highlander or even the Lowlander of Scotland who has not read *The Flight of the Heron* and *The Gleam in the North* must, I am sure, be one of a small minority.' The Jacobite Trilogy made Broster a household name in the country, as the writer declared, 'D K Broster is for most of us a name to conjure with, for she has made the '45 Rising and the years of its aftermath into a living story of our own people' (Anon 1928). Her Jacobite novels remained in wide circulation in Scotland well into the 1990s.

Broster continued to publish historical novels throughout the 1930s and 1940s. Many have naval settings, possibly influenced by her father being a shipowner, which in turn led to Broster's continuing love for the sea. These include *Ships in the Bay!* (1931), *The Sea Without a Haven* (1941), and *The Captain's Lady* (1947). In August 1924, shortly after the publication of her novel *Mr Rowl*, the *Bookman* ran a brief feature on Broster's work accompanied by a rare published photograph of the author. The piece highlights her ability to lend psychological complexity to her characters within the context of a historical novel, which, according to the writer, tend to be 'costume novels' with little character development (Anon 1924, 267).

D K Broster was, by all accounts, a private person and rarely gave interviews or appeared at public functions. One exception was an interview with Jean Boyd which appeared in the 1 July 1928 issue of the Scottish weekly paper *The Sunday Post*, fittingly titled 'Who *Is* This D.K. Broster?' In this, she discussed her writing practices and the amount of work that went into researching and writing her historical novels. She claimed to be a perfectionist when it came to historical accuracy, saying,

> It is certainly no easy job writing historical novels. You cannot let your characters gallop off on their own as they always seem to want to do. The movements of all the troops have to be historically correct, yet I don't suppose half of my readers realise that when they read my books. And I don't suppose they care a damn whether they are correct or not. It would worry me, however, if they were not. (Boyd 1928, 17)

This attention to detail meant that Broster typically spent years on a book before it was ready for publication. She said, 'I work regularly and hard, but it takes me at least two years to finish a book, because I put a great deal of hard study and research into everything I write' (Boyd 1928, 17).

Other biographical details about Broster's life remain sparse. She lived for many years with her close friend and companion, Gertrude Schlich, in Catsfield, Battle, in Sussex. Schlich was the daughter of Sir William Schlich, a professor of forestry at Oxford. Broster dedicated her novel *The Yellow Poppy* to Schlich in 1920. Broster and Schlich also collaborated on the mystery novel *World Under Snow*, published by Heinemann in 1935, which is credited to Broster and 'G Forester' (Adrian 2001a, xxiv).

There are occasional mentions of both women in local newspapers. In 1937, the *Hastings and St Leonard's Observer* reported that Broster gave a talk at the local literary society on the seventeenth-century priest Father Gilbert Blackhall (Anon 1937b). In May 1937 and April 1939, Broster and Schlich were recognized for their gifts to Buchanan Hospital, located in St Leonards-on-Sea (Anon 1937a; Anon 1939). Broster died on 7 February 1950 at Bexhill Hospital. In 1957, Schlich endowed a scholarship at St Hilda's College in Broster's name.

D K Broster collected her weird and supernatural fiction in *A Fire of Driftwood* (1932) and *Couching at the Door* (1942). *A Fire of Driftwood* is divided into two sections, with the first section dedicated to historical tales. The second section contains a few stories centering on supernatural events, including 'All Souls' Day', 'Clairvoyance', and 'The Window'. Other stories in this section verge on dark or macabre narratives with no supernatural content. These include 'The Book of Hours', 'Fate the Eavesdropper', and 'The Promised Land.' Another story, 'The Crib', features a nativity come to life and verges on parable. The stories in *Couching at the Door*, with the exception of 'The Pavement', a dark tale of obsession, are all supernatural in some way. In addition to the title story, this collection includes 'The Pestering', 'From the Abyss', and 'Juggernaut'. These stories were published from 1907, when 'All Souls' Day' appeared in the September issue of *Macmillan's*, up until the publication of 'From the Abyss' in *Chambers's Journal* in December 1940, suggesting that Broster had a continuing interest in the weird and supernatural modes. The fact that she was a bestselling novelist during these decades and financially secure also implies that the stories were not written purely for money.

Reviews for both *A Fire of Driftwood* and *Couching at the Door* were generally positive. In an April 1932 review of *Driftwood*, the *Bookman* singled out 'The Promised Land' as 'by far the best in the whole book,' calling it 'pure Tchekov [sic]' and a story that 'could not have been better written' (Anon 1932). H C Harwood, writing in the *Saturday Review*, preferred the stories in the second half of the book, noting that these showcased Broster's gift for writing such narratives: 'In Miss Broster's short stories there is, however, a lot of kick. I refer more particularly to 'Clairvoyance' and 'The Promised Land', either of which should have established the author as a really first-rate horrifier, a petticoated Poe. [...] The sadly fantastic is what she does best' (Harwood 1932, 349). Cecil Roberts, in his review for the *Sphere*, likewise noted the 'extraordinary Poe-like gruesomeness' of 'The Window' (1932, 418).

In its review of *Couching at the Door*, the *Scotsman* noted that the stories were a departure of sorts from her usual historical themes, but nonetheless declared that she had 'certainly achieved success'. The reviewer also appreciated the range of the stories contained in the book, from the 'definitely supernatural' to the 'borderland of mystery which, while stopping short of the supernatural, serves as a reminder of how much of strangeness human life may contain' (Anon 1942). Vernon Fane, writing for the *Sphere*, recommended the collection and drew attention to 'Couching at the Door' and 'The Pavement' for coming closest to what is called the 'authentic effect' of good ghost stories, that is, 'the slight prickling of the scalp and the rather self-conscious nonchalance of that look round the room to make sure one's quite alone' (Fane 1942).

Though both collections are now out of print and first editions are increasingly difficult to find, Broster's supernatural writing has enjoyed more sustained recognition than that of several of her contemporaries. Interest in her weird fiction began almost immediately after the publication of *Couching at the Door*. Peggy Wells's adaptation of 'The Pestering' was broadcast on BBC Home Service Radio as a 4.15 afternoon matinee on 12 December 1945 (Anon 1945). In her *Times* obituary, Broster's historical novels take priority, but the obituary ends with a mention of this facet of her career: 'History apart, Miss Broster had an imaginative predilection for the supernatural and the occult' (Anon 1950). Of all the stories, 'Couching at the Door' is the most frequently anthologized. Shortly after appearing in the *Cornhill*, Dorothy L Sayers included it in *Great Short Stories of Detection, Mystery and Horror* (3rd Series, 1934). It was later included in Philip Van Doren Stern's *The Midnight Reader* (1942) and again in Stern's *Great Ghost Stories* (1962). Alfred Hitchcock selected it for two anthologies: *Bar the Doors! Terror Stories* (1946) and *Stories They Wouldn't Let Me Do on TV* (1957). The darker elements of the story led John Keir Cross to include it in *Best Black Magic Stories* (1960). 'Couching at the Door' gained more recognition after it was collected in *The Penguin Book of Horror Stories* (1984), edited by J A Cuddon. Broster's supernatural and weird fiction were collected in two more recent books that are now out of print. These include *Couching at the Door*, edited by Jack Adrian and published by Ash-Tree Press in 2001 as a limited hardcover edition of 600 copies. In 2007, Wordsworth Editions published another collection, also called *Couching at the Door*, as part of their 'Tales of Mystery and the Supernatural' series.

Jack Adrian has discussed Broster's gift for the macabre, noting the lack of redemption and depiction of graphic violence that is such a departure from the themes and concerns of her longer fiction. For Adrian, this mysterious dichotomy has unexplainable (and therefore tantalizing) possible connections to Broster's personal life:

> She is, in every way, the master of her craft, writing of a distinctly uncomfortable world in which ugly things appear without warning, and sudden, shocking, and (what's far worse) entirely arbitrary psychic violence occurs. And why Dorothy felt the need to create such stories is just one more vexing question to do with a life that teems with vexing questions. (Adrian 2001a, xxx)

Though we may never know the extent to which Broster brought her own fears and anxieties into these dark narratives, it is clear that she transferred her ability to create distinctive characters – a defining quality in her novels – into her weird fiction. Individual character is at the heart of these stories, which are always just as much about the human as they are the weird and supernatural.

The first two stories in *From the Abyss* show Broster's early interest in history and are closest in theme and setting to her later novels. 'All Souls' Day' is a unique twist on the traditional 'Day of the Dead' as it uses the supernatural to enact a form of ghostly penance between two sworn enemies. The story 'Fils D'Émigré' takes place in 1795 during the French Revolution, and Broster reused this story, without the supernatural element, as Chapter 28 of her 1918 novel *Sir Isumbras at the Ford* (with thanks to Kate Macdonald for spotting this). Its central character, the young Anne-Hilarion, exhibits an inherent nobility and personal reserve beyond his years as he attempts to find his father, an exiled French royalist who has returned to his native country to take part in the ill-fated invasion of France by counter-revolutionary forces. Though the supernatural is not a major part of the story, Anne-Hilarion's accidental act of scrying proves vital to the events of the story's conclusion. Both stories illustrate Broster's early attempts to describe weird events in her short fiction and serve as important instances of her development of the weird and supernatural that she would use to an even greater degree in her best (and far more disturbing) weird fiction of the 1930s and 40s.

Other stories introduce us to territories of pure horror. In 'Clairvoyance' the extreme order of the drawing room is juxtaposed against the chaos of violence that suddenly erupts there. This is one of Broster's bloodiest stories and all the more shocking because the violence is enacted by a child. The frightening pull of the past and its intrusion into the present weighs heavily on this story. The brutal history of the Japanese sword invades the present day, and the trauma within the house lingers through rumours and speculations of the 'unrest' that may still be present.

The haunted bathchair in 'Juggernaut' leads to a violent end for a character who cannot free themself from the dangerous influence of a former personal connection. Obsession, a recurring theme in these stories, results in a relentless struggle of an employee to keep their dead employer happy. The guilt caused by a past crime is an impetus for their repeated actions, performed as a type of never-ending penance. 'Juggernaut' exhibits Broster's ability to infuse her stories with a bleakness – firmly grounded in the everyday existence of these characters – that elevates the sense of fear and doom brought about by the paranormal events. Broster also structures her weird fiction to maximize the feeling of disorientation felt by the reader. The nonlinear plot development of both 'Clairvoyance' and 'Juggernaut' helps to build the mystery surrounding the terrible events causing the respective hauntings.

'The Window' likewise concerns a violent event from the past that returns to haunt the living. In the story, a young British army officer is trapped when a large sash window in a deserted French chateau closes on his arms. The physical pain of his wounds is compounded by the visions of previous bloodshed concerning a family's betrayal during the French Revolution that cleverly cycles back to the 'guillotine window' which traps him. 'The Window' is one of the few times that Broster used the First World War as a setting in her fiction.

'The Pestering' represents Broster's foray into haunted house territory as the past again intrudes into the present. It is also the longest story in this volume. Broster takes full creative advantage of this length, however, to slowly and effectively develop the supernatural 'pestering' that gives the story its title. What starts as a slight bother as a mysterious man wants to be let inside a couple's Tudor-era house gradually becomes something much darker and more insistent. In truly creepy passages, Broster describes the man pursuing the terrified Evadne Seton as she reaches the entrance to her house: 'But she did not seem to have to pass him; he was not where she expected; he was beside her, shuffling along through the fallen leaves at the edge of the path, and keeping up with her as she went' (107–8). Broster puts her own twist on traditional aspects of the haunted house story as the troubled past of the house is gradually revealed to the Setons. Creative elements in 'The Pestering' include the changing appearance of the ghost who must be 'invited' inside, and his mysterious connection to a hidden chest containing a bronze statue of a woman dressed in rotting clothes, with a dagger through her heart.

'Couching at the Door' encompasses both haunting and horror. This time, Broster describes the more immediate past of the 1890s through the career of the decadent poet Augustine Marchant. Like his name, the life of Marchant is a performance, his infamous celebrity and hedonistic reputation is an identity he has crafted and sustains at all costs. When Lawrence Storey is enlisted to illustrate a lavish new edition of Marchant's poetry, he falls under the poet's spell and is urged to visit Paris in order to experience the spiritual 'liberation' that Marchant captures in his work. Yet this liberation comes at a cost. Marchant is haunted by the (re)appearance of a fur boa that returns as a reminder of a ritual which involved sacrifice and a female sex worker during a 'glamorous, wonderful, abominable night in Prague' (149):

> All at once he felt a tickling sensation on the back of his hand, looked down and saw that featureless snout of fur protruding upwards from underneath the rustic bench, and sweeping itself backwards and forwards against his hand with a movement which was almost caressing. He was on his feet in a flash. (155)

The animated object and its intimacy with Marchant, juxtaposed with the feeling of revulsion it inspires in him, become all-too-tangible reminders of that night in Prague. Dabbling in the occult has its consequences, but for Marchant, so too does putting his poetic art above those he deems 'unworthy' of his concern.

Several stories are concerned with the blending of personality and identity and what happens when the boundaries of one person are dissolved into another. The tension in 'The Promised Land' steadily builds as we witness the slow mental unraveling of Ellen, an aging woman who must share her house with her overbearing cousin Caroline, who threatens to completely subsume Ellen's sense of self. Ellen's lifelong dream of visiting Italy quickly turns into a nightmare as Caroline increasingly controls every aspect of her daily life. The violence which erupts is momentarily liberating for Ellen, until her world becomes increasingly smaller and more claustrophobic as she tries to instill a sense of order into a life that is slowly disintegrating into physical, mental, and emotional chaos.

In 'The Pavement,' an ancient Roman mosaic depicting Hebe, the goddess of youth, consumes Lydia Reid to the point where she cannot bear for anyone else to see her. The narrator remarks on this growing obsession: 'Actually the word "fond" was ludicrously inadequate. It was adoration which Lydia Reid felt for that pictured floor, whose bond-servant she had made herself' (197). The violence of the story's conclusion represents a desperate attempt by Lydia to keep the ancient pavement – and even more importantly Hebe – to herself and, in so doing, maintain the fragile foundation on which she has based her life. Possession and obsession are often interchangeable in Broster's weird stories and act as an impetus for the troubling (and often violent) events that conclude these narratives, which often result in a psychological or emotional breakdown – or physical death – for their respective protagonists.

'From the Abyss' examines the idea of 'dual personality' as the living and apparitional forms of Daphne Lawrence seemingly exist at the same time, yet in two different places. In the story, Daphne's fiancé, from whose perspective the events are related, attempts to solve the mystery of her strange reappearance after a supposedly fatal car accident. Like the attention to detail that is such a defining characteristic of her historical novels, Broster includes wonderfully detailed pieces of information about her characters. For instance, in 'From the Abyss', the narrator is able to identify his missing fiancée through a blurry photo where she is seen stroking a cat:

> There was surely only one girl in the world who stroked a cat like that, with the back, not the palm of the hand? Daphne, a cat-lover (it was one of the points on which we differed), always upheld – perversely, I thought – that one felt the charm of the fur better that way. And, execrable

as the photograph was in other respects, it did show this
anonymous figure using that singular caress; I could just
see the tips of the slightly upcurled fingers ... (228)

The vivid picture Broster paints of Daphne only increases the
uncanny qualities of her ghostly double. The dreamlike nature of
the story is balanced with a sense of foreboding as the multiple
meanings of 'the abyss' take on terrible significance. As this
narrative makes clear, the bottomless chasms of the world can be
both physical and metaphysical.

The troubled return of history – or prehistory – is a central feature
in 'The Taste of Pomegranates', in which the sisters Roberta and
Arbel Fraser find themselves the victims of a timeslip while visiting
the caves of the Dordogne. Jack Adrian is credited with discovering
this story, which exists as an unpublished, undated manuscript
in Broster's personal papers held at St Hilda's College Library,
Oxford. Adrian dates the story's composition to around 1945 or
immediately after (Adrian 2001b, 216). Lascaux cave, in the Vézère
valley near Les Eyzies in southwestern France, was discovered in
September 1940. It contains hundreds of prehistoric paintings
dating to c. 15,000 BCE, including depictions of bears, deer, horses,
mammoths, and wolves. In this clever reworking of the Persephone
myth, Arbel Fraser attempts to escape the 'underworld' of the
ancient caves before falling victim to a gigantic prehistoric beast.
This is another meditation by Broster on the connection of the past
and the present as the caves represent a thin veil between history
and prehistory. The disorientation of the Fraser sisters within the
caves aligns perfectly with their dislocation within history itself. If
the saying is that 'in historic places, we are not separated by space
but by time', then 'The Taste of Pomegranates' considers what might
happen if both spatial and temporal barriers suddenly collapse.

Throughout her long and successful career, D K Broster was
able to bring history back to life within the pages of her novels.
Whether it was the events surrounding the Jacobite Rebellion in
mid-eighteenth-century Scotland or the intrigues of Napoleonic

France in the early decades of the nineteenth century, attention to historical detail and finely-drawn characters are defining qualities of her writing. History returns in Broster's imaginative fiction, too, but takes on new meaning as it emerges into the present. In these stories, the past literally returns to haunt the characters, who must contend with otherworldly forces that invade both the present time as well as the ordered, rational world these protagonists inhabit. Yet Broster also makes us question how rational our everyday world actually is. As a contemporary reviewer of *Couching at the Door* noted in 1942, her fiction shows 'how much of strangeness human life may contain'. The eleven stories in *From the Abyss*, representing nearly forty years of Broster's work in weird fiction, showcase the myriad ways this 'strangeness' finds its way into human lives.

Works cited

Adrian, Jack (ed.), 'Introduction', in D K Broster *Couching at the Door* (Ashcroft, British Columbia: Ash-Tree Press, 2001a), ix–xxxi.

Adrian, Jack (ed.), 'Sources', in D K Broster *Couching at the Door* (Ashcroft, British Columbia: Ash-Tree Press, 2001b), 215–216.

Anon, 'First Oxford Women Graduates', *The Times* (15 October 1920), 7.

—, 'The Bookman's Diary', *The Bookman* (August 1924), 265–268.

—, 'Miss Broster Comes to the Highlands', *Dundee Courier and Advertiser* (26 June 1928), 6.

—, Review of *A Fire of Driftwood*, *The Bookman* (April 1932), 81.

—, 'Buchanan Hospital', *Hastings and St Leonard's Observer* (15 May 1937a), 2, 19.

—, 'Three Noble Ladyes', *Hastings and St Leonard's Observer* (4 December 1937b), 19.

—, 'Buchanan Hospital', *Hastings and St Leonard's Observer* (22 April 1939), 2.

—, Review of *Couching at the Door*, *The Scotsman* (4 June 1942), 7.

—, 'Wednesday December 12 Home Service', *Radio Times* (7 December 1945), 12.

—, 'Miss D K Broster', *The Times* (10 February 1950), 9.

Boyd, Jean, 'Who *Is* This D.K. Broster?', *The Sunday Post* (1 July 1928), 17.

Fane, Vernon, 'New Novels and Ghostly Visitations', *The Sphere* (18 July 1942), 92.

Harwood, H C, 'New Novels', *The Saturday Review* (2 April 1932), 348–349.

Roberts, Cecil, Review of *A Fire of Driftwood*, *The Sphere* (12 March 1932), 400, 418.

Spear, Hilda D, 'Broster, Dorothy Kathleen (1877–1950), novelist', *Oxford Dictionary of National Biography*, 4 October 2012, Oxford University Press, date of access 16 December 2021.

Bibliographical details

The texts for all stories in this volume have been taken from
A Fire of Driftwood (William Heinemann, 1932) and *Couching at the
Door* (William Heinemann, 1942), unless otherwise noted.

'All Souls' Day' was originally published in *Macmillan's* in September
1907 and was later collected in *A Fire of Driftwood*.

'Fils D'Émigré' was originally published in the *Cornhill* in July 1913.
The present text is based on this edition.

'The Window' was originally published in *Chambers's Journal*
in December 1929 and was later collected in *A Fire of Driftwood*.

'Clairvoyance' was originally published in *Nash's Pall Mall* in January
1932 and was later collected in *A Fire of Driftwood*.

'The Promised Land' was collected in *A Fire of Driftwood*.

'The Pestering' originally appeared in *Good Housekeeping* in December
1932 and was later collected in *Couching at the Door*.

'Couching at the Door' originally appeared in the *Cornhill* in December
1933. It later became the title story in *Couching at the Door*.

'Juggernaut' originally appeared in *Chambers's Journal* in January
1935. The story was later collected in *Couching at the Door*.

'The Pavement' originally appeared in the *Cornhill* in January 1938.
The story was later collected in *Couching at the Door*.

'From the Abyss' originally appeared in *Chambers's Journal* in
December 1940. The story was later collected in *Couching at the Door*.

'The Taste of Pomegranates' exists in an undated, unpublished
manuscript held at St Hilda's College, Oxford University. The
composition date is most likely around 1945. The present text
is based on this manuscript copy. Obvious typographical errors
and inconsistencies have been silently corrected.

1 All Souls' Day (1907)

The old priest was out when we called at the *presbytère*, but we were told by his housekeeper that he would soon be back, and were invited to wait in the parlour. We had come there, Horsfield and I, because when our friend Travers was working at the history of the Morvan, he had said that the Curé of Chatin-en-Brénil had been extremely kind to him, and was very pleased to see visitors, especially English visitors, in his quiet corner of that green Burgundian land with its astonishing memorials of the Middle Ages, those little walled towns and the great abbey church which is one of the glories of France. So Horsfield and I, who were doing a walking tour from Sens to Dijon by way of Auxerre, had settled to call upon the old man as we passed through Chatin-en-Brénil.

Nor were we sorry to rest awhile in that dark and very cool parlour, hung with a few bad sacred prints and having straight-backed chairs arranged with precision below them. After a little, however, Horsfield got up, drawn as he always is by the presence of a bookcase, and went to the small row of shelves on the wall by the window.

'Our Curé has one or two good bindings here,' he remarked. 'In fact, if this isn't a seventeenth-century English tooling I'll eat my hat!' Moved by the holy enthusiasm of the bibliophile he stretched up a hand, plucked forth a book, surveyed and opened it. 'Look!' he cried triumphantly, and spread it open on the table in the middle of the room.

It was a Dutch-printed Latin copy of *The Imitation of Christ*, of the year 1620, and though I know little of bindings I saw the significance of the faded inscription on the fly-leaf. *Mildmay Fane* – presumably the name of the original owner – was written high up in the right-hand corner; and then lower down, and evidently at a different time, *hunc librum ad LRE de V dedit anno MDCXXXI in memoriam misericordiae non obliviscendae*; and lower down again, *Ora pro anima NC*.

'That's interesting!' I exclaimed – 'given by an Englishman to a Frenchman in 1631! I wonder what it is doing here, and who NC was?'

But as I spoke the door opened, and the Curé hurried in, full of gentle apologies for keeping us waiting, of pleasure at making our acquaintance, and of enquiries after the wellbeing of Travers, 'cet aimable écrivain si passionné pour l'histoire et les antiquités de notre beau pays du Morvan.' He was himself the most charming old man possible, to whom it was easy to utter our rather shamefaced excuses for having made free with his bookcase – for the à Kempis was lying open on the table – and our avowals of curiosity regarding its original possessor.

'Ah, there you have a great treasure,' he said, smiling, taking the *Imitation* with a certain reverence into his fragile old hands. 'It has been a kind of heirloom in my family since it was given to an ancestor of mine – Messieurs, a bargain: if you will stay and take *déjeuner* with an old man to whom it is a pleasure to meet an Englishman, I will tell you the story of your countryman and of the inscription in his book.'

We were only too pleased to stay, and though I fancied the housekeeper was not so pleased, and that I heard vociferations from the kitchen, we had an excellent little *déjeuner*. The old priest was so charming a mixture of shrewdness and naïveté, of humility and knowledge of the world, that his conversation was wholly delightful. After the meal we went into the little walled garden, and sat under a pear-tree, where our coffee was brought out to us, after we had assisted the Curé to hunt a fowl out of his bed of seedling wallflowers. 'I think the blessed St Francis must have omitted to preach to the *basse-cour*,' he said ruefully, as we came back. 'For my part I often feel most unchristian to my sister the hen.'

When we had finished our coffee he drew the book out of the pocket of his cassock. 'I must warn you that this is a story for the fireside in winter, and not for all this' – he waved his hand to include the little green garden, the warm and fragrant air, the stocks and wallflowers, flagging a trifle in the sun, and the drowsy cooing from an unseen dovecot – 'but it does not matter.

'This book, then, was given to a member of my family by its owner, Mr Fane, an English gentleman of great gifts both of mind and body, a very noble person – *une âme d'élite*, as we say – whose good qualities were like to suffer ruin through a disaster which befell him in early manhood. This calamity, brought about through no fault of his own, plunged him into circumstances which were leading him in a direction very different from the path wherein he had early set his steps, and to which, by the mercy of God, he afterwards returned, through what strange agency you shall hear.

'About the end of the year 1629 Mr Fane, then a little more than thirty years of age, was visiting Paris on his return from a foreign tour, when he had the misfortune to incur the enmity of a certain Chevalier de Crussol, a man of notoriously evil life. They had met but a few times when a violent quarrel took place between them, in which Mr Fane, so far as human judgment goes, had undoubted right upon his side. As a result of this disagreement Mr Fane held himself in readiness to receive a challenge from the Chevalier. The expected cartel was never sent, but M de Crussol took other means to avenge himself. As the Englishman was returning alone at night from a ball he was set upon by the Chevalier and several of his lackeys, who, after a brief struggle, left him for dead in the street.

'The door at which Mr Fane fell, with half a score of wounds upon him, was that of the house which Carl' Egidio, the Grand Duke of Parenza, was making his residence during a private sojourn in Paris. By the Grand Duke's domestics, then, Mr Fane was found in the early morning, and, being carried within, was there cared for during the space of two or three months. For many weeks of this time his life was despaired of, and he was unable to give any account of himself. However, the Grand Duke, seeing that he had to do with a gentleman of condition, whose appearance, moreover, had from the first attracted him, spared nothing of his hospitality and care. It so chanced that Mr Fane had despatched his servant to England before he entered Paris, and that none of his acquaintance in the city was aware of his presence there, nor, in consequence, of the disaster which had befallen him. There was no person therefore to make enquiries concerning him, nor to reveal his identity, which he, lying for weeks unconscious, was equally unable to disclose. The result of this general ignorance, when he returned at last to sense and life, was not long in reaching Mr Fane's ears. His friends, in England and France alike, believed him dead, slipt out of life by some such door, perhaps, as that through which he had so nearly passed; and in England the lady whom he had hopes of winning was married to another.

'Mr Fane now fell into a great despair and blackness of soul. So much did he feel the faithlessness of her whom a few short months' silence could so alienate, that the idea of a return to England was abhorrent to him. Nor to his disordered mind did it appear to signify that he had, after all, escaped the sword of his enemy. He persuaded himself that his friends had forgotten him, and when the Grand Duke, who had conceived a violent attachment for his company, implored him to return with him to Italy, Mr Fane consented with a sort of indifferent pleasure, saying bitterly that a dead man had no right to come to life again. He accordingly left Paris in the train of the Grand Duke.

'Dead he was, in another and a more real sense – not, indeed, so dead as the majority of those with whom he now consorted, but with scarcely a trace remaining of that interior life which had once been to him the only existence worthy of the name. Carl' Egidio, a prince of cultured vices, called him saint and recluse, and strove to draw him more intimately into the circle of his own pleasures, but that Mr Fane was of a different fashion from most of the grand-ducal associates did not, after all, confer on him any real title to those names. Yet the pleasures of the court held little savour for him, and sometimes, on his knees with the others at the sumptuous masses which they all attended (for Carl' Egidio was extremely orthodox), faint and bitter memories of better days broke into his soul. And the shy little Grand Duchess Maria Maddalena, the poor little bride who regretted her convent, talked to him at times on themes which had once been more than a name to him; and these conversations, he could not but know it, were almost all she had to prevent their becoming names to her also. It was for her sake that he suffered the mention of things once dear, now inexpressibly alien to him, and perhaps a little for her sake too that he kept himself clean of the grosser forms of vice.

'But these could not fail, in time, to close upon him. The ladies of the court were none too difficult, and he had every gift to commend him to a woman. Before the winter was come Donna Flavia Ranuccini, a married kinswoman of the Duke's, had lured him along a perilous path of intimacy to a disastrous end. He did not love her, but she had wrested from him as much as he had in those days to give to any woman; and to an intimacy of such a kind, at that time and in such surroundings, there could be but one conclusion. Mr Fane was only fulfilling, alas! what his world expected of a gentleman of fashion, when after a year's residence in Parenza he made preparations for becoming Donna Flavia's acknowledged lover.

'It was ten o'clock on the second evening in November. October, so lately fled, had carried off few leaves from the trees in the Duke's beautiful gardens, into which Mr Fane sat looking from a window-seat of his apartment in the palace. A half-moon, sometimes obscured by light fingers of cloud, shone on the statues among the trees, the dryads and fauns, and the Silenus in the middle of the nearest plot, and through the open casement came now and then the shiver of the leaves. Half lying on the deep seat the Englishman propped his chin on his hand and looked out. Something in the tall cypresses reminded him of a graveyard, and the white and silent statues of monuments – or ghosts. Ghosts might well walk in the palace gardens, the ghosts of those who had played out their lives there, on the lawns and terraces in summer, or in winter in the apartments on the other side, now alight with revelry from which he had withdrawn himself – for what? Donna Flavia's letter was in his pocket – in a few years she, too, would be a ghost of the garden – and he? But he was already dead, and had a right to walk already. And then he remembered – what indeed he had forgotten merely for an hour or two – that it was All Souls' Day.

'Even as he remembered it the heavy window-curtain swayed slowly out from its place, as a curtain by an open window will do either with a gust of wind or with the opening of a door. But the wind was nothing save an occasional light shudder in the garden, and the door at the end of the long dimly-lit room had in truth been opened, for, turning his head on the instant, Mr Fane heard it softly closed. Looking down the room he discerned the figure of a man coming towards him, and with some vexation wondered who entered unannounced at such an hour. But as the intruder came nearer he started from the window with his hand on his sword. It was the Chevalier de Crussol.

'He was dressed, as always, with some elaboration, in rich and pale satins, with his dark lovelocks falling over Venice point, a jewel in his ear, and a medal, or an order, on a broad ribbon about his neck. Bare-headed, with his left hand, sparkling with rings, resting lightly on his sword-hilt, he came slowly down the room towards his foe, and his short velvet cloak swung from his shoulder as he walked. But when he was within a couple of yards from Mr Fane he suddenly halted, and stood looking at him with an air of extraordinary seriousness. Mr Fane's last recollection of him was very different, and of the wild passions and vindictive triumph which had then been imprinted on his countenance there was now no trace, nor indeed of any other emotion. All expression seemed to have been wiped, as with a sponge, from his face, which yet bore everything by which a man may recognise one whom he has loved, or hated.

'"What do you want here?" asked Mr Fane, finding his voice at last under his amazement.

'The Chevalier made no answer, nor moved, but continued to look at him with eyes of a strange flickering greyness.

'"Speak, in God's name!" cried Fane. "What are you here for? Are you mad?" And indeed there could scarcely be any other explanation of his audacity.

'"Do you not know," said the Chevalier in a low tone, speaking French, "that it is the *jour des morts*?"

'The sound of his voice carried Mr Fane back in an instant to the dark street in Paris, the torches, and the swords. "I know it," he returned in the same tongue. "And you have, perhaps, a fancy to join them?"

'His visitor paid no heed, but continuing to look at Mr Fane with the same indescribable calm, said gravely: "I am come to warn you of peril."

'"Another assassination!" exclaimed the Englishman bitterly.

'"Rather self-murder," replied the Chevalier, with not the faintest sign of blenching at the taunt.

'His composure, but still more the reference to his own private affairs, was too much for Mr Fane. "Now, by Him that made me," he began, springing towards him. The Chevalier retreated a step and put up a hand to stay him; but Mr Fane never touched him. In afteryears, I believe, he could never satisfactorily account for the reason of sudden enlightenment; the figure, even in the subdued light, was so distinct, so real, with all the visible attributes of breathing humanity about it. But on his closer advance he knew.

'He recoiled very slowly, crossing himself almost mechanically, and the dead murderer and his living victim stood looking at each other across the riven veil. There was no fear in Mr Fane's heart, but awe certainly, and a great wonder. Why had the creature come – to ask his forgiveness? No, for as the thought shot through his mind (he forgetting for the moment what had already passed between them) the apparition answered it. "I am beyond the reach of human pardon, Mr Fane; but I entreat you, by Him you named just now, not to do this thing."

'The strange dead eyes were full upon him, passionless and yet compelling. Fane was shaken, but to be brought to book by one whom he could not but know to be infinitely worse than himself touched his sore and haughty soul too sharply. The human passion swept away with it the sense (which one might have supposed overpowering) that he was speaking to no living man. "Enough," he said shortly, and added: "You find yourself, surely, on a strange errand, Monsieur de Crussol!"

'"The messenger," returned his visitor almost inaudibly, "is not accounted of – And you will not listen, nor stay your steps before it be too late?"

'Mr Fane, without replying in words, made a gesture of negation, and a clock in some recess of the room struck the quarter. It was the hour at which he had ordered his chair to await him. The figure of his visitant stood between him and the door through which he must pass to gain the courtyard, not that door at the end of the room by which the Chevalier had entered, but a *porte de dégagement* on the left of the window. He looked towards it impatiently, in a way that would have been plain to an earthly guest.

"'Mr Fane," said the figure, holding up his hand, while for the first time a trace of emotion thrilled in his low and even voice, "Mr Fane, I will call another to stay you. You shall not dare to pass that door."

'And with that he turned on his heel, as naturally as a living man might turn. On the wall, not far from the door, there hung a beautifully carved crucifix of ivory and silver, Carl' Egidio's gift to his favourite. Before Fane had time to interpose, the spirit of his enemy had it in his left hand, and in his right, the light glinting dully upon it, a little dagger which he drew from his breast. Now he was at the door, and put the crucifix high up against the central panel, and, holding it thus, drove the stiletto through the ring deep into the wood. Then he half turned, looked round at Fane, and – was gone.

'Mildmay Fane wiped the sweat from his forehead. The room was empty, just as it had been a few minutes ago, save for the white Christ hanging over against him, nailed to the wood by an assassin's dagger. The sense of having dealt with the unseen was a thousandfold more potent now than when he had spoken with the phantom. Great God, what did it mean? – and yet he knew.

'Then he told himself that he was dreaming. But the crucifix upon the door – was it real, or was it not? He went slowly up to it, not daring to touch it. Yes, surely, it was as real as sight could prove it, and the little dagger, with the ruby in the hilt

– the dagger which he knew, which had once had his own blood upon it – was fast in the panel. He put out his hand and drew it back again. "I will leave the Christ there until I return, and if it be there still I shall know that I am not dreaming. I am not afraid of ghosts," he thought to himself. But he stood for a moment looking fixedly at the Figure so strangely suspended in his path.

The clock struck the half-hour, and he turned away to get his cloak from the window-seat. When he had his back to the barred door he thought with a smile of his visitor's defiance, "You shall not dare to pass that door!" He put the cloak about him and walked steadily to it again.

'Ah, God! how the Christ looked at him, under the thorn-crowned brows! And as Mildmay Fane stood with his hand upon the handle, in the act to turn the latch, he suddenly drew back trembling. Not knowing why, but as one dreaming, he put out his hand instead to the Chevalier's poignard. His fingers encountered nothing but the panel of the door, but the crucifix, as though its support were removed, slipped instantly down the polished wood. He caught it as it fell, and, as his fingers closed on the symbol which an incredible act of divine mercy had placed to bar his way, the temptation dropped dead in his breast like a shot bird, and with an overmastering sense of awe and gratitude he sank upon his knees with the crucifix pressed to his lips.

'A week later he had left Parenza for ever. Of all the Grand Duke's gifts he carried away with him but one, and left nothing behind of permanency but his memory to the little Grand Duchess.

'So you see, my children,' said the old priest, smiling upon us, 'that even if on All Souls' Day you met the ghost of one who had been your enemy – though I hope that neither of you has such a thing – you would not need to think he came to do you harm.'

'But, Father,' said I, infinitely touched by the sweetness of his tone, 'why should it have been his enemy that was sent to Mr Fane? Do you think it was in expiation of his crime?'

The priest shook his head. 'That is not for me to say. Let us hope so. I think that when Mr Fane prayed before the altar for the repose of the Chevalier's soul, as he did to the end of his life – as he here asked his friend to pray' – he lifted the book – 'that must have been a hope with him ... when he prayed also (as I am sure he did) that he himself, to whom so great a mercy had been given – *misericordia non obliviscenda* – might not be found wanting in the day of the Lord.'

2 Fils D'Émigré (1913)

1

'Grandpapa,' said Anne-Hilarion, please to tell me what is 'ven-al-ity'?'

Mr Elphinstone looked up. 'Eh, what, child?'

'I read in this great book,' proceeded Anne-Hilarion, in his clear, precise, and oddly stressed English, 'This ven-al-ity co-in-cid-ing with the spirit of in-de-pend-ence and en-cro-ach-ment com-mon to all the Pol-y-gars pro-cur-ed them – '

'God bless my soul, what book have you got hold of?' demanded the old man, but before he could finish pulling himself out of his arm-chair by the fire there was a knock at the library door, which, opening, revealed an elderly woman in a cap.

'Master Anne's bedtime,' said she, in a Scotch accent and severely, and stood waiting. Almost at the same moment there appeared by her side an old man of obviously Continental nationality. In his hands was a salver; on the salver, a china bowl. '*M le Comte mangera-t-il ici avant de monter, ou dans sa chambre?*' he inquired.

The little Franco-Scottish boy who was both 'Master Anne' and 'M le Comte' looked from his retainers to his grandfather. What he desired was so clearly visible in his expression that Mr Elphinstone, whipping off his spectacles, said, 'He will have his bread-and-milk down here, Baptiste. I will ring for you, Elspeth, a little later.'

The housekeeper retired, with a tightening of her tight lips, and Baptiste, advancing victoriously, placed the steaming bowl on the table, beside the volume of Orme's *British India* which had been engaging the child's attention. Anne-Hilarion, who had screwed himself round in his chair, turned his dangling legs once more table-wards.

For a few minutes nothing was heard in the large book-lined room but the noise of a spoon stirring the contents of a bowl, while the old gentleman by the fire resumed his reading. But presently the spoon grew slower in its rounds, and Mr Elphinstone, looking up, beheld a large silent tear on its way to join the bread-and-milk.

'My child, what is the matter?' he exclaimed in dismay. 'Is it too hot?'

M le Comte produced a handkerchief, 'I think,' he said falteringly, 'that I want my papa.'

'My poor lamb,' murmured the old man, 'I wish to God I could give him to you! See now, my bairn, if you were to bring your bowl here, and sit on grandpapa's knee?' He held out his arms, and the small boy slipped from his chair, went to him, and, climbing to his lap, wept a little, silently, while his bread-and-milk steamed neglected on the table. Mr Elphinstone's faded apple cheek was pressed tightly on the top of the brown, silky head, and the deep frilled muslin collar round Anne-Hilarion's throat was crumpled, unregarded, against his breast.

It was a July evening of 1795 that filled the big London house with dying radiance; but though it was high summer there was a fire in the library, because Mr Elphinstone was an old man and a sedentary, and still felt England cold after long years in India, and because M le Comte de Flavigny had had whooping-cough in the spring. By that fire there sat now with Mr Elphinstone two shadows. One was a real shade, Janet Elphinstone, Marquise de Flavigny, whom her son could scarcely remember, though to her father it seemed only yesterday that she, a child, had slept thus on his knee, all rosy and tumbled. The other, God help him, might be a shade too by this time – her husband, the French émigré, René-Constant, Marquis de Flavigny, gone with hundreds of other Royalist exiles on that ill-fated expedition to Quiberon concerning which sinister rumours were even now afloat. And that was why, however much Anne-Hilarion desired it, he could not have his father back this evening …

2

'I wonder how far it really is to France,' speculated M le Comte next day, sitting at the window of his nursery and looking down into the square. 'It does not help that Elspeth should say "a great way" and that Baptiste should tell me how very ill he was when he came over with M le Marquis years ago. I know that one goes there in a boat; I wish I had a boat. I might have asked the gentleman who told me stories about the sea that day at Richmond, when grandpapa took me there in the spring, for he was lieutenant de marine. I wish that M de Soucy would come here again, and I would ask him. If he were not so poor he would consent to dine with us more often, grandpapa says.'

The Comte de Flavigny had a fairly extensive acquaintance among the colony of French émigrés in London. Mr Elphinstone keeping open house for any of his son-in-law's friends. Among these more or less destitute gentlemen Anne-Hilarion especially favoured a former companion-in-arms of his father's, a certain Chevalier de Soucy, older than the Marquis, but almost fantastically devoted to him, yet prevented, by a wound recently received in one of the many small gun-running expeditions on the Breton coast, from enlisting with his friend in the émigré regiments destined for Quiberon. So he was still in his lodgings in Golden Square, eking out a living by teaching his native tongue.

And Anne-Hilarion, sitting this morning on his window-seat, thought a good deal about M de Soucy. He had no chimerical visions of setting out for France by himself, for his was a singularly sane mind. But it did appear to him that, with a little encouragement, M le Chevalier, who had seemed so disappointed at having to remain behind, might be induced to go, privately as it were, and to take him with him – not, of course, to fight, but just to find papa. The difficulty was that the Chevalier, ruined by the Revolution, was very poor. Grandpapa said so, and indeed M de Soucy himself, always with a laugh. But if he, Anne-Hilarion, proposed such an expedition, it was surely his duty to defray its cost. Could he do this? He had, in his money-box, a crown-piece which would not go through the hole in the lid, and which grandpapa had therefore introduced by means less legitimate, means which had revealed the presence of many other coins in the receptacle. There might be as much as a guinea there by this time. Anne-Hilarion could not get at this wealth, but if he went to interview M de Soucy he could take the box with him, and perhaps M le Chevalier would open it.

The preliminary step would certainly be to consult M de Soucy. But how to do that alone? How to get to Golden Square without the escort of Elspeth or of Baptiste? Elspeth in particular had a wary eye and a watchful disposition. There seemed no way to evade her but to call in miraculous intervention, and this Anne-Hilarion resolved to do.

Little, however, did Elspeth Saunders, that staunch Calvinist, imagine, as she impatiently surveyed the bairn at his 'Popish exercises' that evening, what it was that caused their undue prolongation, nor what forces were being invoked against her. Little did she realise to what heavenly interposition was due, at least in Anne-Hilarion's mind, the fact that the next afternoon, at half-past one precisely, she slipped on the stairs and twisted her ankle rather badly, so that she had to be conveyed to her room, and Baptiste went to fetch the doctor. M le Comte had not in his orisons specified the hour of the miracle (nor, of course, its form), but he was on the alert. Mr Elphinstone was nowhere about, so he slipped into the library and penned, not without labour, the following note:

> Dear Grandpapa – I think to go to France with M le Cher de Soussy, if God permits and there is mony suffisant in it, to find my papa. It must have been my ange gardien that pushed Elspeth; she must not mind; perhaps even it was St Michel lui-même. I will not be gone for long, dear Grandpapa. I love you always.

He stood upon a chair and put this communication on the library mantelpiece; then, clutching his money-box, he struggled successfully with the front door, and set out towards the hackney coaches standing for hire on the other side of the square.

<h1 style="text-align:center">3</h1>

Anne-Hilarion met no dragons on his adventurous way. The hackney-coachman was most agreeable, and willingly agreed to wait, on arrival at Golden Square, in case he might be wanted again. The only obstacle to progress was the purely physical barrier of a stout and slatternly woman who, at that unusual hour, was washing down the dingy staircase, and whom he was obliged to ask to let him pass.

'Bless my soul!' ejaculated the woman, turning in clumsy surprise. 'And what are you doing here by yourself, my little gentleman?'

'I have come to see M le Chevalier de Soucy,' answered Anne-Hilarion. 'He is above, is he not?'

'The French gentleman? Yes, he is. I'll go first, dearie; mind the pail. To come alone – I never did! And who shall I say?'

'The Comte de Flavigny,' responded the little boy with due gravity.

Strange to say, M de Soucy, in his attic room, did not hear the announcement, nor even the shutting of the door. He was sitting at a table, with his back to the visitor, his head propped between his hands, a letter open before him. There was that in his attitude which gave Anne-Hilarion pause; but he finally advanced, and said in his little clear voice, 'M le Chevalier.'

The émigré started, removed his hands, and turned round – 'Grand Dieu! toi, Anne!'

His thin, haggard face looked, thought Anne-Hilarion, as if he had been crying – if grown-up people ever did cry, about which he sometimes speculated. But he was too well-bred to remark on this, and he merely said, in his native tongue, 'I have come to ask you, M le Chevalier, to take me to France, to find my papa.'

M de Soucy, putting his hand to his throat, stared at him a moment. Then he seemed to swallow something, and said, 'I am afraid I cannot do that, my child.'

Anne-Hilarion knew that grown-up people do not always fall in at once with your ideas, and he was prepared for a little opposition. 'Your health is perhaps not re-established?' he suggested politely (for he was master of longer words in French than in English). But M de Soucy made a gesture signifying that his health was of no account, so Anne-Hilarion proceeded.

'I have brought my money-box,' he said with a very ingratiating smile, and, giving his treasury a shake, he laid it on the table at the Chevalier's elbow. 'I do not know how much is in it. Will you open it for me?'

M de Soucy snatched up the letter, jumped from his chair, and went to the window. He stood as if looking out on the leads and the chimney-pots, but as he had put his hand over his eyes he could not, thought Anne-Hilarion, have seen very much. And gradually it began to dawn upon the little boy that the Chevalier must be offended. He remembered having heard grandpapa say how impossible it was to assist him with money, and he felt very hot all over. Had he done something dreadful?

But M le Chevalier suddenly swung round from the window. His face was as white as paper.

'Anne,' he said in a queer voice, 'money won't find your father for us. He ... my God, I can't tell him ... Come here, child. Bring your money-box.'

M le Comte obeyed.

'First we must see whether there is enough in it, must we not? It costs a great deal of money to go to France, and, as you know, I am poor.'

'I think there is a great deal, but a great deal,' said Anne-Hilarion reassuringly, shaking his bank. 'Will you not open it and see, M le Chevalier?'

'Yes, I will open it,' answered M de Soucy, 'And ... if there is enough, we will go to France. But if there is not enough, Anne – and I fear there may not be – we cannot go. Will you abide by my decision?'

'*Foi de Flavigny*,' said the child gravely, giving him his hand.

How wonderful are grown-up people! M le Chevalier had the strongbox open in no time. Together they counted its contents.

'Seventeen shillings and four pence – no, five pence,' announced M de Soucy. 'I am afraid, Anne ...'

M le Comte drew a long breath. The muscles pulled at the corners of his mouth.

'It is not enough?' he asked rather quaveringly.

'Not nearly. Anne, you are a soldier's son, and you must learn to bear disappointment – worse things perhaps. We cannot help your father in that way.' Again M de Soucy struggled with something in his speech. 'I do not know, Anne, how we can help him.'

Fortunately it was not given to the Comte de Flavigny to read his friend's mind, but he perceived sufficiently from his manner that something was not right. He reflected a moment, and then, remembering the celestial intervention of the afternoon, said, 'Perhaps I had better ask la Très-Sainte Vierge to take care of him. I do ask her every day, but I mean especially.'

'You could ask her,' answered de Soucy, bitter pain in his eyes.

'You have no picture of Our Lady, no statue?

'Not one.'

'It does not matter,' said the little boy. 'Elspeth has taken away my picture of her. They do not know her over here, but that,' he added with his courteous desire to excuse, 'is of course because she is French … M le Chevalier, I think after all I had better ask St Michel, because he is a soldier. It would be more appropriate for him, do you not think? I will pray St Michel to take great care of my papa, and then I shall not mind about the money not being enough.'

So, standing where he was, his eyes tight shut, he besought the leader of the heavenly cohorts to that end, concluding politely, if mysteriously, 'Perhaps I ought to thank you about Elspeth.'

'I had better go back to grandpapa now?' he then suggested.

M de Soucy nodded. 'I will come with you,' he said.

4

Anne-Hilarion had not been missed, for the domestics were still occupied about Elspeth's accident, and Mr Elphinstone, though he had returned to the library, had not found his farewell letter. The only surprise which the old gentleman showed was that his grandson should be accompanied by M de Soucy. He got up from a drawing of one of the gates of Delhi that he was making for insertion in the great MS volumes of his memoirs, at which he had now been working for some years, and welcomed the intruders.

'Anne has been paying me a visit,' said the Frenchman. 'He wanted to go to France, but I have persuaded him to put it off for a little – Can I have a word alone with you, Sir?'

'Did you not get my letter, grandpapa?' broke in Anne-Hilarion, clinging to Mr Elphinstone's hand. 'I left it on the mantelpiece, behind the little heathen god. I did not run away, *foi de gentilhomme!*'

'Send him out of the room,' signalled the émigré. But Anne-Hilarion, having perceived Mr Elphinstone's occupation, was now in great spirits. 'Let me look at the *livre des Indes*, grandpapa! I so much love the pictures. *Faites-moi voir les éléphants!*' And he jumped up and down, holding on to the arm of his grandfather's chair.

But the old man had followed M de Soucy to the window.

'What is it, monsieur?' he asked in a whisper. 'Bad news from France?'

'Read this,' said the Chevalier, thrusting the letter into his hands. 'It could hardly be worse. D'Hervilly attacked the Republican position at Ste Barbe five days ago, and was beaten off with frightful loss. God knows what has happened by now – what has happened to René – the worst, I have small doubt –'

Mr Elphinstone unfolded the letter with shaking hands, but ere he had got to the bottom of the first page Anne-Hilarion's voice, oddly changed, broke in upon them.

'I can see my papa! I can see my papa! He is lying on a great white beach by the sea. There are many people – many ships, soldiers. Papa is ill or asleep; he has a cloak over him –'

Both men turned hastily to see the child kneeling on his grandfather's chair, his elbows on the table, staring down intently at something directly under his eyes. It was the saucer of Indian ink with which Mr Elphinstone had been drawing. The old man caught the younger by the arm, for he at least, after years in the Orient, knew what was happening. M de Soucy, making a long disused gesture, crossed himself.

'Now he's waking up. He has a pistol in his hand. I do not know what – *Papa! Papa! ne faites pas cela! Papa!* Anne-Hilarion's voice rose to a scream; he flung out his arms and fell forward on the table, his curls in the stream of ink from the broken saucer.

5

And at that hour the rain was falling steadily on the white sand of Quiberon Bay, on the long low dunes, on Hoche's triumphant grenadiers, on the tiny crumbling fort which had seen Sombreuil's tragic surrender, on the useless English ships, on the lines of Royalist prisoners, and on the upturned face of René-Constant, Marquis de Flavigny, who lay, shot through the thigh, a short stone's-cast from the rising tide. All about him were the evidences of the great disaster, but for long he had not heeded them, lying where he had been left, by a little spur of rock that had its extremity in the sea. He had been unconscious when two men of his regiment – Loyal-Emigrant – had carried him there, hoping to get him on board one of the boats of the English squadron. But the rescuing boats were already overladen; the getting off to them was very difficult, and there was no chance for a fainting man when even good swimmers perished. So they had laid him down by the rock; he was no worse off than hundreds of others, and neither the cries of the drowning nor the boom of the English cannon wakened him.

But now he had drifted back to pain and the thirst of the stricken and the numbing remembrance of catastrophe. He knew not at first why he lay there, for he had got his hurt up on the sandhills. He had tried to raise his head, but desisted from the pain of the effort, and the fingers of his left hand ploughed idly into the sand. As it dribbled through them, white as lime, he remembered everything...

The Marquis's eyes, so like Anne-Hilarion's, darkened. Since there was no one to make an end of him, he would do it himself, not so much to end the pain and to hasten a lingering death as because everything was lost. And he would go to Jeannette.

But his senses were playing him tricks again. One moment he was here, a piece of driftwood in the great wreck; the next, he was in Mr Elphinstone's library, going again through that dreadful parting with Anne-Hilarion, promising him that he would soon return, and the boy was clinging to him, swallowing his sobs. He could hear them now, blent with the plunge of the tide. Better end it, and go to Jeannette.

He thrust down a hand, tugged a pistol out of his belt, cocked it and put it to his head.

But ere the cold rim touched his temple sky and sea had gone black. Flashes of radiance shot through the humming darkness, steadying to a wide sunflower of light, and then ... he saw distinctly Anne-Hilarion's terrified face, his little outstretched hands. His own sank powerless to the sand, and he was swept out again on the flood of unconsciousness.

6

'Not a single blessed patrol, by gad!' thought Mr Francis Tollemache to himself. 'That means they have got at the port wine and beer we landed at Fort Penthièvre; trust the sans-culottes for scenting it out. But, O gemini, what luck for us!'

For Mr Tollemache, the youngest lieutenant of the *Pomone*, the English flagship, was at that moment, midnight, steering a small boat along the shore of Quiberon. On his one hand were the lights of the English squadron, yet in the bay; on the other, the Republican camp-fires among the sandhills. The files of Royalist prisoners had started hours ago up the peninsula on their march to death, but Sir John Warren was still hoping to pick up a fugitive or two under cover of darkness, and Mr Tollemache's was not the only boat occupied on this furtive errand. But it was emphatically the most daring; nor had Sir John the faintest idea that Mr Tollemache was hazarding his own, a midshipman's, and half a dozen other lives in the search for one particular Royalist. Mr Tollemache, indeed, never intended that he should.

A rescued Frenchman sat already in the stern-sheets – one of the soldiers, picked up earlier in the day, who had carried M de Flavigny down the beach. Truth to tell, Mr Tollemache had smuggled him into the boat as a guide, for the task of finding the wounded man in the dark would otherwise have been hopeless. But the Frenchman could direct them to the little rock by which his leader had been laid, and, rocks being uncommon on the long handy shore, he did so direct them. Unfortunately, as Mr Tollemache, no expert in tongues, could not always follow his meaning, they had not yet found it. Already, indeed, they had made hopefully for some dark object at the water's edge only to ascertain that it was a dead horse, and Mr Tollemache's flowers of speech at the discovery had not withered till the body of a drowned Royalist slid and bumped along the boat's side. But meanwhile, even though the shore was unguarded, it was getting momentarily more difficult to see; the tide was rising once more, the men were getting impatient. After all, it *was* rather a wild-goose chase.

The French soldier tugged suddenly at his arm. '*V'là, m'sieur!*' he whispered hoarsely. There is the place – that is the rock!'

The young lieutenant peered through the gloom, gave a curt order or two, and, lifted on the swell, the *Pomone*'s boat greeted the sand of Quiberon Bay. Another moment, and Englishman and Frenchman had found what they sought. But only Mr Dibdin's special maritime cherub averted the discharge of the cocked pistol which the Marquis de Flavigny still grasped, and which Mr Tollemache had some difficulty in disengaging before they got him into the boat.

The middy, now in charge of the tiller, desired as they pulled away to be informed why his superior officer had been so set on saving this one poor devil.

'Oh, I met him once in England,' replied Mr Tollemache carelessly and quite untruthfully. '(Here, give me the tiller now.) It makes a difference when you have known a man, you see.'

For he was ashamed to avow the real motive power – his chance acquaintance that afternoon at Richmond with a younger member of the family. At any rate, it was not a safe thing to let a midshipman know.

They were nearing the *Pomone* when the Marquis de Flavigny, at their feet, his head on his compatriot's knee, began to mutter something. The middy bent down.

'The poor beggar thinks he's talking to his wife – or his sweetheart,' said he, pleased at being able to recognise a word of French. 'Anne, her name seems to be.'

Mr Tollemache, in the darkness and the sea-wind, turned away his head and smiled.

✳

Many weeks later Anne-Hilarion, from the haven of his father's arms, suggested yet another use for the contents of his money-box. He proposed to make over the receptacle in its entirety to Lieutenant Francis Tollemache, of His Britannic Majesty's Navy, now on leave, the same to be employed in whatever manner that officer deemed best.

'*Dites donc, papa,*' he said, nestling nearer, 'when he comes this afternoon to see us, can I give my box to him for saving you – for he is not poor, like M de Soucy, and therefore it is permitted to me to offer him money, is it not?'

The Marquis folded him closer. 'Keep back then one little coin for thyself, Anne.'

'But *I* did not save you, papa!'

'I would not be too sure of that,' said the young man dreamily.

3 The Window (1929)

1

'We absolutely must see the inside of that jolly old house some time,' said Romilly, not only almost daily to himself, but nearly as often to Charles and Meakin, who were staying with him, fishing and sketching, in the little Norman inn. Yet when Charles replied, 'All right, old chap, we will,' and Meakin said, 'Why on earth, then, don't you get hold of the key or something?' Romilly invariably replied that there was plenty of time yet. And so there was, only each day a little less of it, until at last there was none – none, that is to say, in which they, plurally, could enter the house, because Charles had gone back, groaning, to London, and Meakin, with the sister who had come over to join him, had proceeded south to Tours. So Romilly was left alone to finish, if he so willed, the sketches which he was rather fond of leaving unfinished, and to weave and unweave verses round the theme provided for the week by the Saturday *Westminster Gazette*.

But the house, of course, was still there – long, grey, blind-eyed, unnaturally deserted in a tangle of garden and of rank grass. Romilly passed it yet again on his return from seeing off Meakin, for it stood a matter of three or four kilometres away from the hamlet, and once more he uttered under his breath his parrot-cry about the necessity of entrance, adding to it a not unmerited condemnation of himself as a 'slacker'.

At the 'Coq d'Or' that night he asked the patron to whom he ought to apply for leave to visit the house.

'What, the old Manoir de Boisrobert!' exclaimed M Bonnet. 'Surely Monsieur does not think of going to see that?'

'Why not?' asked Romilly.

'*Mais* – because there is nothing to see!'

'*Entendu*. I did not expect to find it a museum. I want to see inside it all the same.'

'But – but –' began the good Bonnet, seeking for words to express the emptiness of the manoir, and finding instead a simple illustration. 'Inside,' he said, holding out the palm of one hand and tapping it with the forefinger of the other, 'inside it is all bare as this. Perhaps even a little falling to pieces – I do not know. No one goes in there.'

'Then I shall be the first,' retorted the young Englishman. 'Where can I get hold of the key?'

The patron did not think there was a key.

'But, hang it all!' exclaimed Romilly, 'the house, which is pretty big, must belong to somebody! There's an escutcheon on the gateposts.'

Thus pressed, M Bonnet admitted that he believed it belonged to the State. He had always heard that the old family whose property it once was had been dispossessed in the Revolution.

'Come now, that is quite romantic,' observed Romilly cheerfully. 'I shall take steps to get in tomorrow somehow, even if I have to climb through a window.'

But Romilly had procrastinated too long.

He came in to déjeuner at noon next day to find two newcomers seated at the one long table on which, according to the custom of the 'Coq d'Or', meals were indiscriminately served. They were a young good-looking Frenchman – obviously a gentleman – and his wife … or sister? The long table stood close to the wall, and as the wall was hung with the votive offerings of those amateur artists who at one time or another had stayed at the 'Coq d'Or', Romilly, who sat facing it, was perpetually confronted by a little thing of his own for which he confessed a partiality, a painstaking rendering by Meakin of the ornate church at Caudebec, and Charles's humorous Vorticist picture of which no man had ever been able to guess the subject. This was not surprising, since Charles himself did not know, having painted it for fun. Ninette, the large elderly chambermaid, came as near as anyone to describing it when she said, with a shudder, that it was what things looked like when she had a bad migraine.

And that nightmare of Charles's devising was directly over the dark head and slender neck of the beautiful French girl. She had no colour in her face, but the clearest, most transparent complexion, and when he looked at her Romilly conceived that he should never admire a vermeil cheek again. He longed to see her without a hat. Oh, wholly adorable!

Her name seemed to be Gabrielle – a lovely name. But what was her relation to the young Frenchman who forestalled her every want, and at whom she smiled so enchantingly out of those long, dark, mysterious eyes? He was much fairer than she, which seemed to point to the disastrous conclusion that he was *not* her brother. Unfortunately, a pot of flowers on the table prevented Romilly from seeing her rings. It was not the first time that he had suddenly lost his heart, for he had some natural facility in the exercise, and it was calculated by ribald friends, such as Charles, that since he came down from Oxford three years ago he had fallen in love thirteen times. Certainly he was in a perfect fever by the end of déjeuner, and rushed off to interview M Bonnet.

'They who came *en automobile*?' asked the landlord. 'It is M Gaston de Précy and his sister.'

'*Not* monsieur and madame, then!' exclaimed Romilly with relief.

M Bonnet smiled. 'Monsieur thinks they would make a fine pair?'

'Not at all!' replied Romilly fervently. 'A detestable thought!'

'There is something else which will interest Monsieur,' proceeded M Bonnet, rubbing his hands. 'It is really a most strange coincidence. They are of the family who once owned the Manoir de Boisrobert, and they have come over to see it. It appears that they have bought it back – I am not quite sure from whom.'

'Better and better!' cried the enthusiast. 'What a setting for that beautiful creature!'

Indeed, M de Précy and his sister had vanished immediately after déjeuner, presumably in the direction of the manoir. Happy young man, to have such a companion! Romilly forthwith began to picture himself wandering through the deserted rooms side by side, if not actually hand in hand, with the exquisite descendant of the no doubt exquisite ladies who had lived and loved at Boisrobert. As, however, he had yet to make that descendant's acquaintance, this consummation appeared improbable.

Nor did he make it at dinner that night, though he had the satisfaction of seeing her without her hat, and of feeling at rest on the question of her relationship to the young Frenchman.

It was next morning, about half-past ten, when the newspaper came in, that Romilly first awoke to the fact that everyone was looking very grave. For the shadow of approaching war had been stretching further with every sun that set, and he was perhaps the only person in the inn whom it had not yet touched with its feverish and icy fingers. M Bonnet in particular was plunged in woe, because in the event of mobilisation he would lose Ernest, who did everything at the 'Coq d'Or' except cook. Romilly, remaining at the inn against the return of his divinity, who had gone off very early with her brother to Boisrobert, tried to reassure the patron. 'It is impossible that there should be a great war nowadays,' he asserted, having read Norman Angell. 'It is opposed to all modern interests.'

'Pour ça, vous allez voir, Monsieur!' was the patron's lugubrious reply. 'And look, for instance, at this telegram which has just come for M de Précy. I would send it to the chateau after him did I not fear it might miss him. It is undoubtedly bad news, for I have discovered that his father the Comte is a retired general, and he would hear sooner than we ... Our beautiful country will be invaded, and I shall lose Ernest! That God may punish that wicked old man, the Emperor of Austria!'

Romilly was disposed to echo this hope, if Hapsburg machinations were going to be the cause of the untimely departure of Mlle de Précy. The telegram looked like it, and it therefore more than ever behoved him to obtain speech with her while yet he could.

It seemed caddish, however, to hang about in the entrance to witness the reception of the telegram, so, when he heard the car approaching, Romilly withdrew into the garden, or rather kitchen-garden, and, ensconcing himself in the arbour among the raspberry canes, tried to occupy himself with a book. And presently the brother and sister came out there too, and walked up and down the plot of grass near the gooseberries, talking earnestly in low tones. Mlle de Précy had her handkerchief in her hand, and dabbed her eyes with it once or twice, but that was all. Then Gaston de Précy hurried away, but she remained a moment at the far end of the plot, her back to the observer, twisting her handkerchief in her fingers. Now was Romilly's chance, if he could only find some excuse for addressing her. And on the path by which M de Précy had retreated there lay, by good fortune, what would serve his purpose – the opened telegram. Romilly slipped hastily out of his retreat, secured it, and advanced over the grass.

'A thousand pardons, Mademoiselle, but I think that monsieur *votre frère* has just dropped this,' said he in his best French, raising his hat and holding out the little pale-blue scrap of paper.

Mlle de Précy turned with a start, looking so much surprised that for one awful moment Romilly, with recollections of French novels in his mind, thought that he had put his foot in it, and was handing to his innocent sister some not innocent evidence of M de Précy's possible amusements. Then she relieved him by smiling and holding out her hand for the missive. 'Thank you very much, Monsieur,' she said, in the voice that was of a piece with the rest of her. 'This is, alas! a telegram that we should be very glad not only to have dropped, but never to have received. My brother must return to Paris at once – it is war.'

'It *is* coming, then?' observed Romilly in a tone of suitable solemnity, thinking in reality only of her approaching departure. 'Is M de Précy in the army?'

'Not more than every Frenchman, Monsieur. When he is mobilised he is a *sous-officier* in the 153rd of the line. And my father believes that mobilisation will take place on Sunday.'

'So soon!' murmured Romilly.

'So soon!' echoed she, sighing, and began to move towards the inn. Romilly accompanied her, intoxicated to be treading the same plantains. But suddenly she stopped, and, looking at him very directly – she was nearly as tall as he – said, 'And if there is war, will England fight?'

Romilly had not had time to weigh that contingency. But with those eyes upon him there could be but one answer. 'Mademoiselle, how can you ask such a question?' he replied reproachfully. 'What of the Entente?' And then he found himself, with almost appalling suddenness, the prey of a startling resolution. 'Why, if there is war, I shall become a soldier myself, and fight side by side with the soldiers of France. And every Englishman, I am sure, will do the same.'

For the wholesale conscription of himself and his countrymen Romilly was more than rewarded by the smile which it won. 'Monsieur, you are indeed *un preux chevalier*,' said Gabrielle de Précy, and along with that token of her approval she gave him her slim white hand with the marquise ring on the forefinger. And Romilly, his head turning, kissed it as naturally as a Frenchman would have done, and with certainly no less fervour. His own most eager wish at this moment was for instant bloody war – to be involved in some violent personal conflict (so she were witness of it) – to save her brother's life, perhaps, at the risk of his own …

Her voice interrupted these romantic visions. 'You speak French very well, Monsieur.'

The commonplace compliment took on a new value from her lips. 'I believe I may claim some French blood, Mademoiselle,' replied the young man, and for the first time rejoiced in that heritage. 'My great-grandmother was French, though, as I naturally never saw her,' he added, with a smile, 'I cannot exactly say that I learnt your beautiful tongue at her knee.'

But they were at the inn now, and Gaston de Précy, suddenly reappearing with a leather case of some kind in his hand, cut short the inquiry which Mlle de Précy was beginning about this ancestress, and confirmed Romilly's worst fears.

'Gabrielle, have you told your maid to pack at once? I beg your pardon – I did not see that you were engaged.'

'I was just coming in to tell her, *mon ami*,' replied his sister. 'Let me first present you to – to an English gentleman who is going to fight on the side of France.'

The young Frenchman shook hands heartily with the three-minutes old volunteer, said a few graceful words, and carried off his sister, with apologies, to make her preparations.

So, although Romilly was able to see the last of them as their Vinot glided away through the dust half an hour later, that interview in the kitchen-garden of the 'Coq d'Or' was the nearest he got to wandering hand in hand with Gabrielle de Précy anywhere.

2

Romilly's one-time desire had come to pass. There was, quite undoubtedly, war of the kind he had specified, and he himself was fighting side by side with the French – or, to be more accurate, living side by side with them in Rouen. And of this he was already tired.

He got his commission in the spring of 1915, and went out in July. And now, in mid-August, he still abode with his battalion in the City of the Maid, that haunt of tourists, now unimaginably changed, which surged with soldiers of both nations and with nurses – one kind, covered with brass buttons, looking like a female fire-brigade; which gave you tea in the big oak-furnished tea-rooms, just like home, but with better cakes; where the standards of the Allies hung in the Cathedral; and where the familiar red and blue of the French uniform was gradually giving place to the new *bleu d'horizon*, even as the picturesque attire of the Zouave regiments had become a particularly ugly mustard shade of khaki. And Romilly, 'fed up' with these impressions, wished with all his heart that he was a despatch-rider, like Meakin and some other Oxford contemporaries.

He had not forgotten Gabrielle de Précy, but he *had* forgotten that what had first moved him to resolve on volunteering was a wild desire to please her, an impulse which had soon been swamped under more serious motives for the same act. One day he saw an officer who looked like Gaston de Précy turn into the old curiosity shop by the 'Grosse Horloge', where a burly English NCO was visible choosing a medal of Jeanne d'Arc as a brooch for 'the wife', and he had followed the officer in before he remembered that M de Précy was only a *sous-off*. But as he came out it occurred to Romilly that he was no very great distance away from the old manoir.

What if he were now, by means of a motor-bicycle, to pay it that oft-deferred visit? Perhaps by this time Mademoiselle de Précy was living in it! Why had that glorious possibility not struck him before?

Three days later, having snatched at the first available opportunity of a few hours' leave, he was tearing noisily away from Rouen on a borrowed motor-bicycle, with a sketching-block and a box of water-colours behind him, and in his heart a hope that he would not need to use either. Still, they made a good reason for going to Boisrobert.

Alas! when he dismounted after thirty-five minutes' furious riding, at the high old rusty gates, he knew that he had been too sanguine. The place was no more inhabited than it had been a year ago. The only difference was that he could now enter the garden, because the gates were no longer chained together and padlocked. So he wheeled the motor-cycle dejectedly through, wishing that he had not come. Still, as he had come he might as well see the house, if he could force an entrance – for, obviously, any key would be in the possession of the Précys, and it was not worth while trying to find it in the village. He would go there afterwards, and have a chat with M Bonnet.

He leant the motor-cycle against the curving flight of discoloured steps which led up to the main entrance, and picked his way through the tangle of weeds to the back of the house, where there might be a better prospect of entry. And at the back, after due search, he discovered a little painted door which looked promising, and which, indeed, after some vigorous shoving, fulfilled its promise and admitted him. The woodwork seemed swollen with damp, and that fact had apparently prevented the door from being properly closed and fastened; but it must have been for years in that precarious condition, for several long tendrils of ivy were plastered like hinges across its surface.

That rather melancholy little portal seemed to Romilly to strike the keynote of the whole place, such an impression did it give of age-long desertion and neglect. There was the smell of dry rot in the dark passages at the back to which the door had given him entrance, and he hurried towards the front of the house and finally came, to the right of the entrance-hall, on a room which did not feel in the least sad or damp. It had a delightful carved mantelpiece, all scrolls and Cupids, two long windows looking towards the gates, and, opposite the door, a large square one through which could be seen the tangle of garden shrubs backed by one or two straggly cedars. The sun was pouring through this window, and thereby contributing not a little to the effect of life and warmth in the room, the charming proportions of which moved all the artist in Romilly. What he had had in his mind was a sketch of the exterior of the house – if he made a sketch at all. But now he knew that what he wanted to draw was this room. It had so much atmosphere that he could imagine its furniture and fittings, and over the hearth should be the portrait of Gabrielle de Précy, as one of her own ancestresses – unless, indeed, he tried to put her into the room itself. How entrancing she would have looked in a hoop and panniers! He got out his materials and set to work.

✕

Was it the idea of painting Gabrielle, he wondered, which made him begin to feel, after about half an hour's feverish work, that the room really *was* peopled, and by a considerable number of persons? It was almost as if he were painting without permission in an inhabited house, and as if the inmates, naturally enough, resented his presence. Try as Romilly would, the feeling grew, until at last he fancied that the persons in the room – who could exist only in his own imagination – were regarding him with a steadily increasing hostility.

At last he stopped work; it was too uncomfortable. 'What rot!' he thought, fidgeting with his brush, and looking almost defiantly at the great square window which faced him. For it was round that window that the hostility seemed to be concentrated, almost as if there were a group of people there, staring at him accusingly. 'This room has too *much* atmosphere!' he said to himself, trying to laugh, and resumed his painting. But the conviction of some invisible enmity became at last so insistent that, for the first time in his life, Romilly felt in his breast a spasm of real, naked fear.

'This is too dashed silly!' he exclaimed, springing to his feet; and with the words it dawned on him what was, perhaps, the origin of his state of mind. The room had been getting hotter and hotter as the sun sank; a little fresh air was what he needed; and, relieved at the idea, he went to open one of the long windows on his left hand. But a brief struggle with the long bolt-like fastenings common on windows of the sort convinced him that this was impossible. They were rusted immovably into their sheaths, and the handle would turn neither way. The only hope of fresh air was the other, the big sash window, the one through which the sun was streaming, the one where those people … He would certainly prefer not to open that window, nor even to approach it.

He walked across to it, however, with more apparent unconcern than he was feeling. The catch was stiff, but eventually slipped aside; and with some difficulty, for it was large and most abnormally heavy, Romilly raised the bottom sash, pushing it up almost as high as it would go. Then it occurred to him that it would be a good thing to pull down the upper a little also, and he laid hold of this in the only way possible, by putting up his hands outside. This upper sash was very obstinate, and so, bending his arms, and throwing as much weight upon them as possible, Romilly tugged resolutely at its framework.

All at once, with the suddenness of a thunderbolt, something gave way, or rather, some irresistible force wrenched away his hands from their grip on the upper window-frame, and in a second he was brought violently to his knees, receiving at the same moment a stunning blow across his forehead and the bridge of his nose. He had only time to realise that both his arms, just above the elbows, were held immovably in a grip which was causing them excruciating pain, ere he lost consciousness.

✳

Romilly came back, however, very quickly, to the knowledge of what had happened. The lower sash of the window, its old, rotten cords having presumably given way, had come smashing down and pinned him to the sill by his arms; it was its sudden fall which had dragged him to his knees and brought his head into contact with its central rib of framework, and with the glass also. The blood dripping from his right eyebrow and mingling with the broken splinters on the grey paint of the woodwork testified to that. It took Romilly a few seconds to realise it all, for the blow had somewhat stupefied him. Then, armed with a vivid sense of resentment, he set about releasing himself …

At the end of four terrible minutes he was still kneeling there, dripping with the sweat both of physical and of mental anguish. He rather fancied that one of his arms was broken, but the pain of the struggle to get them out from under the fallen sash had not deterred him from putting every ounce of strength into the effort. It was useless. The heavy window had him fast; hampered by his position, he could not so much as stir it.

Romilly leant his bruised and bleeding forehead a moment

against the glass, and gave a laugh. Here was he, a second-lieutenant in the Fourth Fellshires, in his new khaki, kneeling like a suppliant at the window of an empty room in an empty house, his imprisoned arms outstretched, unable to wipe away the blood from his face, unable to do anything save wait in this ridiculous and constrained attitude till someone came to release him from his pillory. And when would someone come?

It flashed on him suddenly that the French called this kind of window, so much less usual with them than in England, a 'guillotine' window. Very funny that! A further reminiscence came from some French Revolution novel, how the women who knitted round the scaffold, like – who was it? – Madame Defarge in *A Tale of Two Cities*, would humorously refer to the guillotine, on the other hand, as the 'national window'. Again very funny! Before his mind's eye wavered a moment the well-known poster of Martin Harvey as Sydney Carton on the steps of the scaffold. But neither he nor anybody else ever put his *arms* under the falling knife; it stood to reason that they couldn't, because their arms were tied behind them.

A suspicion that he was talking, or rather thinking, nonsense made Romilly shift his position – to the very slight degree that he could shift it. Better not to think of guillotines, because, after all, this was only a window … 'Magic windows, opening on the foam' – no, how stupid, of course Keats wrote 'casements'. He began involuntarily to suit the lines to his own case:

> Magic casement, opening on the green
> Of perilous woods (since 'gardens' did
> not scan) in faery lands forlorn –

And, by Jove, they *were* forlorn! Did anybody ever come here now, since the war had, presumably, stopped whatever plans the Précys might have made for the future of the place? Oh, if only he had gone for the key, which would at least have made known to somebody in the village his intention of getting into the accursed house! If only he had not kept it so dark in camp where he was going! He had borrowed Field's motor-cycle, it was true, but he knew that Field had not the remotest idea of its destination.

Unless someone came, then, he would be found here, months hence – a skeleton, perhaps. (How long did it take to become a skeleton?) Not the skeleton in the cupboard, the skeleton in the window – yes, literally, in it, as a fly is in a web, or a mouse in a trap, or a wild creature in a snare. There was a stoat in a gin, once, at home, which ... Never, never again should a trap be set round Greystoke! He would probably have a long argument with the pater about that, though – if he ever saw him again to argue with.

And the pater mightn't know the truth for years, if ever. Would the Colonel have the decency, after the regiment had gone to the front, to write to the pater and pretend that his son was 'missing'? He *would* be missing. Or would it be desertion, when he never turned up again at Rouen, with Field's motor-bicycle?

Outside the window, a little dimmed by the dusty glass, he saw his own hands emerging from the cuffs with the single star. The pain in his bruised and lacerated arms was less now, so long as he kept quiet, but from the elbows down he seemed to be losing feeling in them. They would turn black in time, he supposed, that meant mortification, gangrene. In hospital, limbs like that were cut off. 'If thy hand offend thee, cut it off.' Good God! if only he could! How did it go on – something about its being better to enter into life maimed, than having two hands to be cast into hell, into the fire that should never be quenched ... Sunday morning at home, with the Rector reading the lessons ...

Another few minutes of torture supervened here, as Romilly entered on a second and fiercer struggle to release himself. It only served to confirm the hopelessness of his position, and left him more exhausted than before.

And then he wondered why he had never thought of shouting. The window was already broken, but if necessary he might be able to enlarge the hole by the agency which had created it, his own head. He managed, however, to get his lips to the star-shaped gap in the glass and shout long and desperately, *'Au secours! au secours!'* ... His own voice died lamentably away in the empty garden, and nothing but the wood-pigeons answered him. He *was* to stay here for ever, then – to die here, pinned to the window-sill in a position which, because he could not change it, was on the way to becoming unbearable. Not in those trenches which he had never seen, not by a German bullet, not for England, nor – foolish dream! – for Gabrielle, but in an empty house, to no purpose, and alone ...

Romilly strangled a sob, and his head went down on his stiffening shoulder.

Once years ago, so it seemed – he had fancied that there were people in this hateful, sunny room, gathered round this very window. And though he had thought of them as in some way hostile to him, he would have been glad of them now; they would at least have been company in this utter desolation, even if they had exulted in some shadowy fashion over his plight. But the room was empty beyond all thought, and would be empty tomorrow. And first there was the long night to get through. When the sun next streamed through this horrible window, tomorrow evening, how would it be with him then, and how many more sunsets would he have to look at, kneeling here? Please God, not many!

That same sun, indeed, now low, seemed to be beating into his brain, till all inside his head was the colour of blood, and his thoughts, no longer under complete control, began once more to circle round the idea of the guillotine and its fruits. For out there in the garden, against the orange sky, which showed through the forlorn cedar boughs, was suspended a head, a fiery head – the sun itself, Romilly told himself, against which he had no protection save to close his eyes. But he saw the head all the same through shut lids ... The head kept changing, too. Sometimes it was a man's, sometimes a woman's; once it was an old woman's, with dabbled grey locks; once a young man's, having something of Gaston de Précy's look. And once, great God! was it not hers, Gabrielle's? – the wonderful black hair all dull, the delicate little mouth hanging open, a trickle of blood oozing from one nostril, the eyes ... Horrible, horrible! ... Black hair again, round a face which revealed that shrivelled Indian head in the Pitt-Rivers Museum at Oxford, that dreadful tiny head no bigger than a doll's, which once had been a living man's ... Romilly's heart seemed to be stopping; his ears buzzed; the light through his closed lids turned from red to black, from black to red. The thought visited him that he was dying. But death, he knew, would not come for days yet ... Night – a broken night – descended upon him.

3

What was this strange room, small and bare, and who was this stout, slightly moustached lady all in white sitting by him? Why was he in bed? ... What on earth had happened to his arms? ... Had it all been true, then?

But his guardian (whom he discovered to be French) would answer no questions, and indeed Romilly soon ceased to ask them – he felt so overpowering a drowsiness. At any rate, whether the business with the window were nightmare or reality, he was alive.

The deep sleep into which he then fell so refreshed him that five hours or so later the Dame de la Croix Rouge, as she fed him with some very welcome bouillon, announced to him that the doctor had authorised his receiving a visitor, if he wished it, who would answer his recent questions better than she could. And, Romilly intimating his readiness to receive any number of visitors, she vanished, and after a while there entered in her stead a young man in the misty horizon-blue uniform, wearing one of the new trench helmets painted blue to match, with the abbreviated gold stripe of a sergeant on his lower arm, and the *croix de guerre* on his breast – Gaston de Précy.

He saluted with a smile, looking very soldierly and handsome, then advanced, holding out his hand. '*Bonjour, Monsieur!* All goes well this afternoon, they tell me. Ah, I forget, you cannot shake hands yet.'

'For heaven's sake, sit down,' cried the invalid, 'and tell me where I am, and how I got here!'

M de Précy obeyed him. '*Mon lieutenant*, you are in the French auxiliary hospital at Lerville, and you are here because my sister Gabrielle had so violent a fancy for turning the old Manoir de Boisrobert into just such another, that she carried off my father and a distinguished military surgeon of our acquaintance to view it for that purpose. And as I happened to be *en permission* from the front, I went also. M le Major's time being precious, we motored over there from Rouen early this morning – fortunately – and found you trapped in the window.'

'I was there all night, then?' observed Romilly faintly.

'*Parbleu!*' said Gaston de Précy with interest. 'We wondered how long – my father and I thought you were dead at first; you gave us a fine fright. It took all our united strength to get the window up. I assure you, it made a moving spectacle – a pity that you could not see it.'

'Why?' asked the chief actor. 'I had seen enough.'

'I, the *poilu*,' went on M de Précy dramatically, 'kneel on the floor supporting you, *jeune officier anglais*, insensible, with blood down your face. Over you bends M le Major, slitting up the sleeves of your *vareuse* to see what damage the infernal window has done to your arms – by the way, I am relieved to hear that they will not be permanently injured. Standing near is my father, looking anxious – and he looks also rather chic, my father, in his general's uniform of the old style, *un peu plus gai que celui-ci, vous savez*. To complete the picture, there is Gabrielle, ready to assist M le Major, for she is Croix Rouge, *brevetée*. We must have looked like a cinema company rehearsing something pathetic and patriotic about the Allies.' Gaston laughed, pushing back the helmet that became him so well, but Romilly was conscious that he now made light of the scene, just because he had, at the time, known another emotion.

'And then?' he asked. (So *she* had been there!)

'Then we put you into the car, where you took up a great deal of room, and brought you here, where Gabrielle is nursing. It was the nearest hospital.'

The colour rushed over Romilly's face. 'She is here, then, your sister?'

The young aristocrat of a sergeant smiled, a rather mischievous smile, and twisted his little moustache. 'Yes, but I wished to see you first, *mon cher lieutenant*, since this is my only chance of doing so. I return *là-bas* to-night – to those dear trenches.'

The Englishman began to murmur apologies, and to thank him for his visit. (*First* – did that mean that she was coming too?)

'Oh, I came partly from curiosity,' said Gaston de Précy airily. 'There is something I want to ask you – no, not what you were doing at the manoir, for that was quite explained

43

by your paint-box, your sketch. What I should like to know – if you will pardon the question – is why you opened that window?' And again Romilly fancied that he detected under his visitor's light tone a note of anxiety.

'Because the room was so hot,' he replied.

The young Frenchman made a gesture. 'Ah, you English! Always the fresh air! See what comes of it! But, seriously, *mon ami*, that window has a history – of the most unpleasant.'

Their eyes met. Things were beginning to come back to Romilly – the dimmed horrors too of that broken night. Gaston de Précy was not smiling now.

'Has the story,' asked Romilly at last, 'anything to do with – with heads – decapitated heads?'

'Everything in the world,' replied the young sergeant gravely. 'Shall I tell it to you – yes? … In the year 1793, then, there were living in the Manoir de Boisrobert my great-great-grandfather, the Comte de Précy, then an old man, his wife, his eldest son and daughter, two other daughters a good deal younger, and his eldest son's boys, of nineteen and twelve respectively; and (I think) four servants. None of the family had emigrated, but the second son, François, had gone to fight for the Vendéans. One night, soon after the Vendéan defeat at Cholet, he came home a fugitive and wounded, with a price on his head. They concealed him for some time in various hiding-places in and around the manoir – you can see some of them still – aware, of course, that if he were found it would probably mean the scaffold for all of them. But the servants were proved, and the only other person who knew that he was hidden there was a friend of his in whom he had confided during his flight up to Normandy – a man called St Varent. *Pardon*, did you say something?'

'Nothing,' answered Romilly hoarsely. 'Go on!'

'*Eh bien*, one evening at sunset, when the family were

assembled in the room that you know, a frightened servant rushed in to say that the house was almost surrounded – the Republican soldiers were upon them. François de Précy slipped out into the garden, where there was an underground hiding-place. A few minutes later the Revolutionary authorities were in the room, questioning and threatening. The Comte de Précy and the rest denied all knowledge of the fugitive, asserting that the whole family were present. You can imagine the scene, with its anguishes. It was cut short by the crash of glass, and through the window – *that* window – was flung the bleeding head of François de Précy, splashing the dresses of his young sisters as it rolled to his mother's feet.'

Romilly gave an exclamation of horror.

'Dramatic, was it not?' remarked Gaston de Précy grimly. 'The soldiers had killed him in the garden, and hacked his head off then and there. I forgot to say that it was his friend, St Varent, who had betrayed his whereabouts – some past rivalry over a woman, I believe. His vengeance ought to have satisfied him, for every soul in that house, except the boy of twelve – my great-grandfather – went to the guillotine because of his treachery – because of that head thrown through the window.'

✳

There was silence. Romilly, looking extremely pale, was lying with his own bandaged head turned away.

'So you see, it has memories, that window,' finished the latest of the Précys. 'And you seem, *mon cher*, to have awakened them. But I am at a loss to conceive why you, an Englishman –'

'Monsieur de Précy,' interrupted Romilly in a queer voice, 'you will hate me, but I must tell you. I never heard this story before, not a whisper of it, but it is clear to me now why I got caught in that window, and why I saw – those heads. My great-grandmother was French. I know nothing of her but her name – but that name was St Varent.'

'*Bon Dieu!*' exclaimed Gaston, staring. And he added, after a moment, 'It must have been his daughter. There was a daughter, I believe, and there is a legend that she fled to England. You have written a postscript of the most unexpected to our family story!'

Romilly, biting his lip, tried miserably to summon up what he knew of his great-grandmother. But, as he had said, it amounted to nothing. There might have been two families of the same name, he supposed. If not, then in his veins ran the blood which had betrayed Gabrielle's. What had happened seemed to prove it beyond any doubt.

'There was good reason, after all, for the behaviour of the window,' said Gabrielle's brother musingly. 'Yet, who would have thought that a *house* could cherish vengeance for more than a hundred and twenty years.'

'I feel,' said the wretched Romilly, 'that I can never look … any of your family … in the face again.'

'That scruple is unnecessary,' said Gaston earnestly. Have you not expiated in your own person, Monsieur Romilly, a crime in which you had no share? Those ghosts should be laid henceforward; there is your blood now on the window-sill. It is not the window's fault that you got away alive. But I wish I had not told you the story. You need not mention your ancestry to – any other member of my family,' he added, with the glimmer of a smile.

'But I told Mlle de Précy, the day I first met you, that I had French blood in my veins. It seems to me,' said Romilly, 'that I have it on my hands!'

'You can wash it out, then, in the blood of the Boche,' retorted the young soldier instantly. 'Believe me, *I* bear you no ill-will, and I know how to hold my tongue. Someone is knocking – another of my family, no doubt.'

It was. In the doorway, more divine than ever, to Romilly's thinking, in the white dress and the white veil which, nun-like, showed not a glimpse of her glorious hair, stood Gabrielle de Précy.

'Madame la Directrice permits me to visit you, Monsieur, for one minute,' she said, looking at Romilly with a smile in her eyes. 'I must make, must I not, Gaston, the apologies of our poor old house for using you so ill?'

'*Monsieur le lieutenant* and I have settled all that, my sister,' replied Gaston quickly. And he held up a momentary finger of warning at the Englishman.

※

'Perhaps I shall tell her when we are married,' said Romilly later to himself.

4 Clairvoyance (1932)

1

'Yes, it's certainly a lovely place,' said Mr Alfred Pickering, the Australian wool-grower come 'home', as he looked out through the open French window of the library of Strode Manor on to the great lawn with the lake in the distance. 'Of all the houses I've seen in the last couple of months, this is the only one which in the least bears out the description sent me. I think you house agents have mistaken your job, you know; you ought to go in for writing fiction.'

Mr Simpkins (of Pottinger, Simpkins and Marrow) sniggered. 'Oh, come, sir! We have to do our best for our clients.'

'Well, you don't seem to have succeeded here,' retorted Mr Pickering, 'attractive as the place is. I can't understand its having stood empty all this time. How long did you say it was since Mr Strode went abroad – five years?'

'Fancy his leaving all the beautiful furniture in the house, too!' commented his wife.

'But it has all been well cared for, as you can see,' replied Mr Simpkins, looking complacently round. 'As you say, madam, there's beautiful things in the house – antiques, too. Mr Strode was a noted collector. But his best china – pots they call Bing, or Ming, or some such comic name – is lent to the Victoria and Albert Museum.'

'Those, too, are the sort of things you see in museums,' remarked Mr Pickering, with his eyes upon the fan-shaped arrangement on the only wall where bookcases did not rise too high for such a display, and where the elaborate inlay of an early seventeenth-century German arquebus shouldered the tapering length and complicated hilt of a Spanish rapier or the unfamiliar mechanism of a wheel-lock pistol.

'This is the study, I suppose,' said comfortable-looking Mrs Pickering. 'But I am sure that if I tried to read in here, I should always be looking out at that beautiful view.'

'Yes, madam,' agreed Mr Simpkins, towering over her in his long, light overcoat; 'yes, especially when the famous rhododendrons by the lake are in bloom. And, of course, if the house was occupied the grounds would look more as they used to do – not but what the lawn is mown regularly now. But a property always appears to much better advantage when there is someone in it.'

'What I can't understand,' reiterated the Australian, 'is why in five years there hasn't been someone in it, or why it hasn't been bought, since you say Mr Strode would prefer to sell.'

'Well, sir,' responded Mr Simpkins, with a slight tinge of constraint, 'it's not everyone who requires a large place like this, all furnished. Gentlemen who would take a lease of a property of this size usually have their own furniture; still more so those who might wish to purchase it.'

'Yes, I suppose that's true. But when a man comes back from the under-side of the globe like me, he's glad to find a home all ready to step into. And I should have thought there might have been other chaps in the same position. Have you had *nobody* after it in five years?'

'Oh, several people, Mr Pickering, several,' the house agent assured him in haste. 'But for some of them the Manor was too big, for others too small. There's always a something, as the saying is.' He broke off suddenly. 'Would you kindly excuse me for a moment, sir? There's the gardener out there wanting to speak to me, I see, before he goes home to his dinner.'

'I call it charming,' repeated Mr Pickering, as the agent hurried out into the verandah and vanished. 'Don't you think so, too, Polly?'

But plump little Mrs Pickering did not seem to share his

enthusiasm. 'If you ask me,' she said slowly, 'I believe there *is* a "something" about this place which frightens everyone away, for all it seems so bright and has been so well kept up. Just now, when I was looking out at the lake there …' She stopped.

'But it was you, little woman, who said you'd always be looking at it if you lived here!'

'I'm not so sure, now, that I should,' responded his wife, drawing her breath in sharply. 'And, Alfred, didn't you notice, when we stopped the car at that little farm outside the village and asked the way, just before we met Mr Simpkins, the girl looked almost scared? I wonder if the Manor is supposed to be haunted?'

Her husband chuckled. 'The only objection to haunted houses that I've ever heard of is that you can't get servants to stay in 'em. Otherwise I should be no end pleased to have an ancestor clanking round in chains, even if it wasn't my own ancestor. If there's a Johnny of that sort here, so much the better!'

'Alfred, are you really thinking of buying the place?'

'I'm inclined to, if you're agreeable, old lady. I like it fine. The house may not be as old as these fellows make out, but it's none the worse for that, and the grounds only want a little attention – almost a park, they are, too. I should like to buy it lock, stock and barrel, furniture, books and curios – including those queer old guns (if they *are* guns) and swords and things there.' He surveyed the trophy of weapons for a moment. 'I could put my two bushmen's spears in with them … Hullo, why has this sheath got no sword in it? Japanese work, by the look of it, like that figure in armour over there near you.'

Mrs Pickering was now by the door, looking down at something. 'I don't think this cheap rug is worth buying!' she observed critically. 'An absolutely shoddy thing – on a valuable carpet like this, too!' She stooped, turned back the rug in question, and became quite silent.

At that moment the lank form of Mr Simpkins reappeared at the French window, and him Mr Pickering, still examining the display of weapons, addressed over his shoulder. 'I say, isn't there a sword or something missing from here?'

But the house agent did not answer because at the same instant Mrs Pickering also said, in a voice so queer that her husband immediately turned round: 'I see now why this rug was put here. But ... what made that stain?'

Mr Pickering came over to view the place. The representative of Pottinger, Simpkins and Marrow followed, more slowly. Colour had sprung into his cadaverous cheeks. 'Well, madam, it's hard for me to answer that question, isn't it?' he asked, in a manner attempting the semi-jovial. 'Not having lived in the house, you see ... Oh, something spilt, I should say, by one of the caretakers we've had here; and, after trying to get the mark out, the woman's gone and bought that cheap rug and put it down to cover the damage. But the carpet could easily be turned round, in which case that side of it would be –'

'Yes, of course it could!' broke in Mr Pickering cheerfully. His Polly really looked quite strange and upset. 'What's come to you, my girl? Accidents will happen!'

'I want to know what the accident was!' repeated his wife, with an odd, pale persistence most unlike her.

'My dear, how can Mr Simpkins possibly tell us? It's unfortunate there should be a stain, but I can't see that it's of any importance how it came there.'

'Allow me, madam,' quoth Mr Simpkins, stooping and replacing the rug. 'I will instruct the present caretaker to have a try to get the mark out. I suggest that you come out into the garden now, sir, and have a look at this side of the house ... Madam, I am afraid you are feeling indisposed; shall I fetch you some water?'

'My dear Polly, what's got you?' exclaimed her husband in

alarm, putting his arm round her plump contours. 'Here, I believe I have my flask with me; yes.' And with one hand he pulled it out. 'Sit down there, dear, on the sofa, and have a drop of this, perhaps with a little water, if Mr Simpkins will kindly fetch some.'

'No!' said Mrs Pickering, shuddering violently. 'No, I won't sit down in this room. Take me out of it quickly – no, no, *no*, Alfred, not through that window – that's worse, much worse! And for God's sake don't have anything to do with the house! Something dreadful has happened in this room.'

And as her husband, thoroughly frightened (for she was not by nature an hysterical or fanciful woman), hurried her through the door, she burst into tears.

'Most unfortunate,' said Mr Simpkins about an hour and a half later to his partner in their office in the little county town. 'Blanked unfortunate! He was all for taking it, perhaps even for buying it, the Colonial.'

'I hope you didn't call him that, Simmie,' replied Mr Marrow, who in shape resembled his name-sake of the vegetable kingdom. 'Dominions they are nowadays, Australians.'

Mr Simpkins took no notice. 'Yes, I believe he would have bought it if that blessed wife of his hadn't gone off into hysterics in the library. Perhaps I oughtn't to have taken them in there; but if I had made any difficulty about it that would have seemed odd, too.'

'What made her go into hysterics?'

'She had moved the rug. It's true that it is in an unusual place for a rug to be. But God alone knows what put the suspicion into her head, because the mark don't look like *that* now – not to my thinking. Funny thing was that at the same moment – the very same moment, mind you – the chap himself saw that the sword was missing; said something about it, too, but I took no notice. (The sheath ought not to be on the wall at all.) And then in a minute or two he had to take her out of the room, fairly howling. Queer creatures, women, damned queer!'

Mr Marrow, about to light a cigarette, paused. 'I think, considering what you and me know about the library of the Manor, we may say that they are. And now it almost looks as if it was a case with this Mrs Pickering, too, of – what do they call it? – the thing that caused all the trouble five years ago.'

'You surely don't mean that she is what they said at the inquest that poor girl was?'

'No, no; I mean the business that started it – clair ... what the devil is it called? – clairvoyance.'

'Oh, that! But if this Mrs Pickering had had clairvoyance she would have seen –'

'What it's a good thing for her that she didn't see,' finished Mr Marrow, achieving the lighting of his cigarette. 'But, damn it all, we've lost yet another possible tenant. I suppose they must have heard something, in spite of all the trouble we took that they shouldn't speak to anyone in the village and get wind of it like the last people did.'

'I don't think it was that. And yet when he had soothed her down and got her into the car – for she said she must go straight back to London – he asked me right out, there in the drive: "Has there been a murder or a suicide taken place in that room? Now tell me the truth, as man to man."'

'And what did you say, as man to man?'

'I told him the truth, of course. I said: "No, no murder or suicide took place in that room, I give you my word." So he asks: "What did take place there, then?" looking a bit as if he had caught the horrors from his wife, though he didn't seem at all that sort. (No more did she, to do her justice.) I says: "My dear sir, the house being Queen Anne, lots of things that we know nothing about must have happened in that library." "Queen Anne!" says he. "Queen Victoria, more like! But something very unpleasant took place there, and at a guess five years ago. I shall not take the house. Send in your bill for any expenses you may have been put to over this visit." Then he got into his car and slammed the door; and that was the last I saw of them. All the woman's fault, like the … the affair in the library.'

'That's a bit hard,' observed Mr Marrow judicially. 'It wasn't really the poor girl's fault; if anybody's, it was Strode's – at least, he was responsible. You may remember that if the medical evidence hadn't been so positive that it was impossible to hypnotise a person into doing a thing like that, he might have been sent for trial – Did these Pickerings find out that he left the very day after the inquest; just walked out of the house and has never been near it since, in all these years?'

'Not from me, you bet … Well, there's nothing to be done but to go on with that advertisement, *To Americans and others*, because it seems pretty hopeless to get anybody else – unless the place could be given another name. No one in England is likely to have forgotten the "Strode Manor tragedy".'

'We might head the ad with this, which I saw used the other day, and by a London firm, I fancy: *Situate amid inconceivable rurality*. Not true of the Manor, exactly, but that's no matter. It's a taking expression, that's the main thing.'

Mr Simpkins did not reply. His eyes had a rapt, glassy look; an idea was being born.

'I believe,' he said at last, 'that if we could hook an American we should do better *not* to keep the story quiet, but to boost it to him for all it was worth. Wouldn't a hundred percent Yank be likely to find it full of "pep"?'

'Simmie,' exclaimed Mr Marrow, 'you've hit it! We might even get more for the place … when we find the right oil-king!'

2

The close-shaven lawns were brilliantly green, the great rhododendrons in their full rosy magnificence, when the horror happened, five years before. The villagers said that the bushes had never bloomed so luxuriantly since; but then they never went into the grounds to see. They were afraid of meeting her, the delicate pale girl with *those* hands, or perhaps the little boy ...

It was not exactly a party; Edward Strode did not like them. But Persis, his seventeen-year-old daughter, had her friend Cynthia Storrington staying with her, even as Mr and Mrs Strode had the elegant Mrs Fleming stopping with them; and three girls and a couple of youths of Persis' acquaintance had come to tea and tennis. Moreover, Catherine, the youngest child – the two boys in between were away at school – was celebrating her birthday and playing with half a dozen small companions of both sexes, under due supervision from nurses, down by the lake and its red and pink bastions of blossom. But though Mrs Strode had earlier presided over the tea-table in the drawing-room on the other side of the house, she was now sitting with some embroidery on the sofa in the library, where were also Mrs Fleming, in a Paris frock of extreme simplicity and expensiveness, smoking a cigarette in a long amber holder, and Edward Strode himself, with his little pointed Elizabethan beard, carefully mending a torn page in a recently acquired manuscript.

'Where ever did you get that charming design, Marian?' suddenly asked the guest, coming to the sofa and stooping over Mrs Strode with a lazy, boneless grace. 'Not from any shop, I am sure.'

'No. I adapted it from a *tsuba* of Edward's.'

'Mercy on us, what's a *tsuba*?'

'The guard of a Japanese sword,' replied Mrs Strode, stitching away. 'He has quite a quantity of them, some with very agreeable designs indeed. I have used the best already. This one is actually from the guard of his precious Sadamune *katana* on the wall there, and, not being detached like the others, was a little more difficult to copy, since I would not let him take it off for me.' She held up her work. 'Any design on a *tsuba* must fit into its more or less circular shape, you see. These little drooping stems are rice.'

'But it is exquisite!' exclaimed Mrs Fleming. 'A miracle of design – and of ingenuity. I should like to see the original. A trifle out of place on a sword-hilt, though, somehow – rice.'

Edward Strode looked up. 'Some hilts have plum blossoms, bamboos blown by the wind, peonies or twisted water-weeds. I will get the sword down for you with pleasure, Erica; it is one of my proudest treasures. I have not had it long, however. The *tsuba*, as it happens, has been rather a sore point ever since Jenkinson was here a fortnight ago, for he had the impudence to say that he was not sure if it was genuine.' He made a wry face.

'But the sword –'

'Oh, the sword is genuine enough, and rare, and very old; a poem in steel – a signed poem, too. It's infernal nonsense about the guard, of course; still, I shall not be quite at ease until a better authority than Jenkinson has seen it.'

'But, Edward,' protested Mrs Fleming, 'surely you are an authority on … what do you call the things?'

Edward Strode smiled his infrequent smile. 'There are seven hundred different specimens of these guards in the South Kensington Museum alone, for there exist about seventy different schools and sub-schools in the art of *tsuba*-making.' He was bringing down the sword, scabbard and all from the wall – a long-sword, a *katana*, slightly curved, with the usual long pommel wrapped round and round in an open pattern with dark silk braid, which allowed the pearly incrustations of the ray-skin mount to show through its interstices. The sheath, of magnolia wood ornamented with strips of cane, was old and shabby; but had it been lavishly decorated one would not have looked at it again when the blade was out – as its owner, almost reverently, drew it out now; so mirror-bright was the steel, so perfect in line, so smooth and flawless its marvellous surface. Indeed, Mrs Fleming, forgetting her desire to examine the guard, said, with something like a gasp: 'You say this is very old – it can't be!'

'It was forged about six hundred years ago; it is dated. Sadamune, the famous swordsmith who made it, worked in the early part of the fourteenth century.'

'In the thirteen hundreds! Edward, it's impossible! It might have been made yesterday! Why, the blade of that slim, pointed sword on the wall there – I happened to be examining it yesterday – which I suppose is not so old, looks far older, for it is all flecked and pitted.'

'And yet that rapier is three hundred years the junior of this sword. It is a reputed Toledo blade, too. But, my dear Erica, compared with the work of the great Japanese swordsmiths, even the swords of Damascus and Toledo are, as a French authority puts it, but the efforts of children. Japanese swords are incomparably the most beautiful that the world has ever produced. Do you know that no European sword has ever possessed an edge like this, because if it had the whole sword would be as brittle as glass (since European swords are of the same hardness all over). But here the body of the blade – the very bright part – is of softer temper to avoid the risk of breakage. I have cut through a floating scarf with this beautiful thing, and I daresay it would go with the same ease through a man's leg, bone and all – I have not tried.'

'What is that kind of wavy mistiness along the edge?' asked Mrs Fleming, bending over the weapon.

'That is the *yakiba*, the tempering, patterned so on purpose. There are thirty-two main designs of *yakiba*.'

'Good heavens!'

'Now I will show you an interesting thing,' said her host, well mounted on his subject. 'You see where the *yakiba* comes round to the point of the blade – the *boshi* – and takes a different pattern?'

'Yes, if you can call anything so ghostly and indeterminate a pattern. I suppose you will tell me that there are several different classes of that?'

'As a matter of fact, there are. Well, this particular one is characteristic only of the smith who made this sword, Sadamune, the great Masamune's favourite pupil; and the shape represents the upper part of the head of Jizo, the god who looks after children, and who is generally represented as a young and handsome man with a beautiful smile.'

Mrs Fleming laughed. 'Alas, I can't make out anything remotely suggesting the head of any man, handsome or ugly. But I do see that the sword is a thing of beauty, cold and deadly perhaps, but exquisite – Now I must look at the guard.'

'You do recognise the sword's beauty?' said Edward Strode eagerly. 'I am glad of that. As to its coldness, there is a Japanese poem which says that a drawn sword brings a cool breeze into a house even at midsummer. Swords, you know, were formerly in Japan objects of veneration, almost of worship; the swordsmiths lived a semi-religious life, and the forging of a sword was practically a religious ceremony, requiring a ceremonial costume.'

'The forging then,' commented the visitor, 'was hardly of a piece with that in the *Ring* – I mean when Siegfried, clad in his customary hearth-rug, bangs away at Nothung on Covent Garden stage! So these are your bending rice-stalks, Marian. What workmanship! What metal is the guard made of, Edward?'

'Iron – pierced iron.'

'And what are these tiny gold dragons on the hilt, under the binding?'

'Those are the *menuki*, to give a better grip,' explained Mr Strode. 'The hilt, of course, is more recent than the blade, the *tsuba* too, even if it is really of the school of Miochin, as it purports to be – Hallo, Persis, have your visitors gone?'

'Yes, Daddy, but only just,' replied his elder daughter, appearing at the French window, and sniffing at the big creamy rose which she had plucked from the verandah. 'They said they were too hot for any more tennis, lazy pigs, so we went back to the drawing-room and played the "willing" game – you know. Oh, and Daddy,' she stepped into the room, 'such an interesting thing happened. You know how you blindfold a person and put your hands on their shoulders, two of you, and "will" them to do something or other. Yes,' as her father frowned impatiently, 'I know you think it silly, but listen! Cynthia said she was ready to be "willed"; so we blindfolded her and told her to make her mind a blank, and we settled that she should go to the little table with the snuff-boxes and vinaigrettes, and pick out the china snuff-box which has that darling little landscape, and take it over and put it in a particular place on the mantelpiece. Well, after we had willed a bit she started off, slowly, and went to the table with us – it was Joan and I – and picked out the box from the others all right –'

'I detest this playing with the fringes of a serious subject like hypnotism,' growled Mr Strode.

'Yes, I know, darling, but listen! Directly Cynthia got the snuff-box into her hands she began to feel it all over in a curious way; then, instead of taking it to the mantelpiece, she suddenly sat down and held the snuff-box tight, and began to talk very fast; we could not make out much of what she was saying, and, in fact, it hardly sounded like her voice.

Presently the tears began to run down her face, and she seemed so unhappy that we took the snuff-box away from her, and unbandaged her eyes; and after a bit she woke up and was just the same as usual – Daddy, I shan't stay to be looked at like that. Smell this, and you'll feel better!' She thrust the great rose into her father's face, laughed, and sped out again by the way she had come.

'That's rather a curious thing, Edward,' remarked Mrs Strode after a moment, laying down her embroidery. 'Cynthia could not have known the story of the last owner of the porcelain snuff-box.'

'The girl is apparently a sensitive,' replied her husband, sliding the Japanese sword carefully back into its sheath … 'She's what is commonly called clairvoyante – though to my thinking clairvoyance can nearly always be explained by thought transference from the mind of some other person present.'

'But not in this case,' said Mrs Strode quietly. 'Persis knows nothing about that little box.'

'Cynthia's tears were justified, then?' enquired Mrs Fleming.

'The last owner of the porcelain snuff-box was certainly very unhappy,' replied Mrs Strode. 'But only Edward and I know that.'

'Then the girl is undoubtedly a sensitive!' exclaimed Mrs Fleming. 'It seems to me a gift that should be cultivated; it would be invaluable to a collector, for instance … Why, of course, Edward, here is a splendid chance of getting some light on the problem of your *tsuba*! Have Cynthia in and see what she says!'

'I am afraid I should not attach much weight to it. I am sceptical about clairvoyance, for the reason I have mentioned.'

'Yet you admit that the girl must be a sensitive. Test her!'

'Another time,' said Mr Strode. 'Have you finished looking at the *tsuba*, Erica?'

'But Cynthia is leaving tomorrow, Edward,' his wife reminded him, as she selected a fresh thread of silk. 'By the morning train, in fact, directly after breakfast.'

'So you see that there is no time like the present,' urged Mrs Fleming with a laugh. 'You could try her on something else first. Robert' (she was referring to her husband) 'would be so pleased, poor jealous darling, to hear that your Mino da Fiesole Virgin and Child, for instance, was only "of the school".'

'I don't imagine,' said Edward Strode dryly, 'that, however jealous Fleming is, he would be satisfied with such an ascription on the authority of an ignorant girl of seventeen. But the manifestation is interesting, none the less.'

'Then for heaven's sake let us go and see it!' cried Mrs Fleming. 'Perhaps Cynthia is even now describing the past occupants of those William and Mary chairs in the drawing-room!'

'You forget, there is only Persis with her now,' remarked Mrs Strode. 'The game is over.'

'And in any case, I should not have joined in that childishness,' observed her husband. 'If I made such an experiment at all it would be quietly in here. But of course it is arrant nonsense to imagine that the child could tell one anything of value on a disputed point – anything about the maker of this *tsuba*, for instance.'

'One Japanese looking much like another Japanese, even to a clairvoyante,' suggested Mrs Fleming. 'On the other hand, suppose the *tsuba* was turned out in Birmingham – don't look so outraged, Edward, I'm sure it wasn't. But do have Cynthia in and see what happens! Marian, do make him!'

Mrs Strode put down her work. 'I will go and ask her to come in here if you are so set on it, Erica. Shall I, Edward?'

Half reluctantly, her husband nodded, and she left the room.

'This should be most interesting,' said Mrs Fleming, laying aside her cigarette-holder. Taking up a strip of old brocade from the back of the sofa, she spread its faded silver gilt and roses over the whole length of the sheathed *katana*, still upon the table, leaving only the guard exposed. 'You know how to start her off, Edward – since it seems that *is* the method to start her? I have played at it, too ... But I was forgetting,' she added on a different note, 'I was quite forgetting that you know something of hypnotism, as of most things; so she ought to respond very readily if you "will" her to see a Japanese of the proper period working at those charming ears of rice!'

The door opened.

'Here's Cynthia, ready to oblige,' announced Persis. 'What can she do for you, Daddy?'

Her father fingered his little pointed beard. 'My dear,' said Mrs Fleming, coming forward, 'it is really I who want you to – oh no, I must not tell you exactly what. But we hear that you were so clever about ... something in the drawing-room.'

'Was I?' asked Cynthia Storrington, opening wider her innocent, dreamy-looking eyes. She was a girl for whom the word 'ethereal' might have been especially minted, a tall slip of a girl with ash-blond hair and very delicate features, wearing a green dress the colour of an early beech-leaf.

Mrs Strode reappeared. 'There is something on the table here, Cynthia, that my husband wants to make an experiment about, if you will help him.'

'But how can I?' asked the girl. She glanced shyly at Mr Strode. 'Oh no, I'd rather not, I think. It was only a game, you know, just now in the drawing-room.'

'And *I* don't consider it any more than a game, Cynthia,' said her host quickly. 'And if you would really rather not –'

'Oh, Cynthia, do!' pleaded Mrs Fleming.

'Cynthia, don't be a goat!' admonished Persis more bluntly and perhaps more efficaciously. And she added in an audible whisper, as she went nearer to her friend: 'You can make up what you jolly well please!'

'But I don't make up!' protested Cynthia, wrinkling her white forehead. 'I don't know what I say!'

'Or do, either? Didn't you know you were crying?'

Cynthia turned crimson. 'Don't torment her, Persis!' said that damsel's mother. 'My dear Cynthia, take no notice of her, or of anybody else; go back to the drawing-room!'

But Edward Strode had his eyes fixed upon the girl. Perhaps it was the first time that he had ever been quite aware of her particular quality, though it was not her first visit to the Manor. And Cynthia, supersensitive as she evidently was, seemed to be conscious of something unusual in his gaze. She looked at him, then away. 'I will try if you like, Mr Strode.'

'Thank you,' said he briefly; and Mrs Fleming added: 'That is very sporting of you, Cynthia.' Then Persis produced a silk handkerchief of her elder brother's which had evidently served the same purpose previously, and tied it over the dreamy eyes.

'Who is going to do it?' she asked, knotting the ends. 'You and I, Daddy?'

'No, not you, because you do not know what the problem is. Mrs Fleming, who does, will assist in this … game of Blind Man's Buff.' It was plain that he was ill at ease, ashamed, almost, at taking part, to please his old friend, in what he considered a childish performance.

The two laid their hands lightly on the girl's slim shoulders, and for a few minutes there was complete silence in the room itself. But from without floated in the cries and laughter of the children chasing each other about the rhododendrons, away by the lake, and the sleepy, liquid notes of distant wood-pigeons. Cynthia in her leaf-green frock had stood at first like an image; then, all at once, but still with an automaton-like stiffness, she, and the couple with her, began to move towards the library table. Mrs Strode and Persis watched them. A little pressure easily directs a blindfolded and susceptible young thing, thought Mrs Strode sceptically; she had resumed her seat on the sofa and her embroidery.

As she made this reflection there came a knock at the door – for Mr Strode's sanctuary was never entered without permission. Persis darted out.

She returned. 'Bother!' she said in a low voice to her mother. 'It's Major Whittingham, come about a licence or something. He wants to see Daddy most particularly, Morton says, and can't wait. He wouldn't keep him more than a couple of minutes. He's in the drawing-room.'

Edward Strode heard. 'Then I am afraid I must go to him. We had, however, hardly begun.' He removed his hands. 'My dear Cynthia, a thousand apologies! If you can spare the time to stay here we can resume when I return; I shall not be long.'

'Shall I take off the handkerchief?' asked the disappointed Mrs Fleming as their host left the room; and without waiting for an answer she untied it. 'There, sit down, Cynthia; I don't expect Mr Strode will be more than a few minutes.'

Still as if she were in one piece Cynthia obeyed, seating herself in the chair drawn up to the table; and almost immediately one long slender hand began to search over the table's surface. The other she had put up to her eyes. It occurred to Mrs Fleming that the girl was further 'gone' than she had thought, and that perhaps it was not altogether good to have called her back so abruptly.

'I know,' said Cynthia suddenly, in a slightly unusual voice, 'what you want me to touch. It is here somewhere.' She brought down her other hand, and that, too, began to pass over the nearer portion of the table, sweeping about like a blind person's. Together they reached, one the shrouded and sheathed blade, the other the shrouded pommel of the Japanese sword.

'Cynthia, what are you keeping your eyes shut for?' asked Mrs Strode sharply, leaning forward from the sofa. 'Open them, child!'

But Cynthia's eyes were still shut when her left hand clutched the sword through the strip of brocade; still shut when with a couple of imperious gestures she first flung off the strip and then, somewhat to the consternation of the two ladies, drew off the sheath of the *katana* and threw that, too, upon the floor. The long, keen blade gleamed naked on the library table.

'You'll cut yourself,' remonstrated Mrs Fleming almost nervously. 'And it isn't the blade that we want to know about – Whatever is the girl playing at?'

For while the fingers of Cynthia's right hand were clutching the braided ray-skin of the pommel, the fingers of the left felt along the blade, leaving little patches on the unsullied steel.

'You'll catch it for doing that!' muttered Persis, who knew that no ungloved hand must ever touch that sacred surface.

'Sadamune made it,' said Cynthia in a hoarse whisper. 'He never made a better blade. My great-great-grandfather carried it in a sheath of inlaid iron; my grandfather had a scabbard of gold lacquer made for it, and I –'

She broke off and opened her eyes. They had changed colour and character alike; bright and fierce, they were staring out of the window in front of her, and her mouth, the young, fresh mouth of seventeen, was set in a thin, cruel line.

Mrs Strode was already off the sofa. 'Cynthia,' she said in a tone of authority, 'put down that sword at once!'

Cynthia had not in truth taken it up; it still lay on the table, though the pommel was in her grip. But instead of obeying she laughed, and broke into a run of meaningless syllables, in which the word *wakizashi* kept recurring. Mrs Strode, if no one else, recognised the Japanese name for the lesser sword which always accompanied the *katana* in a *daimio's* sash.

'Persis,' said Mrs Fleming breathlessly, 'go for your father quickly! She – this must be stopped!'

'Oh, Cynthia, don't be a goat!' adjured Persis, for the second and last time; and with the words laid a rather timid hand on her friend's shoulder from behind.

And at that Cynthia jumped up, brandishing the *katana* as though it were of straw, her eyes, which were not her eyes any more, blazing with an unholy rapture, and the strange language still hissing from her altered mouth.

'Daddy, Daddy!' screamed Persis, hurling herself through the doorway, 'Daddy, come at once … *Daddy!*'

'She's gone crazy,' said Mrs Strode quickly. 'We must get the sword away from her! Catch her arm, Erica!'

'I shall make a sheath for it of my enemies!' sang Cynthia, reverting all at once to English. She had backed to the edge of the open French window, dragging with her Mrs Fleming, who, unable to get hold of her right arm, had seized the left. On the threshold Cynthia flung her off, and as she stumbled brought down that flashing miracle of sharpness. It did not need a man's arm behind it. Catching Mrs Fleming between neck and shoulder, going with joy through the soft blue Doucet gown and the chalcedony necklace which matched it, the incomparable edge sliced through the artery and half the neck. Mrs Fleming fell outside in the verandah, screaming; and there, in a very short time, died.

For one instant Mrs Strode had retreated towards the sofa. She might, if she had been very quick, have got unharmed from the room – for she had forgotten the children at the far end of the lawn – but she was by nature a brave woman. Catching up in a bunch the heavy bear-skin rug at her feet she came on again, intending to throw it over that terrible young figure by the window, now whirling the long *katana* about in all directions and chanting unintelligibilities at the top of its voice. 'Edward will be here in a moment,' Marian Strode was telling herself, 'Edward and no doubt Major Whittingham, too. If I can just get this over her head ... or over the sword even ... O God, if only Erica were not screaming like that!...'

But bear-skins were nothing to the Sadamune blade. It flashed once; hair, pelt and mounting parted like butter, and the head of Jizo bit deep into the top of Mrs Strode's left arm. She dropped the rug, and this time made a rush for the door. The sword instantly pursued her. But she was saved by the figure in Japanese armour standing in the corner, for even as she sank down, almost against the door-panels, she heard Cynthia striking madly at the grinning mask under the helmet, and the steel clattering on the lacquered body-plates. That, too, ceased, as she went into darkness ... Two minutes more, and her husband, bursting in, had caught her up in his arms, while out under the pale roses of the verandah Major Whittingham, as pale as they, was just realising that it was of no avail to linger over what lay there. And where was the girl?

Cynthia was gone – to worse. The children by the rhododendrons, thinking it a game, had run to meet her. But Jizo, the protector of children, killed only one outright, and he a rather uninteresting little boy. The rhododendrons saved the rest, even the maimed. She could not easily get in among those flowering fastnesses, or did not trouble to attempt it, slashing at their heads of bloom instead. So the Sadamune blade was stained with green as well before consciousness of what she had done came to the girl ... if it ever came. She may have jumped from the diving-board still in the full frenzy of whatever centuries-old blood lust the touch of the sword had communicated to her, or she may have awakened. One of the children's nurses, herself injured, was the only witness of the end. The young Death gave a cry which might have been either a laugh or a shriek, then, holding the wet *katana* high above her head, jumped straight off the spring-board into the lake. The nurse, before she herself fainted among the rhododendron stems, saw that she went down like a stone.

When the slayer was found she might have been Ophelia. There were no stains on the green dress and her hands were empty and clean. The poem in steel lies quiet at the bottom of the lake, with its lovely lustre tarnished and water-weeds growing through the tracery of the disputed *tsuba*. Perhaps when the right oil-king is found to take Strode Manor he will have it retrieved, for it is very valuable.

5 The Promised Land (1932)

In the church of San Domenico at Siena, on a certain fine spring day not long ago, two ladies and a young man were studying and appraising, not for the first time, the great 'Swoon of Saint Catherine' there. The young man, who looked like a budding don, spoke as one to whom all pictorial art is as an open page, and the ladies held their own on almost equal terms. None of them carried guide-books of any kind, since all were specimens of the truly cultivated traveller.

Two other people were presently heard to enter the empty church. At the sound of steps the cultured looked round apprehensively, lest that horror of horrors, the voluble and loud-speaking guide, should be one of them, and they themselves should be assailed by his detestable English and his still more detestable flow of information. This indeed they were spared, though something almost as repugnant befell them.

The newcomers were two middle-aged ladies in dust-cloaks and mushroom hats, the one large and stout, the other small and thin, and before ever they reached the famous fresco the greater was reading aloud to the less out of a betraying red volume.

'This is by Sodoma, and double-starred, Ellen. Baedeker says –'

Shuddering violently, the cultured trio instinctively retreated, and before much of what Baedeker said had polluted their ears, they were outside San Domenico altogether, leaving Saint Catherine to the elderly Philistines. The young man took off his pince-nez with a judicial air.

'What good purpose can possibly be served,' he remarked, 'by the visit to Italy of such travellers as those, one's mind fails even approximately to conceive. What can Siena mean to them – Siena of all places, with her delicate, evasive charm, Siena who sits within the walls which have grown too vast for her … and smiles? I sometimes see a resemblance in this wonderful town,' he finished, 'to La Gioconda.'

His companions gave this rare thought their attention and criticism. Then they all went for the fourth time to the Baptistery. It was while they were looking at the Knight of Malta that the younger of the two ladies suddenly said, 'I remember now, Cecilia, where I have seen those two old Baedekerites before. They are at our hotel.'

'Oh, are they the old things sitting at that table in the corner? I thought last night that the stout one looked intelligent in a rough-and-ready sort of way. She must have dragged the smaller with her against her will, I should say – *she* didn't look as though she were enjoying Siena much. Did you notice them, Ralph?'

'No, why should I?' asked the young man. 'But I shall notice them henceforward, in order to avoid them. "Double-starred by Baedeker!" Oh, ye gods!'

※

In due time 'the two old Baedekerites' also emerged into the sunshine, and the larger put that invaluable companion into a small corn-coloured satchel adorned with red and green wools.

'Now, Ellen,' she said cheerfully, 'I think you have seen enough for this morning. We must leave Fontebranda, and all that, till this afternoon, and then we can take our time over Saint Catherine's house.'

Ellen said, 'Yes, Caroline'; and their sensibly clad feet began to carry the couple away from San Domenico. But had Ralph Shilleto and his cultured ladies known of the dull, despairing revolt beneath the lace-draped hat of the smaller Philistine, whom they surmised to have been 'dragged abroad' by the larger, they might possibly have been more interested, for the moment, in her than in the masterpiece which she and her companion had desecrated.

To have the dream of a lifetime fulfilled – and spoilt in the fulfilling; to enter at last the Promised Land, and find it a desert; that was the tragedy which, in her sixty-first year, had befallen meek, unimportant Ellen Wright, and was heavy on her now. At every turn the murdered dream cried aloud to heaven: Fontebranda, name like a lovely and heroic poem … but not when her cousin Caroline Murchison uttered it; the tower of the Mangia, that tall lily which could take your soul soaring up with it into the blue … but not when Caroline stood beside you reading out its dimensions. The same blight everywhere – over Perugia, with its fierce, beautiful, massacred Baglioni, even over Assisi the holy. In two days Florence would be added to the holocaust, and then the tour in Italy, the lode-star of thirty uneventful years, would be over, and the two of them would be back in their little house – Caroline's little house – at Lower Waddington, and what remained of wonder in the experience would finally evaporate as Caroline retailed it to callers over the teacups.

'You are very silent, Ellen,' observed Miss Murchison when they reached their room in the hotel. 'A bit tired, aren't you? I should just sit quiet a little before lunch if I were you. I shall go down to the lounge and read the English paper. That book on Saint Catherine is under my knitting over there.'

'Yes,' said her cousin. Her lips were trembling. She began to pull the pins out of her hat.

'You'd better keep your hat on for lunch, hadn't you?' suggested Caroline, turning at the door. 'Or else do your hair again. That hat of yours always presses it down in such an unbecoming way.'

'I will put it on again for lunch,' agreed Ellen meekly. 'But I must take it off now, my head aches.'

'It always will if you go out with the wrong glasses, as you did today,' returned practical Caroline, and she departed, giving the door a cheery bang.

Miss Ellen Wright finished taking off the hat. From habit she went to the mirror, not because she wanted to see herself there, nor even in order to judge whether her cousin's condemnation of the effect of her hat on her coiffure were justified. She took no interest in her own appearance beyond wishing that it should be a tidy one; she knew that she was just a plain, skimpy, dowdy, uninteresting old maid of sixty, tolerated in Lower Waddington only because she was, so to speak, a part of the larger, better-off and masterful cousin with whom she lived and had her being. A part of Caroline – yes, that was the trouble … and a part which was not allowed to have its own existence, scarcely its own thoughts, and which now had had its life-dream killed by Caroline's insisting on sharing it with her.

The eyes of withered speedwell grew for a moment fierce. Then the light died out of them. Ellen sat down and leant her scantily-covered grey head against the chair, reproaching herself for her ingratitude. Caroline was so kind, so practical, and arranged everything so efficiently.

But oh, if she could only sometimes get away from her! If only her own tiny annuity had permitted of a separate cottage, even though it were in the same village. Well, once 'Rosemead' *had* been hers, till she had made that dreadful muddle over an investment, so that in some way still incomprehensible to her there had been nothing left of her money at all. But Caroline, kind Caroline, had somehow bought 'Rosemead' from her, and sunk the purchase money on her behalf in this annuity, and, since the little house was then hers, had come to live in it as well. And everybody had said what an excellent arrangement this was for Ellen, and how much better Miss Murchison ran the place.

That was seventeen years ago. And for seventeen years Caroline had continued to be kind and capable and overbearing; and Ellen always, of course, so grateful to her. And yet … she had come to hate Caroline.

Ellen sat up quickly in her chair. How dreadful! Had she really thought that? No, no, no!

But she *had* thought it; at least, she feared so. And if it were true, it was Italy which had shown her the truth, Italy of the clear air and the bright, unclouded skies … and naturally, for it was over Italy that the nearest approach to a pull of wills had come in all those seventeen years. Of course, like a much weaker side in a tug-of-war, Ellen had been vanquished, for all her resistance. She had fought hard against Caroline's accompanying her to the Promised Land; yet Caroline had come.

Sitting there in the big upholstered arm-chair, clasping and unclasping her bony, veined hands, Ellen Wright went over the affair for the hundredth time. Long before she and her cousin had lived together, in the days when she herself was a little, timid, inadequately-paid governess, already nearing thirty (and no more able to cope with the unruly ways of children than at eighteen) a visit to Italy had begun to seem to her, though of course unattainable, worth – as people said – selling one's soul for. Each year she had contrived to save a pound or two towards the improbable realisation of such a scheme, but these meagre economies being nearly always swallowed up the next year, she desisted at last, disheartened. But for nearly thirty years she went on reading about Italy; its history and its art, and by the latter some seedling love of beauty in her ordinary little soul was sustained at a higher level than, to look at her, one would ever have suspected. When, about the middle of those years, 'that good Miss Murchison' descended upon her like an eagle, and plucked her and her little house out of the abyss, it had not taken

Ellen long to discover, on the evidence of photographs, that to her cousin Italy was not an unattainable dream, for she had once spent a month there. And Caroline on that had found out Ellen's secret, and chaffed her about it.

'Fancy you, Ellen, wanting to go to Italy! I can't see you there, somehow; you'd be frightened of the bullocks and their long horns, for one thing!'

Nourished by the photographs, several of which now hung framed in the drawing-room (but not by Miss Murchison's descriptions), Ellen's dream went on. And then, this last autumn, had come from the skies the most romantic event of her drab existence – the means of its realisation.

About five years earlier there had turned up one afternoon at 'Rosemead', a stranger, a young-old man driving a big car, who had asked for Ellen, had told her that he was the son of her elder brother Charlie who had 'gone out to the Colonies' when Ellen was a girl, and who had, it now appeared, made money in that vague region. He was dead; Charlie the Second had inherited his means, had returned to England, and was thinking of marrying and settling down. With the instinct of the Colonial he had sought out his only remaining relative in the old country. By good fortune Caroline was out when he called, and from the timid, stammering little spinster who was that 'Aunt Nellie' whose ten-year-old presentment in a tartan dress, and with long sausage curls, had been familiar to him since his boyhood, and whose sole completely articulate utterance for some time was a regret that he had missed Caroline – or that Caroline had missed him – he did contrive, thinking the photographs on the walls hers, to draw the admission of her Italian longings.

'Funny!' he said. 'I've always had a wish to go there too. Tell you what, Aunt Nellie, I'll take you there one of these days. Come for a spin now; my car's Italian, as it happens.'

But no, on the whole Ellen had thought, no, she would not

go for a drive. Caroline might very well return, and think it strange that she had gone out without telling her; she might even see her, driving in a large motorcar with an unknown man. Yet she would dearly have liked to go, for she had never entered anything more sumptuous than a taxi.

'Well, I'm real sorry, Aunt Nellie,' declared the visitor. 'But remember now, when I've got fixed up with a house, I'll take you to Italy – sure thing!'

The car bore him away from the gate of 'Rosemead' … into complete silence. For four years at least Ellen waited for that summons to Eldorado, at first expecting it every day, then once a month or so, then … 'Of course he didn't mean it,' Caroline would declare. 'How could you be so silly, Ellen! Master Charlie's off to Italy long ago with someone else – and not with a middle-aged aunt, you may be certain!'

And Miss Murchison, as ever, was right – save about the epoch of Charlie Wright's visit to Italy. For one morning last October, after she had relinquished the smallest glimmer of hope, Ellen had found on her breakfast plate a letter with an Italian stamp.

'That must be from Charlie,' observed Caroline, who, after due examination, had put it there. As Ellen's distant cousin she claimed the latter's nephew as well as everything else pertaining to her. 'Well, he's taken long enough to write to you, and you see, I told you so – he's gone to Italy without you!' She took off the tea-cosy, while Ellen with shaking fingers opened the letter. 'What has he got to say for himself?'

He said, penitently, that he was ashamed to think that Aunt Nellie must believe that he was a chap who didn't keep his promises; that he fully meant to have come to see her again, but that he had not settled in the old country after all – he did not state where he had settled. And now he *was* in Italy, it was true, but on his honeymoon, so that Aunt Nellie would understand that he could not well ask her to join him. But, to make good his offer as best he could, he was sending her a cheque to enable her to go there in the spring for a month or five weeks, and was, with his own and 'Belle's' love, her affectionate nephew.

The cheque had fallen from Ellen's hand to the tablecloth, so Caroline saw it at once. But in any case she would have known all about it ere the day was out.

'That's generous of Charlie, I must say – but stupid too,' commented Miss Murchison. 'There's your egg getting cold, Ellen. For how are you going to find anyone to go with you, paying their own expenses? The money he's sent won't take two people.'

'Oh, I'll find someone,' said Ellen hastily – all the more hastily because she instantly saw what would happen if she did not succeed. But she *would* succeed, and pay for the 'someone' out of the cheque, and go to Italy for a shorter period, rather than have Caroline accompanying her!

She did not sleep a wink that night for excitement, and that was only the first of many wakeful nights caused by her nephew's letter. For of course she could not find anyone to go with her. She had no friends of her own in Lower Waddington now; all who came to the house were Caroline's associates. A ghostlike couple from her girlhood's days were summoned up by letter, but one proved to be crippled with rheumatism, and the other the wife of an underpaid clergyman, who wrote that it was quite impossible to get away, and anyhow it was poor John who needed a holiday, not having had one for eight years. But Ellen could not go with 'John' to Italy. And all the time she felt that her cousin was waiting for what she knew must be the outcome of this quest.

Caroline's attitude, too, while she waited, had been so inevitable, like a stream of lava, slow, but bound to get you in the end. It had progressed from the initial: 'Of course *I* should be the best person to go with you, having been to Italy before, and knowing all your little ways so well; and if I could afford the money, and could leave the house and the garden and the Boys' Club and the Zenana working party, I really should not mind going again,' to the final: 'I can't bear for you to be so disappointed, Ellen, and I'll manage it *somehow*. Miss Colson will take the Wednesday evening classes for me, and Ruth Brown cuts out quite well now that I've taught her. I have some money put by. Yes, I'll manage it, and come with you. There now, you needn't worry any more!'

In vain Ellen had said that rather than take Caroline from her many activities in Lower Waddington she would go to Italy alone. Caroline simply laughed in her 'breezy' way – how tired Ellen had become of the local ladies who found Miss Murchison 'breezy' – and it was plain that she would never be allowed to carry out such an idea … no, even though she had thoughts of stealing away to London, by the night train, and so starting. Caroline would only have come after her. She had to give way, to say it was very kind of Caroline; and to let her make all the plans.

And the whole marvellous experience was, as Ellen had known it would be, ruined.

Nor would she ever be able to come again. This journey was, or should have been, the one shining oasis in the sand of a dull life, and instead it had been but a bitter mirage. Everything that Caroline touched lost its charm, its beauty, its freshness. Even the lower church at Assisi, when Caroline explained the Giotto frescoes which Ellen had loved, in reproduction, for years, took on the feeling of some suburban place of worship, and St Mary of the Angels became a sort of South Kensington Museum, with the Portiuncula, to Ellen a veritable shrine, placed in it for intelligent preservation … And yet what fault could be found with Caroline? She was kind in her masterful way, thoughtful for Ellen's health, bargained with the cab-drivers and the shopkeepers in the way that Italians respect, made the money go as far as possible, arranged everything admirably.

Arranged! Yes, that was it. What would it not be to have a week, even a day, when she, Ellen, could go out by herself and wander as she pleased amid all this beauty, sit down when she liked, go on when she liked, miss some sight, even if it were 'starred', because she wanted to linger over one that was not! But the day after tomorrow they would go on to Florence – to Ellen's expectation the crown of all their seeing – and she knew exactly what would happen there. She saw herself being trotted through the cells of San Marco, past those white wonders of frescoes of which she had thought for years, with 'Come on, Ellen, you're so slow – here's another!' The idea was intolerable! She would rather not go to Florence at all, so that *that* at least could remain a dream for ever, even though her eyes never rested on its loveliness.

Would it be any good suggesting their leaving out Florence?

✕

Of course it was not. She half proposed it at lunch. 'I *said* you were overdoing it!' exclaimed her cousin. 'Leave out Florence – you must be mad! Why, there's more to see there than in all the other places put together! But if you feel like that, we can easily take an extra day here in Siena, where it is quieter, so that you can get a good rest before going on.'

'No, no – I'm not at all tired,' declared Ellen. But she looked very white, and sent away the last two courses untasted.

After that Caroline, of course, insisted on her lying down that afternoon, announcing that she herself would not go out either. They could do Saint Catherine's house on the morrow.

It was easier not to resist, and Ellen very unwillingly climbed on to her half of the double bed in their room. This was the first time they had shared a bedroom. Caroline had insisted on it here, in order to economise for Florence, which she said they would find expensive. The measure had not saved much, and Ellen hated it. She lay there, her dress off, in her petticoat bodice and stout moreen underskirt, very hot, inside the mosquito curtains which, early in the year though it was, had been specially put up at Caroline's request, and Caroline read aloud an extremely gushing book on Florence. But, Ellen summoning up enough courage at last to say that she would like to go to sleep, Miss Murchison obligingly stopped, and, taking up her knitting instead, for she was never without occupation, proceeded with the manufacture of her winter stockings.

The monotonous clicking of her needles might have soothed a really sleepy person, but to Ellen, who was not sleepy, the sound was like the crossing and recrossing of hot wires inside her head.

'Won't you go out, Caroline?' she ventured at last. 'My head does ache a good deal. I think I will stay here, but I don't want to prevent –'

'Something you've eaten has upset you, I can see,' commented Miss Murchison, continuing to knit steadily. 'I wonder if it could have been –' and she ran over various dishes to which the crime might be assigned. 'Or else you've got a touch of fever. No, I certainly shan't go out and leave you.'

After a long time it was evening, and they were going to bed. Kind Caroline had not left her for a moment, just as she would be sure not to leave her in Florence.

Now they were in bed. Caroline blew out the candle, because Ellen must get to sleep, and in the morning she would probably quite have got over her 'upset'.

But it was Caroline, not Ellen, who went to sleep. Those knitting-needles seemed to go on and on … or was it mosquitoes humming, though they said it was too early for them? She was enclosed under the same mosquito-net with Caroline for ever – shut up in a sort of bag with her – being

slowly suffocated, because Caroline used up all the air …
more and more. She *must* breathe! She would make a hole in
the net on her side of the bed. In the dark she tried to do this
with her hands, but the mesh was much too stout. She pulled
the net aside, and, reaching out, felt about until she had her
nail scissors, which happened to be by the side of the bed,
and with these she clipped a small hole near the pillow. That
was better; better, too, than leaving the curtain drawn aside,
because Caroline would be sure to say that mosquitoes had
got in. They could not get in through this little hole, surely.

There, a mosquito *had* got in! Or at least something –
something that buzzed and clicked and all but talked. Indeed,
as the hours dragged by, it did talk, repeating sentences out of
Baedeker, and saying: 'You are upset! you are upset!' It went
on all night, hot and clicking, all night till the dawn came,
and then it flew down Caroline's open mouth and stopped.

But Caroline snored instead – so it was almost the same
thing. The uncertain light showed her bulk beside Ellen in
the bed. She snored not loudly but maddeningly, with a kind
of choke in the rhythm of it. She is never silent, thought
Ellen, never quiet; either she talks or reads aloud or knits
or snores … and besides, at night she flies about buzzing. I
know that now.

And suddenly she pulled aside the mosquito-net and
slipped out of bed. Could she never get away from her? And
would she insist on their sharing a room in Florence, too?

Florence … Firenze … Fiorenza … Dante's city! To wander
there in the dawn alone – to wander even in this spoilt Siena!
But if she dressed now and slipped out Caroline would very
soon discover her absence and come after her and scold her.
There was no escape.

She looked at the face half buried in the pillow, and knew
quite certainly at last, and with a certain exultation, that she
hated it and its small, blunt, purposeful features welded into

that expanse of pale fat. And why did not Caroline, who after all was two years older than herself, wear a collar to her nightdress? Her neck was creased with age. So was Ellen's own, but she kept it covered. 'Cover up your neck, Caroline, and shut your mouth – you are not talking now!'

No, but she would soon begin again.

Oddly enough, at that moment the sleeper did stop snoring, and, stirring slightly, brought her lips together. And Ellen, in her long solid night-gown with its uncompromising buttons and durable machine-made embroidery down the front, stood staring at her, amazed. Was it possible that she could make her miserable puny will dominant over Caroline's when the latter was asleep ... that she could then make her cousin do what she liked? In that case ...

Yes, yes, yes – it might be wicked, but she *did* wish it! ... just for this once ... just for Florence ... she *did* wish Caroline dead!

But that would not make her die. No, 'no fear', as she had heard the milkman at home say. She looked at her sleeping cousin with an air of command which sat strangely on her grey-haired, shrunken little figure. 'Caroline, I wish you to be dead, so that I can see Florence by myself ... dead, dead, dead!'

Caroline moved again, and started to snore afresh. She wasn't dead – wasn't going to be dead!

※

There was a man, an Italian, who had strangled his mistress with a silk stocking. Ellen had read about it in the newspaper a few days ago. Caroline had no silk stockings, still less Ellen. But here was a woollen stocking, the one which Caroline had been knitting with all that clicking, yesterday afternoon. Not long enough.

But need it be a stocking? Somewhere in a drawer was a

certain brown and white artificial silk scarf of Caroline's …
No, not in a drawer, for here it was in her hands … Fasten
one end to something immovable – the young man had done
so, to get a good pull, and a young man was likely to be much
stronger than she.

Now the scarf was knotted to the arm of the heavy
tapestried arm-chair, which could move no further because it
was already against the bed. But she would never get the scarf
passed round that creased throat without waking Caroline,
especially as the mosquito curtains were rather in the way.
'O God,' she prayed, 'help me, so that I can see Florence by
myself … If she is alive again afterwards, I don't mind so
much. Only help me now!'

'God does answer prayer,' she thought, thirty seconds later.
'She must be very fast asleep … I hope the scarf won't break
… No, God won't let it.'

✕

You can pull and pull at an artificial silk scarf. It stretches, but
it does not break, even when you have your knee, your whole
body straining against the side of the bed for better purchase.

✕

Ralph Shilleto was up early that morning, walking to and fro
in the strip of garden before the only just opened hotel. He
was meditating an article on Duccio di Buoninsegna, and
while he was trying to recall to his memory exactly which
panels of that master's great picture were in the National
Gallery, one of the swing doors was opened, and the smaller
Philistine came forth, in her black lace-covered hat and grey
dust-cloak, carrying a corn-coloured bag adorned with bright
wools.

Mr Shilleto reflected idly that it was the first time he had
ever seen her without the other, and wondered where she was

off to, so early, and alone. And as she emerged from the grove of little yellow iron tables before the door, he was moved to salute her with a *Buon giorno* and a lifted hat. The old lady glanced at him as she went quickly past, but it was evident to Mr Shilleto that she vaguely took him for some Italian. She inclined her head, and murmured a very British-sounding *Buon giorno* in her turn.

'Jove, I should never have guessed that the old thing's eyes were so blue,' he said to himself, and returned to his meditations on early Sienese art.

✖

Siena at this hour of the morning, when the air was cool and pearly clear, and the ox-carts were lumbering in from the country ... how like heaven! But the really heavenly flavour of it was this new, ecstatic sense of being alone, and free.

During that vigil ... and afterwards ... Ellen had had ample time to make her simple plans for getting off to Florence alone, without exciting surprise. (It had been wonderful to find how clear her brain was, she whom Caroline had always called muddle-headed.) Luckily they had always come downstairs in the morning for their coffee and rolls; these were never brought up to them. Luckily also Ellen knew that after their bedroom had once been rather perfunctorily 'done,' it was never again entered by any domestic, unless summoned, until next morning. She had therefore merely to say, when she went downstairs later on, that the other signora in number 6 was not very well, and wished to be left undisturbed until she rang, to ensure that no one would enter number 6 before tomorrow morning, and perhaps not even then.

As to getting to Florence, she had abandoned the idea of going with luggage, because she could not carry even their lightest suitcase downstairs unassisted; besides, to go with luggage meant a real departure, and paying the bill. Without luggage they would think nothing of her going out of the hotel alone, even rather early. But, though they would imagine that she was only going for a walk, she would get just enough necessaries for the night into that satchel of Caroline's. They had already taken rooms ahead at a pension in Florence; she would go to that, explaining that the other lady was following next day with the luggage. And as for money, of which Caroline had the charge, she knew where that was.

It had only remained, then, after dressing, to wait until the hotel should be opened, and to make herself a cup of tea on the spirit-lamp. Quite calmly she had brewed, and drunk this, even eating a couple of biscuits, and putting as many as she could stuff into the already packed satchel. For she had no fear now of Caroline, who had stopped snoring when she told her to, and scarcely a memory of what she had done to ensure this, except that it had been difficult, but that God had helped her, because He knew how important it was for her to see Florence by herself. Besides, not liking the look of her handiwork, she had heaped as much as she could of the mosquito net upon it and hidden it.

And so, having told the waiter downstairs, in her stumbling but recognisable Italian, just what she had planned to tell him, here she was, with Siena looking so smiling and friendly that she was almost tempted to linger in it. Yet, in spite of thoughts of the Mangia, it was wiser to get on to her goal by the Arno.

Taking her ticket at the station bothered her a little, because she had never done so before in Italy, and she had to hurry at the last moment to catch the Florence train, which was just going – a piece of good fortune, however, since she had not known if there would be one. But, once in it, what a marvellous feeling of peace and security! The very landscape was clad at last in just that beauty and brightness which she had pictured for years, and which until this morning of freedom she had not seen upon it.

And at a quarter-past twelve she was standing, like an exile come home, on the Ponte Vecchio at Florence, gazing at the snows far away above Vallombrosa. The wind was cold, but there was no one to say: 'Now, Ellen, you'll get a chill!' nor to restrain her from spending as long as she liked over the trays of cheap ornaments in the booths there. Ellen had been fortunate in this, that, on leaving Santa Maria Novella, which, being near the station, had been chosen for her first glimpse into Paradise, she had fallen into the hands of a kindly and competent cab-driver, and, knowing that she had plenty of money, and seeing already that Florence was a great deal larger, and incomparably more noisy than Siena, had agreed to charter him by the hour. And he had not only saved her from being swept off the pavements in the narrower streets by the trams which run so alarmingly close to them, but he had conducted the little mushroom-hatted murderess with a minimum of trouble and fatigue to the Duomo, the Baptistery, and to San Marco. For the prolonged midday siesta, when public buildings close and most sensible people enjoy a meal – but the *vetturino's* fare only ate biscuits out of a bag – he agreed to drive her slowly about that she might see the city, merely stipulating that he should have some short interval for refreshment, and it was during this period that Ellen stood on the Ponte Vecchio and knew that she was indeed in Florence.

Then her driver reappeared and drove her up to San Miniato, and with tears in her eyes Ellen saw below her that unforgettable vista of the whole city with its mellow roofs and domes and towers, round which the very mountains seem to have disposed themselves as best to enhance its beauty. And she could look at this as long as she pleased. For one moment, indeed, a tiny thought whisked its tail, minnow-like, in the troubled pool of her brain: 'Caroline would have liked this.' But another, larger one flicked instantly past: 'How glad I am she is not here!'

After San Miniato, down again, to the warm-hued spaciousness of Santa Croce, and thence, after a considerable time, to the tiny chapel in the Riccardi Palace where the most joyous and lovely of processions wends its way to so gay a Paradise. And now it began to seem that the sight-seeing would shortly have to stop for the day, since it was nearing the closing hour, the *vetturino* hinted that he had had enough of this odyssey, and Ellen herself was feeling exceedingly tired. She would just go to San Lorenzo, since it was near, to see the famous Michael Angelos, and then she would be driven over the river to the Pension Spalding, for she intended to devote tomorrow to the picture galleries, and recent experience had taught her that of all forms of sight-seeing this is the most exhausting.

As she came back into the empty church from the sacristy, Ellen stopped and began to reckon up what she would have to pay the driver, and though she had, she thought, more than enough in her purse for the purpose, this seemed a convenient opportunity to get at the flat holland pocket of Caroline's which she had with her, and bring out another fifty-lire note. This pocket, designed for the safe carrying of money upon a journey, hung under her skirt from a webbing strap round her waist. Seeking a secluded corner, she pulled up her alpaca dress to get at her store.

But there was nothing hanging there. The holland pocket was gone.

✕

As she professed herself, nevertheless, able to pay him what he demanded, the *vetturino* was sorry for the little old English lady when, some quarter of an hour later, she came down the steps to where he was waiting for her, and falteringly told him what had happened. *Dio mio*, what a misfortune! And had the signora searched all over the church and the two sacristies and the Chapel of the Princes? Yes, every guardian whom she could get hold of had been searching ... and coldly had the great Night and Dawn in Michael Angelo's sacristy looked at this incapable member of their sex whose money had not even been stolen from her, but had been allowed to drop off – if indeed it had ever been put on. But Ellen told herself that she remembered having put the pocket on. She must have fastened the buckle of its strap insecurely. She *was* incompetent, as Caroline had so often told her.

Standing there on the bottom-most step under the still unfinished façade of San Lorenzo, almost crying, while the cabman with terrific zeal moved and banged the dusty cushions of his vehicle, Ellen saw but one course open to her – to take the night train back to England. She had her return ticket – it was sewn into her stays – and enough money, after paying the driver, for incidental expenses; at least she hoped so. Without more money than that, as well as without any luggage, she suddenly felt that she could not face explanations at the Pension Spalding. In her panic and her weariness she longed all at once for the shelter of 'Rosemead', where she would not have to give explanations or make arrangements, and where she would not need money.

Golden was the light that swam over the bustling, untidy Borgo San Lorenzo – over all Florence, which she must now leave without a glimpse of its wealth of pictures, its thousand and one yet unvisited treasures. But she had seen the best, and she had seen it with her own eyes, unhampered and unchilled by another presence. She had had one whole day in the Promised Land by herself.

More than one day, surely, it seemed to her during the night, sitting upright, hot, very tired, and sleepless, in the swaying train where room had only been found for her with difficulty. She must have had several days in Florence, she had seen so much. And that was how she had spent the money in the holland pocket, for it was a complete mistake to suppose that she had lost it, as Caroline would be sure to say she had.

And at any rate, she was going back to a 'Rosemead' which she would have for a while to herself, as she had had it seventeen years ago, and so very, very often since wished that she could have it again.

✕

The fly from Upper Waddington station deposited Ellen at the gate of 'Rosemead' about thirty hours after a stricken chambermaid had rushed shrieking down the corridor of the hotel at Siena, and just about the exact time that the local police were deciding that the murder, the work of some unknown criminal, had been committed *after* the other signora had gone quietly out for an early walk, as witnessed to by an English signor staying at the hotel, as well as by a waiter. This signora had not, it was true, returned, and meanwhile all trace of her had been lost; and they knew of no relatives with whom to communicate. Moreover, national *amour-propre* prompted them to keep the matter as long as possible out of the English newspapers.

But Ellen was not troubling herself over what might be happening in Italy; she was sufficiently taken aback to find 'Rosemead' securely shut up and the blinds down. Somehow she had not expected this ... and were the lowered blinds for Caroline? Nor did she know to whom her cousin had entrusted the key, nor what had been arranged about their little servant. After standing for some time irresolute on the neat garden-path, she remembered Mrs Biddle, a charwoman of such superior probity and cleanliness that it seemed likely the key of 'Rosemead' might have been confided to her keeping; so to Mrs Biddle she went.

Mrs Biddle, just washing up her own dinner things, was much surprised when Miss Ellen, 'looking fair tired out and above a bit untidy', came to ask her for the key. It 'give her quite a turn'.

'Back already, Miss!' she exclaimed. 'Why, Miss Caroline did say … dear, dear, and no fires lit nor nothing … nor no beds aired! She'll not be best pleased, but 'ow was I to know, Miss? It wants a full week yet to the time she said as she should come back.'

'Miss Murchison has not come back,' said Ellen, without a quaver. 'She is coming later, as arranged. It does not matter about fires or beds, Mrs Biddle. If you will just let me have the key I can manage quite well.'

'Why, Miss, you don't look fit to do that!' exclaimed the charwoman. 'After all this furrin travelling, too! And Mary Price gone home to her family, as Miss Caroline arranged, and only yesterday I hears from 'er as 'er sister has got the diptheery, so she can't come back not if she was wanted ever so.'

'I shall not require Mary Price in any case. It will do if she comes back when Miss Murchison arrives,' said Ellen, who, besides being very tired, was all impatience to get into and possess 'Rosemead' before Caroline came back … as she was afraid she would do sooner or later.

Still talking, still lamenting, Mrs Biddle put on her bonnet – which was part of her superiorness – and came with Ellen, insisting on opening the house herself, drawing up the blinds (so, if they had been drawn down for Caroline, thought Ellen, at least the funeral was over), making a fire, fetching milk, bread, butter, and eggs from her own home. Nothing could be got in that afternoon, since it was Thursday, when commerce ceased in Lower Waddington. 'Drat that there early closing, I always says; it come far too often!' remarked Mrs Biddle.

When she had gone Ellen went all over the little house with something of the ecstatic feeling she had first known to its full in Santa Maria Novella. Her own, her own again, to do what she liked with! She sat down in Caroline's favourite chair in the drawing-room, and, after crying a little, partly from fatigue and partly from sheer happiness, fell asleep.

By next day, however, she had discovered that there were certain disadvantages in being at 'Rosemead' without Caroline, of which the chief was the lack of ready money. It was not true, as she had told herself in the Italian train, that she should not need any money at home. When she had paid the fly from the station she had in her possession three and eightpence in English currency, four excessively dirty Italian lira notes mended with stamp-paper, and a Belgian franc which had been given her in the restaurant-car for a French one. She perceived that she could not keep house, even for herself alone, on that. Caroline, of course, could have had what Ellen knew was called 'credit' anywhere in Lower Waddington, but she herself felt, with her usual sensation of insignificance revived in the familiar surroundings, that she was not Caroline. Moreover, her cousin always discharged her bills weekly, and indeed Ellen believed that at the butcher's and the grocer's she always paid money down, distrusting their book-keeping. And as Ellen had not for years been permitted to do any household shopping, because she always muddled up the different kinds of sugar and did not, so Caroline declared, know scrag end of neck from leg, she felt it would be too great an ordeal to face shop-people now, especially since this would almost necessarily require explanations of Miss Murchison's absence. There was, however, a supply of tinned provisions in the house, and Mrs Biddle, without being told to do so, had ordered milk and bread to be sent in daily. She had also shown Ellen how to light the gas-stove in the corner of the kitchen – which Ellen had never done before, and only did now with great apprehension – and the weather was so warm that a sitting-room fire was not necessary.

Even so it was borne in upon Ellen that there might come a day when, unless she could procure some money for herself, she might almost wish Caroline back again. She did not know when the next instalment of her little annuity was due – she never did know. She had no cheque-book as Caroline had, no account at the bank … But while she thus brooded over her financial position, the thought of Aunt Sarah's Bracelet rose suddenly in her mind like a beneficent sun. That would save her, that wide gold fetter or cuff, of unexampled ugliness, adorned with a large though inferior diamond, which Caroline had insisted on depositing at the bank when, some years ago, a nonagenarian aunt had bequeathed it to Ellen. Now the legatee, who had temporarily forgotten the Bracelet's existence, thought with relief of its size and the brilliance of the diamond, and was glad that it had never occurred to her to sell it before now, and go to Italy on the proceeds. (But Caroline would certainly have prevented her.) If she could only nerve herself to go and ask for her property back, she would take the train to Shilton, their market town, the fare being only eighteenpence, and sell it to a jeweller there.

It was while Ellen was picturing, with a good deal of alarm, her visit to the bank, and what she should say to 'the banker', that something about a receipt came into her mind, and this bright vision was promptly annihilated. It was Caroline who had taken the Bracelet to the bank, and Caroline to whom the receipt had been made out; she distinctly remembered, now, that Caroline had told her this, adding: 'You would only have lost it if it had been made out to you, so if you ever want the thing, you must tell me, and I will go and get it for you.' She could not even come at her own property without Caroline!

The tears began to trickle down Ellen's cheeks. How unfair it was! But she *must* have money. Did Caroline wish her to starve, just because she was not here?

It was at this point that Ellen's new idea came to her. Why should Caroline *not* be here – at least, why should *she* not say that Miss Murchison had returned, but was unable to see visitors … indisposed … keeping her bed, in fact? If she could make people believe that, it would be far better than acknowledging that Caroline had not come back with her, and would lead to much less awkwardness. She wished now that she had adopted this line at first, and given Mrs Biddle this version. It was not true, she recognised, like the other one, about which the only doubtful point was the actual day of Caroline's return – for return she would of course, in the end. But this new idea, Ellen now saw, was better. For one thing, she could go into a shop and order anything she wanted to be 'sent to Miss Murchison', and they would send it, and it would not matter that she, Ellen, had no money, nor would the shop expect Caroline to pay if she were in bed.

She had an opportunity of practising her new story that very afternoon on a crony of Caroline's who appeared about tea-time, and whom, as Ellen answered the door herself, she found herself obliged to admit, at least as far as the little hall, before she could tell her that she had come in vain. 'I heard you were back, Miss Wright,' said the visitor effusively, 'so I thought that I might venture to look in, and see how you and dear Miss Murchison have enjoyed yourselves.'

'I am sorry to say that my cousin is not very well,' replied Ellen a shade nervously. 'I am afraid that she cannot see anyone at present.'

'Dear, dear!' exclaimed the caller. 'Have you had the doctor?'

'No, it is nothing serious. A touch of influenza, I expect – Italian influenza,' pronounced Ellen, who had heard of the so-called Spanish variety. 'And I think I had better not ask you to stay to tea, for it is very catching.'

The visitor went. This was certainly the better line to take about Caroline.

Having settled that her cousin was in bed in her own room, Ellen had unwillingly to admit to herself that evening that there was a sort of comfort and stability in the idea. A slight feeling of loneliness which had been growing on her was thereby checked. She would make Caroline some nice hot bread and milk to-night; that would be good for her influenza.

Having made it, she carried it, all steaming, into Caroline's empty bedroom and set it down by the unmade and shrouded bed. Then she went downstairs again, lit the lamp, and resumed her peaceful reading of *A Wanderer in Florence*, which brought back to her so delightfully the many pleasant days she had spent there – alone.

※

Before she ate her own breakfast next morning Ellen took a cup of tea, an egg and some buttered toast up to Caroline's bedroom, and brought down the cold bread and milk. Its untouched condition troubled her no more than it would have troubled a child who places food before an unresponsive doll. During her own breakfast she began to compile the list of edible and other objects which she intended to order 'for Miss Murchison'; it was becoming quite a long one, and perhaps before she took it out with her she would do well to show it to Caroline.

She was just thinking of adding to it, she was not sure why, 'new silk scarf (artificial)' when she heard an agitated knocking at the back door. Since it could not be a friend of Caroline's, and was probably only the baker, she went to open it. But it was Mrs Biddle, who stood there, with her bonnet on one side, and her face all red and pale in patches.

'Oh, Miss,' she began at once, "ave you seen this in the paper about poor Miss Caroline? Oh, Miss, she won't come 'ome no more! Why ever did you go and leave her alone in them 'eathenish parts ... poor Miss Caroline, as always says to me, "Mrs Biddle," she says, and if she said it once she's said it a 'undred times, "Mrs Biddle, you do turn out a room as it *should* be turned out!" Now I shan't never 'ear 'er say that no more!'

'"Won't come home no more" – what do you mean, Mrs Biddle?' demanded Ellen. 'She *is* home.' But Mrs Biddle, struggling with hysteria, pointed to a newspaper which she had let fall, and Ellen picked this up from the kitchen floor. It was of the sensational type dear to Mrs Biddle's class, and on the front page was to be seen in large letters: *Shocking Discovery in Italian Hotel. English Lady found Strangled.*

With a growing sensation of indignation Ellen glanced down the column to the accompaniment of the charwoman's sobs. Caroline's name was there (spelt wrongly) and her own (even more incorrectly though phonetically rendered) and their place of residence. Moreover, it appeared that this Miss 'Rait' had been traced to Florence, where she had spent the whole of the day sightseeing. The murder had been committed with a scarf belonging to the deceased lady –

A wave of anger burst over Ellen, and she read no further. How dare Caroline put such things in the papers ... but it was just like her ... Caroline safe in bed upstairs eating a good breakfast! And how did Caroline know that she had gone to Florence, and what she had done there?

'Stop crying, Mrs Biddle!' she said, in a tone almost approaching the imperious, at any rate, so unlike anything which Mrs Biddle had ever heard from her before that she did cease from her lamentations, and looked at her in astonishment. 'Stop crying, and go, and take that wicked, lying paper away with you! I am surprised at your reading and believing such things! Miss Murchison is here in bed with influenza; I have just taken her breakfast up to her.'

At this Mrs Biddle's surprise blossomed into sheer amazement. 'But you said, Miss, on Thursday, as 'ow you had left 'er behind!'

'I said that she was coming home later, and she has come. But she is not at all well, and she will be very much annoyed at all this. Please go at once, or she will be calling down to know what the noise is about.'

Thoroughly bewildered and half frightened, Mrs Biddle left.

But when she had gone the anger which had sustained Ellen ebbed from her, and she crawled trembling out of the kitchen, clutching the newspaper, which Mrs Biddle had left behind after all. She was thinking: 'If this dreadful lie is in the newspapers, all the village will read it, and people will be coming here to ask me about it ... I can't, I won't see them!' And with a feverish determination she locked and bolted both the front and back doors.

She was only too right. Before ten o'clock had struck from the wheezy cuckoo clock in the hall, three ladies of Caroline's acquaintance had tried severally to gain admittance, then a man whom Ellen (peering cautiously from an upper window) imagined might be a reporter. But, as long as she made no sound and did not allow herself to be seen, people might think the house was empty. They would not, surely, break into an empty house, however inquisitive they might be! Caroline in her room was quite quiet. But it was her part to take thought for Caroline now, and she was rather proud of the responsibility involved in the change of role, so she wrote on a sheet of notepaper in large letters: *'Please go away, so much knocking and ringing disturbs Miss Murchison!'* and, choosing a moment when no one was in sight, darted out and pinned this to the front door.

A little later she had another good idea, and, cutting out the 'Shocking Discovery', she wrote on another piece of paper *This is quite untrue!* and, having stuck it to the newspaper cutting with an adhesive luggage label, affixed this also to the door. And from eleven onwards she watched the stream of people who were, she feared at last, attracted rather than kept away by her notices, which now there was no chance of removing – the people who knocked, read the notices aloud and made comments, and then gathered in groups on the path talking. At one time Ellen counted twenty-three persons either inside or outside the gate of 'Rosemead'. But she saw with glee that they dared not, could not, enter the house.

The end came about three o'clock in the afternoon. Feeling rather tired with all this excitement, her vigil, and the absence of any midday meal, Ellen was dozing in the drawing-room below the Italian photographs, when she was roused by a tremendous ring at the front door, followed by a most purposeful knocking. Startled and indignant, she jumped to her feet and went quickly upstairs to her post of observation. Ere she could get there the summons was repeated, even louder. 'Be quiet!' she said angrily under her breath, pulling aside the window-curtain with caution.

Next moment a scream rang through the quiet little house. 'Caroline, Caroline, come quickly! There's a police inspector at the door … and I don't know what to say to him! Why has he come? Caroline, *you* go down and see him! Caroline, *come!*'

They found her in Miss Murchison's empty bedroom, tugging distractedly at the sheeted-over bed, and crying: 'It is mean, *mean*, to pay me out like this! *If you don't come I'll do it again!*'

6 The Pestering (1932)

When Evadne Seton and her husband bought the old cottage at Timpsfield known as Hallows, it was not only because they had fallen in love with its charming half-timbered exterior, but also because it was remarkably cheap for its size. For they had very little money to spend. The war had ruined Captain Seton's health, and left him at one and forty a man who had, most unwillingly, to take care of himself; and his wife possessed no particular talent save a light hand with cakes. The lease of their small and inconvenient flat in West Kensington having come to an end, a chance visit to Worcestershire, joined to a growing conviction that country air would be better for gassed lungs than the petrol-laden atmosphere of London, had resulted in the transference to them of the ownership of a house which Evadne described in all her letters as 'absolutely heavenly'.

And though the Setons always spoke of Hallows as a cottage, it was really large enough to claim the more important title. Off its little square hall there opened on one side Ralph Seton's 'den', which had a long French window – a later feature, of course; on the other quite a large sitting-room with engaging latticed casements; there was also a third small room to serve as dining-room. Above were three bedrooms, and an attic running over all; but the rooms were low, so that in total height Hallows did not much exceed the dimensions of an ordinary two-storey house. All this accommodation, together with an attractive garden, rendered its very modest price a matter of self-congratulation, more especially as it was in good condition and had indeed been recently redecorated, even to the distempering of the attic.

All the Setons' friends who came to see it spoke enthusiastically of the extraordinary bargain which Ralph and Eve had picked up. 'Poor dears, they needed it!' More than one made the remark (which caused Evadne to shudder) that the extreme picturesqueness of the place almost called for the title of 'Ye Olde' – something or other; and it was left for Ralph Seton occasionally to wonder at the fact, which the title-deeds revealed, that Hallows had so often changed hands after comparatively short periods of occupancy or ownership. The agents, however, were able to give quite satisfactory reasons for this, and in any case the drains were all right, for he had had them tested.

The cottage, however, had one slight disadvantage; it stood almost on the high road, at the turn just outside Timpsfield village, and though in that by-way of a notably placid countryside there was less motor traffic than would have shrieked or pounded past elsewhere, still, when summer came, cars bearing the rheumatic visitants to the neighbouring spa developed a habit of pulling up outside to admire the 'sweetly pretty' cottage, the roses clambering on the black and white, and the tall fluted Tudor chimneys, of which two survived in their pristine elegance. The Setons were a little annoyed; and one day when a car-load of lusty holiday-makers from Birmingham rang and asked if they 'did teas', Mrs Seton dismissed the inquiries with some curtness, and entered her husband's sanctum with a heightened colour.

'What's the matter?' asked Captain Seton, looking up from the printed foolscap document at which he had been frowning. Evadne told him.

'Rage becomes you, I declare!' he observed; and indeed Evadne, who was thirty-six and whose thick unshingled brown hair was threaded with grey, looked for the moment quite handsome. But her husband's smile was transient. 'Come here a moment, will you, and look at this. It's from the Silverdale Trust. Even the mortgage debenture-holders will not receive a penny this half-year!'

The flattering colour left Evadne's cheeks. 'Oh, Ralph – another investment gone wrong! ... No, no, my dear; of course I'm not blaming you; I know it's only the bad times, but – And I did so want you to have some of that new treatment this autumn!'

✕

Captain Seton had his new treatment in the autumn, even though he received no dividend from the Silverdale mortgage debentures. The demand of the trippers that afternoon had given Evadne an idea; and the more her husband fought, the more she upheld it. She *would* 'do teas', and he was absurd and abysmally behind the times to think of objecting to it. 'Heaps of people like us do it; and you know I *can* make scrumptious cakes, and Hallows does attract motorists. We can use the garden if it's fine, the large room if it's not; I could probably hire tables, for it will only be for a couple of months or so.'

So very soon old Jacob Friend, the builder, spectacles on nose and tongue following the movements of his hand, was creating, with an intensity no less concentrated in its way than was behind that brush which once swept the ceiling of the Sistine, that one word TEAS, in large letters on a small signboard, which was to provide Timpsfield with a topic of conversation, to please thirsty wayfarers, and in about a month's time to cause opulent sufferers at the spa to say to their chauffeurs: 'I think we might drive round by Timpsfield today, Smithson; I hear there are very good cakes to be had at that tea place there – "Ye Olde Tudor House", I think it is called.'

The Setons had not at first realized that this particular spa had practically a ten-months' season, a fact which, while it proved financially profitable to them, meant that Evadne was never surprised to be asked for tea from half-past three onwards even in October. So it was only with a mild surprise that she had heard the bell ring as she was seated by the hearth late one afternoon, reading *The Silver Spoon* by firelight, and rather unwillingly got up; yet the surprise deepened when she realized that it was already dusk outside. However, it took no time to boil a kettle on a primus, and her cakes were always freshly made.

Ralph had gone to Birmingham for treatment that afternoon, and the village maiden who helped her had departed home some time ago; but as Evadne was always prepared to serve teas herself if need arose, she went to the door without more ado, only regretting leaving the fire and the society of Michael Mont. When she opened it she was surprised again at the depth of the dusk outside. The creeper leaves which fringed the porch were drained by it of their bright colour; the porch, small as it was, seemed quite shadowy; and shadowy, too, was the figure who stood in it – an old man (as far as she could see) in a hat as wide as those beloved of the Chelsea artist and a cloak to match. Only she was not even quite sure about that – the light was so bad.

'Good evening,' she said briskly. 'I suppose you want tea?'

There was complete silence for a moment. Then the visitor said in a low, slightly hurried tone: 'I am come about the chest, mistress.'

'Chest?' repeated Evadne, puzzled. 'What chest?' Then she remembered that a chest of tea ordered the previous week from London had not yet arrived. 'Oh, are you the carrier? You have got it there, then? I was afraid it had gone astray.'

The man moved a little. 'Aye, it has indeed gone astray. And I want it. I wish to take it with me ... if you'll kindly allow me, mistress.'

'There's some mistake,' replied Evadne. 'I'm expecting it – from Twining's. There's no question of sending it back – particularly as it hasn't arrived yet!'

The old man had come quite close to the door now. Somehow Evadne did not like his nearness, and wished that Ralph were not out, and she alone in the house.

'Not arrived!' he exclaimed; and still his voice sounded just as far off as before. 'I was told that it was brought to this inn long ago, when –'

'But this is not an inn!' interrupted Mrs Seton. 'You have certainly made a mistake. Good evening.' Yet she still held the door open, for despite her half-dislike of her visitant, she was curious about him.

'Not an inn!' he repeated. 'When folk come here every day for refreshment! Mistress, pray, pray let me have the chest!'

'How can I?' asked Evadne, more and more puzzled, 'when I don't know anything about a chest?'

'I am so weary of asking,' sighed the far-away voice. 'Have pity on me, sweet lady, and let me come in and fetch it away!'

'No, you cannot come in,' said Evadne, with decision, suddenly, she knew not why, afflicted not with pity but with a strange trickle of fright. 'There is no chest here.' And she shut the door.

After a while slow, dragging footsteps went out of the porch. The old man, thought Evadne, listening on the other side of the door, was probably a little crazy. She would make inquiries about him in the village. He gave, somehow, the impression of considerable age, like Hawkins, the ancient bee-keeper; only that old boy certainly had all his wits about him, as witness the price he had asked her for his honey! And the idea of thinking that Hallows was an inn! She only wished that she were not obliged to admit strangers and give them tea. But there, beggars could not be choosers, and financially her enterprise was well on the way to fill up the hole left by the missing dividends.

When her husband came back about an hour later she told him of the old carrier body or whatever he was, and his request, and how he had stood in the porch asking –

Ralph Seton interrupted her. 'Eve, you must have been having an orgy of cocktails in my absence! Porch! What do you mean? Hallows has no porch!'

The Silver Spoon fallen to the floor, she stared up at him. 'No more it has! What can I have been thinking of?' She passed a hand over her forehead. 'But, Ralph, I … I saw it … I saw the edge of it, the leaves …'

'You might make your fortune if you could remember what you put in that cocktail,' was all her husband would say. 'No good assuring me that you didn't have one! Don't look so worried, old thing!'

'But I am worried!' responded Evadne. 'Ralph, do you think I can be going mental?'

'No; I think you were dazed with reading, and fancied yourself back at your old home, where I seem to remember there was a porch, or somewhere … No, I won't get you certified yet!'

✕

October passed into November, and Evadne still dispensed a few teas. Ivy, the 'help' from the village, now stayed later, and it was about six o'clock one evening that she came up to her mistress, who was drying her just-washed hair by an oil-stove in her bedroom, with the intelligence that there was a queer sort of man at the door asking summat about a chest what he was to take away.

'What!' ejaculated Evadne, flinging down her towel. 'A chest! What was the man like? Never mind, I'll get your master to go.' And with her half-dried hair streaming over her dressing-gown she ran downstairs quite perturbed. It was, nevertheless, a fact that she had hardly given her visitant of last month much thought; his queerness had been swamped at the time by the fact of her own, in imagining an architectural feature which did not exist.

She burst into her husband's room. 'Ralph, there's that man again at the door – at least there's *a* man – after that chest. Do go to him!'

'Can't Ivy see to it?' asked her husband, who was writing a letter. A glance had shown him that his wife could not, at least with decorum. 'Oh, all right.' He got up and left the room. 'I wonder if Ralph also will see something that isn't there,' thought Evadne.

In a moment Captain Seton was back. 'There's not a soul at the door,' he said rather crossly. 'What did that little fool mean?'

'I suppose he has gone away again,' said Evadne, with a sense of relief. 'So sorry, dear. And I apologize for coming in like this!'

In the hall she encountered Ivy and, mildly upbraiding her, was met with the reply: 'Oh, mum, but it was the back door. And he's there still; I can 'ear 'im.'

'You haven't left it open?'

'Oh, *no*, mum!'

'Well, go back and tell him that there is no chest for him here, and that it is no good his coming like this. There's a mistake somewhere, as I told him before.'

Ivy hesitated, getting very red. 'Please, mum, I don't like to.'

'Nonsense! I can't disturb your master again; and *I* can't go like this.'

For all answer Ivy burst abruptly into tears. Interspersed with this watery and far from silent protest were phrases which sounded like: 'It's begun again … everybody said as it would …' and more intelligible ones displaying an immediate desire to go home to her mother.

'If you can't answer the door you'd certainly better go home!'

remarked Mrs Seton dryly, only to be met with fresh sobs and the declaration that for nothing on earth would the sobber go outside the house this night, now that It had begun again.

With a gesture of vexation, Evadne left the weeping nymph, ran upstairs, caught up her discarded towel, twisted it round her head and came down again.

'Since you are so useless I must go to the back door myself!' she said severely, half hoping to shame Ivy into doing her duty. 'And in any case, the man will have got tired of waiting by now.'

The handmaid lifted a flushed, scared face. 'Oh no, he don't never get tired; he's bin at it too long!' And she burst into a fresh howl, demanding her mother and lamenting that she had ever come to Hallows.

Thoroughly annoyed, Evadne Seton in her turban-like headgear marched through the warm homeliness of the kitchen with its gleaming saucepans and stolid ranks of canisters comfortingly labelled: 'Rice', 'Flour', and 'Sugar'. The outer door was fast shut; she could see that Ivy had shot the bolt. But what was that clinking sound proceeding from it? Evadne stopped, her hands tightening on themselves. The thumbpiece of the latch was lifting in a continuous and regular jiggle, as though someone were shaking it from outside.

Evadne drew her breath hard. Must she open that door? Yes, if only because she had scolded Ivy for her cowardice. And besides, there was always Ralph within call. Bracing herself, she set one hand on the bolt and took hold of the latch with the other. Under her thumb it thrilled gently to that pressure outside. 'I can't do it!' she whispered, suddenly frightened to her inmost soul; though all the time something in her brain was saying reassuringly: 'Rubbish; it's only a crazy old man … or the wind.'

Setting her teeth she plucked open the kitchen door. And she would have been glad after all to see that crazy old man, for there was no one there – no one whatever, only empty, windless darkness.

'I was an idiot, of course,' she said half an hour later in her husband's den. 'But I really was scared for a moment – infected by that silly Ivy, I suppose. By the way, did she apologize at all as you took her home?' For it had ended in Captain Seton's having to escort his timid domestic back to her mother's cottage.

'She? My dear girl, is it likely? I don't think we either of us spoke, as a matter of fact. I confess that I was too much bored by the whole business. Mrs Miller was a bit apologetic. Come to think of it, I should never have imagined a country girl would get the wind up so easily. They must be more or less used to tramps.'

'If it *was* a tramp,' said Evadne in a low voice, as she bent to poke the fire.

✕

Apparently Ivy Miller, country-bred though she was, had no fancy for possible further dealings with old men at back doors, or else her nervous system was unusually highly strung, for she did not turn up next morning. In the middle of luncheon, however, arrived a remarkably ill-spelt note from Mrs Miller, intimating that 'my dorter dount feel as she giv' – a word which from the context must have been 'satisfaction' – 'up at halloses and will you kinly tak her weaks nottis an will not hask no wags yours trueley Mrs miller.'

'Look at that,' said Evadne angrily, passing the missive across the table. 'Tiresome woman! I must go and reason with her. And Ivy was just getting nicely into the way of the teas.'

'Why go and reason?' asked her husband, cutting himself a piece of cheese. 'Ivy's a brainless chit. You can easily get another, can't you, and one who won't go into hysterics if she is asked to go to the door in the dark?'

'And have all the bother of training her? I shall make an effort to get to the bottom of this business first. I'll go this afternoon, before any tea-ers can turn up.'

But a party of these individuals came very early that afternoon, and it was not until dusk had begun to set in that Evadne was able to invade Mrs Miller's dwelling. Her interview there was most unsatisfactory. No, Ivy hadn't nothing to complain of; she had always been treated most kind by you and the Capting, mum; but she didn't feel she give satisfaction, and she didn't like coming back in the dark, and it wasn't in reason that the Capting should bring her home every evening, poor gentleman, him with that cough and all; in fact, she'd rather not stay out her week; we can quite manage, thank you, mum, without the wages; sorry to put you about, but we all know there's difficulties about Hallows and no offence intended, I'm sure, and I hope none taken.

'Difficulties?' exclaimed Evadne. 'What do you mean by that, Mrs Miller? What sort of difficulties? The people who come for teas? But most of them give Ivy a tip, and I make all the cakes myself. If it's the extra washing-up ...'

Mrs Miller looked down and smoothed her apron; she was a neat body, which was one reason why Ivy had been selected for her post. 'Oh no, mum; it's not the people who come for teas; oh dear no!'

The slight peculiarity of her tone spurred on Evadne to further investigation. 'Then what people do you –' she was beginning, when unfortunately Mrs Miller's labourer son clumped into the cottage, home from work, and the sentence and the investigation were cut short. Evadne thereupon took her leave, not having seen the recalcitrant Ivy at all.

As she went homewards in the dusk she thought that perhaps Hallows from standing empty (though it had not so stood for long) had gained a bad reputation as the haunt of tramps or undesirables. Yet it was not a solitary piece. Anyhow, the affair was most annoying, and not too reassuring for the prospects of replacing Ivy. It was getting too late now to go round to other cottages and endeavour to find some female to come the next day. But tomorrow was Saturday; together with Sunday the heaviest day for teas. Wrathfully musing, Evadne went past the churchyard with its spiky yews, came to the turn of the road, and saw the light from the living-room at Hallows slipping out cheerfully through the half-drawn curtains.

Then she saw, too – but could only just see – that someone was standing inside the gate, as if waiting for her. Foolish of Ralph to do that in the damp! 'Go in, you old silly!' she called out. 'How long have you been there?'

The person standing inside the gate did not answer, so it was not Ralph, and she wished she had not called out to him. It was not until she actually had her hand on the gate to push it open that she recognized something familiar about the outlines of the figure – about the headgear in particular. Feeling rather sick, she paused with her hand on the wood. It was he, the ... the tramp, and he was on the inner side of her own gate. She would have to pass him, and she most distinctly did not want to do so.

But she could not allow herself to be a second Ivy. Besides, he was in her own garden, where he had no right to be. Horribly afraid, all the same, that he was going to try to keep her out ('and if he does, I shall hit him!' she thought, with a tremulous vindictiveness), she pushed open the gate and went through. 'What do you want?' she demanded, without stopping; for the faster she walked the sooner she would pass him.

But she did not seem to have to pass him; he was not where she expected; he was beside her, shuffling along through the fallen leaves at the edge of the path, and keeping up with her as she went. 'What do you want?' she asked again sharply, looking straight ahead as she spoke, and continuing up the path. 'I can't have you coming here like this!'

'You have just told me to go in, mistress,' said that flat, faraway voice. 'It is true that I am old and silly, as you said; but you told me to go in. You are kind, after all!'

At that Evadne stopped. 'I never told *you* to go in! I thought it was my husband. Go away at once, or I will call him!' She was shivering with a sudden unnamable disgust. And she began to run.

The becloaked old thing kept up with her. 'Kind, kind!' the voice repeated, almost in her ear. 'You told me to go in ... you asked me how long I had been waiting ... Kind ... kind!'

Evadne struck out with her left arm, but she must have miscalculated the distance. Her hand merely brushed the lavender bush by the door. So she knew she was quite near safety. 'You shall not come in! You shall not come in!' she cried. Then she turned the handle, huddled through, banged the door and fell on her knees inside, pushing against it with all her might and shrieking – for at last she could keep it in no longer: 'Ralph, Ralph, come and lock the door. Ralph, come quick – he's trying to get in – Ralph, for God's sake ...'

'Well you did give me the dickens of a fright!" said Captain Seton. He was standing over his wife with brandy, and Evadne, to her surprise, was uncomfortably disposed on the little sofa in the living-room. 'Here, for heaven's sake, get this down!' Ralph was pale himself, paler even than he usually was.

Through chattering teeth Evadne swallowed the brandy, and felt better. 'I'm ... I'm like Ivy, aren't I?' she said, trying to smile. 'You'll have to go to the police, I'm afraid.'

'But, look here,' said he, 'weren't you imagining things? No one was trying to get in, I'm sure.' He began to rub her hands.

'You're as cold as ice, my dear girl! Did he try to stop you coming in – was that what you meant?'

'No. He wanted to come in, too. He said I told him to … as if I should!' She shuddered. 'I thought it was you at first; he was standing just inside the gate.'

'But I can't think why you should have got the wind up so, if he didn't really threaten you?'

'He said I was kind! Me kind … to that creature! And Ralph, he sort of shuffled along beside me … and his clothes smelt so musty …'

'I shall go and light the stove in our bedroom and you must go straight to bed. Yes, I've locked the front door, and the kitchen door is fastened, too. Now, my good girl, you cut off upstairs, and I'll bring you up some hot soup. You said you had made some, didn't you?'

✕

'No, sir,' responded Sergeant Cook, whom Captain Seton had the luck to meet next morning in the village. 'No, I never heard of any old tramp in a cloak such as your lady describes, about these parts; nor I never heard as tramps was partial to Hallows. Now if you'd seen him yourself, Captain Seton –'

'Unfortunately I haven't, Sergeant. My wife, however, is not a fanciful person, nor one easily frightened. I wish you'd keep an eye lifting for a few evenings?'

'I will sir, certainly … Might he perhaps be a loonatic, do you think?'

'I haven't any theories, Cook. For all I know he might be; but there's no asylum near here. The first time this fellow came my wife says he appeared to think that Hallows was an inn. Does that throw any light?'

'Ah!' said the Sergeant deeply. 'Well, it might or it might not!'

'*Was* Hallows ever an inn?'

'Couldn't say, sir. Best ask some of the old villagers about that. Friend, for instance, or old Hawkins, him that keeps the bees.'

'Oh, the rustic with the protectionist ideas about the price of honey! And Jacob Friend ... Now that I come to think of it, my wife reported a curious thing which Friend said to her when she gave him the order to paint us a sign. He told her that she was a brave lady – braver than she knew. She thought he meant – well, undertaking that sort of thing, you know.'

'Quite so, sir. But it may be as he meant more. Them old villagers ... I'm not a Timpsfield man myself. But this here undesirable hasn't ever come to ask for refreshment, has he, sir?'

'No. What he wants, apparently, is a chest which he seems to think we have.'

'Ah, a chest! That sounds old-fashioned, don't it! I'd go and see Friend or Hawkins if I was you, sir.' And on that advice they parted.

Captain Seton had little knowledge of what bees did in winter, but it was plain what a beekeeper did, if he was of the age of Mr Hawkins; he kept by the fire and was careful not to admit the slightest breath of air into his retreat – for months probably, said the visitor to himself as he entered it. Hibernation, if not suffocation ...

However, Mr Hawkins was not even hibernating. His little eyes were quite alert, and the hat which he presumably kept as a permanency on his aged head, lest after all his precautions some faint breath of air might visit it, lent him the appearance of being ready to set off out of doors, the more so since, sitting by his fireside, he leant both hands upon a stout stick. He had to the life the air of a stage rustic, and a badly made-up one at that. Captain Seton could have sworn that spirit gum was the medium which kept in place the unconvincing collarette of white beard which surrounded his pallid moon face, singularly unwrinkled for his age, which was reputed to be close on ninety. A little woman who referred to him once as 'Granfer', but otherwise, with some coldness, merely as 'He', did the honours of the cottage.

'Good morning, Mr Hawkins,' said his visitor; and so strong was his sense of taking part in amateur theatricals that he nearly added: 'And how be bees?' or something in that strain. However, he restricted himself to: 'I hope you are well?'

'Good marnin', sir,' responded the ancient in a little cracked voice, 'I be doin' nicely, thank 'ee.'

'He's not so troubled with the rheumatics as some winters,' observed the hostess, dusting a chair. 'Please to take a seat, sir.'

'Sometimes,' remarked 'He', taking up the cue, 'I has the lumbago pitched in me baack something cruel, so that I be fair stuck like.'

'You are a good age, Mr Hawkins, aren't you? – though you carry it remarkably well,' Ralph hastened to add.

The moon face emitted a chuckle. 'Aye, I be a hundred and three come next month – or be it a hundred and four, Bessy?'

''Tain't neither,' replied Bessy sharply. 'Don't take no notice of him when he talks like that, sir,' she advised the somewhat startled Ralph. 'He ain't no good at figgers.'

'No,' complacently agreed the ancient – for at any rate he was that – 'I never could be bothered with 'rithmetic. Rheumatics is more in my line now – hee, hee! But 'tis bees as I knaws about. Will it be aught to do with them little critters as ee've come about, sir?'

'No, Mr Hawkins. But whatever your exact age, you are undoubtedly, I believe, the oldest inhabitant of Timpsfield.'

'Aye, that I be,' responded the *soi-disant* centenarian proudly, and, possibly with the idea of prolonging this distinction, he settled his hat more firmly on his head. 'Years and years older than the rest of 'em put together, I rackon. Now, Bessy, hold thy tongue! I kin remember old Passon as allus wore a wig, and the big floods eighty years ago, and the times when a loaf of bread costed –'

'And a good deal about the houses in the village, too, I dare say,' put in Captain Seton, to whom general reminiscences were of no value. 'For instance, there's my present cottage – Hallows, you know, at the turn of the road – I'm naturally interested in that. Do you remember any old stories about that?'

The face within the collarette changed in some indefinable way; to Captain Seton it looked as if Mr Hawkins had said to himself: 'Now you be careful!' 'Ah, so you be the gentleman as has bought 'Allows,' remarked he slowly. 'And how do 'Allows suit 'ee, sir?'

'Very well, thank you, Mr Hawkins. But I should like to know something of its past history.'

'A many would like to knaw that,' responded the beekeeper, propping his chin on the top of his stick. 'Now, Bessy, quit fiddlin' there; 'tis time sure, 'ee went for to do some shopping!' And, to Ralph's surprise, Bessy rather resentfully withdrew.

'I can't abide wimmen,' observed Mr Hawkins as the door closed. ''Tis a great pity a man has to put up wi' 'em, buzzin' about like so many bees on'y not near so sensible. And so 'ee likes 'Allows, sir; don't find it to have no inconveniences?'

Ralph looked at him steadily. 'That depends on what you mean by inconveniences.'

Mr Hawkins tried to scratch his head without removing his hat, a proceeding which a good deal disturbed the poise of the latter. 'Well, sir, being as I'm so old, I remember there was talk of folk being pestered like … But that's a long time ago.'

'Pestered by what?'

The old man leant forward over his stick, glanced round and dropped his voice. 'By *him*, sir.'

Ralph's heart gave a queer little jump which surprised him. There *was* something in it, then – or was supposed to be. But he merely asked, after a moment: 'What "him"?'

'Him as is always asking for it,' replied Mr Hawkins, his piping voice sunk almost to a whisper. And then, as Ralph gave no sign, he went on hurriedly and with an air of relief: 'Oh then, sir, if you ain't been worried, no need to say no more about it. There's some as is, and some as isn't.'

'It's true that I personally have not been worried,' said Ralph, after a moment's consideration. 'But I must admit that my wife has.'

'Ah!' Mr Hawkins sucked his lips. Then he leant yet further forward in his chair, and said, still in a tone as if he feared to be overheard, 'Best tell her never to let the young man in – see as she never does that!'

'But – but as far as I can gather it's not a young man, it's an old one; at least that was my wife's impression. Though, of course, the whole thing is probably an illusion,' he added, half to himself.

'I wouldn't call it no names, sir,' advised Mr Hawkins gravely. He drew back in his chair and appeared to reflect. 'So it seems old now, do it? Well, it have been askin' a mort of years, by what folks do say. My father now, he remembered it; and my mother allus swore she saw it one evening knocking on the door of 'Allows … But as long as no one don't never, never ask it in, sir, I reckon 'tis all right; fur it seems it can't come in wi'out 'tis invited, like. 'Tisn't as if 'Allows was an inn –'

'Was it ever an inn? My wife said the – the man at the door spoke of "this inn" the first time he came.'

'Did he now! … I don't remember of its being an inn, nor my father didn't, but some says it was, once.'

Ralph Seton, puzzled, uncomfortable, turned to another point. 'This chest, now, that he asked for – a chest which he said had been left there –'

'Aye, he would,' murmured Mr Hawkins, nodding his head. 'Allus the same thing – a chest, it be.' And by this time Ralph no longer saw him as a comic rustic. He really did seem to have some roots back in a curious past which had small affinity with a present of unceasing loud-speakers and weekly record-breaking aeroplane flights.

'There *is* a tale about a chest, then?'

'There's a tale about him allus askin' for a chest. But there wasn't no man livin', even in granfeyther's day, as knew aught about a chest, and no chest ain't never bin found in 'Allows.'

'Then it's not much use his keeping on asking for it!'

'No, sir, it ain't. But I suppose that's just what he will do, keep on askin', seein' as he don't never get it!'

'A nice look-out, that, for the occupants of Hallows!' exclaimed Captain Seton. 'We have lost a maid over this business already, and I very much fear that my wife may have difficulty in finding another in the village if this tale gets about!'

''Tain't no question of its "gettin' about", sir,' corrected the sage. ''Cos 'tain't no new tale, if you unnerstans me. Only, him not havin' been seen for some time, it might have bin a bit forgot. I wonner now what could 'a started him off again?'

The words woke an echo of what Evadne had reported Ivy to have said on that score. Evidently even the young people of Timpsfield knew, at any rate in theory, of the 'pestering' of Hallows. A cheerful prospect if Evadne failed to get a maid – just now, too, when they were making a little money over the teas ... much as he himself disliked that method of earning it!

'But what is the legend, the tale, behind this ... this ...' he really did not know what to call it, and finally came out with, 'this nuisance? Can you recall having heard anything as to its origin? Who brought the chest to Hallows, and when – and what was supposed to be inside it?'

The old beekeeper was probably not conversant with the vulgarism of 'Now you're asking!' but his expression conveyed that sentiment as he slowly shook his ancient, behatted head.

✕

Captain Seton went out through the blackened Michaelmas daisies and dahlias of Mr Hawkins's crowded little garden, not knowing what to think. By the time he got home he was almost wondering whether Evadne's importunate old man could be accounted for on the theory of mass suggestion. If not, he was faced by an uncomfortable dilemma: either he must believe in this spectre and his 'chest' which he could not bring himself to do, or else Evadne, of all people, was developing nerves or hysteria – delusions, in fact. His mind revolted from both alternatives. The immediate question was, what was he going to tell her about his inquiries? Wouldn't the best thing be to say that neither Sergeant Cook nor the oldest inhabitant knew anything about the business? But then he had not the habit of lying to his wife – nor to anybody else, for that matter.

He was relieved to find that he need not come to an immediate decision on this point. A notice was pinned on the front door which said: 'No teas provided today', and on the hall table he found a note informing him that his wife had had no luck servant-hunting in the village, and had taken the little Austin and gone over to Worcester to a registry office. 'May not be back to tea, so don't wait,' it concluded. 'Cold lunch (sorry!) on the table.'

So she *had* failed to get a maid in the village! Of all the cursed nuisances!

He went for a walk after lunch, by the old canal, long out

of use and undisturbed, as picturesque under its drooping trees as any river. It had no trace of movement in its unstirred waters – so little, indeed, that the drift of red beech leaves and of green ash leaves lay upon its surface as upon ice – the stillest water he had ever seen. The beech trees in their last glory made of it an enchanted waterway. Ralph turned off from it after a while and did a round. When he got back to Hallows it was practically dark.

Evadne had not returned, evidently, for the little garage door was still open and the house was unlit. Captain Seton let himself in and went towards his own den, extracting his pocket-lighter. Just outside, however, it slipped from his fingers, and while he was groping for it on the floor he became aware, to his surprise, that there must be someone in his room, for he could distinctly hear a noise in there. He raised himself and listened. Yes – a series of dull thuds or thumps, apparently against the panelling of the wall. Evadne must be back, then; but what on earth was she doing? He gave up hunting for his lighter, since Evadne would presumably have lit the lamp in there, opened the door, and said, 'What in thunder are you up to, Eve – and in the dark, too?' For the room was not lit, save by the merest scrap of glow from the hearth.

But no one answered him. The thudding had stopped; there was not a sound, nor could he see anyone in the room. Yet that someone was there he was certain. By the draught which the opening of the door had caused he knew that the long French window must be partly open. Had he left it so when he went out?

'Who is it? If it's you, Eve, don't play the silly ass!'

For the only answer he heard what sounded like rough-skinned hands rasping over the panelling. It wasn't Eve in here! 'Here, you!' he called out threateningly, 'get out of this!' and made a dash for the corner whence the rasping appeared to come. He touched nothing, it is true, but he had the impression of something bundling rapidly to the other side of the room, something that diffused a mouldy smell as it moved; he even thought that he saw it, very indistinctly, cross the somewhat lighter oblong which was the uncurtained French window. Filled both with rage and with something of which he had known the like before ... in Flanders – Ralph hurled himself in the dark towards his bureau, on top of which he kept an electric hand-lamp for emergencies, found it, switched it on and threw its strong but narrow beam into the corner on the other side of the window. Nothing there! He swept the room with it – nothing. A long breath of relief shook him. Now if *he* had been having cocktails ...

Then, as he was starting, electric lamp in hand, to leave the room in search of his dropped lighter he did see something ... something that sat, huddled almost into a ball, in his own chair by the dying fire, something covered with what looked like a rotten and tattered dark-brown sack, something that had earth-coloured hands clasped over the shrouded head which was bowed to its very knees ... if it had knees ... something that was whimpering to itself in a dusty, far-away voice, 'Not here ... not here ... not here ...'

Ralph Seton, in a worse place than the trenches, and almost beside himself with fear, hurled the electric lantern like a bomb at the thing which sat in his chair. The heavy lamp hit the stone jamb of the fireplace, shivering its glass and bulb at once. A second afterwards, Ralph heard the window flung wide in the darkness; then he bolted from the room and, with the sweat running down his spine, fell into a chair in the unlit hall, his heart beating almost to suffocation.

After a while he sat up, pulled out his handkerchief and began to mop his forehead, and it was then that he heard the horn of the Austin. A moving beam of light traversed the hall. Ralph got up. Evadne must not find him like this;

besides, It might be lurking outside and frighten her. He opened the hall door, and was disgusted to find that his legs would not carry him down the path.

'All in the dark, old thing?' exclaimed his wife a moment later, appearing with her arms full of parcels. 'Why ever haven't you lit up?'

'Just going to ... dropped my lighter,' mumbled Ralph. 'Haven't found it yet.' To himself his voice sounded extraordinary.

'But there are matches on the hall mantelpiece,' observed Evadne, dumping her parcels on to the table. 'Are you only just in, then? ... There!'

She was lighting the hanging Aladdin lamp. Thank goodness, one had to leave the flame low at first. Anyhow, perhaps he wasn't looking as queer as he felt, and she wouldn't notice.

'Yes. I've been for a walk ... Where are you going?'

'I've bought a new waste-paper basket for your room,' replied his wife briskly, picking up one of her parcels, 'and it might as well be put in there at once ... Goodness, Ralph, two people can't get through this door at a time!'

For her husband had pushed past her without ceremony. It might still be in there for all he knew. But directly he had the door well open he stopped, unable to go a step farther, though he could see that the room was empty. And the fact that he *could* see this was exactly what paralysed him. One of the two never-used candles which decked the old pewter candlesticks on his mantelpiece had been lit ... or was he dreaming? Evadne slipped past.

'Well, you managed to get some kind of illumination,' she observed. 'Oh, you criminal, what a mess, though! You poked the candle into the fire, I suppose, by the look of it!'

Staring at the bowing flame, her husband shook his head. A ... that Thing light a candle! But no, either it was ... not what he felt it was, or some human being had come in through the window and lighted that candle – God knew why! Yet on the other hand, was it likely that anyone … But had the Thing come back, then?

'Hallo!' said Evadne, stooping down to the hearth. 'How did this come here? My goodness! It's all smashed to pieces!' She held up in one hand the damaged oak-cased hand-lamp, and in the other a piece of the stout glass of its shattered bull's-eye.

Before he answered, Ralph went to the French window, shut it and pulled the curtains. Then he came back to the hearth and the solitary candle which he had not lit. 'I'm afraid I'm the culprit about the electric lamp. I don't know whether I'm taking leave of my senses, but – no, for God's sake, don't sit in that chair, Evadne!'

'But why ever not?' exclaimed his wife in utter astonishment, catching the arm which had grabbed at her.

Ralph told her why not.

✕

It was of no avail to turn the matter over and over, as they did that evening; they could come to no stable conclusion. On the one hand it seemed as if 'It' had really won entry to Hallows, and was searching there on its own account; on the other, Captain Seton had the fervent desire to banish the picture of the sitter by his fireside as a trick of eyesight, the memory of the dry earthy hands rustling over the wall and the whimpering voice as a trick of hearing, and the affair of the candle as a jest played by someone who had subsequently slipped in through the open window. He slept ill that night, worse than Evadne.

It was not until next day that his wife told him of the likely woman she had heard of in Worcester the preceding afternoon, whose references she had taken up in person, and whom she proposed to engage at once by letter. This domestic would naturally have to live entirely at Hallows, since she was not of the neighbourhood.

'But what shall we say to this Mrs Minter when she comes?' asked Evadne as she was brushing out her hair at bedtime. 'If we tell her never to leave anything open after dark she'll get frightened about burglars or something, and won't stay.' Neither of them had been out since tea-time that afternoon, and every door and window had then been securely fastened.

Ralph finished winding up his watch and gloomily surmised that anyhow she would hear talk about Hallows in the village.

Two days later the new servant arrived, respectable, middle-aged, and (they hoped) unimaginative. Peace descended again, though that Evadne's nerves were jangled was abundantly proved on the occasion when Minter came in to announce that 'a man had come for the chest –' and got no farther. Mrs Seton had sprung up with a half-suppressed scream, so that the worthy woman stared at her astounded.

'Chest?' cried Evadne wildly. 'No, no, Minter – send him away at once! We have no –'

Luckily her husband came at that instant into the room. He broke in with a loud laugh which did not ring very genuine. 'It's all right, Minter. Your mistress has forgotten that the sofa has to go away to be mended. The man is here with the van from Petty's, Evadne, to fetch the chesterfield away.'

Evadne had recovered herself with a gulp. 'I'll go and see about it,' she mumbled, and fled from the room.

✖

The approach of St Martin's Summer, fine as usual, was bringing visitors again to Hallows, and for a few bright days teas were again in demand; Evadne was glad of the distraction. On Armistice Day itself there were quite a number of 'tea-ers' in the living-room (for no longer, in mid-November, could they be accommodated in the kind of arbour which had sheltered them in the summer). They all arrived about the same time, but there were three parties of them, that is, two parties and one solitary young man who had a table to himself. Evadne, who was helping Minter with the waiting, thought that he looked like an artist; his hair was rather long, his tie large, his collar soft and loose, and his hands almost a woman's – so long and slim and with such tapering fingers that they might, thought Evadne, as she served him, have come out of a Van Dyck portrait. He asked for coffee, and would have nothing to eat; and while he stirred it, sat looking round the room with evident interest. And as Evadne passed again with a tray, he addressed her:

'You have a beautiful old house, madam. Is it ... do you permit your guests to see over it?'

'No, I'm afraid not,' answered Evadne, somewhat taken aback. 'Not more than this room. You see, we live here.'

The young man looked disappointed, much more disappointed than he need, thought Evadne, seeing his handsome face darken until it was almost sullen. Perhaps he was a connoisseur of old houses; but, all the same, they could not undertake to make their home a spectacle to unknown trippers who came for tea – though, indeed, 'tripper' was not exactly the word to apply to this young man. 'I am sorry,' she added.

His face still dark, he made her a sort of bow. 'It is your house, madam,' and she passed on, feeling that she had been discourteous. Next time she came into the room he had finished and gone – and paid (which was the important thing) since the sixpence for his coffee lay on the cloth by the cup.

It must have been about two o'clock in the morning when

Evadne woke with a jump and the impression that she had heard a noise somewhere near her bed. She lay a moment with her heart beating; but in another there came the long rumble of thunder. It had no doubt been a previous clap which had awakened her, and, though she disliked thunder by night, she felt relieved. The wind was rising, too; she heard a door bang downstairs. Yes, a night thunderstorm always affected her with a sense of something sinister. If it went on she would wake Ralph, who was sleeping through it. There seemed to be no lightning, which was odd; she never knew which she disliked the more – at night.

Ah! a flash at last, a slight one; and almost on its heels another, of tropical intensity, blue and searing, which lit up the whole room. But it was not the lightning which drew Evadne's scream and flung her upon her sleeping husband in the bed by her side. The flash had shown her, standing at the foot of her own bed, his hands on the oaken rail, with a half-mocking smile on his face, the young man of the afternoon. And his hands were –

'Ralph, Ralph, wake up! He's here in the room with us … but he's *dead* … his hands are all bones … I saw them … a skeleton's hands … Ralph, he had coffee here this afternoon …' Babbling on in terror, she was clinging so hard to him that it was difficult for Captain Seton to free himself and reach out for the matches, but he succeeded, and managed to light the candle just as a tremendous peal of thunder reverberated over Hallows.

'My dear girl, you've had – a bad dream. There's nothing, Eve, you are – you really are – strangling me!' And he broke into one of his uncontrollable fits of coughing.

It was perhaps lucky; nothing else could so have recalled Evadne to herself.

In the morning the theory of a nightmare seemed the only

plank to cling to, if sanity were to be retained by either of them; and as they counted over the week's takings, Ralph Seton elaborated it with a great show of common sense.

'You know, Eve, how you hate thunder in the night; and the fact that you imported into the dream which it gave you a harmless young tourist or what not from the day before proves ... That lot is ten florins, yes; and six half-crowns – you have been doing well! ... and sixpences – all right, I'll count them again. I make them eighteen, but one of them's a dud. You've been had, old lady! Look at that! Is it foreign, or what?'

Evadne took up the rejected coin and looked at it closely, on both sides; examined it again, got very red, then pale, and let it fall on the table with a little gesture, as though it were something that would sting. 'It's not foreign; but it says "Jacobus Rex" ... it's *his*, Ralph, that he left for the coffee. Oh, what shall we do, what shall we do?' And laying her head upon her arms, she burst into tears.

✕

Dr Mildmay came out of the bedroom and followed Captain Seton down to the latter's den.

'Yes, I will certainly send your wife a sedative. And what about yourself – you're looking none too grand?'

'We're both in the same boat, my wife and I,' said Ralph, smiling mirthlessly. 'And unless this horrible business can be stopped, I really don't know what is going to happen. We can't give up the house; we've only just bought it.'

Dr Mildmay was a newcomer to the district, a slight, hatchet-faced, forcible man in his forties with a little beard and a sallow, dried-up skin. He looked keenly at the haggard man standing before him. Of his physical disabilities he was aware, for Ralph had consulted him soon after settling in

Timpsfield, and it was Dr Mildmay who had put him on to the new treatment in Birmingham.

'Then you must make the … visitant leave,' he said briskly. 'Have you ever heard of exorcism?'

'Yes. But don't tell me that you, a twentieth-century medical man, believe in it! Besides, isn't the object of exorcism to "lay" a ghost in a house? There's no ghost in this house – at least, not permanently. He's outside it – though he evidently intends not to remain there. And after last night it seems as though nothing will keep him out.'

'Then the only course is to take away his reason for coming. What was it he began by asking for – a chest?'

'Look here, Dr Mildmay,' said Ralph roughly, 'I don't want to be humoured! I'm not insane – yet. You know quite well that you put down all I have told you to some kind of hallucination or delusion. It isn't possible for you, with your training, to do anything else. I'm not a child –'

'How do you know what my training has been?' interrupted Dr Mildmay coolly. 'I spent ten years as a medical missionary in East Africa. No man who has done that, unless he is unbelievably stupid or invincibly prejudiced, can dogmatize about hallucination or delusions. He has seen far too many strange things himself out there.'

Ralph stared at him. 'You – you really think that I actually saw what I thought I saw, feeling round these walls, sitting in that chair, and that poor Evadne –'

'I would not rule out the possibility. And so, one must take steps to put an end to this invasion. It is serious – for you and Mrs Seton.'

'God knows it is!' muttered Ralph. 'Look here, Mildmay, can't you use some of your African spells or incantations – or exorcize the house yourself – no, as I said, exorcism probably wouldn't answer.'

'It certainly wouldn't in my hands; I'm a layman, Captain

Seton. Also, you see, I'm a Christian, and can't go in for spells. No, I suggest we start by using common sense. Have you ever tried to find this "chest" yourself?'

'No. But there's nowhere it could be; the place was as bare as my hand when we came into it.'

'No bricked-up cellars, no old wells, no hiding-places in the chimneys, or in the thickness of the walls?'

'I don't think so.'

'Well, get a good builder and go round the house with him and make sure. Don't have a local man; get someone out from Worcester or Birmingham. I will look in again tomorrow morning; or you can send for me if you want me. Meanwhile, I'll write off to a historically-minded friend of mine in Oxford who has a fairly extensive knowledge of the literature of haunting, and see if he can throw any light on this case. Good morning, and don't frighten yourselves with the far worse bug-bear of incipient mental trouble.'

The builder whom Ralph had out next day from Worcester possessed a certain amount of intelligence, though he was extremely sceptical. 'Folks is always dying to find what they calls "priests' holes" in these here old houses,' he observed disparagingly. 'Can't see what they wants 'em for – nasty onsanitary little places when found, what no one but them old cunning Jesuits would have wanted to live in!' Ralph, who had not revealed the ultimate object of the search, replied that such retreats were not inhabited from choice, but was evidently not believed.

It was not until the quest, fruitless so far, was almost over that Mr Wiggins had his great idea, and descending from the attic, went outside the house, stared upwards for some time from the garden, and returned with an expression of satisfaction on his face, to the dispirited Ralph, who had been watching him from one of the attic windows.

'Have it ever occurred to you to wonder, Captain Seton,

why this 'ere right-'and casement,' he slapped its frame as he spoke, 'is set so much nearer to the wall than t'other is to t'other wall?'

'No, I can't say that it has,' returned Ralph. 'Hallows is an old house, and many things in it are not symmetrical.'

'That's right. But it might have give you an idea, sir, same as it 'as me' – 'if you had my experience and intelligence', seemed to be understood. 'Now, listen to this!' Mr Wiggins struck a resounding blow on what appeared to be the end of the attic nearest to the right-hand window. ''Ark at that, sir! It's false, that wall is – lath and plaster. There's space beyond, as can be calkilated from the outside; not much space, hundoubtedly – but enough for one of them skinny Jesuits, I dare say. You've only to give the word, sir, and a haperture's easy made.'

But Ralph had no intention of interior researches being pursued by Mr Wiggins, and did not respond to the suggestion. He himself came and thumped the wall, however, puzzled. 'It's got a beam down it, though,' he remarked doubtfully, for a wavy black beam, just a slice of a tree, like many of the timbers in Hallows, divided the distempered surface into two. But this, according to Mr Wiggins, was but camouflage on the part of them Jesuits (to whom he seemed to attribute the power of continued existence even after what would have amounted to walling up alive).

When Mr Wiggins had departed, Ralph Seton returned to stare at the shut-off slice of the attic. This could surely only be very narrow, and the departed Wiggins had really been sharp to deduce the possibility of its existence. Dr Mildmay was coming tomorrow morning; possibly he might induce that somewhat unorthodox, or at least singularly unprejudiced medical man to help him break in upon whatever was concealed there – if there were anything.

He went to tell Evadne, still in bed, that there was now a

faint hope of the lifting of the siege.

Unfortunately there was also evidence that the blockade was becoming straiter. When the worthy Minter brought Ralph his solitary tea that afternoon she asked him, in a somewhat indignant tone, whether it were by his wish that the builder's man, as she supposed he was, should be sitting on the attic stairs in the dark, moaning to himself – drunk he must certainly be, and she would never have let him into the house in that state, but as it happened, she did not let him in. Her tone seemed to imply that her less observant master must have done so.

Ralph put back the tea-cosy which he had begun to lift off. 'On the attic stairs, in the dark!' he exclaimed, with a sinking of the heart. 'But I never ordered –' Then he checked himself. 'All right, Minter, I'll see to it. He can't stay there, of course. But don't you tell him – I will.'

'Thank you, sir,' replied Minter, with dignity, and retired, while Ralph lay back in his chair and groaned. 'Sitting on the attic stairs … moaning to himself!' There could be no doubt what was doing that. And now he must go and dislodge the creature.

There was one gleam of comfort – Its being where It was seemed to show that Wiggins had been correct, that the attic was the right venue. It also seemed to show that It knew of their doings this morning, and that It could reason …

His teacup, the hot toast, the easy chair and the fire cried strongly to him to remain where he was, and let the horror sit and moan on the attic stairs for as long as It liked. The danger was, not a fright to Evadne, who was, he believed, asleep, but to the precious Minter, lest she got an inkling of the real nature of the 'builder's man' … No, it wouldn't do; though how he was going to expel the thing he knew not, and his flesh crept at the idea of even approaching the narrow stairway leading to the attic. However, he pulled himself out of his chair.

Hardly had he got into the hall when he heard a shrill scream from the direction of the kitchen. Great heavens! He hurried there and found Minter, with a face like a sheet, leaning panting against the dresser clutching a pastry-board shield-wise in front of her.

'What's the matter?' asked her master, with a miserable attempt at jocularity. 'Have you seen a rat or something?'

'Oh, sir, oh, Captain Seton – the most 'orrible, 'orrible thing! No, not a rat – much worse!' She shuddered and let slip the board, which fell with a bang between them. 'I'd just got out me rolling-pin and put it on the table there by the door, and 'ad me back turned to reach the pastry-board when I 'ear a kind of a swish and a scratching like, and out of the corner of me eye I see something come round the hedge of the door and make a grab at the rolling-pin ... something like a 'and with a bit of sacking over it, and –'

'Nonsense, Minter,' interrupted Ralph stoutly. 'It was a stray cat, of course! Pull yourself together, woman!'

'Then p'raps you'll tell me, sir,' choked Minter, 'how a cat could carry off me rolling-pin – because it's gone!'

There was certainly no rolling-pin visible anywhere, even on the floor. An attempt at a suggestion on Ralph's part that she had never put it on the table at all was met by a firm rejoinder that she was, as the Captain knew, a member of the Church of England and a strict teetotaller. Then Ralph said, with a sudden air of enlightenment, that of course it was that drunken fellow upstairs playing her a trick; he would send him about his business in double-quick time.

Never did anyone feel less like carrying out such a threat than Ralph Seton as he went slowly upstairs with his repaired electric lamp. All was quiet above – cheering thought, perhaps the invader had not returned to his place of vigil! No moaning, nothing. But just as he got to the corner on the landing which he must turn before he could see the attic stairs, he stood rooted. What was that rapid series of bumps, one after the other? His hair rising on his head, Ralph set his teeth, slid round the corner and flashed the lamp on to the steep empty stairs ... down which was trundling sedately a pale, cylindrical object – the kitchen rolling-pin.

It came to rest a few stairs from the bottom. Ralph had no wish to pick it up, but stood staring at it as if it had been a cobra. What in the name of heaven – was It descending to the level of a *poltergeist* ... had It been here a moment ago and dropped the thing ... why had It taken it?

Evadne's voice on the landing, sleepy and rather querulous. 'Ralph, I do think you needn't have chosen just the time when I had got off to sleep to do hammering up here!'

'But there's been no –' he was beginning, when it occurred to him that perhaps there had ... on the attic door ... with the rolling-pin. But he could offer neither that explanation nor the other possible one of the bumping descent of that object. He went and induced Evadne to return to bed, humbly apologising for his thoughtlessness; he had not thought she could hear.

But he did not go to bed at all that night; he sat up till dawn in their bedroom with Jeans's *Mysterious Universe* (which he did not read) and, foolishly enough, his service revolver – loaded.

✕

'It seems almost a pity, though,' said the doctor, surveying the new distemper. 'It will cost you something to have this mended up again, even if we only make a sort of doorway in it.'

'I don't care what it costs,' returned the owner of Hallows, hatchet in hand. 'I'm going to hoof that damned "chest" out of here before we both go mad, my wife and I. Come on!'

129

And he struck the first blow.

It was a messy job, but not very difficult, to cut an entranceway through the lath and plaster; and when it was done the two men, candle in hand, stepped one after the other into a narrow, darkish place – wider none the less than Ralph had expected. It was neither cold nor damp, but felt very stuffy. 'Wonder the candles will burn!' muttered Ralph, but the air was not really foul. The rafters showed vaguely on high, but draped with cobwebs so filthy that they looked like dirty cloths hung out to dry, and the floor might have been covered with equally dirty flannel, for the foot sank soundlessly into its thick sediment of dust. In one or two places the candlelight gleamed on small white scraps of bone – relics of bird or mouse or bat. But of a chest, nothing – nothing at first, till Ralph pointed out, at the left-hand end of the slice of room, a small oblong mound on the floor, a shape not more than fifteen inches high and three feet or so long.

'I will fetch the broom I brought up,' he said, stepping back through the gap into the attic. He had foreseen dust, but not so much of it.

Dr Mildmay had vetoed Evadne's presence in her unstrung condition, and she was downstairs helping Minter in the kitchen. Nevertheless, Ralph had bolted the attic door – there was no key. It was wrong of her, therefore, to disobey orders, and, after trying the handle, to keep on tapping like that.

'Go away, Eve!' he shouted. 'You can come in afterwards. Yes, it's all right, we've found something.'

'You promise that I may come in afterwards?' came indistinctly through the door.

'Yes, yes; but go away now!' And to his relief he heard her going down the stairs again.

'I believe this may prove to be a child's coffin,' observed Dr Mildmay, as Ralph, back in the narrow candle-lit space, started cautiously to use the broom on the dust-covered mound which, save that the sides were straight, had an outline that gave colour to the doctor's surmise.

At last Ralph got rid of most of this age-long deposit, and both men, coughing a little, stooped with their candles over a narrow box covered with hide or leather fastened with blackened nails to the wood beneath. In many places this leather was cracked and curled, and the little 'chest' was held together by a couple of thin iron bands going right round it.

'Let's get it out into daylight,' said the doctor. 'By Jove, it's heavy!'

'Treasure, perhaps,' commented Ralph; yet, though a memory of *Treasure Island*, brought 'pieces of eight' for a moment into his mind, he did not really believe in such good fortune. And as he got his hands under the narrow leather-covered box he was conscious of such a spasm of aversion towards it that he had much ado to retain his hold. If it were not that the weight was much too great he would have said that it contained a skeleton – only, surely, the skeleton of a dwarf. Together, with difficulty owing to its weight, they got the receptacle through the aperture in the false wall. And when they set it down in full daylight on the clean bare boards Ralph was aware that Dr Mildmay, too, looked strange. Their eyes met.

'Whatever is in there is evil,' said the man from East Africa in a low voice, and Ralph nodded. Nevertheless, he selected from the tools he had brought up with him, a stout chisel and a hammer.

'I wish I had asked Eve for a duster when she came to the door just now,' he thought, for the box was still pretty grimy. With some difficulty he got the chisel under the first of the iron bands, which, at any rate, was thin and almost rusted away; and indeed, it soon gave, starting up with a *cling*. The other band was more difficult and required the aid of pincers as well, but in the end he got it off. And then, as the lock was broken and the leathern hinges rotted away, there was no more to do than raise the lid.

'I suppose we had better?' suggested Ralph, hesitating, after all.

'I think we must,' answered his companion firmly; and with that he lifted it off and laid it on the floor.

A strange smell, half of damp, half of some withered perfume, came out of the narrow box, out of the folds of rotting brocade, crimson and gold, which loosely covered what was within. And what was within showed enough of its shape to testify that it was a human body – but a body only three feet long. Summoning all his resolution, Ralph Seton pulled the tinder-thin stuff aside; and there met his eyes the greenish shape of a perfectly formed woman, clad only in a thin pleated kirtle from waist to knees, save where a fold climbed upwards over one breast and shoulder ... a woman, yes, but one who had never lived. For after one wild second's thought of some impossible process of embalming, both men together gasped: 'Why, it's ... it's a statue!'

It was; a bronze statue of rather more than half life-size of beautiful workmanship, a nymph, perhaps, for one hand held an arrow, and there were buskins on the feet. But it was not the work of the ancient world, that was clear; and, though the statue was perfect and unworn, it was not modern, either. There was a smile on the face, subtle and enigmatic, a little like the smile that Leonardo knew how to paint, and Luini and Boltraffio, too; but it was not an evil smile. Why, then, had they both been conscious of that feeling of repulsion and almost of fear?

'What is this?' asked Dr Mildmay suddenly, pointing. 'That, surely, is no part of the original design!'

For between the breasts of the figure, the one covered, the other exposed, protruded a blackened, cross-shaped object, like the hilt of a small dagger – a silver-hilted dagger, perhaps.

Below it, indeed, when they looked closer, some half-inch of rusty blade was visible, fitting but ill into a jagged rent a little larger than itself. But there was more than the dagger blade in the bosom which had never felt the wound; there was a strip of paper wound about the rusty steel. The dagger itself would not come away; but Dr Mildmay with neat fingers picked and unwound the flimsy piece of paper. Even so, when he began to unfold it, it tore. Very silently he held out the tattered thing to Ralph. Captain Seton could not make sense of what was written on it – words which seemed no words, and signs that conveyed nothing. Shaking his head, he gave it back.

'This is rubbish, doctor. Or, well, I suppose it may prove of interest. What are you after?'

He got no answer for a moment. Dr Mildmay, looking grim, went back into the recess and returned with one of the still lighted candles.

'Oh, wait a minute!' cried Ralph. 'Isn't that a pity? The paper may be –'

'If you want to be free from that unhappy creature I fancy this is the way,' answered the doctor. 'Don't you want to be free?'

'God knows I do!' answered Captain Seton, who, after all, was no antiquary. Evadne's health and peace of mind, not to speak of his own, were a great deal more to him than cabalistic writings. So he watched the candle-flame making short work of what Dr Mildmay had unwound, and saw, falling to the floor, a few blackened flakes flimsier than the cobwebs in the place which had hidden – for how many years, he wondered – this poniarded nymph lying there before them, with that changeless and secret smile, her head on a little green satin pillow spotted with mould.

✕

It was night. Evadne's even breathing showed him that she

was soundly asleep; but Ralph could not imitate her example. She had been told everything, had viewed with astonishment and admiration the secret of the 'chest,' and, like her husband, had thankfully accepted Dr Mildmay's opinion that with the burning of the strip of paper wound about the dagger, they might reasonably expect Hallows to be free from its importunate visitor. Nevertheless, Ralph was restless; he almost felt fevered. That little statue; he lay picturing it set up on a pedestal. It would surely look even more beautiful so. They had not yet lifted it out of its bed, its coffin. What was to be done with it eventually? Had they a right to keep it? He supposed so. Then he would have that evasive smile to look at always, and the turn of the head, which must be more lovely, more significant, if the nymph were as she was created to be, upright against a forest tapestry of greens and browns …

For nearly an hour he lay thinking about her, and then rose very quietly from his bed, put on his dressing-gown and crept out of the room carrying a candlestick; he did not strike a match until he was outside. Why not be the first to see what she looked like, standing in her half-naked loveliness up there in the bare attic? Though she was heavy, she was not large; he was sure that he could lift her out of the coffer unaided.

Odd, he thought, as he went stealthily up the attic stairs, that that antiquated word should have come thus unbidden into his mind. He wished now that he had not allowed the strip of paper with the writing to be burnt. It might have told him something about his nymph – for she was his now. Dr Mildmay was … well, he had been a missionary, apparently; he was a man of very narrow ideas. Yes, he himself had been a damned fool to let him burn that writing!

This reflection reminded him of the dagger, that cruel dagger whose thrust had not destroyed her imperishable life, but which he hated to think of. He would have another try at getting it out – an excellent, an almost imperative reason for this nocturnal visit. All the same, he must be a trifle feverish, for he opened the attic door almost as though he were entering a shrine; he was aware of this, and knew the feeling to be absurd, more especially as the goddess which it contained was lying tied up in a box. For, the attic door having no key, Dr Mildmay and he had fastened up the chest again in two places with stout cord. However, he could soon undo it.

But even that was not necessary. He gazed down, astonished. The cords were no longer round the coffer ... though they were still underneath it, lying spread upon the floor. And by the ends of them he saw – he could not help seeing – that they had neither been untied nor cut; they had been burst apart. Who on earth could have done such a thing – who could have had the strength?

Ralph set down the candle with a shaking hand and dropped to one knee. For a moment he dared not move the lid, which was still in place, though a little crooked. It was obvious what had happened; someone had got into Hallows and stolen her! She was no longer there; he should never see that smile again. There would only be the empty coffin.

Steeling himself, he took away the lid. His heart leapt up – she was there still, she was there! He took up the candle from the floor and held it over her, drinking in her beauty. And it was only after a moment or two that he noticed something different about her. The blackened dagger hilt was gone – the weapon was gone altogether ... there was only the tiny rent between her shapely little breasts ...

Ralph Seton felt an immense relief and gladness. Now there was nothing to mar her beauty ... and nothing any longer to cause her pain! He could kneel on for ever, just looking at her ...

Not, however, if he continued to have this strong conviction that he was being watched, and watched by someone or something hostile. He tore his gaze away and sent it searching round the dark and empty attic. No one, of course ... nothing ... unless that *was* a face peering at him through the breach in the false wall. No, mere fancy! He looked down again fondly at that perfect visage. Her hair rose high above her lovely brow – higher than in classical statues which he had seen; she was more human than they. The Gioconda smile seemed to flicker about her mouth as the candle-flame bent and wavered in the draught; it seemed to invite him. And had he not a right to it, he who had freed her from her long entombment, who was restoring her to the light of day and to her meed of admiration, to a background of woodland tapestry, with perhaps a crystal bowl of flowers at her feet?

'My beautiful one!' he whispered, and bent to kiss the smile.

How cold she was; how long and unsatisfying the kiss; how curious the sensation that a heavy weight upon the back of his neck, almost like a hand, was pressing his head down into the coffer, against the unyielding bronze and the rotting, faintly scented brocade! ... But there *was* something gripping him there and pressing, pressing unmercifully! He tried to shout, but it was like a nightmare, for he was dumb; he struggled as desperately and as powerlessly as one struggles in a nightmare ... Then, thank God, the nightmare broke, and he was crouching on the floor by the box, sweating all over, his hands to his neck.

What had he been doing, he, Ralph Seton, stealing up at dead of night to kiss a statue – a *statue!* He must have gone mad, quite mad, shamefully mad! ... But was it madness, or returning sanity, which brought to his ears a sound like a low laugh, which seemed to come from that dark place of discovery at the end of the attic? No, he was not mistaken – he *had* been watched at his indefensible worship!

Shame and sudden fury set him on his feet. Leaving the

candle where it was on the floor, he made a rush at that dark cavity. 'Come out, whoever you are – come out and don't snigger in there!'

He caught his foot as he rushed in and half tripped, so that only the close proximity of the opposite wall saved him from falling; then, as he recovered and turned, beating about in the darkness to discover the invisible mocker, he thought instantly: 'Mustn't stop in here more than a moment ... the air *is* foul ... my poor old lungs won't stand it!' So he swung round to face the opening – and then stood motionless. Framed by the jagged aperture, bright and clear, though the only light there was the candle on the floor, a young man in a ruff and a short black velvet cloak was kneeling by the open coffer, his head bowed, his hands outstretched in a gesture that looked like entreaty. Every slash of purple in his green doublet, every stiffened fold of his ruff, every curl of the gold galon round the edge of his cloak was as distinct as the details in a pre-Raphaelite picture, even to the glint of a jewel in his left ear. His face Ralph could not see; and the whole vision, sharp-cut though it was, lasted but the space of a lightning flash ... and when it was gone, left the dark of a night of thunderstorm behind it.

Captain Seton gasped, put a hand for a moment over his eyes, and then groped unsteadily for the aperture. Though the candlelight in the room beyond had been so unaccountably swallowed up he could find the gap by feeling, since, for one thing, it could not be more than a foot or two from his hand ... God! what had become of it? He could feel nothing, not even the false wall ... there was nothing round him anywhere, in any direction, but darkness, a thick, soft, choking darkness. And now his heart, his brain, were beating fit to burst; when he tried to draw a deep breath there was nothing to breathe but dust, dust. He fell on his knees in dust, dust was whirling down upon him in the warm gloom, dust was up his nostrils, in his mouth, in his very vitals. The way out of this place was lost, blocked, gone … with his damaged lungs he must stifle here … he *was* stifling. 'Dust thou art and to dust shalt thou return!' But *she* had not been dust … and that was why this had happened … Poor Eve … but his life was insured … 'Gas-masks, men – gas-masks, quick!' … He went down and down through spinning eternities of dust and suffocation.

※

If Evadne had not wakened and missed him, if she had not heard the sound of hasty feet in the attic above, if her husband had not left the attic door ajar, so that the light shone down – who knows? But these things told Evadne with voices of alarm, and with another candle she ran up the stairs, and saw the first one still burning on the floor by the side of the open coffer.

It did not take her long to find Ralph; but, strong though she was, she had to tug hard to pull him out, asking herself all the time what could have possessed him to enter that place at such a time. She flung the attic windows wide, she fetched remedies; gradually the blueness ebbed from his lips and he began to come round. She helped him to bed, asking for no explanation. As soon as it was daylight she went herself for Dr Mildmay.

What Ralph told the doctor she did not know; to her, later, he merely said that he had undoubtedly had a touch of fever – had had it before he went to bed, but had not bothered to tell her. But he avoided her eyes, and seemed altogether strange as well as ill.

However, he recovered, and recovered so completely as to be able to inform her a few days later that he was going to supper with Dr Mildmay and might be back rather late. She herself had helped the doctor to fasten up the nymph again and to wrap the whole chest in brown paper, so that it looked an entirely modern and ordinary parcel, though out of the ordinary heavy; and the doctor had had it fetched away to his own house. She understood that some art dealer was coming to look at it there.

But on the evening that Captain Seton supped with him, Dr Mildmay fetched out his car afterwards, and he and Ralph lifted the box into it, and they drove through the sleeping village without a single touch on the horn, until they came to the old canal where earlier the autumn leaves had lain unstirring, as on some road of glass. They took the wrapped coffer out and carried it along the verge to the old wooden high-arched bridge which – somewhat shakily now – spanned the canal; and from the middle of this they lowered what they carried with a rope – so much precaution to avoid the sound of a splash in the still autumn night. The heavy thing slid gently into the sluggish water, and the rope, weighted at the end, followed it down; thick bubbles came up as it reached the mud, bubbles of marsh gas. After that the water rocked a little and the widening circles spread out more and more faintly under the stars, and that was all.

Dr Mildmay wiped his forehead. 'May she rest in peace, and he, too!'

Ralph Seton was silent for a moment. After that night he had never wished to look upon the face of his nymph again, nor had he.

'Do you think he will sleep ... or will he look for her here?'

'Who can tell? At least he can vex no human now. But I think that after he had withdrawn the dagger it was over for him, and that you witnessed his very last appearance. Come back with me now, and I will show you what my friend at Oxford has sent me, and you shall judge.'

✕

The doctor's study was homely and comfortable after the sleeping canal and that midnight drowning.

'Come to the fire; you are shivering,' said its owner, and when he had settled his guest in a chair and mixed him a whisky and soda – against his principles, as he informed him – he drew out a letter.

'This is what my friend, Dawkins of Corpus, says. I must tell you first, though, that I only put the case to him as a ghost story which I had recently heard; I did not state that it was actually the present experience of a patient of mine.

I have identified your ghost for you, I think, though I have not come across its name. I remembered to have read the tale you passed on to me some years ago in a book called *Curiosities of the Supernatural*, a collection made by a rather credulous Victorian parson, the Rev Thomas White, who died about 1860. I got out this volume at the Bodleian and found (what I had forgotten) that the reverend author of the *Curiosities* had not told the story in his own words, but had lifted it bodily from a seventeenth-century pamphlet containing, apparently, several such yarns. But the tiresome old cleric omits to mention either the title of the pamphlet or the name of its writer. Here, however, is the passage as he gives it.

'And what shall be said of that young Gallant of the time of good King *James*, who, being violently enamoured of a young and fair *French* gentlewoman that would none of his suit and but mocked at him, caused make a copy in bronze of that beauteous *Diana* wherein that sculptor of so great parts, Monsieur *Jean Goujon*, did immortalize both the lady *Diane of Poictiers* and himself, the which statue was held to resemble as closely this young scornful Beauty as once it had resembled that famous bedfellow of a king; what shall be said of this disdained lover, that took with him to *England* this simulacrum of his lady in a coffer, and, being come there, did wickedly pierce the breast of the twice likened *Artemis*, and in that bloodless wound set a silver dagger wound about with charms; which charms, whether by his knowledge and consent or against it, did cause the death of his proud mistress within the year. And he, being gone (it is thought) to the *Indies* or the *Spanish Main*, knew naught of it; and then, in captivity of the *Spaniards*, still less than naught; but, after many years, returning to England, and desiring to see again the image of his dearest love whom he had done to death, sought it over the length and breadth of the land and could not by any means find it: till, about the time the late bloody tyrant *Oliver* began to raise his horn, he was near finding it; but by ill fortune, before he came at it, was himself slain, being then about sixty-five years of age, bearing arms for our late sovereign Lord King *Charles the Second* at *Worcester* fight, and that by a mortal thrust in the very spot where he had so impiously transfixed the statue. Which statue continues lost until this day, and 'tis said that he still seeks after it, sometimes in the semblance of a young man, sometimes as an old one. Yet, since it appears that he may enter no place in search of it that he be not bidden to enter, 'twould seem that this poor Phantome must continue his quest for ever. Nevertheless, 'tis certain that the effigy lies somewhere hid in the county of Worcester.'

'I was right about the paper, you see,' said Dr Mildmay, laying down the letter.

'Yes, you were right. And so the nymph was Diana herself. And now we have drowned her … Goujon was a famous Renaissance sculptor, wasn't he? But she was a copy, the … the one we found?'

'Yes, and a copy, apparently, of a work of his which is now lost. I don't know much about him myself, but Dawkins, who is a perfect mine of information, has a postscript on that point.' Dr Mildmay took up his friend's letter again and turned it sideways. 'He says that it has been supposed by some critics that there existed another masterpiece besides the famous Diana now in the Louvre, the one where the goddess is seated with her arm round the neck of a stag, because in the eighteenth century somebody called – can't quite make it out, but it looks like Piganiol – spoke enthusiastically of another nymph in the orangery of the château of Anet, where the Diana of the Louvre comes from.'

'Yes, I see,' said Ralph Seton, looking fixedly at his untouched glass. 'But why did you wait until after our expedition of this evening to read me this, doctor?'

'To be perfectly frank with you, because I thought the nymph was better out of the way. But if you regret what we did, if you think that she is valuable and that you could sell her – why, she is not yet sunk so deep that she cannot be fished up again!'

Dr Mildmay spoke cheerfully, but he was looking at his visitor with a gaze not devoid of anxiety.

'No, no,' answered Ralph Seton with a slight shiver. 'I would not condemn even an art collector to the possibility of going through what we have been going through … I suppose, by the way, that *he* was encouraged to begin again by our opening a teashop at Hallows, which gave him a kind of right of entry, as into an inn … And I myself must have invited him into the attic, for my wife denies that it was she at the door when I shouted, "You can come in afterwards" – No, let's have no more of that! I'm all for the Englishman's castle, now, the sanctity of the home and that sort of thing!' And with a rather strained laugh he drank off his whisky and soda.

7 Couching at the Door (1933)

1

The first inkling which Augustine Marchant had of the matter was on one fine summer morning about three weeks after his visit to Prague – that is to say, in June, 1898. He was reclining, as his custom was when writing his poetry, on the very comfortable sofa in his library at Abbot's Medding, near the French windows, one of which was open to the garden. Pausing for inspiration – he was nearly at the end of his poem, *Salutation to All Unbeliefs* – he let his eyes wander round the beautifully appointed room, with its cloisonné and Satsuma, Buhl and first editions, and then allowed them to stray towards the sunlight outside. And so, between the edge of the costly Herat carpet and the sill of the open window, across the strip of polished oak flooring, he observed what he took to be a small piece of dark fluff blowing in the draught; and instantly made a note to speak to his housekeeper about it. There was slackness somewhere; and in Augustine Marchant's house no one was allowed to be slack but himself.

There had been a time when the poet would not for a moment have been received, as he was now, in country and even county society – those days, even before the advent of *The Yellow Book* and *The Savoy*, when he had lived in London, writing the plays and poems which had so startled and shocked all but the 'decadent' and the 'advanced', *Pomegranates of Sin*, *Queen Theodora and Queen Marozia*, *The Nights of the Tour de Nesle*, *Amor Cypriacus* and the rest. But when, as the 'nineties began to wane, he inherited Abbot's Medding from a distant cousin and came to live there, being then at the height of an almost international reputation, Wiltshire society at first tolerated him for his kinship with the late Lord Medding, and then, placated by the excellence of his dinners and further mollified by the patent staidness of his private life, decided that, in his personal conduct at any rate, he must have turned over a new leaf. Perhaps indeed he had never been as bad as he was painted, and if his writings continued to be no less scandalously free and free-thinking than before, and needed to be just as rigidly kept out of the hands of daughters, well, no country gentleman in the neighbourhood was obliged to read them!

And indeed Augustine Marchant in his fifty-first year was too keenly alive to the value of the good opinion of county society to risk shocking it by any overt doings of his. He kept his licence for his pen. When he went abroad, as he did at least twice a year – but that was another matter altogether. The nose of Mrs Grundy was not sharp enough to smell out his occupations in Warsaw or Berlin or Naples, her eyes long-sighted enough to discern what kind of society he frequented even so near home as Paris. At Abbot's Medding his reputation for being 'wicked' was fast declining into just enough of a sensation to titillate a croquet party. He had charming manners, could be witty at moments (though he could not keep it up), still retained his hyacinthine locks (by means of hair restorers), wore his excellently cut velvet coats and flowing ties with just the right air – half poet, half man of the world – and really had, at Abbot's Medding, no dark secret to hide beyond the fact, sedulously concealed by him for five-and-twenty years, that he had never been christened Augustine. Between Augustus and Augustine, what a gulf! But he had crossed it, and his French poems (which had to be smuggled into his native land) were signed Augustin – Augustin Lemarchant.

Removing his gaze from the objectionable evidence of domestic carelessness upon the floor, Mr Marchant now fixed it meditatively upon the ruby-set end of the gold pencil which he was using. Rossell & Ward, his publishers, were about to bring out an édition de luxe of *Queen Theodora and Queen Marozia* with illustrations by a hitherto unknown young artist – if they were not too daring. It would be a sumptuous affair in a limited edition. And, as he thought of this, the remembrance of his recent stay in Prague returned to the poet. He smiled to himself, as a man smiles when he looks at a rare wine, and thought: 'Yes, if these blunt-witted Pharisees round Abbott's Medding only knew!' It was a good thing that the upholders of British petty morality were seldom great travellers; a dispensation of ... ahem, Providence!

Twiddling his gold pencil between plump fingers, Augustine Marchant returned to his ode, weighing one epithet against another. Except in summer he was no advocate of open windows, and even in summer he considered that to get the most out of that delicate and precious instrument, his brain, his feet must always be kept thoroughly warm; he had therefore cast over them, before settling into his semi-reclining position, a beautiful rose-coloured Indian *sari* of the purest and thickest silk, leaving the ends trailing on the floor. And he became aware, with surprise and annoyance, that the piece of brown fluff or whatever it was down there, travelling in the draught from the window, had reached the nearest end of the *sari* and was now, impelled by the same current, travelling up it.

The master of Abbot's Medding reached out for the silver hand-bell on the table by his side. There must be more breeze coming in than he had realized, and he might take cold, a catastrophe against which he guarded himself as against the plague. Then he saw that the upward progress of the dark blot – it was about the size of a farthing – could not by any possibility be assigned to any other agency than its own. It was *climbing* up – some horrible insect, plainly, some disgusting kind of almost legless and very hairy spider, round and vague in outline. The poet sat up and shook the *sari* violently. When he looked again the invader was gone. He had obviously shaken it on to the floor, and on the floor somewhere it must still be. The idea perturbed him, and he decided to take his writing out to the summer-house, and give orders later that the library was to be thoroughly swept.

Ah! it was good to be out of doors, and in a pleasance so delightfully laid out, so exquisitely kept, as his! In the basin of the fountain the sea-nymphs of rosy-veined marble clustered round a Thetis as beautiful as Aphrodite herself; the lightest and featheriest of acacia trees swayed near. And as the owner of all this went past over the weedless turf he repeated snatches of Verlaine to himself about 'sveltes jets d'eau' and 'sanglots d'exstase'.

Then, turning his head to look back at the fountain, he became aware of a little dark-brown object about the size of a halfpenny running towards him over the velvet-smooth sward ...

He believed afterwards that he must first have had a glimpse of the truth at that instant in the garden, or he would not have acted so instinctively as he did, and so promptly. For a moment later he was standing at the edge of the basin of Thetis, his face blanched in the sunshine, his hand firmly clenched. Inside that closed hand something feather-soft pulsated ... Holding back as best he could the disgust and the something more which clutched at him, Augustine Marchant stooped and plunged his whole fist into the bubbling water, and let the stream of the fountain whirl away what he had picked up. Then with uncertain steps he went and sat down on the nearest seat and shut his eyes. After a while he took out his lawn handkerchief and carefully dried his hand with the intaglio ring, dried it and then looked curiously at the palm. 'I did not know I had so much courage,' he was thinking; 'so much courage and good sense!' ... It would doubtless drown very quickly.

Burrows, his butler, was coming over the lawn. 'Mr and Mrs Morrison have arrived, sir.'

'Ah, yes; I had forgotten for the moment.' Augustine Marchant got up and walked towards the house and his guests, throwing back his shoulders and practising his famous enigmatic smile, for Mrs Morrison was a woman worth impressing.

(But what had it been exactly? Why, just what it had looked – a tuft of fur blowing over the grass, a tuft of fur! Sheer imagination that it had moved in his closed hand with a life of its own ... Then why had he shut his eyes as he stooped and made a grab at it? Thank God, thank God, it was nothing now but a drenched smear swirling round the nymphs of Thetis!)

'Ah, dear lady, you must forgive me! Unpardonable of me not to be in to receive you!' He was in the drawing-room now, fragrant with its bank of hothouse flowers, bending over the hand of the fashionably attired guest on the sofa, in her tight bodice and voluminous sleeves, with a fly-away hat perched at a rakish angle on her gold-brown hair.

'Your man told us that you were writing in the garden,' said her goggle-eyed husband reverentially.

'*Cher maître*, it is we who ought not to be interrupting your rendezvous with the Muse,' returned Mrs Morrison in her sweet, high voice. 'Terrible to bring you from such company into that of mere visitors!'

Running his hand through his carefully tended locks the *cher maître* replied: 'Between a visit from the Muse and one from Beauty's self no true poet would hesitate! – Moreover, luncheon awaits us, and I trust it is a good one.'

He liked faintly to shock fair admirers by admitting that he cared for the pleasures of the table; it was quite safe to do so, since none of them had sufficient acumen to see that it was true.

The luncheon was excellent, for Augustine kept an admirable cook. Afterwards he showed his guests over the library – yes, even though it had not received the sweeping which would now be unnecessary – and round the garden; and in the summer-house was prevailed upon to read some of *Amor Cypriacus* aloud. And Mrs Frances (nowadays Francesca) Morrison was thereafter able to recount to envious friends how the Poet himself had read her stanza after stanza from that most *daring* poem of his; and how poor Fred, fanning himself meanwhile with his straw hat – not from the torridity of the verse but because of the afternoon heat – said afterwards that he had not understood a single word. A good thing, perhaps ...

When they had gone Augustine Marchant reflected rather cynically: 'All that was just so much bunkum when I wrote it.' For ten years ago, in spite of those audacious, glowing verses, he was an ignorant neophyte. Of course, since then ... He smiled, a private, sly, self-satisfied smile. It was certainly pleasant to know oneself no longer a fraud!

Returning to the summer-house to fetch his poems he saw what he took to be Mrs Morrison's fur boa lying on the floor just by the basket chair which she had occupied. Odd of her not to have missed it on departure – a tribute to his verses perhaps. His housekeeper must send it after her by post. But just at that moment his head gardener approached, desiring some instructions, and when the matter was settled, and Augustine Marchant turned once more to enter the summer-house, he found that he had been mistaken about the dropped boa, for there was nothing on the floor.

Besides, he remembered now that Mrs Morrison's boa had been a rope of grey feathers, not of dark fur. As he took up *Amor Cypriacus* he asked himself lazily what could have led him to imagine a woman's boa there at all, much less a fur one.

Suddenly he knew why. A lattice in the house of memory had opened, and he remained rigid, staring out at the jets of the fountain rising and falling in the afternoon sun. Yes; of that glamorous, wonderful, abominable night in Prague the part he least wished to recall was connected – incidentally but undeniably – with a fur boa … a long boa of dark fur …

He had to go up to town next day to a dinner in his honour. There and then he decided to go up that same night, by a late train, a most unusual proceeding, and most disturbing to his valet, who knew that it was doubtful whether he could at such short notice procure him a first-class carriage to himself. However, Augustine Marchant went, and even, to the man's amazement, deliberately chose a compartment with another occupant when he might, after all, have had an empty one.

The dinner was brilliant; Augustine had never spoken better. Next day he went round to the little street not far from the British Museum where he found Lawrence Storey, his new illustrator, working feverishly at his drawings for *Queen Theodora and Queen Marozia*, and quite overwhelmed at the honour of a personal visit. Augustine was very kind to him, and, while offering a few criticisms, highly praised his delineation of those two Messalinas of tenth-century Rome, their long supple hands, their heavy eyes, their full, almost repellent mouths. Storey had followed the same type for mother and daughter, but with a subtle difference.

'They were certainly two most evil women, especially the younger,' he observed ingenuously. 'But I suppose that, from an artistic point of view, that doesn't matter nowadays!'

Augustine, smoking one of his special cigarettes, made a delicate little gesture. 'My dear fellow, Art has nothing whatever to do with what is called "morality"; happily we know that at last! Show me how you thought of depicting the scene where Marozia orders the execution of her mother's papal paramour. Good, very good! Yes, the lines there, even the fall of that loose sleeve from the extended arm, express with clarity what I had in mind. You have great gifts!'

'I have tried to make her look wicked,' said the young man, reddening with pleasure. 'But,' he added deprecatingly, 'it is very hard for a ridiculously inexperienced person like myself to have the right artistic vision. For to you, Mr Marchant, who have penetrated into such wonderful arcana of the forbidden, it would be foolish to pretend to be other than I am.'

'How do you know that I have penetrated into any such arcana?' enquired the poet, half-shutting his eyes and looking (though not to the almost worshipping gaze of young Storey) like a great cat being stroked.

'Why, one has only to read you!'

'You must come down and stay with me soon,' were Augustine Marchant's parting words. (He would give the boy a few days' good living, for which he would be none the worse; let him drink some decent wine.) 'How soon do you think you will be able to finish the rough sketches for the rest, and the designs for the *culs de lampe*? A fortnight or three weeks? Good; I shall look to see you then. Good-bye, my dear fellow; I am very, very much pleased with what you have shown me!'

The worst of going up to London from the country was that one was apt to catch a cold in town. When he got back, Augustine Marchant was almost sure that this misfortune had befallen him, so he ordered a fire in his bedroom, despite the season, and consumed a recherché little supper in seclusion. And, as the cold turned out to have been imaginary, he was very comfortable, sitting there in his silken dressing-gown, toasting his toes and holding up a glass of golden Tokay to the flames. Really *Theodora and Marozia* would make as much sensation when it came out with these illustrations as when it first appeared!

All at once he set down his glass. Not far away on his left stood a big cheval mirror, like a woman's, in which a good portion of the bed behind him was reflected. And, in this mirror, he had just seen the valance of the bed move. There could be no draught to speak of in this warm room, he never allowed a cat in the house, and it was quite impossible that there should be a rat about. If after all some stray cat should have got in it must be ejected at once. Augustine hitched round in his chair to look at the actual bed-hanging.

Yes, the topaz-hued silk valance again swung very slightly outwards as though it were being pushed. Augustine bent forward to the bell-pull to summon his valet. Then the flask of Tokay rolled over on the table as he leapt from his chair instead. Something like a huge, dark caterpillar was emerging very slowly from under his bed, moving as a caterpillar moves, with undulations running over it. Where its head should have been was merely a tapering end smaller than the rest of it, but of like substance. It was a dark fur boa.

Augustine Marchant felt that he screamed, but he could not have done so, for his tongue clave to the roof of his mouth. He merely stood staring, staring, all the blood gone from his heart. Still very slowly, the thing continued to creep out from under the valance, waving that eyeless, tapering end to and fro, as though uncertain where to proceed. 'I am going mad, mad, mad!' thought Augustine, and then, with a revulsion: 'No, it can't be! It's a real snake of some kind!'

That could be dealt with. He snatched up the poker as the boa-thing, still swaying the head which was no head, kept pouring steadily out from under the lifted yellow frill, until quite three feet were clear of the bed. Then he fell upon it furiously, with blow after blow.

But they had no effect on the furry, spineless thing; it merely gave under them and rippled up in another place. Augustine hit the bed, the floor; at last, really screaming, he threw down his weapon and fell upon the thick, hairy rope with both hands, crushing it together into a mass – there was little if any resistance in it – hurled it into the fire and, panting, kept it down with shovel and tongs. The flames licked up instantly and, with a roar, made short work of it, though there seemed to be some slight effort to escape, which was perhaps only the effect of the heat. A moment later there was a very strong smell of burnt hair, and that was all.

Augustine Marchant seized the fallen flask of Tokay and drained from its mouth what little was left in the bottom ere, staggering to the bed, he flung himself upon it and buried his face in the pillows, even heaping them over his head as if he could thus stifle the memory of what he had seen.

✕

He kept his bed next morning; the supposed cold afforded a good pretext. Long before the maid came in to re-lay the fire he had crawled out to make sure that there were no traces left of … what he had burnt there. There were none. A nightmare could not have left a trace, he told himself. But well he knew that it was not a nightmare.

And now he could think of nothing but that room in Prague and the long fur boa of the woman. Some department of his mind (he supposed) must have projected that thing, scarcely noticed at the time, scarcely remembered, into the present and the here. It was terrible to think that one's mind possessed such dark, unknown powers. But not so terrible as if the … apparition … had been endowed with an entirely separate objective existence. In a day or two he would consult his doctor and ask him to give him a tonic.

But, expostulated an uncomfortably lucid part of his brain, you are trying to run with the hare and hunt with the hounds.

Is it not better to believe that the thing *had* an objective existence, for you have burnt it to nothing? Well and good! But if it is merely a projection from your own mind, what is to prevent it from reappearing, like the phoenix, from ashes?

There seemed no answer to that, save in an attempt to persuade himself that he had been feverish last night. Work was the best antidote. So Augustine Marchant rose, and was surprised and delighted to find the atmosphere of his study unusually soothing and inspiring; and that day, against all expectation, *Salutation to All Unbeliefs* was completed by some stanzas with which he was not too ill-pleased. Realizing nevertheless that he should be glad of company that evening, he had earlier sent round a note to the local solicitor, a good fellow, to come and dine with him; played a game of billiards with the lawyer afterwards, and retired to bed after some vintage port and a good stiff whisky and soda with scarcely a thought of the visitant of the previous night.

He woke at that hour when the thrushes in early summer punctually greet the new day – three o'clock. They were greeting it even vociferously, and Augustine Marchant was annoyed with their enthusiasm. His golden damask window-curtains kept out all but a glimmer of the new day, yet as, lying upon his back, the poet opened his eyes for a moment, his only half-awakened sense of vision reported something swinging to and fro in the dimness like a pendulum of rope. It was indistinct, but seemed to be hanging from the tester of the bed. And, wide awake in an instant, with an unspeakable anguish of premonition tearing through him, he felt, next moment, a light thud on the coverlet about the level of his knees. Something had arrived on the bed …

And Augustine Marchant neither shrieked nor leapt from his bed; he could not. Yet, now that his eyes were grown used to the twilight of the room, he saw it clearly, the fur rope which he had burnt to extinction two nights ago, dark and shining as before, rippling with a gentle movement as it coiled itself neatly together in the place where it had struck the bed, and subsided there in a symmetrical round, with only that tapering end a little raised, and, as it were, looking at him – only, eyeless and featureless, it could not look. One thought of disgusted relief, that it was not at any rate going to attack him, and Augustine Marchant fainted.

Yet his swoon must have merged into sleep, for he woke in a more or less ordinary fashion to find his man placing his early tea-tray beside him and enquiring when he should draw his bath. There was nothing on the bed.

'I shall change my bedroom,' thought Augustine to himself, looking at the haggard, fallen-eyed man who faced him in the mirror as he shaved. 'No, better still, I will go away for a change. Then I shall not have these … dreams. I'll go to old Edgar Fortescue for a few days; he begged me again not long ago to come any time.'

So to the house of that old Maecenas he went. He was much too great a man now to be in need of Sir Edgar's patronage. It was homage which he received there, both from host and guests. The stay did much to soothe his scarified nerves. Unfortunately the last day undid the good of all the foregoing ones.

Sir Edgar possessed a pretty young wife – his third – and, among other charms in his place in Somerset, an apple orchard under-planted with flowers. And in the cool of the evening Augustine walked there with his host and hostess almost as if he were the Almighty with the dwellers in Eden. Presently they sat down upon a rustic seat (but a very comfortable one) under the shade of the apple boughs, amid the incongruous but pleasant parterres.

'You have come at the wrong season for these apple-trees, Marchant,' observed Sir Edgar after a while, taking out his cigar. 'Blossom-time or apple-time – they are showy at either, in spite of the underplanting – What is attracting you on that tree – a tit? We have all kinds here, pretty, destructive little beggars!'

'I did not know that I was looking … it's nothing … thinking of something else,' stammered the poet. Surely, surely he had been mistaken in thinking that he had seen a sinuous, dark, furry thing undulating like a caterpillar down the stem of that particular apple-tree at a few yards' distance?

Talk went on, even his own; there was safety in it. It was only the breeze which faintly rustled that bed of heliotrope behind the seat. Augustine wanted desperately to get up and leave the orchard, but neither Sir Edgar nor his wife seemed disposed to move, and so the poet remained at his end of the seat, his left hand playing nervously with a long bent of grass which had escaped the scythe.

All at once he felt a tickling sensation on the back of his hand, looked down and saw that featureless snout of fur protruding upwards from underneath the rustic bench, and sweeping itself backwards and forwards against his hand with a movement which was almost caressing. He was on his feet in a flash.

'Do you mind if I go in?' he asked abruptly. 'I'm not … feeling very well.'

✕

If the thing could follow him it was of no use to go away. He returned to Abbot's Medding looking so much the worse for his change of air that Burrows expressed a respectful hope that he was not indisposed. And almost the first thing that occurred, when Augustine sat down at his writing-table to attend to his correspondence, was the unwinding of itself from one of its curved legs of a soft, brown, oscillating serpent which slowly waved an end at him as if in welcome …

In welcome, yes, that was it! The creature, incredible though it was, the creature seemed glad to see him! Standing at the other end of the room, his hands pressed over his eyes – for what was the use of attempting to hurt or destroy it? – Augustine Marchant thought shudderingly that, like a witch's cat, a 'familiar' would not, presumably, be ill disposed towards its master. Its master! Oh God!

The hysteria which he had been trying to keep down began to mount uncontrollably when, removing his hands, Augustine glanced again towards his writing-table, and saw that the boa had coiled itself in his chair and was sweeping its end to and fro over the back, somewhat in the way that a cat, purring meanwhile, rubs itself against furniture or a human leg in real or simulated affection.

'Oh, go, go away from there!' he suddenly screamed at it, advancing with outstretched hand. 'In the devil's name, get out!'

To his utter amazement, he was obeyed. The rhythmic movements ceased, the fur snake poured itself down out of the chair and writhed towards the door. Venturing back to his writing-table after a moment Augustine saw it coiled on the threshold, the blind end turned towards him as usual, as though watching. And he began to laugh. What would happen if he rang and someone came; would the opening door scrape it aside … would it vanish? Had it, in short, an existence for anyone else but himself?

But he dared not make the experiment. He left the room by the French window, feeling that he could never enter the house again. And perhaps, had it not been for the horrible knowledge just acquired that it could follow him, he might easily have gone away for good from Abbot's Medding and all his treasures and comforts. But of what use would that be – and how should he account for so extraordinary an action? No; he must think and plan while he yet remained sane.

To what, then, could he have recourse? The black magic in which he had dabbled with such disastrous consequences might possibly help him. Left to himself he was but an amateur, but he had a number of books ... There was also that other realm whose boundaries sometimes marched side by side with magic – religion. But how could he pray to a Deity in whom he did not believe? Rather pray to the Evil which had sent this curse upon him to show him how to banish it. Yet since he had deliberately followed what religion stigmatised as sin, what even the world would label as lust and necromancy, supplication to the dark powers was not likely to deliver him from them. They must somehow be outwitted, circumvented.

He kept his *grimoires* and books of the kind in a locked bookcase in another room, not in his study; in that room he sat up till midnight. But the spells which he read were useless; moreover, he did not really believe in them. The irony of the situation was that, in a sense, he had only played at sorcery; it had but lent a spice to sensuality. He wandered wretchedly about the room dreading at any moment to see his 'familiar' wreathed round some object in it. At last he stopped at a small bookcase which held some old forgotten books of his mother's – Longfellow and Mrs Hemans, *John Halifax, Gentleman*, and a good many volumes of sermons and mild essays. And when he looked at that blameless assembly a cloud seemed to pass over Augustine Marchant's vision, and he saw his mother, gentle and lace-capped, as years and years ago she used to sit, hearing his lessons, in an antimacassared chair. She had been everything to him then, the little boy whose soul was not smirched. He called silently to her now: 'Mamma, Mamma, can't you help me? Can't you send this thing away?'

When the cloud had passed he found that he had stretched out his hand and removed a big book. Looking at it he saw that it was her Bible, with 'Sarah Amelia Marchant' on the faded yellow fly-leaf. Her spirit *was* going to help him! He turned over a page or two, and out of the largish print there sprang instantly at him: *Now the serpent was more subtle than any beast of the field.* Augustine shuddered and almost put the Bible back, but the conviction that there was help there urged him to go on. He turned a few more pages of Genesis and his eyes were caught by this verse, which he had never seen before in his life.

And if thou doest well, shalt thou not be accepted? And if thou doest not well, sin lieth at the door. And unto thee shall be his desire, and thou shalt rule over him.

What strange words! What could they possibly mean? Was there light for him in them? 'Unto thee shall be his desire.' That Thing, the loathsome semblance of affection which hung about it … 'Thou shalt rule over him.' It *had* obeyed him, up to a point … Was this Book, of all others, showing him the way to be free? But the meaning of the verse was so obscure! He had not, naturally, such a thing as a commentary in the house. Yet, when he came to think of it, he remembered that some pious and anonymous person, soon after the publication of *Pomegranates of Sin*, had sent him a Bible in the Revised Version, with an inscription recommending him to read it. He had it somewhere, though he had always meant to get rid of it.

After twenty minutes' search through the sleeping house he found it in one of the spare bedrooms. But it gave him little enlightenment, for there was scant difference in the rendering, save that for, 'lieth at the door', this version had, 'coucheth', and that the margin held an alternative translation for the end of the verse: 'And unto thee is its desire, but thou shouldest rule over it.'

Nevertheless, Augustine Marchant stood after midnight in this silent, sheeted guest-chamber repeating: *'But thou shouldest rule over it.'*

And all at once he thought of a way of escape.

2

It was going to be a marvellous experience, staying with Augustine Marchant. Sometimes Lawrence Storey hoped there would be no other guests at Abbot's Medding; at other times he hoped there would be. A *tête-à-tête* of four days with the great poet – could he sustain his share worthily? For Lawrence, despite the remarkable artistic gifts which were finding their first real flowering in these illustrations to Augustine's poem, was still unspoilt, still capable of wonder and admiration, still humble and almost naïf. It was still astonishing to him that he, an architect's assistant, should have been snatched away, as Ganymede by the eagle, from the lower world of elevations and drains to serve on Olympus. It was not, indeed, Augustine Marchant who had first discovered him; but it was Augustine Marchant who was going to make him famous.

The telegraph-poles flitted past the second-class carriage window and more than one traveller glanced with a certain envy and admiration at the fair, good-looking young man who diffused such an impression of happiness and candour, and had such a charming smile on his boyish lips. He carried with him a portfolio which he never let out of reach of his hand; the oldish couple opposite, speculating upon its contents, might have changed their opinion of him had they seen them.

But no shadow of the dark weariness of things unlawful rested on Lawrence Storey; to know Augustine Marchant, to be illustrating his great poem, to have learnt from him that art and morality had no kinship, this was to plunge into a new realm of freedom and enlarging experience. Augustine Marchant's poetry, he felt, had already taught his hand what his brain and heart knew nothing of.

There was a dog-cart to meet him at the station, and in the scented June evening he was driven with a beating heart past meadows and hayfields to his destination.

Mr Marchant, awaiting him in the hall, was at his most charming. 'My dear fellow, are those the drawings? Come, let us lock them away at once in my safe! If you had brought me diamonds I should not be one quarter so concerned about thieves. And did you have a comfortable journey? I have had you put in the orange room; it is next to mine. There is no one else staying here, but there are a few people coming to dinner to meet you.'

There was only just time to dress for dinner, so that Lawrence did not get an opportunity to study his host until he saw him seated at the head of the table. Then he was immediately struck by the fact that he looked curiously ill. His face – ordinarily by no means attenuated – seemed to have fallen in, there were dark circles under his eyes, and the perturbed Lawrence, observing him as the meal progressed, thought that his manner, too, seemed strange and once or twice quite absent-minded. And there was one moment when, though the lady on his right was addressing him, he sharply turned his head away and looked down at the side of his chair just as if he saw something on the floor. Then he apologised, saying that he had a horror of cats, and that sometimes the tiresome animal from the stables ... But after that he continued to entertain his guests in his own inimitable way, and, even to the shy Lawrence, the evening proved very pleasant.

The three ensuing days were wonderful and exciting to the young artist – days of uninterrupted contact with a master mind which acknowledged, as the poet himself admitted, none of the petty barriers which man, for his own convenience, had set up between alleged right and wrong. Lawrence had learnt why his host did not look well; it was loss of sleep, the price exacted by inspiration. He had a new poetic drama shaping in his mind which would scale heights that he had not yet attempted.

There was almost a touch of fever in the young man's dreams to-night – his last night but one. He had several. First he was standing by the edge of a sort of mere, inexpressibly desolate and unfriendly, a place he had never seen in his life, which yet seemed in some way familiar; and something said to him: 'You will never go away from here!' He was alarmed, and woke, but went to sleep again almost immediately, and this time was back, oddly enough, in the church where in his earliest years he had been taken to service by the aunt who had brought him up – a large church full of pitch-pine pews with narrow ledges for hymn-books, which ledges he used surreptitiously to lick during the long dull periods of occultation upon his knees. But most of all he remembered the window with Adam and Eve in the Garden of Eden, on either side of an apple-tree round whose trunk was coiled a monstrous snake with a semi-human head. Lawrence had hated and dreaded that window, and because of it he would never go near an orchard and had no temptation to steal apples ... Now he was back in that church again, staring at the window, lit up with some infernal glow from behind. He woke again, little short of terrified – he, a grown man! But again he went to sleep quite quickly.

His third dream had for background, as sometimes happens in nightmares, the very room in which he lay. He dreamt that a door opened in the wall, and in the door-way, quite plain against the light from another room behind him, stood Augustine Marchant in his dressing-gown. He was looking

down at something on the ground which Lawrence did not
see, but his hand was pointing at Lawrence in the bed, and he
was saying in a voice of command: 'Go to him, do you hear?
Go to him! Go to *him!* Am I not your master?' And Lawrence,
who could neither move nor utter a syllable, wondered uneasily
what this could be which was thus commanded, but his
attention was chiefly focused on Augustine Marchant's face.
After he had said these words several times, and apparently
without result, a dreadful change came upon it, a look of the
most unutterable despair. It seemed visibly to age and wither;
he said, in a loud, penetrating whisper: 'Is there no escape
then?' covered his ravaged face a moment with his hands, and
then went back and softly closed the door. At that Lawrence
woke; but in the morning he had forgotten all three dreams.

The *tête-à-tête* dinner on the last night of his stay would
have lingered in a gourmet's memory, so that it was a pity
the young man did not know in the least what he was eating.
At last there was happening what he had scarcely dared
hope for; the great poet of the sensuous was revealing to
him some of the unimaginably strange and secret sources of
his inspiration. In the shaded rosy candle-light, his elbows
on the table among trails of flowers he, who was not even a
neophyte, listened like a man learning for the first time of
some spell of spring which will make him more than mortal.

'Yes,' said Augustine Marchant, after a long pause, 'yes, it
was a marvellous, an undying experience … one that is not
given to many. It opened doors, it – but I despair of doing
it justice in mere words.' His look was transfigured, almost
dreamy.

'But she … the woman … how did you …?' asked Lawrence
Storey in a hushed voice.

'Oh, the woman?' said Augustine, suddenly finishing off
his wine. 'The woman was only a common street-walker.'

A moment or two later Lawrence was looking at his host wonderingly and wistfully. 'But this was in Prague. Prague is a long way off.'

'One does not need to go so far, in reality. Even in Paris –'

'One could … have that experience in Paris?'

'If you knew where to go. And, of course, it is necessary to have credentials. I mean that – like all such enlightenments – it has to be kept secret, most secret, from the vulgar minds who lay their restrictions on the finer. That is self-evident.'

'Of course,' said the young man, and sighed deeply. His host looked at him affectionately.

'You, my dear Lawrence – I may call you Lawrence? – want just that touch of … what shall I call them – *les choses cachées* – to liberate your immense artistic gifts from the shackles which still bind them. Through that gateway you would find the possibility of their full fruition! It would fertilize your genius to a still finer blossoming … But you would have scruples … and you are very young.'

'You know,' said Lawrence in a low and trembling tone, 'what I feel about your poetry. You know how I ache to lay the best that is in me at your feet. If only I could make my drawings for the Two Queens more worthy – already it is an honour which overwhelms me that you should have selected me to do them – but they are not what they should be. I am *not* sufficiently liberated …'

Augustine leant forward on the flower-decked table. His eyes were glowing.

'Do you truly desire to be?'

The young man nodded, too full of emotion to find his voice.

The poet got up, went over to a cabinet in a corner and unlocked it. Lawrence watched his fine figure in a sort of trance. Then he half-rose with an exclamation.

'What is it?' asked Augustine very sharply, facing round.

'Oh, nothing, sir – only that I believe you hate cats, and I thought I saw one, or rather its tail, disappearing into that corner.'

'There's no cat here,' said Augustine quickly. His face had become all shiny and mottled, but Lawrence did not notice it. The poet stood a moment looking at the carpet; one might almost have thought that he was gathering resolution to cross it; then he came swiftly back to the table.

'Sit down again,' he commanded. 'Have you a pocket-book with you, a pocket-book which you never leave about? Good! Then write *this* in one place; and *this* on another page … write it small … among other entries is best … not on a blank page … write it in Greek characters if you know them …'

'What … what is it?' asked Lawrence, all at once intolerably excited, his eyes fixed on the piece of paper in Augustine's hand.

'The two halves of the address in Paris.'

3

Augustine Marchant kept a diary in those days, a locked diary written in cipher. And for more than a month after Lawrence Storey's visit the tenor of the entries there was almost identical:

No change … Always with me … How much longer can I endure it? The alteration in my looks is being remarked upon to my face. I shall have to get rid of Thornton [his man] on some pretext or other, for I begin to think that he has seen It. No wonder, since It follows me about like a dog. When It is visible to everyone it will be the end … I found It in bed with me this morning, pressed up against me as if for warmth …

But there was a different class of entry also, appearing at intervals with an ever-increasing note of impatience.

Will LS go there? ... When shall I hear from LS? ... Will the experiment do what I think? It is my last hope.

Then, suddenly, after five weeks had elapsed, an entry in a trembling hand:

For twenty-four hours I have seen no sign of It! Can it be possible?

And next day:

Still nothing. I begin to live again – This evening has come an ecstatic letter from LS, from Paris, telling me that he had 'presented his credentials' and was to have the experience next day. He has had it by now – by yesterday, in fact. Have I really freed myself? It looks like it!

In one week from the date of that last entry it was remarked in Abbot's Medding how much better Mr Marchant was looking again. Of late he had not seemed at all himself; his cheeks had fallen in, his clothes seemed to hang loosely upon him, who had generally filled them so well, and he appeared nervous. Now he was as before, cheery, courtly, debonair. And last Sunday, will you believe it, he went to church! The Rector was so astonished when he first became aware of him from the pulpit that he nearly forgot to give out his text. And the poet joined in the hymns, too! Several observed this amazing phenomenon.

It was the day after this unwonted appearance at St Peter's. Augustine was strolling in his garden. The air had a new savour, the sun a new light; he could look again with pleasure at Thetis and her nymphs of the fountain, could work undisturbed in the summer-house. Free, free! All the world was good to the senses once again, and the hues and scents of early autumn better, in truth, than the brilliance of that summer month which had seen his curse descend upon him.

The butler brought him out a letter with a French stamp. From Lawrence Storey, of course; to tell him – what? Where had he caught his first glimpse of it? In one of those oppressively furnished French bedrooms? And how had he taken it?

At first, however, Augustine was not sure that the letter was from Storey. The writing was very different, cramped instead of flowing, and, in places, spluttering, the pen having dug into the paper as if the hand which held it had not been entirely under control – almost, thought Augustine, his eyes shining with excitement, almost as though something had been twined, liana-like, round the wrist. (He had a sudden sick recollection of a day when that had happened to him, quickly submerged in a gush of eager anticipation.) Sitting down upon the edge of the fountain he read – not quite what he had looked for.

'I don't know what is happening to me,' began the letter, without other opening. 'Yesterday I was in a café by myself, and had just ordered some absinthe – though I do not like it. And quite suddenly, although I knew that I was in the café, I realized that I was also back in *that room*. I could see every feature of it, but I could see the café too, with all the people in it; the one was, as it were, superimposed upon the other, the room, which was a good deal smaller than the café, being inside the latter, as a box may be within a larger box. And all the while the room was growing clearer, the café fading. I saw the glass of absinthe suddenly standing on nothing, as it were. All the furniture of *the room*, all the accessories you know of, were mixed up with the chairs and tables of the café.

I do not know how I managed to find my way to the *comptoir*, pay and get out. I took a *fiacre* back to my hotel. By the time I arrived there I was all right. I suppose that it was only the after effects of a very strange and violent emotional experience. But I hope to God that it will not recur!

'How interesting!' said Augustine Marchant, dabbling his hand in the swirling water where he had once drowned a piece of dark fluff. 'And why indeed should I have expected that It would couch at his door in the same form as at mine?'

Four days more of new-found peace and he was reading this:

In God's name – or the Devil's – come over and help me! I have hardly an hour now by night or day when I am sure of my whereabouts. I could not risk the journey back to England alone. It is like being imprisoned in some kind of infernal half-transparent box, always growing a little smaller. Wherever I go now I carry it about with me; when I am in the street I hardly know which is the pavement and which is the roadway, because I am always treading on that black carpet with the cabalistic designs; if I speak to anyone they may suddenly disappear from sight. To attempt to work is naturally useless. I would consult a doctor, but that would mean telling him everything ...

'I hope to God he won't do that!' muttered Augustine uneasily. 'He can't – he swore to absolute secrecy. I hadn't bargained, however, for his ceasing work. Suppose he finds himself unable to complete the designs for *Theodora and Marozia*! That would be serious ... However, to have freed myself is worth *any* sacrifice ... But Storey cannot, obviously, go on living indefinitely on two planes at once ... Artistically, though, it might inspire him to something quite unprecedented.

I'll write to him and point that out; it might encourage him. But go near him in person – is it likely!'

The next day was one of great literary activity. Augustine was so deeply immersed in his new poetical drama that he neglected his correspondence and almost his meals – except his dinner, which seemed that evening to be shared most agreeably and excitingly by these new creations of his brain. Such, in fact, was his preoccupation with them that it was not until he had finished the savoury and poured out a glass of his superlative port that he remembered a telegram which had been handed to him as he came in to dinner. It still lay unopened by his plate. Now, tearing apart the envelope, he read with growing bewilderment these words above his publishers' names:

> Please inform us immediately what steps to take are prepared send to France recover drawings if possible what suggestions can you make as to successor Rossell and Ward.

Augustine was more than bewildered; he was stupefied. Had some accident befallen Lawrence Storey of which he knew nothing? But he had opened all his letters this morning, though he had not answered any. A prey to a sudden very nasty anxiety he got up and rang the bell.

'Burrows, bring me *The Times* from the library.'

The newspaper came, unopened. Augustine, now in a frenzy of uneasiness, scanned the pages rapidly. But it was some seconds before he came upon the headline: 'Tragic Death of a Young English Artist', and read the following, furnished by the Paris correspondent:

> Connoisseurs who were looking forward to the appearance of the superb illustrated edition of Mr Augustine Marchant's *Queen Theodora and Queen Marozia* will learn

with great regret of the death by drowning of the gifted young artist, Mr Lawrence Storey, who was engaged upon the designs for it. Mr Storey had recently been staying in Paris, but left one day last week for a remote spot in Brittany, it was supposed in pursuance of his work. On Friday last his body was discovered floating in a lonely pool near Carhaix. It is hard to see how Mr Storey could have fallen in, since this piece of water – the Mare de Plougouven – has a completely level shore surrounded by reeds, and is not in itself very deep, nor is there any boat upon it. It is said that the unfortunate young Englishman had been somewhat strange in his manner recently and complained of hallucinations; it is therefore possible that under their influence he deliberately waded out into the Mare de Plougouven. A strange feature of the case is that he had fastened round him under his coat the finished drawings for Mr Marchant's book, which were, of course, completely spoilt by the water before the body was found. It is to be hoped that they were not the only –

Augustine threw *The Times* furiously from him and struck the dinner-table with his clenched fist.

'Upon my soul, that is too much! It is criminal! My property – and I who had done so much for him! Fastened them round himself – he must have been crazy!'

But had he been so crazy? When his wrath had subsided a little, Augustine could not but ask himself whether the young artist had not in some awful moment of insight guessed the truth, or a part of it – that his patron had deliberately corrupted him? It looked almost like it. But, if he had really taken all the finished drawings with him to this place in Brittany, what an unspeakably mean trick of revenge thus to destroy them! ... Yet, even if it were so, their loss must be regarded as the price of deliverance, since, from his point of view, the desperate expedient of passing on his 'familiar' had been a complete success. By getting someone else to plunge even deeper than he had done into the unlawful (for he had seen to it that Lawrence Storey should do that) he had proved, as that verse in Genesis said, that he *had* rule over ... what had pursued him in tangible form as a consequence of his own night in Prague. He could not be too thankful. The literary world might well be thankful too. For his own art was of infinitely more importance than the subservient, the parasitic art of an illustrator. He could with a little search find half a dozen just as gifted as that poor hallucination-ridden Storey to finish *Theodora and Marozia* – even, if necessary, to begin an entirely fresh set of drawings. And meanwhile, in the new lease of creative energy which this unfortunate but necessary sacrifice had made possible for him, he would begin to put on paper the masterpiece which was now taking brilliant shape in his liberated mind. A final glass, and then an evening in the workshop!

Augustine poured out some port, and was raising the glass, prepared to drink to his own success, when he thought he heard a sound near the door. He looked over his shoulder. Next instant the stem of the wineglass had snapped in his hand, and he had sprung back to the farthest limit of the room.

Reared up for quite five feet against the door, huge, dark, sleeked with wet and flecked with bits of green waterweed, was something half-python, half gigantic cobra, its head drawn back as if to strike – its head, for in its former featureless tapering end were now two reddish eyes, such as furriers put into the heads of stuffed creatures. And these eyes were fixed upon him in an unwavering and malevolent glare.

8 Juggernaut (1935)

1

'I really do think, Aunt Flora, that we shall be comfortable here! This Mrs Wonnacott seems very obliging, and the rooms aren't at all stuffy, and not too *aspidistrian*, as that clever young man we met at the Vicarage last week called it. And there's a splendid view of the sea-front – much better, really, because we are on the first floor; so that will make up, won't it, for your having to go up and down the stairs? Now, you are not resting your leg, as Dr Philpson said you were to, in between! Wait a moment; here's a most convenient little chair, better than that beaded footstool – how delightful to see a beaded footstool again – it reminds me of dear Grandmamma ... Is that quite comfortable? I expect Mrs Wonnacott will be in any moment now with the teapot, as everything else seems to be on the table. Cucumber sandwiches, too – how very nice!'

The active tongue which would shortly sample those sandwiches was not new to either of its principal functions. Speech had flowed copiously from it – nearly always cheerful and good-natured speech – for some five and thirty years. Primrose Halkett, its proprietress, was a spare, dark, alert girlish woman, who shared the kindly temperament, though not the comfortable habit of body, of her Aunt Flora, the elder Miss Halkett, with whom she lived in the country. Miss Flora Halkett herself, the victim of a rather badly sprained ankle, had come to Middleport for a short change of air after her enforced seclusion at Grove Cottage, and since her medical attendant had recommended her to use her leg, in moderation, the cautious ascent and descent of one flight of stairs, together with a certain amount of walking, had not been forbidden her.

The limb in question, of a size capable of supporting her solid frame, extended on the chair provided by her niece. Miss Flora Halkett looked appraisingly round the comfortable ornament-bedecked sitting-room of 'Bêche-de-Mer' – for Mrs Wonnacott's husband, after reading a novel about some Pacific island, had bestowed this singular appellation upon his dwelling under the impression that it was the French for 'sea-beach'. In her late fifties, of the type of British spinster who not long ago would have worn a decent mushroom hat with strings – somewhat longer ago a bonnet with intensively cultivated pansies packed under the brim – Miss Halkett had surmounted her large, square, florid face and greying fair hair with a black béret, more striking than becoming. For though (despite the béret) she looked, and actually was, one of those exceedingly worthy and untiring women who form the standby of a country parish, Aunt Flora might with some accuracy be said to Lead Two Lives, and under different names too. If need arose she would take her niece's place at the organ in church, she reigned almost supreme in the Women's Institute, but she was also a writer, and not a writer of stories for the parish magazine – though in moral tone her books were unimpeachable.

The Gift (as her friends alluded to it) had come upon Miss Flora Halkett suddenly and late, for it was only between six and seven years ago that the Muse had dropped a stray plume from her wing upon Miss Flora's writing-table, near the GFS account book. The pen thus put into so unlikely a hand must have been feathered with crimson, since this good, kindly lady with a sense of humour wrote thrillers of the most improbable type – and sold them too – but not as 'Miss Halkett'. For when she first launched her inexperienced literary craft and discovered the turbulence of the waters which it seemed appointed for her to navigate, she had promptly taken to herself the cloak of a masculine pseudonym, fearing that if the Vicar or some member of the Mothers' Union came upon her real name displayed upon the cover of *The Murder Swamp*, he or she might be scandalized. But to her almost shocked gratification she subsequently discovered that the Vicar had read 'Theobald Gardiner's' thriller with avidity, though unaware of its real attribution, and he later accepted a substantial donation towards the new blowing apparatus for the organ out of the yield of the swamp in question. In the same way the advance royalties of *Tiger or Dagger*, just completed during Mr Gardiner's recent seclusion, were assigned to the financing of this holiday for herself and the faithful Primrose.

Tea now appearing, in a large Britannia-metal teapot enriched with repoussé roses, Miss Halkett removed herself from her chair to the table, with a view to doing fuller justice to the meal. And indeed the chronicling of deeds of terror had never affected her appetite, nor did the 'Things' which in her stories walked behind her heroes on lonely moors, or waited, gorilla-like, to strangle her heroines in underground passages, ever sit beside her bed or deprive her of a single night's rest.

After tea, aunt and niece sat at the open window and looked forth upon the Mecca of their pilgrimage, the ocean, bounded on the hither side by the relentless concrete of the 'front', at the glass-sided shelters full of forms reading, knitting, or merely torpid, and at the remarkable architecture of the new pier pavilion, which recalled at one moment Byzantium, at another Mandalay. Primrose sniffed the salt air appreciatively, her tongue going merrily the while, and Miss Halkett smoked her after-tea cigarette (one of the daily four, which were never exceeded) and asserted that she felt she would soon be able to walk as far as the West Cliff, of whose unspoilt beauty she had heard so much.

'But not for some time yet, Aunt Floral!' expostulated

Primrose, ready to check the ardour which not long ago had conveyed Miss Halkett's bulk half-way up the rough track of Ben Nevis. 'You must go slow for a bit – start with walking to the end of the promenade and coming back in a bath-chair. There are bath-chairs here; I see a little row of them farther along.'

'It will have to be a solid bath-chair, then,' replied Miss Flora, chuckling, as she crushed out the end of her cigarette. 'Primrose, have you counted the number of china ornaments on this mantelpiece? There are twenty-three, including the miniature litter of pigs. I must make a note of it, for I think I might stage my next book in a seaside town like Middleport.'

'Because stories of your kind never happen there!' interpreted Primrose admiringly. 'Oh, Aunt Flora, how original of you!'

'I'm not sure,' admitted Theobald Gardiner, with commendable candour, 'that my particular brand of story could happen anywhere!'

✕

The fine evening of the Miss Halketts' arrival was succeeded by a morning of lashing rain. A leaden sea tumbled in untidy hostility among the long centipede legs of the pier, and slapped vigorously against its inveterate enemy, the wall of the sea-front. Occasionally a burst of spray would come sousing over the pavement of the promenade, and it was Primrose's somewhat childish amusement to sit at the rain-washed window and watch for victims among the very few stalwarts who tramped up and down despite the weather. At the table Theobald Gardiner wrestled, Laocoön-like, with the galley-proofs of a former masterpiece, *The Death Stairs*, of which she had recently sold the second serial rights to a small provincial newspaper. This step she was now near to regretting, for the compositor of the *Bulsworth Gazette and Springshire Advertiser* was endowed with an uncanny faculty for converting her intended tragedy into comedy, a metamorphosis which was not actually very difficult of accomplishment.

'Primrose!' suddenly screamed the outraged authoress, 'this really is the limit! Not content with having made my rich banker a *baker*, the scoundrel has turned "the dreadful bond which linked them" into "the dreadful bone which licked them"!'

But Primrose's gaze did not move from the sea-front. 'How tiresome!' she concurred absently. 'Of course it should be "the bone which they licked", shouldn't it?'

'You are obviously not attending, dear! There is no question of bone-licking by anyone – no question, of a *bone* at all! It should be *bond* – b, o, n, d – Good gracious, here's another misprint at the bottom of this slip – "a man of noble *berth*" – as if it were a matter of a state-cabin! – What is interesting you so much, Primrose, that you have no attention to spare for the incredible villainies of this printer?'

Primrose jumped round. 'I'm *so* sorry, Aunt Flora! How dreadful of me! And your proofs are sliding all over the place.' She knelt down and began to collect some galleys – endued as usual with a slithery life of their own – from the floor. 'I was only looking at a bath-chair going to and fro along the front, and wondering what sort of invalid was brave enough to be out in such weather.'

'Rather foolish, whoever it is. Have you the next galley there? – it should begin: "Feverishly he clutched ..." That's it. Was it a man or a woman in the bath-chair?'

'I could not see, Aunt Flora, because, of course, the hood was up – or down, whichever you like to call it. – Aunt Flora, the printer of this paper ought really to be dismissed! I've just seen something in a slip you haven't done yet – something I'm sure you never wrote: "Taking her hand he conducted her, silly sheep, towards the" ... *Oh!*' Primrose's voice broke off on a note of horror.

'"Silly sheep",' exclaimed Theobald Gardiner, roused to fresh fury. 'Heavens above, it should be "still asleep"! It is where the mysterious Sylvester, having sent Miranda into a hypnotic trance – you remember? – at the séance, takes her into the cabinet which he has arranged to have removed while she is inside, and so to abduct her. Don't tell me this criminal fool has muffed the cabinet too; he *can't* have made anything else out of that word! – What are you so red about?'

'Well,' answered her niece, with a real Victorian blush, 'he hasn't actually altered the word, but for some reason he has put it into italics, so that it looks French … and you know what it means in French, Aunt Flora!'

✕

Miss Halkett did not find walking for any length of time as easy as she had anticipated, and though at first she fought against the idea of taking a bath-chair when tired, she soon came not to dislike this method of transport, save that she wished, for the sake of the bath-chairman, that she weighed rather less. 'Otherwise, Primrose,' she observed after her first experience, 'there is a kind of Cleopatrish sensation about it, except that I am sure Cleopatra's slaves were younger and more upstanding.'

The bath-chairmen of Middleport were certainly neither young nor vigorous, nor did they unduly exert themselves, with the exception of one old man, and he almost the frailest-looking of them all, who seemed always to be either on his way to fetch a fare, or on his way back after depositing one, so that never did the Miss Halketts actually see any occupant of his vehicle, particularly as, whatever the weather, the hood was invariably forward.

'Perhaps that is what is meant by "plying for hire",' observed Primrose one day as they were returning on foot to

'Bêche-de-Mer', and had just espied this particular old man dragging his machine along the front. 'He is certainly more energetic than the other old creatures, and I am almost sure it was him I –'

'*He*, Primrose!' corrected the authoress.

'He (of course) that I saw that day in the storm. And have you noticed, Aunt Flora, that though we never actually see anybody in his bath-chair, he always pulls it – he's pulling it now – as if there were a weight inside? I mean, you can nearly always tell from the way a bath-chairman walks –'

'Yes, yes, of course one can. But, though I personally should never try to hire him, because he doesn't look strong enough, I had not noticed that fact about your old man.' Indeed, Miss Flora's powers of observation had latterly been in abeyance, owing to the cloud spread upon her faculties by the sins of the compositor of the *Springshire Advertiser*.

Two or three days later, however, her attention was drawn, if indirectly, to the 'plying' bath-chairman. She and Primrose had walked nearly to the extreme end of the sea-front, when a heavy shower of rain drove them into a shelter, already nearly full. When the rain had stopped, it left the surface of the promenade so wet that Primrose was afraid of her aunt slipping, while the approach of lunch-time did not admit of their waiting for it to dry. The stand being too far away, Primrose volunteered to catch some cruising bath-chair, and, after hovering about for a little outside the shelter, she returned to announce that she could see one coming along, which appeared to be empty; and was off again.

But when she had posted herself in the route of the slowly advancing vehicle, and it became clear to her that it really was empty, it became clear also that the man pulling it was 'her' old chairman, whom Miss Flora would have qualms about engaging.

'But it's quite a short way to Mrs Wonnacott's,' thought Primrose, and started forward. 'Stop, chairman, stop! There's a lady in that shelter wanting you!'

The old man did not appear to hear, but went on past her with his head bowed forward, slowly tugging, for all the world like an automaton pulling a heavy weight. Yet the bath-chair was quite empty, though shrouded up against the rain. Primrose put herself directly in front of the chairman, and he was obliged to stop.

'There's a lady here wants you to take her quite a short way – and in the direction you are going!'

Without raising his eyes the elderly chairman replied, in a voice little more than a whisper: 'Sorry, ma'am, but this chair is engaged.'

'But if you are on your way to fetch a fare,' insisted Primrose, 'surely you could take this lady in that direction, and drop her? She is lame, and I am afraid she may slip on the wet pavement.'

The bath-chairman raised his eyes. They were of a clear pale blue, an innocent blue, almost like a child's, though no one could have mistaken them for the untroubled eyes of youth.

'Lame? Did you say she was *lame*, ma'am? With a stick?' he questioned, in a tone which for a second suggested yielding to her demand. Then he shook his head, in the old straw hat which contrasted with his decent and little-worn black suit. 'No, ma'am, I'm sorry, but Mrs Birling wouldn't like the chair being used.'

Primrose drew back. 'I didn't know, of course, that it was a private chair,' she said. 'I'm sorry.'

'There is no call to apologise, ma'am,' said the elderly chairman, with courtesy and even dignity, and starting the bath-chair again with a slight effort, went slowly on his way.

'It's no good,' announced Primrose, arriving back, slightly dashed, at the shelter. 'There's no one in his chair, but he won't take you; he said some lady or other wouldn't like it.'

No sooner had she uttered the words than a female of that unmistakable type which abounds in seaside shelters, wearing a long magenta knitted coat, looked up from her book and said: 'It's a waste of time, if you don't mind my telling you, ever to try to get old Cotton to take you in that bath-chair of his. He's been queer, you know, ever since Mrs Birling's death.'

'Mrs Birling – that's the name!' exclaimed Primrose. 'But is she *dead*? He said just now that the chair was hers – or at least he implied it!'

'That's just how he's queer,' explained her informant, who had evidently the advantage of being either a resident or a frequent visitor at Middleport. Everyone else in the shelter woke to attention, with the exception of an old gentleman in the corner doing the *Daily Telegraph* crossword. 'Mrs Birling always used to employ Cotton – had him for years. A bad-tempered old thing she was, but rich – and mean. However, when she died about a couple of years ago she did leave him a legacy in her will – quite a nice little sum, I believe – and since then he has dragged that empty chair of his about in all weathers, and won't let anyone get in … Under the circumstances,' she added to herself, 'I'm not sure that I should care to.' But this remark was caught by neither of the Miss Halketts, particularly as Miss Flora began instantly upon the objection that, as he was a licensed bath-chairman, he surely was obliged to take up persons wishing to hire him.

'Oh,' said the lady in magenta, resuming her book, 'no one bothers about that here. You see, he was always such a respectable old man that people are sorry for him, and he doesn't take up room on the stand. You may have noticed that he is never there.'

It was only after the Miss Halketts had left the shelter that the old gentleman of the crossword looked up and asked:

'Why didn't you tell those women straight away that what keeps most people from worrying Cotton for a lift is that they know what happened in that bath-chair?'

The open mouths of the non-resident listeners emitted one simultaneous '*What* happened?'

2

'Dinner's ready, Dad,' announced Mrs Sims, appearing in the doorway of the shed. 'Now, you can leave dusting your old chair, surely, till afterwards, or you won't get your rabbit-pie hot, and you like rabbit-pie, don't you?'

The shed stood in the yard behind the little tobacco and sweet shop whose proprietor, Mabel Cotton, had married 'from service'. It was nearly two years ago that her father, after the death of her mother, had come to live with them – he and his bath-chair and his 'bat in the belfry' about it. But since Mabel and Will Sims had arrived at the resolve not openly to combat 'Dad's crazy notions', life had become easier in the little house over the shop. No more would Mabel burst out, 'Don't be so absurd, Dad – it ain't right to go on so! You weren't that fond of the old lady when she was alive – old terror, I thought she was!' only to provoke a flash of brittle, evanescent anger in the old man, and to drive him to stay out the longer on the sea-front with his inseparable companion. For her husband had counselled her to leave the subject as much as possible alone; not to encourage the poor old chap, but not to thwart him. And the plan had seemed to work; at any rate, there wasn't the worry involved in continual protests.

'You know,' Mabel Sims had said one evening some months after this decision had been taken – 'you know, Will, if Mrs Birling hadn't left Dad that fifty pounds I don't believe there'd have been any of this trouble. The – the other affair alone wouldn't have made him carry on like this. It's his gratitude – silly kind of gratitude I call it, hauling that old chair about in all weathers, with that crape bow and all! It's getting worse, too.'

They were covering up the shop for the night. 'If you ask me,' said her husband, as he locked the till, 'I don't think he does it out of anything so – so human as gratitude.'

'Goodness, don't you? What is it, then? Just pig-headedness?'

'I don't rightly know,' replied Will Sims. 'But it's my belief, from things I've sometimes heard him muttering to himself in that shed, that he hates the thought of Mrs Birling.'

Duster in hand, his wife stared at him. 'Well, I never! Come to think of it, though, she must have given him a fair shock. I don't wonder, in a way, that he has a special kind of feeling for that wretched chair of his. I've often thought about that day up at the West Cliff. Poor old Dad! Well, anyhow, I'll go on sticking to your advice, Will, and not try to stop him doing what he likes.'

That conversation had taken place the previous winter. Since then some gradual grinding process had been at work on poor old Dad. Every day he seemed a little more whittled away; the neat black clothes which he had worn since the death of his wife hung more loosely upon him, the flesh of his mild, thin face had gained in transparency – and the octopus-like tentacles of his obsession enwrapped him ever more straitly. And yet neither his daughter nor her husband could quite penetrate to the core of his delusion, and indeed it seemed as if old Cotton himself was too confused in mind to do so either. What exactly did he think he was doing pulling the old chair about – did he imagine that Mrs Birling sat in it still?

Mabel Sims had often asked herself that question. It was not far from her thoughts now as she looked at her father across the table, where he sat gazing abstractedly at the half-eaten contents of his plate. They were alone together, for it was early-closing day, and Will Sims had gone over to the carnival at Shenstone, Middleport's neighbour and rival.

'Dad, never mind if you can't finish your pie. There's a nice little milk-pudding in the oven. I'll get it out now.'

The old man, however, pushed back his chair. 'I don't want no more to eat, thank you, Mabel. The pie was very good. I'll go back and finish my polishing – must do some extra polishing after the rain.' He looked at her sideways as she lifted the pie from the table, and went on gravely: 'Something awkward happened this morning – something She wouldn't have liked.'

His daughter did not need to ask who She was. She and It – round those two pronouns her father's conversations (what there was of it) tended increasingly to revolve.

'What was it, Dad? You mean the rain was awkward?' Mabel asked, in the kindly, but only half-attentive, voice of one speaking to a child, and she turned away with the pie.

'No, not the rain itself … though I suppose it wouldn't have happened but for the rain. A lady stopped me on the front and wanted to hire It.'

'Well, that does happen sometimes, don't it, Dad?' commented Mrs Sims brightly, as she went to the oven. 'I suppose you just told her that it wasn't for hire, like you always do.'

Her father was fidgeting with a spoon on the table. 'She didn't want it for herself,' he replied. 'It was for another lady, what wasn't there, who was lame, she said.'

'Well?' asked Mabel Sims, opening the oven door.

'Don't you see, Mabel, what it seems like?' asked the old man in an agitated voice. 'Don't you see what it might be? Like as if She was wanting It again!'

'Dad, I never heard such absolute nonsense!' said his daughter sharply, abandoning the withdrawal of the milk-pudding and her usual neutral attitude at the same time. She was roused by the fear of a new complication in the 'belfry'. 'There's heaps of ladies with game legs about – in fact, I never saw such a place as Middleport for dot-and-go-one old women. Some days there don't seem one as can plant her feet straight! Besides,' she added triumphantly, 'you said just now that Mrs Birling wouldn't have liked this lady asking for the chair, so it couldn't have been her that was wanting it! Go along now, and finish your old polishing, and then come in for a rest and I'll make you a nice cup of tea.'

'I shan't have time for a rest; I shall have to go out again this afternoon,' replied her father, with a little sigh. 'But thank you, Mabel, all the same; maybe I'll come in for a cup first.' He went slowly out of the room, and his daughter pushed the oven door to with her knee rather more violently than became her vow of non-interference.

'Drat that blessed bath-chair!' she said under her breath.

✳

Outside in the little yard Will Sims's nasturtiums, trained against the tarred wall of the shed, were glowing in the sun. Very slowly old Cotton unlocked the door of that edifice, which was always fastened when It was inside and unattended. Will had once kept a watering-pot and a few tools there, too, but now only his bicycle was adjudged worthy to share the repose of his father-in-law's bath-chair. With a hesitation almost amounting to reluctance the old man entered, picked up his polishing materials from a little shelf, and resumed his labours; and though they were practically unnecessary, it was a good quarter of an hour before he desisted from them and stood back to survey the result.

The vehicle was one of the old solid type designed to shield its occupant from the weather as thoroughly as the extinct hansom cab, but it had undergone modifications which had deprived it of the hinged flaps which used to meet over the legs of the passenger and of the kind of window which could be closed at need. A waterproof apron had superseded the former, while the window had gone entirely – both greatly to the lightening of the chair's weight. For the rest, this converted antique was so well kept that it belied its probable age.

After a moment or two's contemplation old Cotton proceeded to address it, rubbing his hands together, his body bowed forward and a pale smile upon his lips.

'The West Cliff, ma'am? Yes, of course, of course, if you fancy it! I'll just beat up the new cushion a bit.'

He bent the hinges of the hood, stiff with disuse, and folded that protection back against the pushing handle behind. It could then be seen that a large crape bow had been pinned across the back of the inside of the chair. Below this reposed, in gaudy incongruity, a cheap new cushion, orange, purple, and black, while a striped rug of silk waste lay primly folded on the seat.

'You're quite sure as you want to go up there again, ma'am, in spite of ... You haven't been up there since, you know ... You really would like to go ...?' he mumbled, bending over these adjuncts.

His monologue, however, came to a close as, appearing to remember something, he hastily unfastened the waterproof apron over the lower part of the chair, and groping about under it, brought up a book in the durable but unattractive uniform of the Free Library. It was labelled *Diseases of the Heart*. Opening it at a page already indicated by a strip of paper, old Cotton read a few lines several times over; then, shaking his head, he thrust the book down again into its hiding-place.

His lower lip was trembling, and he began to mutter again, but this time to himself. 'I believe it *was* Her this morning! Then She will be angry ... Oh dear, oh dear, it's so difficult to know what She really wants!' Yet there was a smile, a fixed, mechanical smile, on his face as he plumped up the ugly cushion, and spread the rug out as if over some person's knees. It vanished, however, as if it had been turned off, as he put the hood forward again, and it was with a heavy sigh that he took his old black-ribboned straw hat off a peg and dragged the bath-chair out into the sunshine.

3

The afternoon was indeed so tempting that Miss Flora and her niece hired a car and went for a country drive. Coming back, they halted on top of the famous West Cliff before descending to the level portions of Middleport. It was a remarkable phenomenon that this headland, with its bracing air, fine sweep of view, and gorse-clad spaces, had neither been appropriated by the local golf club nor ruined by pavilions and houses, a phenomenon only to be explained by the fact that it had been bequeathed to the town on condition that it was always kept in its natural state. It was therefore undisfigured – except, of course, by the usual revolting jetsam, periodically removed, of orange-peel, torn wrappers, and sandwich-paper, by which British democracy commemorates its visits to any place of beauty or interest. There were a few seats, a gravel path or two, nothing more; even the main road cut straight across the landward side of the promontory.

The Miss Halketts were so much pleased to find the West Cliff practically deserted (the result, they surmised, of the attractions of Shenstone carnival) that they decided to dismiss their car, and after enjoying the breezy solitude to walk down to the spot where they could take the tram back to Middleport. Slowly and peaceably the two ladies proceeded therefore over the grass towards the verge, and when they reached the point sat upon a seat and enjoyed the view over a pale and silken sea. Far out on the horizon the smoke of invisible steamers created phantom coasts of cloud; nearer at hand, headlands, which aunt and niece tried vainly to identify, stretched beyond each other into the haze; and at their feet the turf, studded with pink thrift, fell away in a gentle slope to the true edge of the cliff, whence the rock plunged sheer to an inaccessible beach below.

When at last they started back towards the road it could not be denied that the distance thereto seemed to have increased, and while they rested upon a seat a little farther back Primrose gently rated her aunt, and now bewailed the unusual solitude which rested upon the West Cliff.

Not until they rose to continue their way were they aware that Heaven had sent Miss Flora a means of conveyance. Round a large gorse bush at some short distance there came suddenly into sight a bath-chair, drawn – as usual – by an old man.

'What luck!' exclaimed Miss Flora, waving her stick to attract his attention.

'But, Aunt,' interposed Primrose, doubtfully, 'I'm afraid it's that old Cotton, who won't take anyone!'

To her surprise the bath-chairman put on a spurt, and bringing his vehicle to rest a few yards away, came shambling towards them, his hands fluttering over each other. 'I thought I should find you up here, ma'am,' he said, addressing Miss Flora. There was a faint tinge of the fawning in his manner. 'The chair's all ready, nice new cushion and all.'

'You don't mind, then –' began Miss Primrose.

Yet perhaps the old man did mind. His gaze had riveted itself upon Miss Flora's béret, and for a moment he looked like a lost and puzzled dog. 'I don't know, after all,' he said hesitatingly. 'I think perhaps I'd better not.' But he still stood there.

'Oh come, I'm lame, you know – though only temporarily.

You'll take me down as far as the tram, I'm sure!' And, smiling her jolly smile, Miss Halkett advanced towards the bath-chair. 'But I must have the hood back, or I can't get in.'

Quite suddenly, for no reason that was at all apparent, the old man was once more all eagerness to comply. 'Yes, yes, I'll take you down, ma'am; I'll take you down. I was thinking of going myself. It's the only thing left to do, I've decided … so if you really wish it … that is, if She wishes it …' He was already putting back the hood; now he unfastened the apron and stood with the striped rug over his arm.

'Aunt Flora,' whispered Primrose, catching her arm, 'don't go in his chair! Don't let him take you; he's so very queer! And look, there's a crape bow on it!'

'Do you imagine he's going to abduct me?' whispered back Miss Flora, chuckling. 'Only light people are in danger of abduction. Dear me, that's rather witty!' She was so pleased with her unintentional *bon mot* that she took no notice of the funereal adornment beyond saying under her breath, 'Very morbid, poor fellow!' and forthwith clambered in, the chair creaking a little beneath her weight.

'But what's this hard object down by my feet?' she inquired, as old Cotton assiduously spread the rug over her knees.

Stopping, he brought up the obstacle. 'Beg your pardon, ma'am, for leaving it there. It's the book what's made it quite certain and sure that I shall have to go down. I didn't quite believe it before about those drops in the capsicule thing –'

'What on earth is the man talking about?' quoth Miss Flora, but not as if she expected an answer.

Old Cotton stuffed the book with some difficulty into a pocket. 'Are you quite comfortable, ma'am?' he inquired. 'Got your stick and all? I see you haven't brought your air-cushion today. Now we'll go down, then.' He went forward to the handle, and the bath-chair, getting into motion, began to move off in the direction of the sea.

'No, not that way, Mr Cotton!' said Primrose loudly, catching hold of the pushing-handle at the back. 'We want to go down to the tram, not back to the edge of the cliff. Stop, stop! Aunt Flora, get out at once!'

Miss Flora, indeed, was already shouting in unison with her niece: 'Not this way! Turn round, man!' As old Cotton, however, appeared not to hear, but proceeded steadily and with a certain purposeful haste seawards, she began to follow Primrose's advice. Wrapped in the rug as she was, and further incommoded by the waterproof apron, this was not easy, though Primrose did her best to check the advance of the bath-chair by throwing her weight on to the rear handle. The scene ended, after a moment or two of confusion and something of panic, by the conveyance overturning and Miss Halkett rolling out on the ground.

✕

Old Cotton, ashy white and shaking, helped the distracted Primrose to disentangle and raise the prostrate and indignant authoress, whose ankle, most fortunately, had sustained no additional damage.

'Oh, ma'am, I can't think how it happened!' he exclaimed in the accents of one smitten to the heart. 'How dreadful, how dreadful! Was it the wheel gave way? Such a thing hasn't never happened with me before … Oh, ma'am, indeed I hope you are not hurt!'

'Why on earth didn't you stop when I told you to?' demanded Miss Flora breathlessly, her béret at an uncommonly jaunty angle, as she was assisted to her feet. 'If you had done that it certainly wouldn't have happened!'

'But I thought you wanted to go down, ma'am!' replied the old man, looking worried again.

'So I did – down to the tram. I said so!' retorted the exasperated and shaken lady.

A mildly shocked expression came over old Cotton's face. 'The tram! Mrs Birling never went in a tram!' he said reproachfully.

'But I am not Mrs Birling, my good man! – No, Primrose, I am really all right. Don't fuss so!'

The old man passed his hand over his forehead. 'That's just what muddles me so,' he muttered. 'It's true that you couldn't well be Mrs Birling –'

'No, because she is dead, isn't she?' interposed Miss Flora, much more gently.

'She *died* right enough, yes, ma'am,' assented old Cotton in a slightly correcting tone. 'I ought to know that, if anyone does, because it was in this chair that she passed away. Still, I don't know as she's *dead!*'

'Passed away in this chair!' exclaimed both the ladies, their eyes going to the vehicle where it still lay sprawled upon its side on the grass.

'Yes, ma'am. Died of a heart disease with a name I never can get right – something like "engine".'

'Angina pectoris, I suppose,' murmured Miss Flora.

'Yes, ma'am, that was it. But they said that if she'd had the stuff to smell she wouldn't have died – not that day, anyhow.'

'Ah, nitrite of amyl. Yes, I've heard of it.'

'Yes, ma'am, I expect that's what it was. Drops of some kind in a glass capsicule. No, she wouldn't have died.'

The old man, stooping, began to tug at the chair in an endeavour to get it upright again. Primrose, moved by pity, did the same, and together, not without difficulty, they heaved it on to its wheels and replaced its scattered contents.

'And this Mrs Birling,' said Primrose, cutting short old Cotton's humble thanks – 'this Mrs Birling died in your chair, and you could do nothing? How dreadful! No wonder you –' She pulled herself up.

'Yes, it was, ma'am,' assented the old man, looking from one lady to the other. 'Yes, I've often thought it was very dreadful. But, you see, I did want the money so bad; my poor wife was dying then, and there was some treatment as would have made it easier for her that she couldn't get at the Infirmary, and I knew Mrs Birling was leaving me something in her will. Many a time before that day I had thought to myself, knowing she had that bad heart, that if only the bad heart would carry her off soon, perhaps my poor Amy wouldn't have to suffer so.'

Both ladies recoiled.

'You are surely not – surely not trying to tell us that you murdered Mrs Birling!' cried Miss Flora, horrified, she who wrote so glibly of terror and slaughter and had never wittingly come within a hundred miles of any criminal.

The suggestion seemed to shock the old man in the black suit much less than its maker. 'Oh, *no*, ma'am!' he protested mildly. 'Because I didn't really believe about the drops. But this book I got from the Free Library says it's true. *Yes, it's true!*' he added suddenly in quite a different tone, a tone of anguish, and, pulling out his handkerchief, he wiped his forehead.

✗

The scent of the gorse came warm upon the breeze. Primrose, fear in her eyes, was biting her long string of beads; Miss Halkett leant heavily upon her stick, also staring at the speaker, but neither of them moved or spoke. It was the inoffensive old man who broke the silence, looking not at his hearers, but out at the lazy sea beyond the cliff edge.

'Yes, it's two years now I've had to drag this chair about. Sometimes she's sitting in it, sometimes she doesn't come, but it's always heavy – getting heavier, too. Miss Sharpe – that was her companion – always carried those capsicules with the drops about with her in case Mrs Birling had another attack.

She'd only had but two, and long enough ago; there really didn't seem much cha– danger of another. But that day Miss Sharpe had a bad sick headache; she couldn't come walking by the side of the chair; she stayed at home, but just to be on the safe side she gave the glass capsicule to me, and told me how I was to break it under the old lady's nose if she was took bad, which wasn't very likely to happen. She gave me a clean handkerchief on purpose for it. Mrs Birling was all for going up to the West Cliff that day, knowing there'd be nobody much about, because it was the carnival at Shenstone – like it is today – and she made me go, though it was cruel hot. She never had no mercy; she used to say: 'There's fifty pounds down for you in my will, Cotton – you can go and ask my lawyer if there isn't – so you've no call to grumble whatever I ask you to do ...' Amy was very bad that day, so it come to me again, if only I could get that fifty pounds for her before it was too late. But I knew it was no good asking the old lady for it before the time; she would never part with a penny if she could help it. So it seemed such a chance, like, for poor Amy that when we got up here, and nobody about ... same as today ...' Still staring out to sea, he rolled his handkerchief round and round like a ball in his hands and repeated quietly, consideringly, 'It seemed such a chance.'

'What seemed – such a chance?' asked Miss Halkett in a whisper. Her face could not be called florid now.

'That she had one of them attacks up here ... Bad it was ... I hadn't never seen one before. I broke the capsicule into the handkerchief, like Miss Sharpe had told me; I can smell the stuff now ... Then I thought of my Amy, and I – I shoved the handkerchief right down into my pocket, and put the hood of the chair over her quick, so as not to see, nor no one else if they *should* come by ... and went and stood over there by the edge for a bit.' One hand left the other and went out to point. 'Yes, it was just over there ... I told the doctor afterwards the stuff hadn't had no effect, but he said I done what I could for the old lady, because there was the glass crushed up in the handkerchief for him to see. It was Miss Sharpe as was blamed … But Amy died before I got the money … And I know that it's over there Mrs Birling wants me to go; even the chair sometimes seemed to be pushing a bit of late. Anyhow, I shall be glad not to have to pull it about no more; and I'm glad I've told somebody. But I'm sorry I frightened you, ladies, just now … Good evening, and thank you for listening to me.'

His hearers were so frozen that they made no protest as old Cotton caught up the handle of the chair and started off at a brisk pace for the edge of the cliff. Then they woke to his purpose. Primrose again clutched the handle at the back, Miss Flora grabbed at the side of the chair, both by some fatality concentrating their resistance on the vehicle instead of on the old man who pulled it. And for a moment he, tired and spindly as he was, dragged them also forward for a few yards, until they reached the place where the turf, flushed with sea-pinks, began to slope to the ultimate verge, by which time their combined weight was too much for him. Old Cotton dropped the handle, turned on them one brief look of triumph, and holding on his hat, ran quietly down the incline.

No human eyes saw him go over, for they were tightly shut. But half a dozen gulls, screaming louder than Flora and Primrose Halkett, flapped indignantly up from their nests on the ledges below. An instant or two later came a fresh uprush of clamour and white wings, as the bath-chair, released by the two women only just in time for their own safety, ran with a kind of clumsy eagerness down the slope, then, toppling sideways, followed its bond-slave over the cliff.

9 The Pavement (1938)

Adhaesit pavimento anima mea

1

'There's the bell, Lyddy,' said the bent old man, looking up from his newspaper. 'That'll be the third lot this week, won't it?'

The little grey wisp of a woman standing by the dresser in the cottage living-room made no reply. But her hand, outstretched to hang up a teacup, was arrested thus for a moment, like a statue's. Then the blue cup swung on to its hook, and another after it.

The bell, naked in the dark corner by the hearth, jangled anew.

'If you don't show yourself, happen they'll go away again,' admonished the reader.

Lydia Reid turned round from the dresser – small, old, faded, ordinary, save for her eyes. 'Happen I'd as lief they did,' she retorted.

'Ah, you're tired, Lyddy! It must be tedious hot out there today. All the same, you do love to show it, don't ye now?'

'You know I do, Simon – to the right folk. But these ... I'm not so sure...' Her eyes travelled to the old-fashioned black bonnet hanging at the side of the dresser. Yet she made no motion to take it down.

'But, drat it, woman, you don't know who they are!' exclaimed her brother, exasperated. 'There, go, for goodness' sake, if you're going!' For once more the bell gave tongue, and it was clear that the hand which pulled the wire was impatient.

Yet the old woman stood a few seconds, gazing now at the oscillating bell as though that could tell her what she wanted to know. Then, jerking down the rusty bonnet, she put it on, tied the strings, took a key from a corner of the dresser, and, plucking open the cottage door, went out into the August sunshine.

Visitors to the Roman pavement at Chasely usually waited by the gate at the end of the flower-bordered pathway leading to the custodian's cottage. The bell-pull to summon that individual hung from a pole lashed to the gate-post, so why give oneself the trouble of walking up the path unnecessarily? It seldom occurred to visitors that its presence also saved Simon Reid and his sister the annoyance of raps upon their door and of voices asking: 'Do we come here to see the Pavement?' and, 'Is there any charge?'

Of course there was a charge! Was it to be supposed that an old woman of seventy-four was going to leave her warm fireside in winter, or brave the shadeless sunshine in summer, and go nearly a quarter of a mile to unlock the shed which covered the Pavement, spend an unspecified time in explaining the mosaics, point out where the heating flues used to run and other details – and this very likely to a set of ignoramuses who only made silly jokes – all for nothing? It was not likely, especially when she and her half-crippled brother were entitled to the whole of the money paid for admission, since the Pavement stood upon their land – upon the pitiful and shrunken remnant of what had been the many-acred farm which their forebears had owned for some ten generations.

It was in their grandfather's time that the ploughshare had brought to light this relic of those still more distant owners of Romano-British days. A learned antiquarian of the neighbourhood, hearing of what had been turned up on Farmer Reid's land at Chasely, had hastened to the spot, held forth to that Sussex worthy of the distinction which the discovery conferred upon his property, superintended its further uncovering, induced him (not without difficulty) to erect a shelter above the treasure in order to preserve it from the elements, and wrote an article upon it in the *Gentleman's Magazine* of 1798 which gave the impression that the credit of locating and unearthing 'the *triclinium* of what must have been an important Roman Villa' was due entirely to himself.

At intervals during the next five-and-twenty years more antiquarians in broadcloth and, often, in top-hats, came to inspect the Pavement; occasionally young gentlemen from Oxford or Cambridge too. Farmer Thomas Reid gave them all a bluff welcome and the offer of a tankard of home-brewed. But he charged nothing for a sight of they liddle old bits of flooring; he didn't reckon that he'd have cared to have pictures like them to walk about on. There was occasionally talk by the top-hatted of what further discoveries the spade might yield, since it was clear, by the size of the room exposed, that the dwelling of which it formed part must have been of considerable size; but nothing came of these speculations. It was Farmer John Reid, the next in succession, who, beginning in the second half of the nineteenth century to lose money and to sell outlying portions of his land, and having, to his annoyance, to rethatch the roof of the shelter, bethought him of making a charge for viewing what it covered – an innovation, however, which did little to ease his situation.

Farmer John's ill-luck was handed down in the eighteen-sixties, with his debts, to his son Simon, a bad farmer, a bad manager in general and seldom out of the hands of moneylenders. After years of shiftless struggle rendered harder by the fact that he was early crippled with rheumatism, the final crash came with bankruptcy, and the passing out of Reid hands of all the wide acres of tilth and shaw and pasture, and even of the generously planned old farm-house with its weatherboarding and its beautiful tawny roof. With his sister Lydia, who had kept house for him since his wife's death, the childless Simon retired, a broken man, to that one of his cottages nearest to the Pavement. For Lydia had insisted that he should keep back from the sale the field on which it stood, pointing out that since of late years there had been a decided increase in the number of visitors to the mosaics, the small annual sum derived from the entrance money would be a welcome addition to a narrow income.

'Aye, so 'twould be if we could keep it for ourselves,' her brother had agreed. 'But we'd have to pay away every penny of it, and likely more besides, in wages to a man to show the Pavement.'

'Nay, for I would show it myself,' urged Lydia. 'I've often thought I'd like to. I could soon learn up a piece to say about it, and say it, too, a deal better than old Skinner in Dad's time. Then there'd be no need to pay away anything.'

2

A middle-aged woman then – the year was 1886 – Lydia Reid had now acted as custodian of the Chasely Pavement for nearly fifteen years. She had spoken the truth when she announced, at the time of the disaster, that she would like to undertake the task, for ever since she was a child the thatched shelter and what it covered had held a fascination for her. Now, at seventy-four, liking had become a passion. With nothing to build on but the knowledge that the first Romans 'came over with Julius Caesar' and eventually stayed a very long time, and with exceedingly little money to spare for the purpose, she had nevertheless bought or borrowed any book on which she could lay hands about Roman Britain, its inhabitants and the remains which were their sole memorial. Visitors to the Pavement, therefore, who had some acquaintance with similar relics (which the majority had not) were often surprised to find its guardian so intelligent and well informed. Was she not just a withered old woman out of a cottage, speaking with the local burr, and often pronouncing the classical names rather oddly? Yet she appeared quite fond of the Pavement as well as being proud of it.

Actually the word 'fond' was ludicrously inadequate. It was adoration which Lydia Reid felt for that pictured floor, whose bond-servant she had made herself. So long had she lived with its myriad mosaics that she knew by heart its every discoloration and unevenness of surface, and could have found the three or four damaged portions blindfold. Its bluish greys, its browns, its ash colours, its reds could not in her eyes have been surpassed by the greatest of colourists; its intertwined borders were to her the perfection of symmetry. Above all, the figures which it enshrined, whether of beasts or immortals, were her living companions. The peacock picking at a vase, with green and purple in his tail, who would almost eat out of her hand, the twin fishes for ever circling round each other, the panther wreathed with vine leaves – these never died, were never sick or sorry. And in the south-western corner lived her 'darling'.

She was a young girl with flying draperies who held a cup in one hand, and was conjectured by experts to be Hebe (or 'Heeb', as Lydia, having first met the attribution in print, pronounced the name until she learnt better). But for Lydia this airy figure was nothing so unreal as the handmaid of the gods; she was a beautiful girl who had once lived in the Roman Villa, and whose beauty the pavement-layers had perpetuated – the young daughter of the house, in fact, as Lydia herself had been at Chasely Farm more than fifty years ago, but an heiress and courted, as she had never been. Before long she had also persuaded herself, though with scanty justification, that she could trace in those regular and somewhat lifeless features a resemblance to her own, as they had met her in the looking-glass half a century before. And after the wonderful day when she discovered that her own name was Roman, 'Hebe' became 'Lydia' too.

Of late years Lydia had taken to holding conversations with her namesake when no one else was there, talking of lost youth, her own or 'Hebe's', in time so distant from each other, but in place so near, of her own worries, of her lumbago, of Simon's trying ways. She always came away cheered by this commerce, for, as people said, it was good to have somebody young about one, and seventeen hundred years or so had added no visible age to the girl who lived in that enchanted world at Lydia's feet.

If the caretaker of the Chasely Pavement must needs harbour a delusion about any of its figures, it might well have been thought (since she was an old maid, and all old maids, it is a commonplace of popular psychology, must of necessity long for a lover or regret the children they have never had) that Lydia Reid would have chosen for her affection either the Ganymede at the north-eastern corner, although he had lost an arm, or one of the small cupids of the charming group in the centre, chasing the butterflies which for ever eluded them. But it was not so. It was only over Lydia-Hebe that she spread a piece of matting, when she discovered the danger which her darling was running from the leak in the roof which it took her so long to induce Simon to have repaired. From that it was but a short step to keeping a protective covering over her always, and to unveiling her for visitors as the supreme sight of the Pavement. And when Lydia had to admit persons who, in her estimation, were mere trippers, and who abounded in senseless laughter and farcical remarks about the figures, she would refuse to lift the matting from her namesake at all. Nor had any of these unworthy visitants ever dared to raise it for himself, save, on one Bank Holiday, a certain Alf, who, urged thereto by his guffawing compeers with a suggestion that it must conceal something improper which it would be fun to see, had turned it half back – but no more.

'She fair scared me,' he confessed afterwards outside. 'Did you see her eyes, you chaps? Regular old witch she is, and no mistake. And nothing underneath to cover up, that I could see – just a girl holding out a cup!'

3

The two visitors whose summons Lydia had reluctantly answered this afternoon were duly awaiting her at the gate. Accustomed to 'size up' such persons quickly, she saw at once that they were gentlemen. One had a short beard and eyeglasses and appeared to be about fifty, while the other, clean-shaven, pleasant-faced and alert, might have been ten or fifteen years younger.

They were both of pleasant manners also. Each lifted his hat as the old woman came through the gate, and the elder apologised for disturbing her. But when the younger asked with a smile whether, since it was so hot, she would like to hand over the key of the shelter and allow them to go there without her, all his courteous manner went for naught with the guardian of the Pavement – in fact, it counted against him.

'Certainly not,' was her curt reply. 'That's never allowed. This way, please.'

Before Lydia had quite turned her back to precede them she received an impression that the younger man had made a slight grimace at his companion. Let them go alone, indeed, after that! She would keep a pretty close watch upon them. Yes, that strange feeling which had seized her when the bell

rang just now … she would have done better not to answer it
… However, here she was, and they would not easily get rid
of her, nor would they find it easy to slip into their pockets
any of the little odds and ends which had been dug up with
the Pavement, although they were only kept upon a shelf,
open to touch or theft.

Clutching the key, she went ahead along the field path, the
sun beating down hotly on her black-clad shoulders. Behind
her the hills lay drowsing in the heat like gigantic but amiable
beasts, an occasional ruddy fleck on the settled green of the
woods showing that autumn's palette was preparing. And
all around the cornfields which Simon had lost spread like
a golden sea.

'My hat, what a position!' Lydia heard the younger of the
men behind her exclaim suddenly. 'And what fertile land!
The Romans certainly had a flair for a site! But in this case,
Professor, I suppose I should say the Romano-Britons?'

'Hardly, Mr Usher. The consensus of opinion is that the
Chasely Pavement is actually of the first century, of the time
of Vespasian or Titus. This early attribution is one reason why
I have advised the – Ah, through this gate, I see. Allow me to
open it for you, Miss Reid.'

Half an hour later the flame of Lydia Reid's hostility and
suspicion was burning much less fiercely, dimmed in fact
almost to extinction by the appreciation which the two
gentlemen showed of the Pavement, the reverent care with
which they examined every detail, and the wide knowledge
which the elder, especially, showed of the subject of Roman
villas in general. Her own little store was quite sufficient to
enable her to recognize this. Experts such as these might,
after all, have been allowed the unprecedented privilege of
the key. Nevertheless, Lydia was glad that she had refused
it, for otherwise she would have lost the pleasure of listening
to their discussions about the floor, and showing them that

she, too, knew that the subsidence near the centre was partly due to a flue of the hypocaust having given way. The visitors' admiration of the figures, and in particular of 'Hebe-Lydia', was indeed so satisfying that for a fleeting moment she found herself, for the first time, on the verge of communicating what she knew about her darling. But she stopped herself upon that verge.

Since they knew so much about the subject it did not surprise her when the gentlemen finally asked permission to go round the outside of the shelter with a view to reconstructing in their minds the position of the rest of the Villa, which, from the size of this triclinium, must, repeated the Professor, have been the property of someone of considerable importance. Lydia was quite aware of that theory and said so. (Had not her darling been an heiress?) She was in no hurry, she added; they could take their time looking round outside. And, sitting in the sun on the rough bench at the door, she watched them, but not suspiciously now. It had amused other people before them to indulge in these speculations about the extent and lie of the Villa; she did not mind. What might still sleep in Pavement Piece slept peacefully, as deep buried as this banqueting floor had been before excavation, and no one had the power to disturb that slumber.

But after a while she got up and went round the shelter. The couple seemed to be arguing about something; the elder had a plan in his hand at which the younger was looking, and a round brass case containing, presumably, a tape-measure.

'But, Professor,' the younger man was saying, 'if the cryptoporticus was *there*, as Morgan says (following Lysons, I believe), then surely –'

'Oh, conjectural merely, this plan, you know,' interrupted the Professor. 'I may quite well be wrong. Only the spade can show us.' Then, becoming aware of the custodian's presence, he said, rather abruptly: 'But we are keeping Miss Reid too long,' and began to fold up the plan, adding as he did so: 'Perhaps, however, she will allow us to have a final glance at the triclinium?'

Preceding her this time, they left the sunlight for the tempered day and mitigated damp of the shed, and stood there in silence. That, thought Lydia appreciatively, was how the Pavement *should* be taken leave of, in a condition of reverent awe. She fetched from the side the piece of matting which she had not yet replaced over the Hebe. And at that the bearded Professor spoke.

'You do well, Miss Reid,' he said gravely, 'to keep that figure covered. In fact, the whole pavement would be the better for more adequate protection, would it not?'

Lydia could hardly believe her ears. For, perfectly courteous though the tone was, the words were unmistakably words of criticism, even of reproach.

'I don't know what you mean, sir,' she said, stiffening. 'My brother had the shed repaired again only this spring.'

'After the rain and frosts of the winter had done a little more of their annual damage! Isn't that so?' asked the Professor, still quite gently. 'And you know, Miss Reid, next winter they will gain entrance at fresh places – as here, for instance.' He suddenly jabbed with his walking-stick at a decaying plank.

'Yes, of course they will if you make holes in the shed!' retorted the old woman, with acid vigour. 'And, anyhow, I don't see, sir, that it's any business of yours! This is *our* land and *our* shed – my grandfather put it up – and *our*' (she nearly said 'my') 'Pavement.'

'Quite, quite!' interposed the younger man hastily. 'I am sure, Miss Reid, that you fully appreciate the importance of what you have on your property. But Roman work of this early date, with tesserae so uncommon, demands very careful protection, don't you think?'

'Well, it's getting it!' snapped Lydia. Her eyes were bright and hostile. 'Where do you think these tesserae' (the word was quite familiar) 'would be today if it hadn't been for my grandfather in the first place, and my brother and me now? I've given my life for the last fifteen years to caring for the Pavement. If you gentlemen only came here to find fault you'd better have stopped away. And I'll be obliged if you'll leave now!'

Looking distinctly uncomfortable, the visitors simultaneously declared that to find fault was the last thing they wished to do, and that they considered it most laudable of private persons to have gone to the expense of protecting the remains, as the owners had done for three generations. By the time this joint apologia was finished they were outside again, and Lydia, very grim about the mouth, was locking the door.

'You know, Miss Reid,' observed the younger man rather tentatively, 'that there is probably a great deal more of the Villa still remaining.'

'I dare say,' returned the old woman. She pocketed the key and began to walk away. He was obliged to follow her.

'The Professor and I would very much like to have a talk with Mr Reid about it.'

'Simon don't take no interest in the Pavement,' returned his sister over her shoulder.

'Oh, come, Miss Reid,' protested the visitor, 'you are libelling him, surely! At any rate, the question of upkeep must interest him. We should really like to have a word with him. Would he be at home now?'

At that Lydia stopped and turned round. Against the ocean of ripe ears round her the old black dress and bonnet looked rustier than ever.

'Simon's always at home. He's an invalid. Don't you know that, sir, as you're so pat with our name? But he don't see strangers nowadays. Good afternoon.'

After that he had to let her go. The Professor came up, and together they stood watching the small retreating figure in silence. Before long they saw it stop abruptly, rummage in a pocket and fling something invisible on to the path. When, a moment or two later, they themselves came to the spot, the shillings which they had paid for admission were lying on the parched earth at their feet.

4

It was fortunate that Lydia's sudden attack of appendicitis should have occurred, if occur it must, during the latter half of October, for by that time of year there was hardly ever a single visitor to the Pavement. In her bed in the County Hospital to which, intensely against her will, she had been whisked away, she was able to congratulate herself upon that fact, and also upon the stratagem which, even if an odd sightseer or two should turn up, would effectually prevent them from viewing the floor in her absence. For rather than give control of the shed to that chit Molly, the niece who was looking after Simon in her absence, she had brought away the key with her to hospital.

After all it was found unnecessary to operate, and Lydia recovered. More wisp-like than ever in appearance, but spiritually undefeated, she returned to the cottage, dismissed the not unwilling Molly after twenty-four hours, resumed the reins, and on the first opportunity paid Hebe and Ganymede a visit.

'I've brought you some flowers, my dear, to make up for being away so long,' she murmured, looking fondly at her namesake; and laid by the flying figure a bunch of slightly frost-bitten chrysanthemums from the garden. Never before had she done such a thing, and, sensible now of the pleasure which the act was giving her, she wondered why she had never thought of it before. Before she left she put the tribute on top of the matting which she had replaced – but, on actually quitting the shed, was so struck with its resemblance in that position to flowers upon a pall that she nearly went back and took it off again.

'Been out to the Pavement, Lyddy?' enquired Simon, looking up from his eternal newspaper, as she re-entered the cottage. ''Twas a great pity you took away the key like that, because a Government gentleman came down here last week, and when he couldn't get in –'

Lydia stood stock-still, her hand at her bonnet-strings. 'A Government gentleman?' she asked, an icy foreboding coursing through her. 'What was he like?'

'Very pleasant,' answered her brother, misapprehending. 'Very pleasant indeed, and said the Work Office, I think he called it – I've got the letter somewhere, with the name put properly – said this Office was going to take over the upkeep of the Pavement for us. The shed wants a deal of repairing, it seems – you should have told me about that! – and there ought to be some more digging done round about. Talked a lot, he did, about what a splendid big place the Villa must have been. And none of this will be any charge to us, and –'

He broke off with an exclamation; his sister was shaking him. 'Simon,' she almost screamed, 'what have you been doing, what have you been doing? You've surely not sold Pavement Piece – you *can't* have done such a thing!'

The crippled old man cried out in pain. 'Take your hands off me, Lyddy – you're hurting me cruel! No, of course I haven't sold the Piece; it's ours just as it was before, only –'

'You've given leave to strangers, then, to come poking and digging there! So that's what those two were up to that day, sneaking about and measuring!' Hot tears of rage began to run down her wrinkles. 'I *knew* I'd ha' done better not to answer the bell that afternoon. The shed! God knows I've asked you often enough to have it properly gone over – so how *dare* you say I ought to have told you about it? You must take back the permission, d'you hear, Simon? Write at once and take it back!'

'Listen here, Lydia,' said her brother, half-cowed, half-angry, 'I can't take back my permission because I haven't given none. The gentleman explained – Mr Usher his name was. This here Office of Works (I mind now, that's what it's called), this Office has the right to come and look after old monuments and remains and such-like – and a good thing too, say I! I've had enough of your complaints about that old shed! Now they'll be responsible for it, and if they do some more digging in the Piece, as they think they will, there'll be all the more money coming in later. I see I must ha' put the letter that came on Tuesday up there on the chimney-piece; you read it and you'll see it says there was an Act passed last year –'

Lydia looked up, saw behind the clock on the high mantelshelf a long envelope bearing the letters OHMS in lieu of a stamp, snatched it down, and tore out the contents.

Yes, there it was, the unbelievable.

HM *Office of Works*
Nov 7th, 1901

Dear Mr Reid,

As I explained to you on my recent visit, by the Act of 1900 this Department is empowered to take under its guardianship ancient monuments of any description, when such transfer of responsibility seems desirable, as in the case of the Roman pavement upon your land. I must reiterate that no interference with your rights as owner is contemplated, the field and pavement remaining as before –

Lydia read no further. 'Behind my back,' she blazed, 'behind my back you could let them go and do this! You call yourself a man, and you couldn't stand up to them that come to interfere with your own property –'

Feebly rubbing the shoulder which she had gripped, Simon interrupted her. 'I don't know how you expect me to stand up to a Government department, Lyddy, even if I had the right use of my limbs! And look here' – he stopped rubbing, and there was a note of satisfaction in his voice – 'what do you suppose had a deal to do with that chap saying the Pavement would have to be taken over, as he called it? Why, your going off with the key like that, so that he couldn't get in, nor anybody else neither! It was that clinched the matter, my girl, and don't you forget it!'

Shaking with wrath and despair, the little old woman stamped her foot. 'They shall never do it – never! I'll see to that! It's my pavement; they all know me, them that's in it, and I'll have no one, Government or no Government, interfering and disturbing them! A lot of noisy men to come digging round the shed ... and somebody trying to take my place, I dare say, to show the floor! You write to your Office of Works and their spies and tell 'em it can't be "taken over", because I won't have it – and tell them where their letter's gone to, into the bargain!'

Torn across, it went sailing into the fire, and Lydia Reid, with thirty years fallen from her, rushed out of the room.

5

But the shock, and the ravaging emotions which it had brought, on top of her recent illness, restored those years and more. She was prostrate next morning, and a neighbour had to come in and look after the two of them. But in a couple of days the old woman rose from her bed, very white and quiet and unlike herself. Simon did not dare to refer to the subject of the Pavement, and was equally relieved and astonished when, after a while, Lydia herself brought it up, admitting that she had behaved foolishly, and that its guardianship by the Office of Works would be the best thing. Nevertheless, her plans were not only laid to circumvent the office, but were already being put into practice.

Every afternoon, a little before dusk, she slipped out to the shed carrying a portion of the previous day's newspaper and a bit of rag or sacking. The coal-hammer was already there, for she did not want to be seen carrying it to and fro. The risk of some visitor demanding admission in the waning daylight, almost negligible as it was, she had to run. But the work of destruction was much more strenuous than she had anticipated. She had thought that she could actually hack or prise out the tesserae, although in her years of guardianship she had discovered how firmly they were laid. But even so, she had underestimated their stability. A floor which had withstood more than a millennium of neglect was not likely to yield to a rather frail old woman armed merely with a coal-hammer. Lydia could more easily pound the half-inch cubes of mosaic into smaller fragments than she could uproot them from the hard cement in which they were embedded on top of a still more solid eight-inch layer of fine gravel, pounded brick and lime. So she just smashed to the best of her ability, beginning in a methodical way with the least well-preserved portions of the Pavement, and covering over her ravages, as they proceeded, with sacking and the *Sussex Chronicle*.

At that time of the day and year she could not remain too long in the shelter without arousing Simon's curiosity, yet gradually the tide of havoc and newspaper spread, as the peacock and the fishes, the Amorini and Ganymede were submerged. And at last the evening came when of all the glories of the Chasely Pavement only Hebe remained, tranquil and unsuspecting beneath her brown shroud and the browner chrysanthemums.

Panting a little, Lydia laid down the coal-hammer, uncovered her, and knelt for some time gazing, with a heart so torn that its pain was physical, and made her catch her breath. But She could not be left to survive alone … no, least of all could She be left! And time was short now. There had been a further letter to Simon from the Office of Works; somebody was coming down on Monday to make preliminary arrangements for the transfer. He must find nothing then – no trace of that beloved form, so light and airy, that flying scarf, that upraised goblet. She would wish it thus; for was not She one's other self? And it must be done all at once; She must not spend even a few hours half-killed, mutilated. The final ruin would not come till after midnight.

Again and again the old woman bent and kissed the cold mosaic on the cheek. 'Good-bye, good-bye, my darling! You understand, don't you? Good-bye, good-bye …' With tears running so fast that she could scarcely see she took up the coal-hammer and struck the first blow at the sandalled feet. It was like striking at her own …

She was quite composed at supper. The worst was over now. Simon, blindest of men, and convinced by this time of her complete acquiescence with events, talked about Monday's envoy. 'I reckon, by the hours you've been spending out there, Lyddy, that you're getting it all tidy and shipshape for him?'

'Surely,' answered his sister. ''Twill all be ready for him when he comes.'

It was about two in the morning when she crept out of the cottage carrying a gallon tin of paraffin and a flimsy oil lantern with most of its glass missing. The newspapers, sacks and some kindling wood were already in place; they only required a good drenching and a light setting to them. And since Lydia Reid had no intention of including herself in the holocaust – for she meant to taste the bitter savour of her victory on Monday – she was going to throw the lighted lantern on to the central oil-soaked pile from the vantage spot of the open doorway. Then, retreating outside, she could watch the whole shed go up in flames above the smashed and meaningless floor, with the burning thatch shooting feathery drifts of sparks into the night.

Far up in the profound peace of the heavens the constellations with their Roman names looked down upon the place which the Roman had once chosen for his delight, and upon the old woman who loved it trudging towards the accomplishment of a deed not altogether inconsonant with the Roman spirit.

10 From the Abyss (1940)

I remember how indirectly and casually we three men got on to the subject of dissociated personality that evening in Stephen Ellison's flat. It was because, at the end of dinner, Roddy Pearson happened to mention some shipmate or friend of the name of Norton Prince, which brought from Fenning, who is a doctor, a not unnatural reference to the American psychologist Morton Prince, and his celebrated book – of which Roddy, the youngest commander in His Majesty's Navy, had never heard. And when the mysterious and disturbing phenomenon which forms its theme was explained to him, he refused to believe in it. 'Dual personality! You'll have my leg off altogether if you pull it so hard! The idea of two Hitlers or two Mussolinis doing their stuff at the same time would be a nightmare!'

So once more he was told that he had got hold of the wrong end of the stick, that the scission was moral and mental, not, of course, physical, which was impossible. 'If you, my good Roddy, happened – as the result of a shock, perhaps – to develop two, or even three, alternating and quite different selves, you would still occupy only one chair.'

Ellison, who had not uttered a word during these exchanges, here got up abruptly and jerked forward a window-curtain with such vehemence that I involuntarily glanced round at him. On his face I surprised for an instant just the twisted kind of grin that I had seen on a man stabbed in a sudden affray in Malaya.

Fenning and Roddy had to leave early, and I was soon alone with the barrister friend whom I had not seen, and had scarcely heard from, since I had gone out East six years before. Of the four of us who had made up this little reunion Ellison and I had once been the most intimate; yet I believe that I might almost have passed him in the street now without recognising him, so much had he altered. But then, six years is six years.

The incident of the curtain came back to me as he poured me out another drink. Had I not so lost touch with him of late I should have asked him if anything was wrong. As it happened, I had no need.

'I must apologise for behaving in rather a jumpy way just now,' he observed, as he handed me the tumbler. 'I am not really "a bundle of nerves", as the phrase goes. But that one topic, dissociation of personality, happens to hit me on the raw. It isn't once in a blue moon, thank God, that it comes up. I certainly never expected to hear the phrase in Roddy's mouth.'

'Well, you saw that it meant less than nothing to him, good normal chap that he is,' I answered. 'Not exactly an everyday topic in the ward-room mess, I take it. But why should it so affect – I'm sorry! I didn't mean to be inquisitive.'

Ellison gave a queer little smile. 'My dear fellow, who brought the subject up again, you or I?' He went to retrieve the cigarettes from another table, and was some time about it. Then he put the box down at my elbow with the words, rather jerkily uttered: 'You wouldn't of course, out in Malaya, have seen an account of a motor smash which happened in the mountains behind Nice about three years ago – or have remembered it if you had?'

I shook my head. 'You were in it – or someone you knew?'

'Someone I knew,' answered Ellison slowly. 'Someone who escaped by a miracle … only to become the victim of … No, I can't bring myself to put it into words.'

'What *do* you mean?'

He looked down at me very gravely. 'I can best say what I mean by telling you that when you were all discussing "split personality" just now, the ignorant Roddy Pearson was on the right tack, and you and Fenning, when you corrected his misconception, on the wrong. All human history, all human psychology, and all physiology is with you – nevertheless, you are wrong!'

I stared up at him, at first blankly, then with growing uneasiness. That there could be a *physical* split, that one person could, bodily, become two ... no, it was inconceivable that he was maintaining such a monstrous thing!

'Ellison, you can't leave it at that,' I said after a moment.

'Or you will go away and try to get me certified?' he finished, with rather a ghastly smile. 'Yes, I'll tell you the story. I admit I have gone too far now not to. The only other person who knew the truth – if it was the truth – her father, died last year.'

He sat down and took a cigarette from the box; but it was never lighted.

✖

You wouldn't remember the Lawrences at Stottingham (began Ellison); in fact, I think they only came to live there after your people left. They bought that pleasant place, Ridings. But I saw a good deal of them and of their only daughter. I had, in fact, known ... Daphne – (it was clearly difficult for him to name her) – for quite a long time before I induced her to agree to marry me.

I ought to tell you, in view of what happened to her, that Daphne Lawrence was a thoroughly normal, natural English girl, country-bred, excellent at games and at organization of any kind. She liked her own way, yet she was essentially sweet-tempered; she was also well educated, though without any specially literary or artistic bent. (Ellison broke off with an impatient little laugh, and for the first time glanced in my direction.) I know that sounds a hopelessly stilted and cold-blooded description, but I have to try, you know, to see this story from the outside, as though it concerned two people whom I never met, otherwise I can't tell it at all.

We became engaged in January, 1935, just over three years ago. In March Daphne went out with a friend, Mary Frodsham, to the Riviera, and finally came to anchor at Nice – not, as Daphne wrote to me, because they liked a place so large and so sophisticated, but because it was such a good centre for expeditions. One could get up with ease, for example, to the winter-sports centres in the Alpes Maritimes, Beuil, or Peira-Cava, and though they had no car of their own with them, there were daily motor-coach excursions. Moreover, there was a young unattached American at their hotel who had a car, which he more or less put at their disposal. In fact, they were having, she reported, 'a super-excellent time', and I was not to expect many letters.

Thus warned, and aware that Daphne was not in any case much of a correspondent, I thought little of having heard nothing from her for over a week. Then suddenly the news, blazoned in large type on the front page of a daily paper, struck at me from the Temple Station bookstall: 'ENGLISH GIRL IN FATAL RIVIERA MOTOR SMASH – CAR AND DRIVER DOWN BOTTOMLESS RAVINE.'

The caption was meant, of course, to suggest that 'the English girl' (whose face smiled from the page at me) had gone down the ravine too. And for a few seconds the whole façade of the bookstall vanished. Then I found myself quite calmly holding out a penny and wondering how the photograph had been procured. For with electric speed my mind, almost independently, it seemed, of my eyes, had absorbed the fact that Daphne had miraculously been thrown clear when the car in which she was a passenger had collided with a motorcoach in some gorge in the Alpes Maritimes. But the driver, a young American, Curtis Whitaker, had gone down in the car to death hundreds of feet below. Of Mary Frodsham there was no mention.

I telephoned immediately to Mr Lawrence at Stottingham. He had not yet seen the newspaper accounts, but had received a wire, delayed in transit, from Miss Frodsham. He read it to me over the telephone: 'Daphne in motor accident uninjured but coming home easy stages writing.'

'Then it is of no use my starting for Nice – I should miss her,' I observed.

'No, not a bit, my dear boy,' came Mr Lawrence's voice. 'I am very sorry that you should have learnt the news in this rather dreadful way. She will have had a bad shock, poor child, but thank God it's no worse. I'll ring you up directly I know when she is arriving – but there, you'll probably hear as soon as I do.'

But I did not, though I lived in hopes of a wire, or a line, from Miss Frodsham at least. Mr Lawrence, however, forwarded me a letter from her, written at Avignon. It said that Daphne was all right, though not sleeping too well. They hoped to be home in the middle of the week. A brief account of the accident followed, by which it appeared that both she and Daphne had intended going up to ski at Beuil with the young American. On the morning itself, however, Mary woke with a cold, and let them go without her – an abstention to which no doubt she owed her life. On leaving the skiing grounds, young Whitaker and Daphne had decided to return by the longer route through the wild and magnificent Gorge of Daluis, which, explained Mary, was rather a canyon than a gorge. When they got there the American, for the sake of the view, had quite inexcusably taken the outer road assigned to up-coming vehicles instead of that hewn in the rock-face for downward-going ones, and had met a motor-coach coming up, with disastrous results to himself. Some check, from the parapet probably, before the car mounted or broke through it, had thrown Daphne clear, at the cost of bruises and a cut or two, but the reckless young man had been hurled, with the car, sheer down into a spot whence it was quite impossible to recover his body, a spot where no signs of either could be seen. There was no slightest doubt that he had been killed outright.

With this indirect news I had to be content. And when, a few days later, I heard from Ridings by what train Daphne was expected, a case came on which prevented me not only from meeting her at Victoria, but even from going down to Stottingham for the night. On the Saturday after her return, however, I got off.

✕

Rather to my surprise, Daphne was out when I reached Stottingham, although I had telephoned the hour of my arrival. Mrs Lawrence, who received me, apologised for her absence, and said that she seemed a little vague about time, and had probably gone for a walk and not looked at her watch. I *was* a little dashed; but, after all, I thought, the poor child has received a great shock; and I asked whether she had recovered from this, and if she was really physically unhurt? I learnt with great relief that, except for bruises, now disappearing, and a cut on her cheek, which was healing, she was marvellously uninjured.

'And as for the shock,' said Mrs Lawrence, 'she is getting over it as well as could be expected. She was knocked unconscious, you know, and mercifully doesn't remember much about the accident. Which is perhaps why,' she added, lowering her voice, 'Daphne seems to think that she went down with the car to the bottom of the gorge. Of course, if she had' – she shuddered – 'she wouldn't be here today.'

'One doesn't like to blame the dead,' I said rather hotly, 'but that young man's conduct was quite criminal!'

'That is what my husband and I think. And just how Daphne escaped I can't –' Mrs Lawrence broke off and slipped away, as Daphne herself came into the room, a spaniel at her heels. In a blue coat, with a fur round her neck and colour in her face from the cold, she was exactly the Daphne I had seen off at Victoria a few weeks before.

'Hallo, Stephen,' she said with a smile, in a voice that was just not casual. 'You've come for the week-end, haven't you?' And she held out her hand.

Our meetings were not usually so 'modern' in tone. I, at least, could not hide the emotion I felt, though what I said as I took her in my arms was the last word in commonplaces. 'Daphne, my darling! Thank God you're safe!'

Her answer was not so commonplace. 'But am I?' she asked, and very gravely. Her lips were cold; she did not kiss me in reply. 'I can't feel sure yet that I am.'

I drew her down beside me on a sofa, noticing the half-healed scar, more like a long scratch, down one cheek, and the bandaged palm of her left hand. 'Of course you are safe! You have had a wonderful escape, but the most sensible thing is to try to forget all about it. You will do that, won't you?'

She did not look at me. 'Stephen, how can I? I *know* that I am back at Ridings, but unless I am talking to someone, or reading, I am all the time climbing and climbing up those dreadful red precipices. I don't know how I did it. My hands … They never found Curtis, you know, or the car – not a shred of it.'

'But, my poor darling, you never –' I began, and then stopped myself. Better not to argue the point. I did not know what injury was under the bandage on her left hand, but the right, which I was holding, was plainly undamaged. And she was going on.

'It was all because he wanted to go along the outside road, on the left – the wrong side in France, you know – where you can see the view all the time, instead of going through the tunnels, as he ought to have done. He started on it before I could stop him. So it wasn't my fault, was it?'

'No, no, my dearest, of course not! Don't let's talk about it any more!'

'I don't want to,' she murmured. 'It's quite bad enough wondering what bit of rock I am going to try to get hold of next – Go away, Susan darling, you're a nuisance!' She pushed away the spaniel, got up, and became once more the slightly casual young lady who had entered the room. 'I must go and take my things off. See you later, Stephen.'

I went to bed that night puzzled and uneasy, telling myself that I must make allowances. But those allowances were, oddly, of two quite opposite kinds – one for the presumable effects of shock, and one for the present-day dislike of admitting to emotion. For, contrary to what she had said earlier, Daphne seemed at dinner that evening rather anxious than otherwise to talk about the accident, though her parents and I headed her off from the subject as well as we could. On the other hand, by the end of the evening (in which I failed to get her to myself again) I was feeling exactly as if I were not her destined husband, but some recently-made acquaintance whom she had asked down for the week-end.

I could not let matters remain thus, and on Sunday afternoon I asked her to come for a walk with me. She made no difficulties, and we tramped along lanes studded with primroses, in a cutting April wind, talking of this and that, until I approached the question of our marriage, for which a tentative date had been fixed in the early autumn.

At that Daphne, her hands deep in the pockets of her coat, said with more affection in her voice than I had yet heard there on this visit: 'Dear old Stephen, isn't it time you dropped that joke? You *know* I'm not going to marry you in September!'

The lane seemed to give a jolt under my feet, but I did not slacken my pace; I only slipped a hand under her arm. 'Not in September? October, then – but the Law term begins again, you know, about the middle of the month.'

She stopped then and faced me, unsmiling. Yet her voice was gentle. 'Stephen, what makes you talk of *any* month, when you know that we are not going to marry each other at all?'

'Indeed, I don't know it!' I said, indignantly and rather harshly. 'We are engaged; we have been engaged since January! Or was that a joke also? My poor child' – I was suddenly penitent – 'I was forgetting. Forgive me! That damned accident has upset you. Daphne, don't look at me like that!'

She had turned a clear and direct gaze upon me; I had never seen her eyes so blue. 'You think I've lost my memory. But I haven't; I remember exactly how we got engaged. But I see everything differently now. I do like you very much, Stephen, and you are very good to me; but I don't want to marry you, and I never did.'

I suppose I shall never see primroses starred all over a high bank again without feeling that they are listening to everything that is said, as they did that afternoon when I reasoned and pleaded so hard. Yet, for all this complete *volte-face*, Daphne was not exactly obstinate. No, she had not been in the very least in love with that poor Whitaker – for in my pain and bewilderment I asked her that – and there was no one else. She did not want to marry at all. I had overborne her desire when I extracted her promise; didn't I remember how many times I had asked her before she consented?

One plank I did induce her to leave me in this shipwreck: she undertook not to make public the rupture of our engagement at present. I used the plea that the news would distress her parents so much just at this juncture. My real reason was less altruistic; I wanted still to have the right to see her frequently. In time she would surely turn to me again?

She was very sweet about it all, and even compassionate, there in that green lane where the spring smiled at us both; but the cold wind which swayed the hazel catkins seemed to blow through my heart as well.

※

In the middle of the following week I was surprised to receive a visit at my chambers from Mr Lawrence in person. He looked worried.

'I hope I have not called at a very inconvenient moment, Stephen?' he said. 'I could have written, but I wanted to talk to you.'

'Daphne isn't ill or anything?' I asked hurriedly.

'No, no – and it hasn't to do with her ... exactly. But I have just had a letter from Ashcroft, an old friend of mine, a painter, who is staying at Vence, that little place in the hills behind Nice. It has rather disturbed me. He says that, having read of my daughter's recent escape in the Gorges de Daluis accident, he thinks he ought to let me know of a story which is going about in the mountains of a girl who turned up the day after the crash – or, rather, was found exhausted by some peasants – near a place higher up than the gorge called – let me see, yes, Guillaumes. This girl alleges, so it seems, that she was in the American's car, that she went down with it to the bottom of the ravine, and after some unspecified interval of time crawled out from the wreckage and climbed, God alone knows how, up the side of the precipice, which is nearly perpendicular and reputed to be quite unscaleable. (You may remember that no attempt was made to recover Whitaker's body.) This girl appears to have forgotten her name and where she came from – though that may be feigned ignorance – and Ashcroft says that it is reported her accent and looks have led the peasants to suppose her English. What do you make of that, Stephen?'

'Why, that she is some unbalanced creature who has heard of the accident, and either genuinely imagines that she was in it, or – much more probably – is deliberately trying to attract attention to herself. Cases of the latter kind are not uncommon after a disaster or a crime, as you must know. You won't let Daphne hear of it, of course?'

'No, certainly not,' said Mr Lawrence. 'Especially as she clung at first to that queer notion that she herself had gone over – and down – with the car … I suppose there *wasn't* any other girl with her and that unfortunate Whitaker?'

'How could there have been, sir?' I protested. We know both from Daphne and from Miss Frodsham that Daphne went alone with the young man. Besides, had there been a third person in the car, he or she must have shared his fate, since no one, evidently, could survive such a terrible fall.'

'I hope,' said Mr Lawrence unhappily, 'that the tale does not get into the English newspapers.'

I hoped so just as fervently, and after a moment's reflection asked him if he could possibly request his friend at Vence to go into the matter a little further.

'If he could see the girl personally,' I urged, 'one would know much better what one was up against. He might perhaps induce her to drop her impossible story – even if he had to resort to bribery. Once the report gets to the point – if it hasn't already got there – of being investigated by the local authorities, and they think the girl really is English, it is almost certain to appear in the English papers.

And, since this painter was an old friend, and Mr Lawrence had bought some of his pictures, he agreed that he might justifiably make this request.

✕

Yet I was not made so uneasy by this tale of a half-crazy impersonator hundreds of miles away as by the progressive and rapid change in Daphne herself, which I seemed to perceive much more clearly than her parents did, when I next went to Ridings after a fortnight's interval. To me her manner had not altered since my last visit, and she allowed no hint to appear that we were no longer engaged. I almost felt that she was indifferent about the matter. But this was not the case with other relationships. Her old interests appeared to be deserting her, taking with them that happy self of hers. She was beginning to drop her games, was preoccupied and restless, and full of plans for brief visits to her many friends, she who had always been so devoted to her home. She was off to Northumberland on one of these the very day I left; and to this expedition were to succeed flying sojourns in Shropshire and Somerset.

It was on her return from the last of these that I contrived to meet her at Paddington in order to give her lunch and see her off to Stottingham. This time I was struck with the fact that since I had last seen her about ten days before she had altered physically as well. There are some people to whose looks a painter could only do justice in pastels, but Daphne had never been one of those; she would have demanded oils. But not now. In the most extraordinary and yet subtle way both colour and contour seemed to have dwindled, and when in the refreshment-room (for there was not time between trains to take her elsewhere) she removed her hat, the diminution in the glow and sheen of her beautiful red-gold hair was most noticeable.

'What sort of a life have you been leading lately, young lady?' I asked, as lightly as I could. 'You look as if a tonic would do you no harm.'

'A tonic!' she said disdainfully. 'Why, Stephen, I am *perfectly* well! If you think I don't look it then it must be the effect of such a mass of railway journeys. I don't know why I didn't take my car. It's true I haven't had much exercise lately; you know I do like plenty of walking – and by that I don't mean just trailing along the flat, as I have to do at home. I think I'll go up to Scotland soon, because I am beginning to feel that I must have mountains ... But not, of course,' she added after a moment, 'the Alpes Maritimes, because I might run into *her* there.'

I was so startled that I nearly showed it. It *was* in the papers then, that queer tale about the girl out there. Yet, though I had been keeping a careful lookout, I had not seen it.

'Run into whom?' I asked, since I must take some notice of the remark.

'Oh, only someone I keep seeing in a dream I have been having lately about *that* place. There is a girl like me – only she is not me – always standing at the spot where ... where it all happened ... looking down the precipice. Yes, just like me, in that brown Rodex coat of mine, and with my handbag in her hand.'

I forced a laugh. 'But, my dear Daphne, what more natural than that you should see yourself in any dream about that place?'

'But I thought,' said she, wrinkling her forehead, 'that was a thing no one ever did – see themselves in a dream? Besides, I always feel I hate this female, so it can't be me. Heavens, Stephen, my train goes in six minutes! Hadn't we better be making a move?'

We made the move in some haste. I installed Daphne in the Stottingham coach, and got out as doors were being slammed. The train was on the point of moving off when she put her head out of the carriage window.

'That coat of mine and my handbag were in the car, you know, when it went over. They were lying on the back seat.'

✳

I went back to my chambers worried much less about the past, the girl in the French mountains, or even Daphne's dreams of her, than over Daphne's own present waking condition. But worry was changed to something much more dynamic by a letter from Vence which Mr Lawrence forwarded to me a few days later:

Dear Lawrence, *wrote the painter Ashcroft* – On receipt of your letter I went at once to Guillaumes, which is a little place about 2,500 feet up, sitting on a level spot where two streams meet. Unfortunately, the girl had wandered off a day or two previously and had not returned. Moreover, as there was no news of her anywhere else, the authorities were informed of her disappearance, and search is being made, I believe, lest she should have met with some mishap. Meanwhile I learnt some facts about her from the people whose 'paying guest' she has been.

If she is not English she at least – so they said – is not French. She had no passport or papers of any kind, but in her handbag, besides a considerable sum in French money, there was an English pound note. When they found her, lying exhausted on the outskirts of the village, she was wearing a thick coat marked with the name of an English shop – from their efforts at pronouncing it I gathered that this was Marshall and Snelgrove – and English shoes. She was also wrapped in a motor-rug, but – exceedingly oddly – had on no other clothes of any description. As there was nothing against her, except her incredible story of having survived and climbed up from the bottom of the ravine (which these local people said was absolutely out of the question), and she had sufficient money to pay for her keep, the good peasants fitted her out with some of their own best clothes, and displayed no objection to housing and feeding her. She has hitherto spent most of her time out of doors, apparently in taking long walks. Just lately, however, she has been manifesting a great desire to 'return' to England, but whether this is the explanation of her recent disappearance they have no idea.

These people – their name is Verdier, by the way – still do not know what the girl calls herself, but they say she has a single silver 'D' on her handbag. And it seems, too, that the day before she left them she went into the church, which (so far as they knew) she had not previously entered, and afterwards observed that of the saints whose images she had seen there one had her name and another 'his' – without giving any clue to whom the latter pronoun referred. On this I went into the church myself, and here is the list of its canonized population for you to deduce what you can from it. There was the Virgin, of course, and in addition St Roch, St Christophe, Ste Thérèse de l'Enfant Jésus, St Laurent, St Joseph, St Etienne, and St Antoine de Padoue. Apart from the Madonna you will see that there is only one female saint in the list, but I do not know whether one is to infer from this that the vanished girl's name is Mary or Theresa. If I hear anything further of her I will communicate with you at once.

PS – I nearly forgot to enclose this very indifferent snapshot of their lodger, which one of the family had taken of her without her knowledge, and which I begged from them, though it is perhaps not worth sending.

I laid down the letter, my mind in utter confusion. What was I to think? That there really had been another girl in the American's car after all? Here was the reappearance of Daphne's coat and handbag; her shoes too had probably been left in the car if she had not removed her skiing boots. And as for this attempt at identification of the wanderer's name, why suppose that it was her Christian name to which she had been referring? There was 'Lawrence' staring the inquirer from Vence in the face!

And more than that, there was my own name, 'Etienne' – as a Christian one this time. And how could any girl not intimate with Daphne have known of 'Stephen', unless Daphne had spoken of me either to her, or in her hearing … or unless there had been a letter from me in the handbag? But the peasants had declared that the girl had no papers of any kind.

I sat there with my head between my hands. I did not see how, on the evidence of those two saints' names and the possession of what were presumably Daphne's belongings, this unknown girl *could* be entirely unconnected with the ill-fated motor-car. Not that I believed for a moment that she had really gone down with it to the bottom of an inaccessible gorge. Had she perhaps scrambled out before the crash? No, that, too, seemed impossible. Had she, then, got out of the car at its last stop before the accident? Perhaps, indeed, she had never been in it at all, but had stolen the coat, bag, rug, and shoes from it when the occupants were lunching at Beuil, and Daphne had only assumed that her property was still in the back. Or perhaps – though I admitted it was extremely improbable – she was someone out of the motor-coach whose reason had been shaken by the collision. But this hypothesis, very improbable in itself, would not give her possession of Daphne's coat and bag. I inclined to the previous conjecture, of theft at Beuil.

I was, in fact, gradually detaching the girl at Guillaumes altogether from the accident, making her someone unknown to Daphne, someone whom Daphne had never seen. Well, why not? It was the only logical way to view the enigma. Otherwise I should have to predicate either that Daphne had deliberately concealed the other's presence in the car, or that the memory of that presence had been wiped clean from her conscious mind by the shock of the accident. That was, of course, perfectly possible; and it was equally possible that her subconscious self was thereupon bringing up the figure in her dreams, clothing it in her own coat and even giving it her own likeness ...

Clothing it in her own coat! But why in the name of all that was sane was the girl, when found, wearing nothing else, save the shoes? In March, in a high altitude, to have discarded all her other clothes! The only answer to that, as I had stoutly told myself all along, was that she was *not* sane, and had no real connection with Daphne or the smash. Nothing in what one had heard of her subsequent conduct called for a reversal of that verdict.

No, that would not do! For what, in that case, of her oblique reference to me, to 'Etienne'?

I began to feel a little as though, while watching in a detached way the unrolling of an octopus's tentacles in an aquarium, one of them had unexpectedly shot through the glass at me – at me and Daphne. And I folded the letter hurriedly together and thrust it back into the envelope, as though that would get rid of its unwelcome contents. Something, however, obstructed its entry and I remembered that Mr Ashcroft had mentioned a photograph. I shook it out.

It was the smudgy over-exposed product of a cheap camera, a picture snapped at a preposterous angle, from the side, and with the subject's head turned away. It merely showed some female – that was all that could be said of the figure – in a dark dress, stooping, apparently, to caress a cat. The open door of what might have been a stable, and part of the wall of some small stone building, showed behind this absurdly indeterminate figure. I did not wonder that Mr Ashcroft had thought the snapshot hardly worth sending. The person it portrayed might have been any girl – any woman – in the world.

Great God! No! not *any* girl! There was surely only one girl in the world who stroked a cat like that, with the back, not the palm of the hand? Daphne, a cat-lover (it was one of the points on which we differed), always upheld – perversely, I thought – that one felt the charm of the fur better that way. And, execrable as the photograph was in other respects, it did show this anonymous figure using that singular caress; I could just see the tips of the slightly upcurled fingers ...

But this was becoming a nightmare! I broke out into a sweat. A breath of something unbelievable seemed to be playing about me ... I threw the snapshot on to the table, and went straight to the telephone to announce to Mr Lawrence my intention of starting immediately for the Riviera. But a strong feeling that Daphne herself would very likely answer my call checked me – for I had temporarily forgotten that she was once more away on a visit – and I telephoned a telegram instead. Then I told my man to pack as quickly as possible, wrote to Mr Lawrence, returning the letter and photograph and telling him the reason for my action, and with ten minutes to spare caught the train to Dover.

✕

'But yes, monsieur,' said the official in the sous-préfet's office at Nice, glancing down at some papers, 'it is quite clear that there is a girl, an English girl apparently, roaming the mountains. We have had reports of her lately from different places. It seems that she spends one night at a village and goes on next day, carrying a knapsack. Your countrywomen are such famous walkers! Yes, it is quite certain.'

So she had not disappeared entirely. I could have wished that she had. 'I find it hard to believe that she is English,' I returned. 'In fact, I find it hard to believe in her existence at all. Look at that tale she tells – impossible, as I understand – of climbing up the gorge from the wreck of that young American's car! It is a case, surely, of mass hallucination, of the birth of a legend!' (But all the time I saw that hand, palm uppermost, stroking the cat.) 'Or else she is a ghost, a phantasm of some kind.'

'Ghosts do not eat, monsieur.'

'How do you know that she eats?'

He shrugged his shoulders. 'She was more than a month with those peasants at Guillaumes, and *that* was not reported by them!'

'I will go and see them. Or perhaps better – where was the girl last heard of?'

The official consulted his papers. 'She is said to have been at Péone the day before yesterday, but she will not be there now, one supposes. You would undoubtedly get most information about her at Guillaumes. The name of the people there is Verdier. But, *pardon* – monsieur is a relative *de cette infortunée*?'

'The product of mass hallucination can't have relatives,' I muttered to myself. 'I am the fiancé,' I answered, stretching a point, 'of the young lady who had the marvellous escape in the accident in question.'

'Ah, Meess Laurence? *Parfaitement.* I certainly advise you, monsieur, to go to Guillaumes; and if, on your return, I have any further information about your mysterious countrywoman, it will be at your disposal.'

I thanked him and left. But when I got back to my hotel I found awaiting me a telegram from Mr Lawrence: 'Daphne disappeared believed gone Riviera enquire Hotel Rivage d'Or.'

Disappeared! Good God! But it was quite possible that she was on her way out here, although she had implied that the Alpes Maritimes were the last mountains she wished to see. I was thankful that I was in Nice already, and dashed round to the Rivage d'Or, the hotel, I remembered, where Daphne had stayed in March. She had not arrived there, and the management knew nothing, but promised to keep me informed. And since she could not well turn up now before next day, I put from me the impracticable plan of making enquiries at all the numerous hotels in Nice, and decided to rush up to Guillaumes and back again as quickly as I could.

※

In my haste and preoccupation I had not quite realized the distance to the little place with the odd name – between fifty and sixty miles on a winding mountain road; nor did I at once elicit this fact from the driver of the car which I had hired to take me there. I think I was in a kind of coma for the first fifteen or twenty miles out of Nice, until we exchanged the wide stony valley of the Var for a region of steep mountainsides, where almost every crag was crowned by a village. After that the valley narrowed and narrowed until we were in a defile so constricted that there was room only for the river, the road, and the line of the railway.

'This is not the Gorge of Daluis, is it?' I asked my Italian-looking driver, feeling pretty sure, however, that it could not be, since here we were most certainly at the bottom of a ravine, not at the top. The rocky walls above us, projecting in some places close over our heads, could not have been far short of a thousand feet in height.

'Ah no, monsieur! This is the beginning of the Gorges de la Mescla. The Gorges de Daluis are more than fifty kilometres farther on. But monsieur will pass through them, necessarily, on the way to Guillaumes.'

So I should see the ill-omened place. I had not anticipated it.

More gorges, beautiful and impressive. Then the river, green as malachite, ceased to be penned between mountain walls and widened once more. The scenery changed its character.

Once I might almost have imagined myself in Asia, so closely did the very high-piled, tiny-windowed houses of one village that we traversed resemble those familiar in travel books about Tibet; at another time I was confronted by a miniature town strayed from the Middle Ages, walled, moated, and draw-bridged as well, its citadel perched above it on the rock against which it was pressed.

'Only about twenty-five kilometres now to Guillaumes,' said the driver encouragingly.

Once more the widened bed of the river began to contract, and presently the mountains through which it poured towards us had taken on the strangest copper-red hue. The driver waved his hand.

'We approach the Gorges de Daluis.' (For the second time I was struck by the sinister content given, somehow, to the name by the sounding of that final 's.') 'Monsieur will see how superb they are – although the whole is really a canyon, not a gorge.'

I was prepared for this distinction, since Mary Frodsham had already made it, and, indeed, we were rising increasingly far above the stream, instead of being penned in with it. The road was marvellously and daringly engineered, half of its width being tunnelled in some places through the rock itself. As my driver naturally took the right-hand, outer section, there was nothing to shut the magnificent spectacle from my view. I had never imagined that anything of this breath-taking nature existed in Europe. Moreover, as the car was ascending the admirable gradient with increasing slowness, I had plenty of time to take in the scene even before the vehicle, with a very strong smell of petrol, came to a standstill altogether.

'It is nothing, monsieur, nothing!' the driver assured me, springing out. 'Never is there anything amiss with my auto! But monsieur would doubtless prefer to walk on ahead, and be overtaken? Just round the corner is the finest view, and the deepest part of the ravine, le Grand Abîme.'

'Was not that the place where the recent accident occurred?' I asked him, half unwillingly.

He nodded. 'The body of the mad American is down there – for ever,' he replied unemotionally, and plunged his optimistic head into the bonnet of his auto.

I walked on up, almost mesmerised by my surroundings. The road itself was high enough, yet in places the blood-red walls and pinnacles of the canyon lifted themselves still farther skywards. The profile of an occasional projecting spur showed how unimaginably sheer was the drop from road level, straight as a plummet-line. One would have expected the hot-hued rock to be entirely barren, yet to the flanks of this giant fissure there clung an astonishing, metallic-looking vegetation – verdigris on copper. The torrent was so far below that despite the silence one could not hear it.

The road now took me round a corner, a spur. I turned that corner … and my heart stopped.

Against the newly mended parapet farther on, over-topped by one of those gaunt reddish crags, stood the figure of a girl, looking down into the depths. She wore curiously ill-fitting black clothes, but there was no hat on her auburn hair – Daphne's hair. She turned her face towards me at my step; and it was Daphne's face.

So she had already arrived at Nice – and some morbid attraction had drawn her to the Grand Abîme! 'Daphne, my darling!' I exclaimed, hurrying forward, 'why did you not let me know?'

But this was not Daphne – at least, not the Daphne whom I had seen off at Paddington only a few days before! This was the radiant Daphne of the old days, with the vivid and charming colouring, and with no trace of a cut to mar the roses and cream of her cheek. And this Daphne stretched out her hands to me, laughing with pleasure.

'Oh, Stephen, at last! I knew you would come to find me! But what a long time you have been!'

She caught my hands with her own, then her arms, strong and warm, were about my neck as I pressed her to me in those unfamiliar black clothes. 'Take me home with you, Stephen,' said her voice in my ear. 'Take me home quickly. I am so tired of these mountains!'

But though I tried, I could not answer; the words were strangled in my throat. Directly I held her I knew that it was not Daphne ... And yet it *was!* I seemed to have been swirled into some region where, as happens in the world of dreams, one person can be two people and the mind has no difficulty in accepting their identity. Speechless still, I was nevertheless just stooping my head to kiss her when she recoiled violently. The eyes looking up at me as they used to look before either of us heard of this cursed place swerved away, charged with an expression of hate and horror which turned me cold. At the same moment there came a cry behind me, and I looked round.

There stood the Daphne I had left behind in England, gazing, not at me, but at the other, with the same dreadful look on her face.

Involuntarily I stepped back, hypnotised, staring first at one, then at the other. But it could only have been for a few seconds, for a dazzle like the loss of focus of a migraine came over my sight. The two figures confronting each other with the same air of fathomless revulsion seemed all at once to rush together and coalesce, like two drops of quicksilver that are spilt upon a table. I staggered back against the rock wall with my hands over my eyes ...

The next thing I knew was that a man somewhere near me

was shouting to another in French: '*Nom de Dieu*, she has jumped right over, the young lady who came up in your car! You didn't see it? ... I was coming to tell my passenger that the petrol feed-pipe ... Here he is! Monsieur, monsieur, why in Heaven's name did you not try to stop her?'

I was at the edge next moment with both drivers holding on to me; I struggled with them in vain. 'No, no! Once over, there's no chance. *On est coulé! C'est le Grand Abime, voyez-vous – fini!* The young lady must have been mad!'

✖

Nothing but that stupendous chasm at my feet, going down to the very centre of things, to a spot as inaccessible as any on earth; and, now that the drivers' excited voices had ceased as they also gazed into that dizzy red gulf, a silence that was its counterpart in menace and finality. And Daphne's broken body was down there ... for ever.

✖

After that I found myself in bed at my hotel, with only a confused recollection of the long drive back to Nice. I was there for some time; a *juge d'instruction* came to the bedside to take my evidence. I said nothing of the presence of the Other; he would have pronounced me insane. The driver of my car, the only other witness – the *only* witness, in fact – of that leap ... or fall ... to death had obviously seen but the one figure. It was probably his evidence that I had been at some distance from the young lady which saved me from any suspicion of having pushed her over – that and the realization by the authorities, already conversant with the details of the first tragedy in the gorge, that the shaken nerves of a participant in it might well have led her to revisit the spot and throw herself over.

It came out that Daphne had arrived that very day, not at Nice but at Cannes, possibly because Cannes was somewhat nearer, had hired a car, told the man to stop just where circumstances had already forced mine to stop, and had walked on up alone. Why she came will always remain an open question.

And the Abyss of Daluis keeps the greater secret, that of the Other. I have no explanation to give myself which satisfies me. But that her brief existence was not a product of my imagination there is ample evidence; and to prove that she was not a phantom I have the remembrance of the warm and breathing personality whose hands I held, whose lips I all but kissed before it ... she ... was absorbed into Daphne's – or reabsorbed hers – with so terrible a result.

✖

'So you see,' finished Ellison sombrely, 'that the phrase "dual personality" means for me something much more inexplicable than it does to the ordinary man, or even to the psychologist. It means something fundamentally incredible ... Yes, I have managed to retain my sanity – if the increase of my practice at the Bar is a proof of this, which I sometimes doubt ... Shall we go and have supper somewhere?'

11 The Taste of Pomegranates
(c. 1945)

1

'Are you ready to start, Arbel?' asked Roberta, arriving
suddenly from the hotel. 'M Barbier has restored that
particularly devilish note to his horn, and is tying up the
mudguard, so I expect he will be here to collect us quite soon.
I daresay his contraption will get us to Les Eyzies and back
all right.'

Neat, competent and affectionate, she smiled down at her
sister, sitting under a young walnut-tree among the bright
riverside grass and the spike of dark-blue monkshood above
the Dordogne. The walnut leaves had not yet lost their tender
bronzy green, for it was early summer still in Périgord. A little
below coursed the river itself, beautiful, strong and charged
with history, guardian of more formidable castles than the
Loire. Here, indeed, at Beynac, far above M Barbier's little
hotel, which was squeezed in between the river and the cliffs,
rose one of the proudest of these ruined strongholds.

The girl under the walnut-tree did not seem to have heard
the question. 'She is in one of her far-away moods,' thought
her elder sister, looking down at her with love, and a familiar
catch at the heart. That beautiful face of Arbel Fraser's wore
so often in repose a look for which 'tragic' was nevertheless
too strong a word. It was rather an expression of unsatisfied,
perhaps unjustifiable, yearning. With her lovely transparent
skin, her pale auburn hair and eyebrows, her great, rarely
smiling hazel eyes, there was about her something intangible
and apart. She was like an alabaster lamp enclosing an unseen
flame, consuming rather than vivid.

The two girls, orphaned daughters of a London doctor of Scottish origin, were not well off, and had to earn their own livings, Roberta as the almoner of an East End hospital, Arbel in a Mayfair hat shop – a job which she detested as much as Roberta, on the whole, liked hers. The choice of the Dordogne country for their long-promised French trip had been Arbel's; was it not little visited by tourists, beautiful in itself, and full of splendid castles? Professing to dislike the twentieth century, she had a persistent hankering after life in some much earlier epoch, Roberta, on the other hand, considered that existence in any time before the seventeenth century must have been most undesirable, especially for women, and sometimes teased her sister about that vague desire of hers to 'go back'. Nevertheless, Arbel being so precious in her eyes, it often gave her a queer uneasiness.

And certainly they had come to a region apt enough to encourage daydreams of the past, for along the Dordogne the Middle Ages met them at every turn. Today, however, since they were about to set off to see the relics of times unbelievably more remote, Roberta thought that Arbel ought to display more alertness. She stooped over her and shook her gently by the shoulder.

'Wake up! M Barbier will be here in a few minutes!'

And at that Arbel removed her gaze from the river and picked a stem of monkshood.

'In reality,' she said lazily, 'we ought not to drive to Les Eyzies at all, even in that antediluvian car. It would be more appropriate, wouldn't it, to go on foot to "the capital of the prehistoric world", as that young Oxford don who was here last week – and who wasn't the least my idea of a don – told us that it was called?'

'Walking there I refuse to contemplate,' replied Roberta

briskly. 'Especially as I don't see how one can be really interested in people – if they were genuine people and not monkeys – who lived twenty thousand years ago!'

'I'm *not* particularly interested in them,' retorted Arbel, twirling the aconite stem. 'But I do want to see the wonderful drawings they made in those caves.'

Roberta felt a tiny stab at her heart. Had their means permitted, Arbel would have trained as an artist herself. Roberta had once nourished a daydream in which she herself had inherited a substantial legacy from some unexpected source, and had at once rushed off to Madame Séraphine's and insisted upon Arbel's giving her the shortest possible notice. Only somehow the fabric of that dream had a trick of twisting in her hands, for Arbel would have been quite likely to say: 'Terribly good of you, Rob darling, but it's too late now. I shall never do anything more exalted than design a hat worthy of the show window!'

'That Mr Amery,' remarked Roberta now, 'said it was very difficult to make out the drawings unless you were trained to it, like that French archaeologist friend of his whom he mentioned. And I don't share your passion for caves.'

'Passion for caves!' exclaimed her sister, a little colour springing into her face. 'When you know I dislike them intensely!'

'Arbel Fraser, how can you sit there and say that! Think of the job I had in getting you away from the Gouffre de Padirac!'

Arbel rose to her feet. 'Ah, but Padirac was different – a world of its own down there, far beneath ours! That lovely little clear underground river!' The tiniest shiver ran over her, of delight or some other emotion. 'I'm certainly going there again if it can be managed!'

'Again! No!' said Roberta firmly, thinking of that descent by lift into the bowels of the earth, and of that strange,

electrically lit waterway along which they had been ferried, a
sterile transparency bereft of any visible living thing. 'Not, of
course, that it wasn't interest –'

She broke off, for a series of ear-piercing hoots announced
that their landlord had traversed the quarter-mile of road
from the hotel and was waiting for them to embark. There
indeed he was at the grassy verge, holland-coated, Panama-
hatted, and beaming.

'*En voiture, mesdemoiselles, pour les grottes de la Vézère!*'

2

An hour or so later a young Englishman in tweeds was sitting
with a pipe in his mouth and his back to the ruined castle of
Tayac above Les Eyzies. His name was Norris Amery, he
was a Fellow of All Souls, and he had come to the Dordogne
country in search of local material for his forthcoming book
on the Hundred Years' War – which accounted for his visit to
the relic behind him, surrendered by his countrymen to the
French five years before Agincourt. For the moment, indeed,
he was making Les Eyzies-de-Tayac his headquarters, a
good deal because of the presence there of his friend Gabriel
Lenormand, that rising young French archaeologist. It was
in fact for Lenormand's emergence from the little Musée
tucked against the rockside that he was waiting now.

'He's being the deuce of a time with that colleague of his
down there,' he thought. 'He said he wanted to run me over
to the *grotte* at La Palombière before déjeuner, not after. But
I'm too abysmally lazy to go and rout him out.'

Besides, it was uncommonly pleasant just to do nothing
and gaze at the green and smiling valleys of the Vézère and
the Beune, as fresh as if they had just been created. Yet under
the shelter of their overhanging limestone bluffs, or in them,
mankind had lived for hundreds of centuries: cultivated and

pastoral now, this was nevertheless the landscape above all others in which Stone Age man had lived out his difficult and hardly to be imagined existence. The knowledge made Norris Amery's own mediaeval studies seem but a quickly turned page in a book written yesterday, and the era of knight and bowman, troubadour and crusader a mere ripple in the long, long stream which had its source in the mists of prehistory.

But after a while the smoker got up. 'This is reprehensible,' he said aloud. 'I must really go and find out what is keeping Gabriel.'

※

It was no 'colleague', for he had departed, which was delaying M Lenormand in the little Musée d'archéologie préhistorique, but the desire to be of some assistance to two young English ladies, whom he saw wandering about in a rather bewildered fashion in the otherwise empty rooms. His tentatively offered help being gratefully received – he spoke English fluently – he went round with them explaining the more interesting exhibits; and after they had enquired how best they might see some of the cave-paintings of which they had heard, found himself offering to accompany them to one of the 'art-galleries' in the neighbourhood, recommending for this purpose the Font de Gaume.

'Oh, Monsieur, how very kind of you!' exclaimed Roberta gratefully. (He does not seem like a typical Frenchman, she decided, in spite of his little beard – so steady and serious-looking!) 'But shall we not be taking up too much of your time?'

Sacrificing still further the waiting Amery – after all, the arrangement with him had not been very definite – Lenormand assured her that he was entirely at their disposal.

'But before we go, Monsieur,' put in Arbel, 'perhaps you would make it a little clear to us what is the difference between "Mousterian", "Magdalenian", and – what is it, "Aurignacian"? These names, and the others, like "Cro-Magnon", mean nothing to us, I am afraid!'

'Steady and serious-looking' Gabriel Lenormand might be, but he had a very pleasant smile. 'I understand that you wish me to give you a short lecture, mesdemoiselles!' So there and then, in the most famous of its haunts, Roberta and Arbel learnt of that race variously called Neanderthal or Mousterian (itself by no means the earliest known) which, their informant said, had maintained itself upon this planet longer than any other before or since – a matter of some 20,000 or even 25,000 years; and how it had lived through the prolonged rigours of the Fourth Ice Age, the worst of all, at first under the overhanging limestone rocks, the *abris* abounding in this region, then in the draughty mouths of caverns, later in the damp recesses, at constant odds with the terrible cave bear and the cave lion, snaring the elephant and the rhinoceros, themselves ogres no more than five feet high, with a great head poking forward and arms disproportionately long.

'Yet they were men, mesdemoiselles,' affirmed M Lenormand, 'though not, indeed, your ancestors or mine; no, not even though remains of them have been found in other continents, and actually in London itself.'

'But surely London did not exist then!' objected Roberta.

'Indeed, no. It is that during excavations in your Leadenhall Street (I believe for the purpose of building a new bank) there was found a portion of the skull of a woman of that race.'

'And it could be told from *that* that she had been a woman … thousands and thousands of years ago?'

'Not only so, but also that she had been a left-handed woman.'

'And what happened to these Mousterians? They died out, I suppose,' hazarded Arbel, looking reflectively at her own left hand, for she shared this idiosyncrasy.

'No,' said the archaeologist, 'they did not die out, they were wiped out in the first great war in history – or rather, in prehistory. It was very hard on them, after their long fight with an adverse climate and so many animal foes; but they were overwhelmed by the invasion of a far bigger and finer race – indeed history has seen none finer. The poor men of Le Moustier! … But these men who obliterated them, this new race, the Cro-Magnons or Aurignacians, were also the first artists who ever existed, for it was they, with their successors the Magdalenians –'

He broke off at the sound of a step. They all turned, and the Frasers beheld 'the young Oxford don' advancing towards them among the show-cases.

'Mr Amery!' exclaimed Roberta. 'Well, you see we have taken your advice and come to Les Eyzies!'

'And improved upon it by annexing an excellent guide! This is the old friend of whom I spoke to you, M Lenormand. Have you been into any of the caves yet?'

'No, but we are just going. This – M Lenormand has very kindly offered to show us one.'

'Your luck continues,' said Amery, smiling. 'M Lenormand is in charge of the excavations at a *grotte* about seven miles from here. In fact he discovered it in the first place; and I can assure you that the revelation of yet another prehistoric site in this exceedingly well-combed region caused a pretty big sensation in the archaeological world.'

'Mr Amery exaggerates,' said the discoverer modestly. 'Digging is not yet far advanced at La Palombière, but I have hopes of some finds later on, encouraged by a good drawing of a bison in a little *diverticule*. But in Font de Gaume, which I shall now have the pleasure of showing you, you will see really great art.'

'Devoted entirely to zoological subjects,' observed Amery

flippantly. 'The place is a nocturnal Whipsnade – with the difference that the beasts can't run at you ... May I come too?'

✕

It was nearly half-past twelve when the four emerged from the long, narrow, ill-lit series of passages, with their profusion of ranging bisons and processions of hairy mammoths, from the horses, reindeer and the rest, all of so marvellously life-like an execution, whether merely incised upon the rock – and consequently difficult for the uninitiated to make out – or, as in most cases, outlined or painted in the red and black of ochre and manganese. Lenormand's guidance was invaluable to the two sisters, and Norris Amery, more silent than his wont, seemed also to have gone to school with them. But his eyes were actually more often upon Arbel Fraser's living profile than upon the creatures limned by hands so long dead.

'How wonderful and how strange!' said Arbel slowly; and she put her hand for a moment over her eyes as though to shade them from the jubilation of shining river and sunlit foliage in this, the world of outside, the world of today, 'Because it is obvious that all those animals have been drawn from life – or rather, I suppose, from memory, since there could have been no models in the cave itself.'

'Drawn, too, mademoiselle, you must realise,' said Lenormand quickly, 'by men who had no tradition whatever of drawing to help them, no slightest inheritance of art behind them. Cro-Magnon man was in the most literal sense the first graphic artist in the world.'

'And all these drawings were made, I think you said,' put in Roberta, 'to ensure success in hunting through sympathetic magic?'

'And possibly with some ceremonial aim as well. But we know nothing of the religious ideas involved.'

'Well, we can't possibly thank you enough for bringing us here,' said Roberta warmly,

'No, indeed,' murmured Arbel, who still seemed half lost in a dream of her own.

'I think,' remarked Norris Amery, looking at her, 'that the best payment you ladies could make to M Lenormand is to get him to show you his own special cavern at La Palombière. Couldn't we all four go over there one of these days, Gabriel, and make a picnic of it?'

And it is possible that this suggestion was made neither to give satisfaction to his friend, nor to increase the Misses Frasers' knowledge of prehistory.

'If these ladies would really care for it I should be delighted,' returned the Frenchman with a little bow. 'Not, as I say, that there is much to see there yet, but the site is certainly attractive. If a visit would really give you pleasure, mesdemoiselles, then Sunday would be the best day for it, because there would be no digging going on.'

'You agree?' asked Amery of the two girls. 'Then I will come and fetch you next Sunday at about eleven – Lenormand's car is only a two-seater. But you are going to allow us to give you lunch now, aren't you?'

This offer, however, Roberta and Arbel were obliged to decline, since M Barbier – probably already dancing with impatience – had to get back to his duties at Beynac. They must hurry down to him.

✕

'Quite an agreeable interlude!' remarked the young Fellow of All Souls as he and his friend watched the ancient car shudder and rattle itself off. 'I don't blame you, Gabriel, for forgetting that you had engaged yourself (or so I believed) to take me with you to La Palombière this morning. No, don't apologise; after all, I saw Font de Gaume again.'

'And the Mlles Fraser also,' said the Frenchman. 'Since you had met them already, and you may perhaps know something of them – where they come from, for instance?'

'My dear chap, I don't know a thing about them. I merely came across them *chez* Papa Barbier when I spent a couple of nights at Beynac last week. From their name, I suppose they are Scottish.' Amery paused for a moment and then added slowly, 'There is to me a curious charm about the younger (as I take her to be) which I can't exactly define. It is not merely the fact that she is lovely. She reminds me vaguely of someone I have seen before. I had that feeling at Beynac, and again this morning, even more strongly.'

Lenormand looked at him, surprised. '*Tiens*, that is very strange! For I also have that impression. It must therefore be some girl or woman whom we have both met.'

'Yes, but when or where? In Oxford, when you came to that archaeological conference? Or in France, as for instance when I stayed with you in Provence two years ago?'

Gabriel Lenormand shook his head; and remarking simultaneously that it was time to eat, they both turned in at the Hôtel Cro-Magnon and were presently partaking of the excellent Périgourdin food and drinking Monbazillac.

3

The fine weather which had attended the Frasers' excursions to Les Eyzies was broken during the next few days by rainstorms. On Sunday morning however there was prospect of a better, even of a sunny day, although there were still rather ominous clouds in the sky. In view of this fact, Amery, when he appeared on the banks of the Dordogne in his open tourer, advised his passengers to take with them some form of protection against the weather.

'M Lenormand will meet us at this place, I suppose?' enquired Arbel as they started.

'He will. In fact he is bringing the lunch.'

'It is very good of him,' observed Roberta, 'to waste his time on such ignoramuses.'

'I assure you,' said Amery promptly, 'that he does not regard you in that light. He told me that he had been impressed with your intelligent interest, and I know he is genuinely looking forward to showing you his find. It is true that the cave is only partially cleared, and that it is rather rough going in some parts, but at least there is no need to crawl, as I understand was once the case. And he has managed to install a rough system of electric lighting. Jolly country, this, isn't it?'

It was more. It was enchanting. And when they came to the green valley which was their destination they found it a replica on a lesser scale of that of the Vézère, even to having a smaller lateral valley running into it.

'The Grotte de la Palombière is up there,' said Amery as he slowed down; and he indicated the typical limestone cliffs. 'There's quite a good wide path leading up to it, passing an *abri* on the way. But one can't, naturally, take a car up. Lenormand will have left his, as I am going to do, on the level here, round this next bend. I hope we shall find him unpacking the lunch.' He gave a touch to his horn and swung the car round into an almost lawn-like little space bordering the stream.

But to his evident surprise there was no other car there; no archaeologist – and no lunch.

'Shades of Le Moustier! What can have happened to the man?' cried his fellow-host. 'He certainly expected to be here by the time we were, or even before.'

'The cave, Mr Amery – he must be up there,' suggested the practical Roberta.

'Impossible, unless he has been dropped from an aeroplane,

because there is no other place but this where he could have left his car.'

'Might he not have come in a hired one, which then went back?'

'In that case he would certainly have waited here for us. No, he must have been delayed somehow, for I am quite sure that with ladies as guests he would not otherwise be late. And we cannot pass the time by invading his cave, for there is no one there and the barrier will be in place. I think we had better turn back a little and take the *chemin vicinal* which leads to Les Eyzies and reconnoitre. Or,' as he correctly interpreted Arbel's expression, 'would you both rather stay here while I go? Let me open the door then.'

'I thought we might walk about a bit while we have the chance; it is so charming here,' explained Arbel, when Amery had turned his car and left them. 'Prehistoric man seems to have had a liking for beautiful scenery.'

'I wonder, really, if he noticed it,' replied her sister. 'I expect he was too much occupied in hunting for food and in defending himself.'

'Let's go up the cliff path a little way,' suggested Arbel, looking round her. 'We shall get a much better view from there, and still see when Mr Amery returns with his missing friend.'

Five or six minutes' walking brought them to the beginning of the track, and they walked slowly up its easy gradient enjoying the view, and thus scarcely noticed that the sun had disappeared. They were quite two-thirds of the way up when a heavy spattering of raindrops drew their attention to the large black cloud which, seeming to arrive from nowhere, was preparing to empty itself upon the valley.

'What a nuisance!' exclaimed Roberta. 'I'm glad that I have kept my raincoat, for I'm afraid it's going to be a downpour. Oh, Arbel, don't say you have left yours in the car!'

'I've got my sunshade. Let's hurry on and make use of the *abri* Mr Amery spoke of. It can't be much further up.'

They quickened their pace and very soon reached the overhang of the limestone, and thankfully accepted its shelter, as Stone Age man had done before them. The rain was now falling very purposefully over the valley, and soon, there was no denying it, began to be driven in against them by the wind, for the *abri* was not very deep.

'This is no fun!' exclaimed Arbel with some petulance. 'Bother M Lenormand; why couldn't he be punctual? I wish we could get into his cave; then it would be of use as well as of interest.'

'Well, we know we can't,' responded Roberta, 'so we must make the best of what our distant ancestors – oh no, we were told not to think of them as ancestors – had to put up with in bad weather.'

'I shan't!' retorted Arbel. 'I'm going to have a look at the cave anyhow. It must be quite close. No, I *won't* take your raincoat!' And opening her cotton sunshade again, she dived out into the rain.

'But as we can't get in, that's silly!' called Roberta after her wilful sister – and then followed her into the rain. A few moments later they were standing looking at what was undoubtedly the entrance to M Lenormand's *grotte*, an entrance, surprisingly, not so narrow as that to Font de Gaume. But –

'You say we can't get in!' Arbel was exclaiming in triumph. 'Look at that!'

'Something must have happened to that gate affair,' opined Roberta very justly, for the palisading strung on wires, designed evidently to keep out trespassers, had given way beneath the weight of a considerable quantity of earth and limestone which had fallen in the middle of it, presumably from further up the cliff wall. As a consequence one end had been wrenched clear away from the stout post to which it had been attached.

'The effect of yesterday's rain, I suppose,' commented Arbel. 'Anyhow, it's now quite possible to squeeze in.'

"*Défense absolue d'entrer*'!' quoted her sister, pointing at the notice hanging all awry on the twisted palisading.

'Can't be enforced now,' retorted Arbel briefly. 'I'm going to take refuge with Cro-Magnon man; you can stay outside in the rain with your Mousterians if you like.' Gathering her pretty flowered dress round her she slipped through the gap, and Roberta, protesting weakly, 'I don't think we ought to!', followed her into the gloom.

Once in, she instinctively turned to face the outer world and the heavily falling rain, but Arbel, murmuring something about electric light, groped about on the wall. 'I wonder which side the switch is? Ah!' And a click was followed by what seemed a brilliant illumination.

At that Roberta also turned towards the interior and, by the light of the two or three naked bulbs disposed on a flex strung up against the uneven side of the cave, the intruders were able to view what had so far been excavated of the Grotte de la Palombière. At first sight this appeared disappointingly little. The width and height of the place in which they found themselves were in fact considerable, but ahead of them it had only been cleared for some fifty or sixty feet. After that came a solidly packed wall, the detritus of uncounted centuries. No prehistoric drawings of any kind were visible; but then, as the girls already knew, these would in any case be difficult to make out without assistance. Halfway down on the right was what looked like another blocked passage but, rather nearer on the left, excavation had been going on along a side alley of some sort, for an electric light hung over the entrance.

'That must be the *diverticule*, as M Lenormand called it, where the drawing of the bison is,' said Arbel. 'Let's go and have a look at it – No, I'm *not* going out in this wet to see if those two have turned up yet – not till I've seen the bison anyhow.'

'We must be quick about it, then,' said Roberta, still uncomfortable about this unceremonious entrance. 'And we really ought to wait for M Lenormand to do the honours.' Nevertheless, for the third time she followed her sister.

The *diverticule* was narrow and sinuous, and its walls bulged inwards much more than in the main cave, but it was quite well lit.

'Can that be meant for a bison?' queried Roberta, after they had both peered at some indeterminate scratches.

'It looks to me more like a bit of a mammoth, one of those nice woolly mammoths we saw at Font de Gaume – only it's not painted. Isn't it hard to realise that those absurd great things (they must have been absurd) once roamed all over this countryside – reindeer too, at one time.'

'There were other animals less agreeable as well,' Roberta reminded her, 'That horrible sabre-toothed tiger, for instance, that M Lenormand spoke of, and the cave-lion.'

'Yes, and the cave-bear into the bargain. Do you remember that place in Font de Gaume where the wall was all scored over with their claw-marks? – What was that noise, Rob?'

It was a slight rumbling sound, rather like distant thunder, which grew in intensity as they listened. It did not, apparently, come from within the cave, but from outside.

'It must be –' began Roberta, but before she could get further there was a prolonged slithering crash which sent echoes rippling and booming about their ears. Next moment the electric light went out.

For a moment or two there was complete silence in the *diverticule*. Neither of the intruders had uttered a word, but Arbel had gripped her sister by the elbow.

'How jolly!' said Roberta, finding her voice – not a very steady one. 'However, we can quite well feel our way out of here; the floor's not too uneven. Only we must be careful not to bump our heads on the bulgy walls.'

'Quite so,' assented Arbel drily, and gave a little laugh. 'Come on then. I'll go first.'

('Now don't lose your head!' Roberta vehemently adjured herself. 'There's not the slightest need to.') But how starkly alarming absolute darkness could be, and how it could transform surroundings which, though now unseen, were exactly the same as when they were visible.

For some moments the two felt their way back along the rough and sometimes inconvenient wall, and if each was speculating as to the cause of the crash and of the extinction of the lighting, neither gave voice to her surmises. The darkness was so intense as almost to stifle thought. At last Arbel spoke.

'I think I've come to the end of the *diverticule*. Yes, I have. But, Roberta' – her voice grew sharp – 'surely we ought to see some daylight from the cave entrance now … and there isn't any!'

That was just what part of Roberta's own mind had been whispering – no, shouting – to the other half, the half which implored her to keep her head. For ought not some faint glimmer of daylight to have reached them even up the *diverticule*? 'Because, since Einstein, we know that light bends,' she found herself thinking foolishly.

Arbel had now stopped dead. Roberta only knew this for certain because her own outstretched left hand – the right was feeling along the wall – came into contact with her shoulder, a trifle damp from the rain (and if only that rain were falling on them now, outside!). And at her touch Arbel gave voice to their common fear. 'I believe,' she said slowly, 'that the entrance to the cave is blocked – I mean, quite blocked. If it is –'

Roberta's hand tightened on her shoulder. 'Even if it is, Mr Amery will guess that we are in here (because we couldn't be anywhere else) and he and M Lenormand won't be long in getting us out. It can't, surely, have been a very big fall, even if it did make such a noise in here – echoes mostly, I expect.'

'Probably this rain now, on top of yesterday's, has done the trick. Anyhow we'd better get as near the entrance as we can. I'm sorry, Rob, that I was so darned obstinate about coming in here. (Much better have respected the notice!) I'm going on now; I'm turning the corner.'

That accomplished, they continued their shuffling and careful progress. 'If only we had brought an electric torch with us,' lamented Arbel. 'I suppose a wire has been carried away.'

About two minutes later, however, both girls gave a cry of astonishment. The solid darkness in which they had been groping was suddenly no more, annihilated by what seemed at first an almost intolerable radiance, which showed them that they had only a few more yards to go. The electric light had come on again – or had, perhaps, been switched on in some way from outside. It might be that they were practically rescued already!

'Mr Amery, Mr Amery, we're in here!' called out Roberta at the top of her voice.

'And really longing to see you,' finished Arbel.

But there was no reply, save their own voices echoing in the emptiness. Moreover the illumination, which at first had seemed so dazzling, now resolved itself into one solitary electric bulb near them. Roberta looked up at it gratefully.

'It's wonderful to have it,' she murmured. 'And it *must* mean they are outside. Let's get as near as possible to the entrance now that we can see the way.'

Her heart checked for a moment nevertheless, when she saw what the 'entrance' had now become – a mere mass of limestone rubble and small rocks, completely blocking any exit and spreading inwards for some distance along the cave floor. The avalanche was of a very much more formidable nature than that which had wrenched aside the palisading. They were well and truly imprisoned.

'Yes, I see what comes of flouting a notice,' said Arbel reflectively. Roberta slung off the Kodak she had brought with her, removed her Burberry, and folding it up to make a cushion for them both, put it on the floor in the corner. 'Come and sit down, Arbel, and we will both listen hard. It is quite likely that we shan't hear them at all when they begin to dig us out; the fall must be pretty thick. But they *must* be outside by now!'

'Or gone away for spades and things – or even possibly for more help,' supplemented Arbel. Then she looked with apparent amusement at her sister, trying to settle herself comfortably against the limestone wall. '"Calm bearing of two young ladies trapped in a prehistoric cavern." You ought to be photographed. What have you done with your camera?'

'This light would not –' began Roberta, and found herself speaking of what existed no longer. For at that precise moment their miraculous bulb decided to go out again; and instantly the cave became once more a place of potential terrors.

Roberta reached out. 'Arbel, come here close to me! We mustn't be separated ... though I daresay the light will go on again. It's – it's got the jumps, as I shall soon, I think!'

Arbel made no answer, but felt for and found her sister and sat down close by her. For some time both were silent, straining their ears in the unrelieved blackness for some sound from outside. But none came.

'Don't you think it's getting rather airless in here?' said Arbel suddenly.

'No,' answered her sister with decision. 'It can't be. Two people would take ages to use up all the air there must be in this place. Besides, we shall soon be out of it.'

'With all that mass of stuff in the entrance? And why can't we hear *any* sound of its being cleared away? I'm sleepy; that shows the air is close.'

'Well, to go to sleep is a good way of passing the time,' said Roberta with more composure than she felt. 'Lie down and put your head on my knee – like that. I will go on listening.'

And for a time she did listen, acutely, though her vigil was rewarded by nothing more than the occasional tinkling fall of a scrap of loosened limestone, so that after a while her own head began to nod, and she unexpectedly dozed off.

※

She woke with a jump, unbelieving but overjoyed to find that the electric light bulb had resumed its functions. Was that what had awakened her, or was it some noise of shovelling outside? Again she listened hard.

If there had been any shovelling it was not audible now. Yet there was, undeniably, a sound which she had not heard before. Roberta looked down anxiously at the sister whose cherished head lay on her knee. Why was Arbel breathing so heavily? Oh God, did it mean that the air *was* dangerously foul? She stooped over the sleeper. No, she looked perfectly all right, and was drawing her breath quite peacefully; and Roberta herself had no feeling of discomfort. But why, oh why, were the two men so slow? Mr Amery could not have forgotten them! Even if something very unforeseen, such as an accident, had happened to M Lenormand, Mr Amery would have returned to fetch them away.

But … when he came and did not see them anywhere about, how, really, could he guess that they had got into a cavern whose mouth, by the time he reached it, was impenetrably blocked?

As that horrible question shot up before her Roberta felt as if she had received an electric shock. She had so far assumed that their release would only be a question of time; had indeed speculated whether M Lenormand had not gone to fetch some of his workmen to help. Now she had a searing vision of Mr Amery – of both men, perhaps – turning away, quite justifiably, from the choked entrance to continue a vain search elsewhere. In that case … She would not, would *not* let herself face that terrible outcome.

How long had they slept? How long indeed had they been here? Her watch could not tell her that, for it had stopped, when or why she had no idea. Arbel's then? She tried without waking her sister to get a sight of it, forgetting that a broken glass had prevented its being worn that day. And, cautiously as she pushed aside Arbel's sleeve, the touch woke her.

'It's no use trying to see the time,' she said, in the voice which a somnambulist might use. 'Time doesn't exist any longer. And even if it did, there could be no way of measuring it here.'

'Wake up properly, darling,' said Roberta, trying to speak naturally. 'Wake up and don't talk nonsense.'

Yet as Arbel sat up, exclaiming, 'Why, the light is all right again!', Roberta became conscious of the continuance of that slightly stertorous noise which she had already heard. And now the sound aroused in her a different kind of uneasiness.

'Do you hear something almost like snoring?' she asked.

Arbel made no answer. In that stark, unflattering light she looked very pale. Staring straight before her she said slowly, 'Rob, surely there is a lot more of the cave than there was! It didn't reach nearly such a distance when we first came in. And look, on the far side of the entrance, it's quite different!'

Yes, it was true. Roberta could see that. She drew a sharp breath. Beyond the last of the extinct electric bulbs the main passage no longer came to an abrupt end, as before, but stretched away into darkness. And on the right loomed the opening of the new passage. Moreover, on the further side of the blocked cave mouth the wall seemed to have receded, giving place to a kind of bay, not very clearly discernible. Towards this a rocky floor sloped upwards, seeming however to stop before it reached the other side of the recess, and suggesting thereby that there was a cavity of some sort between.

Roberta's senses swam for a moment. 'I can't believe it – I won't believe it!' she repeated under her breath. 'It's only a particularly vivid nightmare! Or else it is bad air after all, making us imagine things.' And she clasped Arbel to her in an access of despair and protection. 'Darling, you shall, you *shall* be got out!'

But it was she, and not Arbel, whose sobs were echoing in that tomblike silence.

'Don't cry, Robbie!' said Arbel gently, putting an arm round her neck. 'We must face it: there's nothing else to be done.'

Roberta gulped and wiped her eyes. At all costs Arbel must not be allowed to share the vision which had come to her just now, and which she was trying to repudiate. 'No, no, it will be all right – you'll see. It may take time to get through, of course; but we shall soon hear them starting to dig us out!'

Arbel removed her arm. She looked all eyes. 'How *could* they dig us out? They do not exist! In this place, *now*, we have gone back twenty thousand years or so, into prehistory – into the time when the woolly mammoth and all those forgotten beasts were alive. Why, it will be centuries and centuries before men called Amery and Lenormand are even born! And when at last this cave is opened, thousands of years hence, we shall just be two female skeletons or bits of skeletons of the

Stone Age … and one of us left-handed, like the remnant of a woman who was found under Leadenhall Street – a left-handed Londoner!' She laughed; it was the most unmirthful sound. 'No, I'm wrong. There wasn't even her skeleton, only the top of her skull. Poor Sleeping Beauty!'

Roberta, who did not like this outburst at all, took a firmer grip upon herself. 'You are talking rubbish, Arbel,' she said severely. 'It is wrong to give way to such morbid fancies. And they *are* just fancies, because if we really had gone back thousands of years, there couldn't be an electric light burning up there!'

Brought up short by this undoubted anachronism, they both gazed in a half mesmerised fashion at the faithful if erratic bulb which still lit the nearer portion of the cavern. And it was at that moment that it came to their ears – a kind of faint, far-away clinking sound. Gripping each others' hands the two girls held their breaths. And the little noise came again. Thank God, thank God! It meant rescue after all, rescue *now* – not the discovery of their bones centuries hence.

'There, you see, darling, how wrong you were!' cried Roberta, her voice shaking. 'They're outside. They've begun!'

'Let's shout!' suggested Arbel. They did so, but got no semblance of a reply. The subsidence was evidently too thick for their voices to travel through it.

'I feel too restless just to sit and listen,' announced Arbel, getting up. 'As we can't do anything to help from our side, and it may be ages before they get through, I'm going to explore a little. For you see, Rob, that when the daylight gets in again – if it ever does – the cave will go back to the size it was before we went to sleep. So M Lenormand will never know about the extra bits and the lie of them (at least not until he has excavated them) unless we tell him. So I vote we try to see what is on the other side of that slope.'

It was rather like walking up the side of a not very steeply pitched roof. The slope came to an end some ten feet from the farther wall of the cave, falling abruptly into a pit of shadow, so inadequately lit by the solitary bulb at their backs that the explorers could not at first see to the bottom of it. But if their eyes did not function, their noses did, and these told them that from this cavity below there was rising up a very disagreeable odour.

'What is that horrid smell?' asked Arbel disgustedly.

'Perhaps,' suggested Roberta, peering down again, 'this is one of the "kitchen middens" about which M Lenormand told us – the refuse, bones and all, of years and years of meals. I thought at the time what an unpleasing idea it was.'

'It rather suggests the Zoo to me,' observed her sister, also peering down. 'And ... whatever is that queer noise?'

For there it was again, that sound almost like snoring which had already disquieted Roberta. There was no doubt that the source of this also was the dark hollow below them. The realisation struck both girls motionless, Roberta at least conscious of a suddenly thudding heart.

All at once Arbel, who had got down on her hands and knees in an attempt to see through the gloom – now less impenetrable as the eye became more accustomed to it – got up quickly, seized her sister's arm and whispered into her ear: 'Keep quiet, Rob, keep quite quiet! There's something very queer down there. Look again!'

Roberta in turn knelt down and craned over. And gradually there became clear to her sight – much too clear – a great dark furry shape lying at the bottom of the cavity. It was no doubt something which the hunters of those incredibly remote ages had slain. On the present fantastic plane of existence which had engulfed Arbel and herself, such a relic was not unnaturally visible to them, just as were the enlargements of La Palombière itself. But the great creature down there was of course dead, had been dead these many,

many centuries. 'Many, many centuries', repeated Roberta to herself, beginning to tremble.

But *was* it dead? As both girls stared fixedly down, a sort of tremor passed over the dark mass. At the same time the steady snoring noise culminated in an unmistakable snort, and then ceased.

'*It's alive!*' Which of them had said it? And which, through equally stiff lips, had got out the words, '*Cave-bear!*'?

They could see down quite well now. The animal seemed to be several yards long, and the rest of its immense shaggy bulk was in proportion. It lay sleeping – if it were still sleeping – on its side, with one gigantic paw over its snout, its dark pelt, between brown and black, showing a little lighter on the belly.

There was no need now to urge each other to be quiet. The two crept back along the tilted rock listening in terror for any sounds of stirring from below. Even so they might not have heard them, since the assault on the obstruction outside the cave had by this time brought the rescuers so much nearer to the entrance that the noise of shovelling could now be quite distinctly heard. Huddled in their former nook near the entrance, the sisters clung to each other, instinctively fighting back the almost overwhelming desire to shout to the men outside, lest they should thereby rouse the monster down there; but Arbel had to cram her fist against her mouth. The idea of taking refuge further back in the cave, in the *diverticule* for instance, they dismissed in a couple of whispers. For not only would they be hiding from their rescuers, but also throwing away their only chance of bolting out of the cave directly a sufficient opening had been made. Yet – O God, let them be quick, let them get through before It wakes!

And this did seem just a possibility, for those outside were now working with such intensity that it sounded as if they had (but impossibly, surely, in the time) brought a mechanical excavator with them. Stones and rubble were being flung aside as if they weighed nothing, and at one moment the diggers' voices, lifted apparently in unison, travelled through the scattering debris with the effect less of shouted speech than of a muffled roar.

But this attempt at communication from without was disastrous. Almost instantly a series of grunts came up from the sleeping chamber below the tilted rock. Its inhabitant, fairly roused at last, was evidently coming up from its lair to investigate. They were lost, for It would be upon them before the mouth of the cave was sufficiently cleared. Dumb with terror, the girls heard the scratchings and scrabblings of the creature's gigantic claws as it somehow heaved its way up. At first they dared not look, hoping, ostrich-like, that thus they ran a better chance of its not seeing them. But in the end they were forced to raise their heads.

There it stood at the top of the tilted floor, its whole unbelievable dark bulk defined by the electric light. It was unimaginably huge, five feet at the shoulder, twice that in length. The biggest bear in any Zoo, even the grizzly, was a mere cub by comparison. Its enormous head, carried low, was swaying from side to side like some evil pendulum, and it seemed impossible that it was not already aware by smell, if not by sight, of the two terrified human beings crouched not many yards away, and that those great heelless feet would not in a moment start to shuffle down the slope towards them.

After what seemed an eternity of agony, however, the cave-bear ceased to swing its head, and the little eyes under the curiously domed forehead fixed themselves upon the entrance, where the commotion caused by the operations outside was increased now by the consequent sliding and scattering of rubbish on the inner side. And suddenly a fresh dread seized Arbel and Roberta. What of the two men themselves as they broke through, to find themselves confronted by this monster from a vanished world – a peril all the greater that they would be totally unprepared for it?

And all the while the sound of almost infuriated digging and of flying stones and earth was continuing in a crescendo. Then a miniature landslide rattled into the cave, and some feet above the floor level the blessed daylight shone at last through an aperture large enough to admit a man. And Roberta, exultant yet desperate, thought that though she was not brave enough to shout a warning, at least Amery and Lenormand would have pickaxes or something of the sort in their hands …

But it was not a man at all who next moment filled the opening; it was the hairy head and shoulders of a creature much vaster, from whose jaws hung something limp and horned, which dripped blood. And at that sight the bear from the cave-hollow, uttering a roar, left her place and lunged down the slope towards her mate, returned with his kill after so furiously clearing the way to his blocked fastness.

✕

At the end of this new dark tunnel-like passage, half seen in their crazed flight from the growling monsters (intent for the moment on tearing their prey to pieces), a ray of daylight was the only hope left. Roberta, stumbling among the jags of limestone or stalactites with which the tunnel was studded, heard herself croak out a word of encouragement to Arbel, close on her heels. This hitherto non-existent passage into which they had plunged communicated, then, in some way, with the outer world; there was no time to speculate how, nor any use in the attempt, since nothing in this unholy nightmare was capable of explanation. Only one thing mattered – speed.

The light, as the girls neared it, was seen to come through a narrow aperture set almost like a window at the top of a slope of earth and rubble, debris which slid under the feet as one scrambled up, so that neither could help the other. A short effort, and Roberta was at the summit, and had thrust her head and shoulders through the slit, meeting with dizzy relief the air of the familiar world which they had left – how long ago? She was looking out, nevertheless, on a little hillside which she had not seen before, and a steep one at that. But some feet below there protruded a grassy ledge, not at all impossible of attainment.

'Darling, we're saved, we're saved!' she called back over her shoulder. 'Look! – No, wait a moment! I'll get right through first, and make sure of the best way down.'

Feet first this time, she got herself completely through the opening, and let herself cautiously down a little way. Then she dug in her toes and peered in again into what seemed by contrast almost absolute darkness. 'It's quite easy. I'll give you a hand.'

But to her dismay there was no sign of Arbel, who had been so close behind her. For a moment Roberta's heart stopped. Could They in those few moments …? But all was quiet. 'It must be that I can't see so well after the daylight,' she thought. But what if Arbel had fainted and slipped back …

'Arbel, where are you?' she cried in anguish. 'Have you fallen or anything? I'm coming, I'm coming!'

But the effort she made to scramble back into the opening was too impetuous. What foothold she had won outside abruptly gave way beneath her, and with a cry she felt herself falling into space.

4

The reason for Gabriel Lenormand's non-appearance, and Gabriel Lenormand himself, were found by Amery about halfway on the road to Les Eyzies. Turning a corner on that most indifferent thoroughfare he recognised at once the stooping figure whose head was buried in the bonnet of a car. The Frenchman's petrol-feed was leaking, he said, with results like the Seine in flood; and so, unless the car was to be abandoned on an unfrequented road, there was no course but for Amery to tow it back to Les Eyzies as quickly as possible. But since neither of them could produce any hawser more serviceable than a piece of very worn rope, in danger of breaking at the least jerk, this undertaking took longer than was anticipated. Once the Citroen was safely in the hands of a *garagiste*, however, the two set forth again at top speed in Amery's car, Lenormand overflowing with remorse at being the cause of their guests having to wait with no shelter from the rain at La Palombière.

Amery pointed out that the shower, though certainly heavy, had not lasted long, and that if they chose to go up to it, they had the *abri* to shelter in, and were no worse off than any Aurignacian young ladies, who, moreover, did not possess mackintoshes. 'You did say the cave was of Aurignacian times, didn't you?'

'The present cave level is Aurignacian, yes; but the *abri* would have been used by older races still … Ah, by the way, my friend, I believe that I have solved the problem of how it was that we both seemed to recognise Mlle Fraser *la cadette*. It came to me, oddly enough, as I was struggling with that wretched petrol-feed just now. Do you remember, during the time we spent together at Nîmes two years ago, my taking you to the studio of a connection of mine, a painter named Quineau?'

'Quite well,' replied Amery, taking a bend with little room to spare. 'But there was no woman there, that I remember – not even a model.'

'Not a living model, certainly. But have you forgotten that lovely fragment of late Greek sculpture which Quineau had picked up somewhere?'

The car's speedometer dropped. 'Do you mean that broken bas-relief of a girl which, he said, had so haunted him that finally he made a picture of her? Yes, yes, of course. And he had painted her knee-deep in flowers, just turning in surprise and fear as she sees the strange and terrible fate which is about to overtake her.' And now the car was almost crawling as Amery went on with animation, 'How could I have forgotten that Persephone of his, just before the lord of the underworld advances to carry her off! He was not shown, I remember – only the terror in her eyes.'

'I was right, then, was I not?' asked Lenormand. 'Mlle Arbel Fraser has a remarkable look both of that sculptured head and of Quineau's reconstruction of it on canvas. She has even the same colouring as the latter. Indeed, I think the resemblance is striking.'

'I quite agree. One ought to try to get Miss Fraser to visit M Quineau's *atelier*; he would be startled, I think. I daresay someone has tried to paint her already; but not, probably, as Persephone.' Amery accelerated again. 'That story, by the way, nature-myth though it be, is quite a satisfying one.'

The Frenchman nodded. 'Do you remember why Persephone, even after her release, had to go back and spend one-third of the year in the underworld?'

'No, I don't.'

'It was because, while she was in the realm of Dis, she had eaten part of a pomegranate. I learnt that at the *lycée*, before I even quite knew what a pomegranate was.'

'A good detail, that! I'll tell you what, to my mind, is most commendable in the story, as story – that it should have been her mother who searched so distractedly, and successfully, after Persephone. It is so much fresher, to a modern palate, than the kindred tale of Eurydice and her lover.'

Lenormand smiled. 'You think so? It is true that Ceres succeeded where Orpheus failed.'

'His failure was Eurydice's fault. But what are myths to you prehistorians!' exclaimed Amery, bringing the car to a standstill at the level space by the stream. 'Your precious old Stone Age knew nothing so poetical! Why, all its graphic art – which I grant is astounding – was purely utilitarian in spirit, designed either to preserve a man's life from his animal foes or to fill his belly! Now, where have those girls got to? Miss Fraser, Miss Fraser! They have probably rambled off somewhere, which is a nuisance.'

'Not, surely, in that heavy rain,' expostulated Lenormand, looking unhappy. 'If only I had not had that mishap!'

'They brought mackintoshes with them. They may be anywhere. *Miss Fra-ser!*'

'I believe I see someone in the *abri*,' observed Lenormand, scrutinising the cliffside. 'No doubt they went there for shelter.'

'If they are there now, they must be deaf and blind,' commented his friend. 'Besides, it stopped raining some time ago.' Nevertheless, he followed him towards the path.

But Lenormand proved mistaken; the *abri* was untenanted. Puzzled and penitent, he surveyed the valley below.

'Better try the cave itself,' said Amery, moving off.

'But, my dear fellow, that is the one place where the young ladies cannot be!' protested the cave's guardian as he followed him, but slowly. So it was Amery who stopped with an exclamation.

'Great snakes! What on earth has been happening here? Did you know of this, Gabriel?'

It was of course quite clear to both that some time since noon the previous day, when work at La Palombière had stopped, there had been a heavy subsidence at the mouth. There was nothing to tell them that there had been two falls, nor, at first sight, that the second of these had completely blocked it. For, the pile of rubble once surmounted, there was ample room to enter, if one stooped a trifle.

'You will of course want to investigate this,' said Amery, contemplating the mound of debris. 'Could those girls, I wonder, have felt moved to climb in?'

'Not, surely, over all this!' objected the Frenchman as, in his friend's wake, he scrambled over the rubble.

'Well, *someone's* been trespassing on your preserve!' called the latter from the summit. 'The electric light's on!' And with a jump he vanished.

A moment later Lenormand joined him on the floor of the lit but apparently empty cavern. Another minute, and he emerged from a hasty and fruitless search of the *diverticule* to see Amery picking up a Burberry and a red and white sunshade from the corner just inside the entrance.

'These belong to the Fraser girls. At least the parasol thing does. I recognise it. So they *have* been in here ... Is that someone calling?'

They both listened, and heard a woman's cry, sharp and desperate, drift again through the half-blocked aperture. This time the words were audible: 'Arbel! Arbel! Where are you? Arbel, Arbel!' Then there was the sound of someone scrambling wildly up the other side of the mound. Both men were halfway up the inner when Roberta Fraser, panting and distracted, appeared in the opening.

'Your sister is not here,' said Amery. 'Have you lost her?'

'She *must* be here! Oh, let me come in! ... The bears ... where have they gone to?' Half sliding though she was, she pushed past the two men as though they were trying to hinder instead of to help her, and sobbing out, 'The passage – she must be in there still!' rushed past them up the cave, and, stopping halfway, beat at the rock-face on the right-hand side with her hands, calling out, almost shrieking her sister's name.

'Bears? Passage?' stammered Amery, considerably horrified at this outburst. 'Miss Fraser, has there been an accident? Have you –?'

'O God! She's in there somewhere, my darling!' gasped Roberta, ceasing to hammer on the limestone, and turning upon him a face almost unrecognisable in its despair. 'In there alone … where we ran to get away from the bears. And now this end is blocked up again!'

'But, Mademoiselle,' said Lenormand gently, 'it has never been unblocked.'

'Where did you last see your sister, Miss Fraser?' asked Amery.

'In here … but at the farther end … just before I climbed out and fell.'

'Ah yes, some accident … that is clear!' murmured Lenormand; and seeing how she was shaking with agitation Amery put a hand under her elbow.

'One moment, Miss Fraser. Are you sure that your sister came in here with you?'

'Of course I am sure!' returned Roberta on a high note. 'We were both caught in here when the rocks came down outside – we both saw them, the enormous bears – the one that was here, and the one that made its way in. Why can't you believe me? That is her sunshade over there … Oh, but this is wasting time! I must get back to the side valley. Please don't keep me!'

'On the contrary, we will come with you,' said Lenormand, glancing at Amery. 'Let us help you over this.' And, once outside, he asked for some indication of the spot where she said she had fallen, and, receiving the same reply, was obliged to say, unwillingly, 'But, Mademoiselle, there is no other exit from the cavern than this.'

'But there is, there is!' retorted Roberta wildly but convincedly. 'In that little valley round there. I tell you I got out there – halfway up the cliff it was. But Arbel didn't …

she suddenly wasn't there … and when I picked myself up again I could not get up to the opening again. So I came to try this end – and it's no use, no use!' And with a gesture of utter hopelessness she started, half running, to go down the path past the *abri*.

'I think I know the place she means,' said Lenormand hastily to Amery. 'There probably was an exit there – in quaternary times. I will go with her, but I suggest that you should stay here, in case Mlle Arbel should return.'

Amery nodded. 'Yes, that is the best plan. The poor girl has evidently got concussion from a fall *somewhere*; all that talk of bears and a non-existent passage shows it, though she doesn't seem to have been hurt. I wonder where her sister has got to?'

※

'That is where I got out … and fell,' gasped Roberta a little later, pointing. 'That is the ledge …' Then her hand dropped to her side. 'But … but I don't see…' For even where the limestone was not shrouded with growth, there was no sign of any aperture on the wall of the bluff.

'No, Mademoiselle,' confirmed Lenormand in a low voice, 'there is no possible way out there. Your dream –'

'But it wasn't a dream!' protested Roberta with a sob. 'It was real – it happened! Oh, why did I go ahead and leave her … though I never, never meant to!' She hurried on up the little valley, weeping, with the Frenchman close behind her.

※

Since, after half an hour's wait, the younger Miss Fraser had not reappeared at La Palombière, nor could be seen anywhere, Amery decided to exchange his vigil for more active search – though indeed, as he told himself, the other two might very well have found the truant by this time. So he wrote a line on a leaf from his pocket-book, and, pinning it down with stones in what he hoped was a prominent position on the heap of debris, set off.

He had gone a good quarter of a mile up the narrow and winding lateral valley before he saw Lenormand and the girl about two hundred yards away, coming towards him, Roberta anxiously scanning the cliff on her right. All at once she stopped, her eyes fixed on a particular spot. Amery easily guessed why, but he could see no opening of any kind. Lenormand came to meet him.

'We have found no trace of her anywhere. Have you?'

Amery shook his head and went on. When he reached her, the ghost of the once ruddy-faced Roberta said, in the kind of voice he hoped never to hear again: 'If my climbing out by the hole in the cliff which is there no longer was a dream, as M Lenormand says, then Arbel must have stayed behind in the cave itself … with the bears … and if so…!' She gave a cry of sheer horror and covered her face with her hands.

'Those bears again!' muttered Amery, turning a little pale himself. 'This whole business is becoming a nightmare! Good God, the girl *must* be found before dark.'

'She has gone back!' wailed Roberta. 'She always wanted to. Only not so far, not so far! But I shall never stop looking for her, never!'

'Nor shall we!' asseverated Amery. He felt a strong impulse to add, 'Round the world, if necessary.' But that was absurd and uncalled for; Arbel Fraser could not be far away. Or … could she?

'I think, Mademoiselle Roberta,' suggested Lenormand, with the gentleness which he had shown her all along, 'that we should now try the main valley, below the cave.'

For a moment Roberta seemed to hesitate. She looked back along the rough track. 'Yes, but we must first look into the narrow gully place we passed just now. You said it would have been impossible for her to climb up there without help, but

I have a feeling that we ought at least to have looked. Please, please come back with me!'

The plea could not be refused, though Amery privately condemned the probable waste of time. They ought rather to carry out Lenormand's suggestion without delay. And when in ten minutes or so they came to the 'gully', it proved indeed to be almost a rock-climber's 'chimney', though wider and more sloping, which the two men would have preferred to negotiate by themselves. But Roberta would not consent to this. It was quite a tough little climb, ending, rather surprisingly, in an attractive little green plateau surrounded by easy slopes, not at all impossible of access from above.

And it was there that Amery, the first up, saw her, lying motionless among the small flowers that love the limestone, her shining hair in disorder, and the hint of a smile on her face. She seemed asleep, very soundly asleep ...

'But she's not!' he said to himself with a bitter pang at his heart as he looked down on her. Yet there were no signs of any injury, only an extraordinary pallor. 'Persephone has gone back ... for ever.' And he could tell, by his silence and immobility, that Lenormand, now beside him, was of the same mind.

But not Roberta. With a cry of ecstasy she fell on her knees beside her sister, kissing her again and again. 'Arbel, Arbel darling, wake up! How *did* you get here? But wake up now! You are safe!'

'No use, no use!' thought Amery, full of pity. Yet to his joy and amazement Arbel, between two kisses, stirred slightly. Then the colour began to come back to her face and her eyelids lifted. She said in a sleepy voice, 'Safe? Safe from what?'

5

Dusk was falling when Amery got back from Beynac, whither he had conveyed the reunited sisters. Lenormand, who had been left behind by his own request at La Palombière, was outside the cave, studying the piled debris with so grave an expression that Amery concluded him to be feeling concern about the extra work its removal would entail.

'I believe that both the girls will be none the worse for their fright in a few days' time,' he hastened to assure him. 'I was hoping that Arbel' (his voice changed slightly on the name) 'would not recall what she was supposed to be "safe from". Unfortunately by the time she got to the hotel it had come back to her – the hallucination, I mean, which she shares with her sister about what they saw in this cave of yours. (Of how she got to that place where we found her she has not the faintest recollection.) However, I think the effect will pass in time. They must have fallen asleep, had a particularly vivid bad dream – or at least Roberta did – and rushing out in alarm, got separated.'

Lenormand made no comment on this theory. 'And Mlle Roberta?' he asked.

'She was much calmer, and had time to be worried about your remaining here alone in this dreadful place, as she called it. But I pointed out that you were used to caves and were not, perhaps, as unduly imaginative as they are.'

The archaeologist, one hand all the time in his pocket, continued to contemplate the landslide. 'Mlle Roberta's concern is very kind.'

Amery followed his gaze. 'Yes, you will have to set your workmen on to that tomorrow. It will take them some time to clear it up.'

'To finish clearing it up,' corrected Lenormand.

'What do you mean? The mess is just as it was when we went in not very long ago!'

'Quite so. But we were in a hurry then. Does it not strike you now, Norris, when there is more time to study it, that quite a large amount of clearing had been done by the time we got here? From the general appearance of the fall it is plain – at least to me – that the entrance must at first have been completely blocked by it. And did not Mademoiselle Roberta give us to understand as much? Yet we got in with little difficulty.'

Amery studied the fall for a few moments. 'Yes,' he said at last. 'Yes, I believe you are right. But who, in Heaven's name, would have set about the job, and why – and when? And why did we not come upon anyone at work?'

'I think there was a very good reason for that.'

'You mean that some person – a rival, perhaps? – has been making a clandestine weekend entrance into your preserve, but that he and his diggers, getting wind of our approach, had cleared out before we came on the scene?'

Lenormand gave a rather grim little laugh. '"Cleared out", yes – if the term is adequate. But there was only one ... digger.'

'Then he must have been pretty hefty!'

'He was possessed of enormous strength. Look at those great lumps of limestone, how they have been flung aside, tossed into positions where the fall could not possibly have carried them!'

Increasingly perplexed by something odd in his friend's manner, Amery nodded. 'Yes, I grant that. I never knew that archaeologists were so muscular! And after that display, did the gate-crasher go in, or didn't he?'

'He went in,' answered his friend, and now he looked at him directly. 'We know that. The Mesdemoiselles Fraser saw him.'

Amery fairly recoiled. 'But what they saw – or thought they

saw – was – Oh, *nonsense!* You are pulling my leg, Gabriel! You cannot seriously believe that a –' He broke off and clapped Lenormand on the shoulder. 'Look here! It's high time we went back to Les Eyzies and had a meal! I could do with one myself. Come on – No, wait one moment. I have just remembered that Roberta asked me to find her camera for her. She left it in the cave, and if you haven't come across it I'd better go in and have a look.'

'Unnecessary,' said his friend briefly. 'I have already found it. But it can never be used again.'

'Why not?'

The Frenchman at last removed his hand from his pocket, and drew out a queer, crumpled black object in which it was indeed hard to recognise that familiar appurtenance of the traveller, a Kodak. Flattened, bent and scratched, the lens torn away from the now dangling bellows usually so neatly concertinaed away in its interior, and with a great hole driven through both sides of the metal frame where once the winding-bobbin had been, its obvious destination was now the dustheap.

'What a pitiable sight!' exclaimed Amery. 'Poor Roberta! I suppose she had left it near the entrance, and it was crushed by the subsidence.'

'No. It was too far in for that. And here is its case – or what remains of it.' And from his other pocket the archaeologist extracted a mangled object which had once been a brown leather case of some solidity.

'Why, that looks for all the world as if it had been chewed!'

'It almost certainly has been. By the same agency which has bitten the camera almost to pieces.'

'Bitten!' Amery looked more closely at the massacred Kodak as Lenormand put it into his hand. Those dents and scores – yes, a formidably armed jaw might – But no, it wasn't possible!

'Gabriel, *mon bon*,' he said earnestly, 'you are giving way to your imagination. How could the tooth of any living beast make a hole this size?' And he stuck two fingers at once into it. 'Are you suggesting that some escaped lion or tiger is roaming the district? But even the big felines haven't teeth that size!'

Lenormand's gaze was at once exalted and sombre. 'You have said it. No lion or tiger – no living beast has such fangs. But in quaternary times there inhabited the recesses of nearly all these caverns another carnivore, as big as a bull – but a great deal stronger-boned than a bull – and *its* teeth –'

Amery felt a sort of icy trickle down his spine. 'But,' he interrupted rather faintly, 'we are not in quaternary times.'

'*Entendu.* We are not. But where were the Mesdemoiselles Fraser some hours ago?'

'My dear fellow, you *know* that their experiences were an illusion. Don't tell me that you, a man of science, are seriously subscribing to some – forgive me – some other quite incredible theory!'

Lenormand was very pale. 'Theory?' he repeated hoarsely. '*Mon Dieu*, how can one make any theory about a tangle like this? The agency which we never met but which, as I believe, cleared a way into the cave before we got here, and which those girls saw – in their joint dream, if you will – you are at liberty to tell me that I am romancing about that. But, with regard to what you hold in your hand, I have a key in the cave, and you shall see how well it fits the lock.'

He turned and began to scramble up the subsidence, and for the second time Amery did the same. Once inside, the Frenchman went to the iron box near the opening of the *diverticule* in which he kept the less valuable fruits of excavation pending their sorting and classification, and unlocked it. He came back holding what looked like a fossilized banana. Taking the ruined camera he thrust this into the hole. It fitted exactly.

'In God's name, what is that monstrous object?' demanded Amery, almost fiercely. But he had guessed the answer.

'It is one of the canine teeth – they are frequently found – of *ursus spelaeus*, *l'ours des cavernes*, the cave bear, which no human eye has beheld for perhaps fifteen thousand years, until –'

'Until this afternoon, I suppose you were going to say? But then only in a drea –'

But he could not go on. And there closed upon them both the numbing silence of that half-explored twilight retreat, a habitation so old that Ur or Cretan Cnossos were in comparison but growths of an hour. Amery was aware that it was no question of the chance survival, in this populated countryside, of a couple of palaeolithic fauna; that was not what Lenormand was postulating. But it was no product of dream or delusion which had vented its fury on Roberta Fraser's camera, nor tossed aside, like a child's bricks, the blocks of limestone out there … Yet, between an impossible survival and an unconvincing theory of double hallucination, what alternative was there?

Only something after which the mind groped without a real clue. Fragments of ideas wavered through Amery's own mind like weeds in a stream. '*Ursus spelaeus*,' he found himself murmuring, his eyes fixed on the great fang in Lenormand's hands. 'That then was the infernal deity, aeons older than the mythical Pluto, which came after our Persephone. She was lucky, thank God; she did not go far … Let's get out of here, Gabriel!'

Notes on the stories

BY KATE MACDONALD

1 All Souls' Day (1907)

In the 1907 Macmillan version of this story the first two pages were replaced by the first six paragraphs of the text reproduced in this volume from the 1932 version published in *A Fire of Driftwood*. The original 1907 opening pages are reproduced below:

> The saint's breviary, we were told at the church, was kept at the *presbytére*, but M le Cure would be delighted to show it to us. So we went thither, and passing under an archway in the wall, and through a tiny garden-corner bright with flowers, found that M le Cure was out but was expected back at any moment, and were requested to wait in the parlour. This we were glad enough to do, for Breton roads in August are hot and dusty, and we were somewhat weary with our long walk.
>
> The parlour was rather dark and very cool; it had straight-backed chairs arranged with extreme precision along the walls, a round table in the middle, and was hung with a few sacred prints. At either end of the mantelpiece, under a glass shade, was a little crucifix of extremely uncouth workmanship. The Curé not appearing, I was wandering aimlessly round the room, when my eyes fell upon the book which we had come to see, in a roughly-made case on a table in the window.
>
> 'Here's our quarry,' I exclaimed. 'I wonder why the housekeeper did not tell us that it was in here.' A card, neatly written, gave us information as to the date and authenticity of the breviary, but we did not like to take the volume from its case to examine it more closely until its guardian should arrive. 'Our host has one or two good bindings up there,' remarked my friend, his eyes travelling to a little bookcase upon the wall. 'Moreover, if that's not an English seventeenth-century tooling I'll eat my hat.'

Moved by the sacred enthusiasm of the bibliophile he stretched up a hand and plucked the book forth. 'Look,' he said.

It was a Dutch-printed Latin copy of *The Imitation of Christ*, of the year 1620, and though I know little of bindings I saw the significance of the faded inscription on the fly-leaf. *Mildmay Fane*, presumably the owner's name, was written high up in the right-hand corner, and then lower down, and evidently at a different time, *hunc librum ad LRE de V dedit anno MDCXXXI in memoriam misericordiae non obliviscendae*; and lower down again, *Ora pro anima NC*.

'By Jove!' I said, 'given by an Englishman to a Frenchman in 1631. I wonder what it is doing here, and who NC was.'

But as I spoke the door opened, and the Curé hurried in, full of gentle apologies for keeping us waiting. He was the most beautiful and fragile old man that it has ever been my lot to meet, and he had spoken but a few words before we knew that he had a mind to match his person. In a minute or so the saint's breviary was out of its case, and we were examining it with attention, while the priest discoursed of it in a manner that showed he had no small knowledge of medieval manuscripts. It seemed to be all that was claimed for it, while its guardian›s pride in it, and his manifest pleasure in showing it to foreigners (of whom one at least was a competent critic) were delightful to witness. But the discussion became at the end too technical for my attention, which wandered off to the Englishman's a Kempis, lying close to my hand, and I turned over its yellow pages musingly until I realised that the examination of the breviary was finished.

'You are very amiable, Messieurs, to have come so far to see this relic,' remarked the Curé, pulling his spectacles lower on his nose, and looking at us over them, 'Especially as you are, I suppose, Protestants?' he added.

My friend and I disclaimed the title so hastily as to cause the old priest some amusement. 'Well, well,' he said indulgently, 'at any rate you cannot have known the same devotion for the blessed Hugues which has brought here most of those who come to see his book.'

'But there is one saint and his book,' I observed, rather sententiously, I fear, 'for whom we all have a like devotion, whatever our country, creed, or age.' And holding out the *Imitation* I asked him if he would be good enough to satisfy our curiosity about it.

presbytère: French, the presbytery, the priest's house.

the Morvan: a mountainous massif in the centre of France.

The Imitation of Christ: a fifteenth-century English handbook for spiritual devotions by Thomas à Kempis.

Hunc librum ... Ora pro anima NC: Latin, This book to LRE from V, in the year 1631, in memory of mercy not overlooked ... Pray for the soul of NC.

cet aimable écrivain si passionné pour l'histoire et les antiquités de notre beau pays du Morvan: French, this delightful writer who is so passionate about the history and relics of our lovely Morvan.

basse-cour: French, farmyard.

stocks: *Matthiola incana*, a lavishly fragrant garden flower.

une âme d élite: French, an elite soul.

a challenge: a duel to settle a matter of honour.

cartel: a diminutive form of *carte*, a visiting card, presumably containing the request for a duel.

Parenza: in the 1907 version the Duke's title is given as P——, intending to suggest perhaps Parma or Perugia, or some other noble name veiled by discretion.

regretted her convent: regretted leaving her convent.

on themes: presumably spiritual matters.

Venice point: Venetian lace.

jour de Morts: French, the day of the dead, All Soul's Day.

his chair: his sedan chair, to take him to his midnight appointment with the lady.

porte d'égagement: a private door leading directly outside, rather than through the public rooms.

misericordia non obliviscenda: Latin, compassion must not be forgotten.

2 Fils D'Émigré (1913)

fils d'émigré: the son of a French refugee from Revolutionary France who was pro-Royalist and of noble rank.

M la Comte ... sa chambre: French, Will the Count eat here before he goes upstairs, or in his room?

Orme: Robert Orme was a popular eighteenth-century authority on the history of the British in India.

Quiberon: a port on the south coast of Brittany. The Marquis is part of the Royalist assault at the Battle of Quiberon on 21 June–23 July 1795.

Foi de Flavigny: French, faith of a Flavigny.

Faites-moi voir les éléphants: French, let me see the elephants.

Ne faites pas cela: French, Don't do that!

Hoche: General Lazare Hoche commanded the successful Revolutionary troops at the Battle of Quiberon.

Pomone: HMS Pomone, a captured French flagship, had assisted the British forces aiding the French Royalists at the Battle of Quiberon.

Warren: Captain Sir John Warren, commander of one of the two British squadrons from the British Navy at the Battle of Quiberon.

3 The Window (1929)

Westminster Gazette: a popular and influential magazine published before the First World War. Its weekly poetry competition was very popular.

escutcheon: a carved coat of arms.

vermeil: anglicisation of vermeuil, French for vermilion or red, here indicating a rouged or made-up face.

Norman Angell: one of the founders of the Union of Democratic Control which opposed war, and author of the influential *The Great Illusion* (1910), which argued that war was impossible due to the interlinked nature of the many European economies.

Pour ça ... Monsieur!: French, 'As for that sir, you just see!'.

sous-officier: a non-commissioned officer.

Entente: the *Entente Cordiale* had been signed in 1804 by France and Great Britain, to strengthen diplomatic and military relations.

un preux Chevalier: French, a valiant knight.

marquise ring: a ring with a stone cut in the shape of an oval with pointed ends.

Vinot: a leading French make of car.

despatch-rider: an army messenger, usually rushing about the countryside by motor-cycle or car, who had a more dashing and adventurous image than the regular infantry officer.

before he remembered: as an NCO de Précy is below Romilly's rank as an officer, so while they were in uniform they would not be permitted to have a public conversation as social equals.

pillory: an instrument of public punishment, in which the standing victim is locked into a wooden frame with their hands and head protruding from its three holes.

Martin Harvey: the English stage actor John Martin-Harvey had his first success as Sydney Carton in Sir Henry Irving's 1899 adaptation of Dickens' French Revolution-era novel *A Tale of Two Cities*, in which Carton goes willingly to the guillotine to allow another character to be saved.

Magic ... foam: line 69 of John Keats' poem 'Ode to a Nightingale' (1819).

gin: a trap for animals.

If thy hand offend thee ... quenched: from the Book of Mark, 9.43.

single star: the star signified his rank as a lieutenant.

en permission: French, on leave.

poilu: a French soldier.

vareuse: French, a jacket.

un peu plus gai que celui-ci, vous savez: French, 'a little more cheerful than this one you know', that is, more brightly coloured.

brevetée: French, qualified.

Vendéans: the Vendée Revolt was a counter-revolution during the French Revolution, beginning in July 1793 in the Vendée region south of the Loire in western France.

Cholet: the Battle of Tremblaye fought near Cholet on 15 October 1793 was a defeat for the Royalists.

4 Clairvoyance (1932)

arquebus: a type of long musket, dating from the fifteenth century.

blanked: a euphemism for a swear-word.

Sadamune: is held to be one of the finest Japanese swordsmiths, active in the fourteenth century.

katana: a Japanese curved steel sword, to be wielded with both hands.

South Kensington Museum: the older name for the Victoria and Albert Museum.

Nothung: Richard Wagner's name for the sword Gram from the *Volsunga Saga*, in his *Der Ring des Nibelungen* (1876).

"of the school": painted by a pupil or follower of a great artist rather than by the artist themself.

daimio: daimyō, a Japanese feudal lord from the tenth century.

5 The Promised Land (1932)

dust-cloaks and mushroom hats: a dust-coat was a thin all-enveloping garment won to protect the day clothes from the dust of the street or the road. A mushroom hat, made popular in the 1870s, had a turned-down brim, and by the 1920s had become ubiquitous wear for women with no pretensions to fashion.

Baedeker: a famous series of nineteenth-century travel guides to the more commonly-visited countries of the world, published by the German firm Verlag Baedeker, and synonymous with the earnest tourist desirous of the correct information about the correct sights to see.

La Gioconda: Leonardo da Vinci's painting, more popularly known as the *Mona Lisa*.

Baptistery: the fourteenth-century ecclesiastical building in Siena, undoubtedly also in Baedeker as one of the sights to see.

speedwell: an English wildflower with petals of a striking blue.

amour-propre: French, self-esteem.

diptheery: diptheria, a bacterial infection of the throat and lungs, which in Victorian times was a common killer.

6 The Pestering (1932)

Ye Olde: Evadne's shudder indicates that she doesn't share the taste for fake medieval that this phrase suggests.

unshingled: she has not cut her hair to the fashionable short crop favoured by women after the First World War.

The Silver Spoon: a 1926 novel by John Galsworthy.

people like us: the Setons are upper-middle-class, and expect to live on their investments, but the economic depression of the late 1920s has made them poor and so they have to break class boundaries and work for some of their income. That Evadne has to work herself is an even stronger breach of class expectations, since in this period married women from the lower middle classes upwards did not work outside the home at all.

The Chelsea artist: probably Augustus John, the famed London artist who wore Renaissance-type sweeping hats and cloaks for dramatic effect.

soi-disant: French, so-called.

Passon: If Mr Hawkins can remember a bewigged parson or vicar he is recalling the very early nineteenth century, which would make him over 120 years old, which he probably isn't.

St Martin's Summer: the English name for a period of warm weather in autumn, often conflated with the North American term 'Indian summer', now disused.

florins, half-crowns: a florin was a two-shilling coin, and a half-crown had a value of two shillings and sixpence. Ten florins or eight half-crowns made a pound.

seemed to be understood: was the implication.

straiter: archic term for more confined, tighter and with fewer options.

The Mysterious Universe: Sir James Jeans was a prominent physicist and mathematician. His 1930 book about the nature of the universe was a popular best-seller.

Luini and Boltraffio: Italian artists who worked in the studio of Leonardo da Vinci.

meed: archaic term for a portion or share.

galon: a decorative braid.

Corpus: Corpus Christi College, Oxford.

Curiosities of the Supernatural: no such title is held by the Bodleian Library at Oxford.

Jean Goujon: sixteenth-century French sculptor.

Diane of Poictiers: Diane de Poitiers, mistress of Henri II and a great patron of French Renaissance art.

7 Couching at the Door (1933)

couching: from the French *couchant*, an archaic Anglicisation for lying down.

cloisonné, Satsuma, Buhl: cloisonné is an enamelled or decorated ornamental metalwork; Satsuma is a Japanese pottery style exported to the West in bulk in the nineteenth century: Buhl, or *boulle,* is a style of French cabinet furniture made famous in the seventeenth century. All these, with the first editions, are expensive collectables signifying money and taste.

Herat: carpets from Herat in Afghanistan are prized for their fine workmanship and design.

country and county society: country society means the gentry and the squires, local baronets, vicars and professionals like doctors and lawyers; county society is further up the social scale, into the aristocracy.

The Yellow Book and *The Savoy*: two of the 'little' magazines of the *fin de siècle*, notable for their aesthetic qualities and tendency to publish scandalous literature and art.

Mrs Grundy: a character in a Regency play personifying social censoriousness, which quickly became a byword for judging one's neighbours for what is nobody's business but their own.

hyacinthine: golden.

pleasance: from the French *pleasaunce*, a pleasure-ground, garden, artificially constructed space for outdoor leisure.

'sveltes jets d eau', 'sanglots d'exstase': half-remembered phrases from last lines of the poem *Clair de Lune* (1869) by the French poet Paul Verlaine. 'Et sangloter d'extase les jets d'eau / Les grands jets d'eau sveltes parmi les marbres. (And makes the fountains sob with ecstasy / The slender water streams among the marble statues).'

sward: self-consciously medieval term for a grass lawn.

culs de lampe: French typographical term for the ornamental design that signifies the end of a chapter.

recherché: French, literally 'research', in this context exotic or refined.

Maecenas: after Gaius Cilnius Maecenas, friend of the future Emperor Augustus, and a wealthy patron and sponsor of the arts in pre-Christian Rome. The name is complimentary since it suggests taste and generosity.

scarified: scarred multiple times.

grimoire: a book of instruction in magic and the dark arts.

And if thou doest well: Genesis 4.7.

dog-cart: an open carriage drawn by one horse, with an open box at the rear to carry dogs, or luggage.

mere: archaic term for a lake, usually a dark and gloomy one.

les choses cachées: French, hidden or concealed things.

comptoir: French, the counter with the cash desk.

fiacre: French, horse-drawn cab.

8 Juggernaut (1935)

juggernaut: the anglicised term for a large wheeled chariot designed to carry a Hindu deity in state among their people, meaning a large and unstoppable object in motion.

GFS: Girls' Friendly Society, a charity originally designed to give girls occupation and an object in life that would prevent them falling into bad habits.

Britannia-metal: a pewter alloy of tin, giving a good shine when buffed up.

repoussé: a design in metal hammered from the inside out, so the pattern is raised above the surface.

glass-sided shelters: early twentieth-century British seaside resorts where the winds could be too chilly for comfort often had a row of benches inside open-fronted shelters built on the main promenade, the 'front', for prolonged sitting.

Laocoön: a character from Greek mythology most well-known from Virgil's *Aeneid*, who with his sons is punished by the gods in the form of an attack by a giant sea-snake and is strangled. They are usually depicted trapped within a tangled mass of snake.

galley-proofs: before digital publishing techniques, authors' proofs of their books were posted as galleys, long sheets of pages in layout, on a slippery paper, that authors had to correct and return to their publisher. They were notoriously easy to get confused and lose.

second serial rights: selling second serial rights was effectively selling the story for the second time to a different newspaper chain or syndication company, for a good fee, with the probable option of collecting that story in a book of short stories or anthology.

in French: *cabinet* is French for, among other meanings, a toilet or WC.

dot-and-go-one: slang for the movements made by someone walking with a limp.

nitrite of amyl: amyl nitrite is a common treatment for heart disease.

9 The Pavement (1938)

Adhaesit pavimento anima mea: Latin, 'My soul clings to the ground'.

as lief: I would rather.

triclinium: the dining-room in a Roman villa.

tilth and shaw: agricultural land and woodland.

lumbago: a disease of the joints, often manifesting in persistent pain in the lower back.

commerce: an exchange of views, although in this case Lydia supplied both sides of the conversations.

Ganymede: a Trojan youth in Greek myth, the most beautiful of humans, whom Zeus stole away to live with the Immortals.

compeers: a vulgarisation of *compères*, French for friends.

crypto-porticus: a covered passageway underground that supports a ground-level structure.

Office of Works: the Ancient Monuments Protection Act 1900 strengthened existing protections over ancient monuments in Britain by authorising the Office of Works (traditionally the department of government that took care of state buildings) to take monuments and notable ruins into their care.

OHMS: abbreviation for On His Majesty's Service, signifying a letter from the government.

10 From the Abyss (1940)

dissociated personality: a disconnecting from the self.

Morton Prince: the leading psychologist in the investigation of dissociation in the personality.

scission: a division or a split.

ward-room mess: the dining-room on a naval ship where the officers ate.

games: sports such as hockey, golf and tennis.

the right to see her frequently: in this period unmarried women still living in conservative homes did not have the freedom to receive visits from the same man repeatedly unless there was an engagement, or a private 'understanding' sanctioned by her parents.

chambers: the narrator lives and works in these rented rooms in the Temple, the legal district outside the City of London.

Rodex: an English luxury brand of overcoats.

Stottingham coach: the train presumably split at a junction, so it would have been important to be sitting in the correct part of the train.

to have discarded all her other clothes: the effects of hypothermia and exposure on the mind can persuade victims that they are overheated.

de cette infortunée: French, of that unfortunate young woman.

On est coulé … C'est le Grand Abîme, voyez-vous – fini!: French, 'We're sunk, it's the Great Abyss, you see. It's finished'.

11 The Taste of Pomegranates (c. 1945)

monkshood: *Aconitum napellus*, also called aconite or wolfsbane, a tall blue-flowered perennial related to the delphinium.

almoner: an archaic term for the monk or nun who takes care of the finances for a religious foundation; a modern almoner is the treasurer or finance officer.

Gouffre de Padirac: a cave system in the Massif Central accessible through its collapsed roof, first exploited for tourism in the nineteenth century.

holland-coated: he is wearing a light jacket or coat of holland, a cream-coloured fabric used for dustsheets as well as protective garments for driving open-topped cars.

En voiture, mesdemoiselles, pour les grottes de la Vézère: French, Your car, ladies, for the Vézère caves.

Fellow of All Souls: a member of All Souls College, Oxford, a research college with no undergraduates. To be a Fellow of the College indicates a high level of academic achievement as well as original thinking.

Font de Gaume: a famous cave system discovered in 1901, with many prehistoric rock paintings.

left-handed woman: an excavation in the Leadenhall Street area in March 1924 discovered 'the London Skull', considered then to be of a left-handed woman (see the *British Medical Journal*, 7 November 1935, p853, for a contemporary account).

diverticule: French, meaning here a small side passage in a cave system.

Whipsnade: one of the first outdoor zoos in the UK, established in 1928 by the Zoological Society as a wildlife park for public education and animal breeding.

limned: drawn, or painted.

abri: French, a shelter.

chemin vicinal: French, a local road.

Défense absolue d'entrer: French, Absolutely forbidden to enter.

la cadette: French, the younger.